CRITICAL ACCLAIM FOR *HEADBANGER*

'*Headbanger* is as surprising as if Nick Hornby had suddenly delivered a Proustian epic... through an accretion of one-liners and humorous set-pieces he sketches a morally ambivalent world which is immensely compelling and engaging. Coyne is a majestic creation... if Flann O'Brien's lunatic Professor De Selby had genetically engineered a cross between the novels of Raymond Chandler and those of Patrick McCabe, this is what the progeny might well have looked like' – *Times*

'Coyne is the most unusual character in Irish fiction for some time: larger than life, a bit of a mess at one level, but a great original, a true flesh and blood man living out his spell of not-so-quiet desperation with terrible conviction' – *Sunday Independent*

'*Headbanger* is an exciting and blackly comic thriller lobbing incendiaries at both the dark corners and sacred cows of modern Ireland... Read it now before it comes to a cinema near you' – **Dermot Bolger**

'With its echoes of the gangsters' bravura and Coyne's ranting sermons, this strident style verges on self-parody, further blurring earnestness and irony. This is just the mindless mess of rhetoric and confusion against which Coyne is banging his head. Hamilton turns the collapse of the hero's world into a nail-biting finish, not a domestic tragedy. He covers his tracks so well that it is impossible to tell whether the book is a thriller with existentialist hankerings or an elaborate joke. Therein lies the appeal'
– *Times Literary Supplement*

'A terrific creation' – *Guardian*

'Hamilton is a great international writer who just happens to be Irish'
– **Anne Enright**

ALSO BY HUGO HAMILTON

Surrogate City
The Last Shot
The Love Test
Dublin Where the Palm Trees Grow
Sad Bastard

Headbanger

Headbanger

HUGO HAMILTON

NOEXIT2

This edition published in 2017 by No Exit Press,
an imprint of Oldcastle Books Ltd, PO Box 394,
Harpenden, AL5 1XJ
noexit.co.uk

A CIP catalogue record for this book is available from the British Library.

This is a work of fiction. Names, characters, places, and incidents either are
the product of the author's imagination or are used fictitiously, and any
resemblance to actual persons, living or dead, businesses, companies, events
or locales is entirely coincidental.

ISBN
978-1-84344-901-0 (print)
978-1-84344-898-3 (epub)
978-1-84344-899-0 (kindle)
978-1-84344-900-3 (pdf)

2 4 6 8 10 9 7 5 3 1

Typeset in 11.65pt Sabon
by Avocet Typeset, Somerton, Somerset, TA11 6RT

Printed in Great Britain by Clays Ltd, St Ives plc

FOR MARY ROSE

THE AUTHOR WOULD LIKE TO THANK DAVID COLLINS
OF SAMSON FILMS FOR HIS GENEROUS SUPPORT
AND ENCOURAGEMENT WHILE WRITING THIS BOOK.

Coyne was a father figure to the city of Dublin, holding his paternal arm around its suburbs, protecting its inhabitants like a family. He was a member of the Garda Siochana, guardian of peace; a cop, pig, rozzer, fuzz, bluebottle, who drove the squad car with both hands on the steering wheel, alert and ready for the next situation. His navy-blue Garda cap lay on the ledge beneath the back window, along with that of his colleague, Garda McGuinness. Now and again, the voice from headquarters broke in over the radio, drawing attention to the city's emergencies, traffic accidents, little rust spots of criminality. It was a bright autumn afternoon, a day on which nothing much had happened yet, and beside him, McGuinness was going on about golf, explaining at length how he had to let Superintendent Molloy win a game.

Molloy couldn't play golf to save his life, McGuinness was saying. It's an act of charity. I had to turn my back and pretend I didn't see him putting the ball back.

But Coyne was only half listening to this golf tirade because he was more concerned with the state of the world outside, observing every tiny detail in the street, waiting for something suspicious to turn up. Coyne – the real policeman – a massive database of ordinary facts and figures, licence plates, faces and social trivia. No detail too small.

Coyne saw the woman in a motorised wheelchair moving up the street. He saw the security van pulling up outside the post office and one of the uniformed men getting out carrying a steel case shackled to his arm. The reassuring emblem on the side of the van, like a Papal insignia – two crossed keys and a slogan underneath saying: vigilant and valiant. At the traffic lights, Coyne scanned the faces at the bus stop as though they were all potential criminals. Everybody looking mysteriously down the street like a bunch of weather vanes to see the bus coming. On the pavement, the usual chewing-gum droppings stuck to the ground in their thousands; flattened discs of dirty off-white or off-pink gum-pennies that people spat out before getting on the bus.

Garda Pat Coyne would be in a position to reconstruct every faithful detail in evidence. Your honour, the youth was seen spitting a grey substance in the direction of the oncoming bus. Your honour, the lady at the front of the queue carried an upturned sweeping brush. When the time came, Coyne was in possession of the facts.

Vigilant and valiant. Somehow, the words applied more to Coyne himself. Mind you, he'd come across some fairly peculiar slogans on the sides of vans lately. Signs like: East Coast Glass – Your Pane is our Pleasure. Or else: Personal Plumbing Services – day and night. And the oddest one of them all was the 'Dip–Strip' van, boasting all kinds of stripping services. I mean, how were you to know it was furniture they were talking about? Were the people of Ireland trying to look like complete eejits or what? Somebody should go up and point out how absolutely absurd they looked. 'Embibing Emporium' was another Dublin idiosyncrasy that sprang to mind. As a Garda, Coyne took an interest in the precision of language, and one of these days he would walk straight into that pub, slap a concise Oxford down on the bar counter and say: you pack of right honourable gobshites, you can't even fucking spell. Look, it's I, not E. Imbibing.

These were the things that mattered to the sensibilities of a cop, not who could or could not strike a golf ball. Whatever way you whacked the thing, it was predestined to seek only one conclusion, that was to go down a hole.

Molloy might as well be playing golf with a shovel, McGuinness went on. He's got this fabulous Ping driver and he keeps hacking the fairway with it. I swear to God, you'd think he was cutting turf.

Coyne remained silent. His attention was drawn instead to the window display of a lingerie shop. He examined its contents of bras and knickers; a purple camisole; an amputated leg doing a solo cancan; a dismembered female torso cut off at mid thigh and squeezed into a beige corset; a black plastic bust wearing a white lace bra and a large sign, written in red capital letters, saying: BRAS REDUCED. Another sign saying: NIGHTWEAR 20% OFF.

What are they talking about – bras reduced?

Coyne slapped his hands on the steering wheel and, for a moment, both men were staring intensely at this new shrinking phenomenon. As though the women of Ireland were heading into some kind of physical recession. *Erin go Bra* – that great cry for national freedom would have to be reassessed.

With the afternoon sunshine sloping across the city, he turned the squad car down the street towards the sea and saw a band of water shimmering like a cool blue drink at the bottom of a glass. Even though it was autumn already, Coyne could vividly remember the summer and the people walking along with rolled-up towels, ghettoblasters on their shoulders; prams with parasols; girls who had forgotten to turn over and went crimson on one side of the face, or crimson down the backs of their legs. Now there was nobody except an old man leaning over the granite wall staring out at the ferry.

The kids were back at school, but Coyne still carried with him the rather sad summer image of an upturned ice-cream cone with a white pool spreading out along the pavement, and a crow with tattered charcoal wings tilting his beak to drink from some child's misfortune. To Coyne it was a symbol for all the invisible tragedy that lurked underneath society. He was there to make sure that the enemies of happiness were banished. Somebody had to deal with all the brutality and misery. And Coyne was going to kick ass, as they kept saying on TV. He was going to sort out some of these bastards. Blow them away. The Dublin Dirty Harry. He had a list of names in his head, like a top ten of local criminals.

Every muscle in his body was spring-loaded and ready for action. He was in a state of cataleptic readiness, lying dormant like a lethal virus that was going to rain down on some of these characters. He had put some of the hoors away before. And he wasn't finished yet either. You know, Coyne thought, while McGuinness was still going through every stroke on the Straffan golf course, life wasn't meant to be stationary. Life was more than a series of shagging holes on a green landscape. It had to have momentum, like music. Coyne wasn't the kind of cop with the cap tilted on the back of the head. No way.

Then it came: the situation. The familiar voice on the radio speaking with precise eloquence.

Ballsbridge area. Armed robbery in progress. Newsagent cum post office. We believe the raiders are still on the premises.

McGuinness picked up the radio mouthpiece and got the exact details, the very post office they had just passed by five minutes ago. Coyne swung the car around. With the siren on, they howled through the streets, blue light flashing back at them from doors and windows as they passed. Maybe this time they would really punch the clock. They arrived just in time to see a motor bike skidding off the pavement out on to the road. Hey Joe, where would you be going with that bag in your hand? Coyne was on the ball, only fifty yards behind.

We have them, Larry, he said. And as he caught up with them, he could have knocked them down with a tiny shove, only that one of the raiders on the back of the bike turned around and hurled a hatchet at them. Coyne took evasive action. Braked and skidded. But the hatchet came crashing through the windscreen like a shark through the side of an aquarium. Glass everywhere. Diamonds cascading all over their laps.

Jesus Christ, McGuinness said, his eyes open wide, staring at the hatchet stuck in the windscreen as if it were alive.

Coyne broke through and cleared away some of the glass with his elbow, then accelerated once more. He hadn't lost them yet, and after the next junction, he caught up with them again, just as they were heading into a small laneway at the end of which the raiders dropped the bike and jumped over the wall into the gardens, engine left running and the back wheel continuing to spin out like roulette. Coyne brought the car to a halt.

Don't be crazy, McGuinness urged.

But Coyne was going after them. No wonder they called him Mr Suicide back at the station. In the attempt to apprehend the raiders he jumped over the wall and came close to being savaged by a dog. He crossed the gardens like an obstacle course. Almost severed his leg from the knee down on a wheelbarrow and, in the end, very nearly got himself killed by the passing DART when he tried to give chase across the railway line. Jumped back just in time.

Bastards. Forced to give up the chase, Coyne limped back to talk to a woman who was standing in shock at the centre of a vegetable plot with her gardening gloves clasped as in prayer. They both faced each other suddenly, as though they were at a shrine together. Coyne out of breath and half kneeling to examine the footprints across the trampled leeks. He was embarrassed that he could not recover his breath more quickly. His chest was so badly out of condition that it felt like he was playing the accordion with himself. A tiny E flat note whistling through the air passages like a bent reed.

There had always been a sort of imaginary audience in Coyne's head. After all, a man's life was a performance. At this moment, the reaction would have been a short, modest applause, tailing off to silence, everybody waiting for his next move. Now and again, at crucial moments, he would talk to his audience, justifying his motives. Now and again, his audience merged with the real people he knew – his wife Carmel, his late father, his mentor Fred, and his friend Vinnie Foley. God knows who else was there in Garda Pat Coyne's audience? His friend Billy who had emigrated to Australia. Even his enemies maybe. And the top ten victims were always there in the front row admiring his tenacity in the face of all odds.

The Novena in the garden. Coyne looked like he'd come for a miracle, inhaling furiously. When he finally regained his breath, he asked the woman if she had been able to identify any of the raiders. She shook her head. But Coyne already had his own suspicions and began to lift some of the soil up in his hand, trying to ascertain if it was organic.

Yes, the woman nodded. Totally organic.

Back in the patrol car, with the sections of laminated glass all over the floor, Coyne thought of his own safety for the first time. He had lost sight of any personal fear and stopped acting like a man with a wife and three children. He was being heroic and suicidal again. More like a younger man trying to impress his friends, or his girlfriend, with nothing to lose.

Pat, you're a mad bastard, McGuinness crooned in his Tralee accent. You're going to get yourself killed.

I nearly had the fuckers, Larry.

You nearly had yourself mangled, you mean.

It's that bastard, Perry. I know it. He hasn't seen the last of me, the little savage.

McGuinness held the hatchet in his hand, and you'd think he was going to burst into song, some kind of Kerry golfing ballad. I don't want something like this in my skull, no thanks. It would be a terrible handicap on the golf course.

Garda Coyne was in his mid thirties, medium build and a narrow, handsome face. More handsome than he knew himself. He had a good smile, but more often bore an expression of great determination which made him look worried, or furious, or just stunned. Like he'd just been whacked on the back of the head with a newspaper and was ready to turn around and retaliate. A man who had his mind made up. A man who knew exactly what had gone wrong with the world.

He was a dedicated cop. Above and beyond the call of duty. He was following invisible goals, set by his own father, by his wife Carmel and by her mother, Mrs Gogarty. One day he would reach the rank of superintendent or commissioner. But Coyne was interested in more than that. He was a crusader and the streets of Dublin had gone out of control, simple as that. He was answering an inner mission to reform the society and clean up the city. And somebody was going to have to do something about the shaggin' environment as well.

The world was fucked, basically. The problem was that Coyne frequently found himself making his case to empty houses. Nobody wanted to know. He was explaining his views to an uninterested audience at a matinée, with popcorn left all over the place and sticky patches where they had spilled Coke in the dark. People with nowhere else to go. There he was, telling them about the kind of world he wanted his wife and children to be able to live in, and the audience would just walk out on him, leaving only the cleaning staff with the sound of their buckets and brushes, letting in a brash blast of daylight, flooding the place with the banal sound of traffic from outside.

At home, Carmel was getting ready to go to her art classes – Painting for Pleasure. The brochure from the local night school had been hanging on the notice board for weeks, beside the gas bill, and surrounded by calendar pages of Chagall and Egon Schiele. Some of her own new paintings were also beginning to take over the kitchen wall.

Carmel was slightly younger than her husband. Small build, blonde hair and a round face. She had sad, light-blue eyes. In her own way, she was full of determination too, and looked like she was fond of arguing, but also ready to laugh at any minute. She wanted to go places. Do something interesting with her life. She was maternal but fiercely independent, and in a modest way, proud of her looks, especially her legs. She knew she had talent.

Her mother was in the kitchen with her, drinking tea. The children were playing in the hall: Jimmy trying to arrest his two little sisters, Jennifer and Nuala, persuading them that they had to go to prison in the cupboard underneath the stairs. He was reading them their rights – you have the right to remain silent, but everything you say will be taken down in evidence. Look, there was nothing to be afraid of, he reassured them. He allowed himself to be incarcerated first.

Carmel was packing her art materials, throwing pencils and brushes into her bag. Made her feel she was seven years old again. Held up the fattest of her brushes and pretended to use it as a blusher. They laughed and her mother almost choked on a mouthful of bitter tea, bringing tears to her eyes, not so much because of the inhaled liquid but because of a sudden sense of pride in her daughter. She blew her nose: a mixture of snot and tears and tea, remembering the little flat tins of water-colour paints Carmel had used as a child. Squares of magenta and scarlet and purple that became mixed into a brown mess after a few days.

You were always gifted, Carmel, she wanted to say, but there was a scream from the hallway and Nuala came running into the kitchen crying, sniffling, sitting up on her grandmother's knee.

There you are, pet, Carmel's mother said, wiping the child's face. That'll teach you never to marry a Guard.

Ah now, Ma. There's no need for that, Carmel said, giving her mother a look.

At the station, Joe Perry had been taken in for questioning and Garda Coyne was pulling him apart over the raid on the post office. He was a young lad of seventeen, with milk moustache still clinging to his upper lip. He was wearing wide jeans and a hooded jacket. Just the kind of generic description they often put out on *Crimeline*. He seemed terribly casual as he was brought into the main office, looking around and smiling as though he was being ushered in for some kind of talk show, waiting for somebody to come and clip the little mike to his lapel. There was a kind of swing in his walk. The Ringsend swagger. He sat right underneath the cannabis poster – 'you've got the wrong man' written all over his face.

Coyne knew how to deal with these clowns. That grin didn't fool him one little bit.

So it's hatchets now, he said, leaning against a filing cabinet like it was the mantelpiece at home. But you could see Perry saying to himself: yah thick Garda gobshite. What do you expect me to say, yes?

Coyne approached Perry and jabbed him in the chest.

Chief Running-Foot, he said, waiting to see if the joke worked. You won't be running very far now, you little savage. Coyne got the hatchet from his desk and held it up to Perry's face. Exhibit A. Did you leave this behind by any chance? His personal audience roared laughing.

I done nothin', I swear.

Let's see your footwear then. Perry's sneakers had massive tongues; maybe they were meant to make him look like one of those mythical horses with white wings on their hooves.

Come here, Pegasus, you little bastard. And Coyne made him stand up while he examined the soles like a blacksmith.

Organic soil, eh?

I want to speak to my solicitor.

Coyne dropped the hoof and Perry's shoe made a tiny squeak on the tiled floor. But he wasn't finished, and Coyne then produced a small bag of soil.

Exhibit B, he shouted triumphantly as he pushed the soil bag into Perry's face. What was happening? Was it the adrenalin from the chase still surging like a narcotic around his head? Coyne suddenly lost his patience and began trying to feed Perry some of the soil, stuffing it into his mouth as though he was concerned about some nutritional deficiency, until some of the other Guards came over to restrain him.

You've made your point, Pat.

Perry was spitting out the black mixture of clay and saliva, proclaiming his innocence. Grimacing at the taste of wholefood.

At this point, Coyne felt a bit of a shit. He was only dealing with small fry. He had let himself down and felt his audience had suddenly switched over to *Come Dancing* in utter desperation. McGuinness even handed Perry a Kleenex, for God's sake, and Coyne held his palms out to his inner public, appealing that he was only human too. There is only so much a man can take. But his ratings had plummeted and his audience were all passed out on the sofa, yawning, half watching a couple strutting around in a high-bottomed tango.

As usual, the real crime was happening somewhere else. Public enemy number one, Berti Cunningham, was driving a spanking new Range Rover through the streets of the city. Just about the same time that Coyne was carrying out the special feeding programme at Irishtown Garda station, Berti Cunningham, his younger brother Mick Cunningham and their chief accountant Charlie Robinson were stopping briefly along Baggot Street so that Berti could pick up a kebab. They were the untouchables. Nobody could lay a finger on them. Berti strolled into Abrakebabra inhaling the smell, drawn to the counter like a fly to a ketchup stain. He had a thin, wiry sort of frame as though he had been underfed as a child. Raised on sliced bread and jam. Chip sandwiches, maybe. Where other crime lords needed a drink before they went out on a job, Berti Cunningham, or the Drummer as they all called him, needed some really evil piece of food, something that would set off a vicious clash of gastric fluids, leaving him with the stench of a tannery on his breath and a slight disfiguration at the edges of his mouth that only barely concealed the boiling bile.

His brother Mick was a little less ugly. Small goatie beard and a reversed baseball cap. He sat at a table with Chief, a stout man with a shaven head, wearing a kind of happy, vegetarian shirt, with lots of colours. It was more like a pizza really, with braces holding up his jeans. They had left Drummer's two Rottweiler dogs in the back of the Range Rover, panting with their tongues hanging out. They sat looking up at MTV – three women standing knee deep in the sea singing: *Don't go chasing waterfalls*, whatever the fuck that was supposed to mean. Right underneath a sign that said: No alcohol allowed on the premises, Chief cracked open a can of beer while Drummer ordered three kebabs, one for himself with lettuce and garnish, and two plain kebabs for his Rottweilers. Abrakebabra. Sure it was only dogfood anyway.

Carmel sat at the back of the class, listening to the art teacher, Gordon Sitwell, with vocation written all over her eyes. An unfinished painting was spread out in front of her and she was mixing up some paint, spellbound by eagerness, soaking up every word that Mr Sitwell uttered as though he was carefully distributing some precious linseed oil you could not afford to lose even one drop of.

Sitwell was a gentleman with a grand accent that somehow went with all that art talk. He had a squat build and wore a green corduroy jacket. He seemed to draw inspiration from his earlobe, which he squeezed gently as he spoke. He was there to spout erudition and to urge his disciples on to greater things. He kept walking up and down the room, talking as though he had a direct link to the great masters, stopping occasionally to hold up his index finger, knocking against an invisible urn and waiting to hear a faint musical note. He was just the kind of art teacher Carmel had expected, somebody with grey temples who was utterly lost in culture.

Sometimes he made eye contact with her, just to see if she understood what he was saying, and she automatically nodded. Once or twice he smiled as he wandered around the classroom, leaving behind him an intoxicating whiff of aftershave, which had to be called something like 'Renaissance' or 'Rubens' and must have been made with some ancient musk extracted from the entrails of a mythical animal. A sphinx or a unicorn. It curled around Carmel's nostrils and inspired her to carry on working on an evening sky over the sea, with a tree to one side. Nothing too fancy. Keep it simple.

Nice, gentle brush strokes, Sitwell was saying. Let me see the brush swing a little in your hand. Remember that painting is like telling a story. The colours are your words.

He turned his back and walked away as though he was leaving the room, then swivelled round dramatically and stopped to look everyone in the eye, individually. Some of the people had come back for a second year and knew by the sleepy grin on his face that he was about to say something funny.

Remember, ladies. It's not a powder puff you're holding, and everybody laughed in recognition as though they had heard this one before. It's an instrument of self-expression.

And when he came up behind Carmel the next time, he leaned

over with his medieval musk and urged her to use some more dramatic colour for the sky. Something really sensuous. A fiery cobalt, perhaps?

That's how it started, Coyne was telling the lads at the station. With tribal rituals.

He was writing in the details on the arrest sheet and stopped for a moment to tell the other members one of his little anthropological facts. Sergeant Devaney was listening with a sceptical smile on his face, buttocks perched on a desk. Life on Earth, with Pat Coyne.

That's how all that art and culture began in the first place. This tribe of people where all the men go out together to have a communal crap.

You're taking the piss, McGuinness said.

I swear, Coyne insisted. Every morning, all the men go out and leave these little sculptures on the landscape. Defecation missions they called it. I read all about it. It's only much later that they began to use materials like wood and paint.

Coyne could not remember where he had developed this obsession with facts. Probably at school, as a form of protection. To fit in with the schoolboy hierarchies. It resulted in a real interest in nature, and he still borrowed books and anthropological videos all the time. He still bought the *National Geographic* and was deeply committed to the environment; anything that affected the future. But none of his knowledge ever brought him closer to people. He had difficulty communicating his vision of the universe to his colleagues. He was not one for bending reality to the demands of story-telling, and in the end, always found himself alone, staring out from his own mind as though he sat on a raft that would never reach the shore. It seemed as if the other Gardai in the station were all listening to him from the far bank.

You wanker, Coyne. You're making this up.

I'm telling you, it's a well-known fact, these lavatory parties in the forest. Can't remember the name of the place.

But Coyne saw them all gazing at him incredulously, as though he was beyond rescue this time. Out of reach. At the mercy of a tide of Garda realism. Maybe it was the way he told it. But as usual, he felt the awkwardness of drawing an unspoken comparison between the actions of tribal men and the toilet-trained men of Ireland with

19

whom he worked. Telling them the unenhanced truth. We're all a bunch of civilised shitters when it comes down to it, each one of us proclaiming our identity, marking our space in the world through waste. It was clear that nobody had any idea what the hell Coyne was going on about. Where was the joke?

Out in the real world, Drummer Cunningham and his gang were making their way along the canal down to Percy Place. Mick Cunningham had taken over the wheel of the Range Rover to allow Drummer to finish off his mobile meal. The Rottweilers had already inhaled theirs. As they pulled up outside a house in flats, Drummer got out and threw the kebab wrapper on to the pavement as much as to say: this is my city. I'll throw my shite around if I like.

Upstairs, in a small apartment facing on to the street, Naomi Keegan was lying in a heap along the bed. She was still in her dressing-gown and the ring on the doorbell was her first contact with the outside world that day. Up to then she had successfully been able to remove reality by watching MTV. Her mind was a sponge, soaked in senseless images, heaving with the endless motion of limbs and lyrics. She went to the window, opened it and threw down the key. Then went back to lie on the bed again with a litre bottle of Ballygowan. Not so much to drink it but to hold it like a teddy bear or some kind of comfort toy that offered a vague notion of innocence and purity.

She was around twenty-five and had been a student of architecture at one stage. A drawing board in the corner of the room was submerged under a pile of clothes and personal items. It had also been misused more frequently as a surface from which she snorted whatever substance Drummer brought to her. A rolled-up James Joyce note was stuck in a penholder as the most essential implement. She was the architect of her own misfortune was the last sentence she heard from her South Dublin parents. To them, the sight of their daughter with an earring in her eyebrow and black fingernails was the end of her education. Not to mention the tattoo on her backside. That was a step beyond.

She could smell the kebab coming up the stairs and finally decided it was time to take another drink of water to recover some real sense of purity. Drummer came in and gave her the shite and onion smile. Looked around with disgust at the state of the room and pushed a mug away with his foot. *Can I touch you there* was on MTV at that moment. Michael Bunburger Bolton floating down some tropical river in a white suit, looking for some woman washing her hair in a waterfall for fucksake. Drummer made a little joke about the lyrics which Naomi ignored until he passed her a tab and she began to perk up. Then he went to the wardrobe and chose some clothes; a gold skirt and a thin black pullover.

I've got a job for you, he said.

Berti, please. Don't ask me. I'll do anything.

Just a little dance, baby. That's all.

She looked at him, and he smiled as though there was a VIP lounge in the back of his head that nobody ever got into. Even in matters of sex there was a Bluebeard room in Drummer's mind which you didn't want to investigate. Some young one had been turned into a kebab and hidden under the floorboards in the past maybe. A challenge to all women. Please discover me. Try and get into my last VIP lounge and find out what no woman has ever seen before.

He was already pulling her off the bed, taking the fizzy water from her and forcing her to get dressed. Slapped the tattoo on her backside just a little too hard to pass for affection, and while Naomi got dressed, he began to dance to the music on the TV. Some kind of profane jerky movements that made him look like he was suffering a mild form of tropical tarantism. He was a shite dancer. It was Tai Chi meets Michael Jackson, holding his crotch and thrusting forward like he'd just received a kick in the sphincter. His body just mocked everything that was aesthetic.

Carmel's art class was coming to an end. Everybody was beginning to wash brushes and put everything away while Mr Sitwell stood behind her, commenting on her tree.

It looks like a chestnut, or an oak, he said. Perhaps you could give it a little more body. Make it look stronger, more muscular. If you get my drift?

Carmel looked up. She didn't know what he meant.

Try a bit of maroon or burgundy, he said, taking her hand and guiding the brush towards the paints, dabbing and mixing with great skill, then applying thin downward lines of burgundy along the tree trunk.

Brilliant, she thought. He had transformed the painting and was already walking away again, talking to the class in general.

Every object has its own personality. Every object has its own dark, romantic secrets inside. When you draw an oak tree, it should look like a mystery man. A tall, handsome, muscular body. You should want to hug him, ladies.

They all laughed. Carmel blushed. The cheek of him.

Superintendent Molloy was in a strange, elated mood that evening. With good reason. He had finally broken through the wall of silence which surrounded Drummer Cunningham's deeds. He was excited by the fact that he now had a conviction in sight. A key witness, Dermot Brannigan, had turned police informer and was prepared to talk in court. Not so much a supergrass as a disaffected former associate of Berti Cunningham's who had given Molloy more than he needed to end the Drummer's reign.

When it came to the armed robbery and the case of Joe hatchet-man Perry, that was a different matter. His lawyer came into the station ranting about his client being assaulted. Superintendent Molloy said there was no harm done and he was happy to release the suspect to show that the Gardai were being reasonable about the whole affair. The lawyer was standing in the office with a long face on him; you'd think it was he who had been force-fed the organic muck. OK, Coyne had gone a little too far on the high-fibre diet, but after risking life and limb to arrest the little bastard, Molloy was now deciding not to have him charged.

He was just helping us in our enquiries, Molloy said.

He has his rights, you know, the lawyer complained. I'm considering a case of serious harassment.

Not at all, there's no need for that, Molloy brayed. We'll be releasing him right away. We're just going through the formalities.

My client has suffered deep distress, the solicitor added.

Well, he shouldn't be waving his hatchet around the post office then, Coyne said, finally losing his head.

What are you talking about, the solicitor fought back. My client was visiting his sick grandmother this afternoon.

So that's where he got the muck on his shoes. That bastard is guilty and you know it.

Coyne found himself pointing his finger straight at the lawyer. But it was like touching an electric fence. Once again he felt his audience had deserted him as though the only person in the world who would understand him was his wife, Carmel. She was there in the audience, about five or six rows back with her crisps and her toffees; a devoted fan with her knees up against the seat in front encouraging him. But Coyne had already gone too far and Superintendent Molloy was urging him to calm down.

Everything is under control, he said.

Coyne couldn't believe it. What was the point in him half killing himself running over those garden walls? As far as he was concerned, the legal profession only interfered with the administration of justice.

Just keep him away from my client, the lawyer said.

And afterwards, when the lawyer was gone, Superintendent Molloy took the opportunity to make a little speech of his own. Telling Coyne he wasn't up to it any more. He had lost his balance and needed to relax. Should go down the country for a few days.

That's not the way to go after these fellas, Molloy said. You can't take any short cuts.

Like Coyne's own father, Superintendent Molloy came from West Cork. Those county by county alliances throughout the Garda ranks had once established a bond between them, protecting Coyne, keeping him in sight of promotion. Molloy was taking on the role of a lost father figure, using the same tired country clichés.

Superintendent Molloy was a true redneck Garda. His hair crossed over from one side of his bald head to the other, like a lid or a trapdoor that had to be put back in place every time he went out in the wind. A hair-door is what it looked like, with a hinge at the side of the head, just above the temple. And Coyne stared at the mole just under the super's nose thinking, how does he shave? He imagined Molloy shaving the mole off and a fountain of blood gushing out. Moleshaver Molloy, walking around all day with a plaster on his face with the blood still seeping through.

You've got to play by the rules, Moleshaver said like a mantra.

I'll get him one of these days, Coyne vowed.

Look, Coyne. We've gone through this before. You can't lean on a suspect like that. Everybody knows he's guilty, but he's got a smart lawyer. Works for big-time sharks like the Cunninghams as well. Lay off until you've got something concrete.

Molloy leaned back, touching the tips of his fingers against each other, shampooing some invisible head in front of him. Coyne could see his own father, with the braces, and the rings holding up the sleeves of his shirt. He could smell the ancient tube of shaving cream, as though it was against the principles of the new republic to change to foam shaving lotion. Molloy took in a deep breath and leaned forward again, with purpose.

A word of advice, Pat. It's like a fart in the sauna. Unless you catch the fucker at it, forget it. It's the legal system in this country. He didn't get away with much anyhow.

That's not the point, Coyne snapped back in amazement. We can't just let him go.

Forget Perry, Molloy insisted. We've got Brannigan talking. He's under protective surveillance at the moment. You know what this means, Pat.

The Drummer.

Moleshaver looked across his desk with great Garda pride. Then he got himself ready to deliver an even more profound piece of advice.

You see, you've got to be able to connect the shite back to the arsehole it came from, he said.

Now that was ten per cent extra talk. That was the new improved formula language. As though Moleshaver had put forward the greatest ecological message of our time. The solution to pollution. Connect the shite back to the arsehole it came from. Molloy winked, and Coyne could not help being impressed by the impact of this new visual illustration. He liked it. It rounded off the faecal discussion earlier on. An inspiring concept which had a crisp cinematic feel to it, like the final words before a deadly subversive mission. Go for it, men. There was nothing to add, only action.

Coyne drove home along the seafront. Over the rasping sound of his own car, the tape deck was playing the blues. A brilliant red sky over Dublin had begun to fade away and it was getting dark. The red glow on the granite walls was gone and there was a pure white moon up in the shape of a half-masticated host. There was a hint of winter in the breeze, which swirled up dust and leaves and sweet wrappers together along the pavement.

Coyne laughed to himself. It was the most inappropriate reaction to the day. But he felt light-headed and washed over by a kind of dangerous exuberance. He saw everything in black and white. It always came down to this – the two directions: top road or bottom road. You could blame the world or blame yourself. You could try and change the environment and the circumstances around you, or you could try and change yourself. Coyne was certain that he was right and they were all wrong. He would show them all one of these days.

Carmel's mother was at home, putting on her coat as soon as he arrived in the door.

Your dinner is in the micro, she muttered.

Chicken Chernobyl, Coyne muttered back.

He felt like doing something outrageous. Like pulling down his trousers and exposing himself to her back; that ridiculous wide hairdo on her, the cloud of Lancôme and the chiffon scarf, for God's sake. Tried the chiffon scarf test lately, Gran? Sorry, Baroness von Gogarty. He made a grimace at the back of her head, pretending to come up and open the door for her. But she caught him.

I can see what you're doing, she said, letting herself out instead. Spinning around on her hind legs to throw him a filthy look. He watched her walking out the driveway, waiting to see if she would allow herself one more vicious look back. Yes.

Jennifer, one of the children, stood at the top of the stairs saying she couldn't sleep. So he went upstairs and found them all awake, waiting for him to tell the stories. He was much better than Gran.

She just tells girls' stories, Jimmy said. And Coyne felt appreciated, knowing that he could re-invent the whole universe for his family audience at least. He was back once more in the bubble of his own home, laughing at arcane little jokes that no other family would understand. Insulated by the warmth of his own group as though the world depended on them to begin all over again.

At other times, Coyne felt he had become his own audience entirely, watching himself on closed-circuit TV; a silent blue figure shifting around in a semi-detached house on a Dublin housing estate, carrying his children into bed, telling them bedtime stories about forsaken places under the sea.

And then the underwater man with no eyelids brought the little pink fishes to a place where they could hide. He lived in a sunken ship where they would be safe. You see the mackerel were smart because they had white tummies and they swam up high where the shark couldn't see them against the light. But the coloured fishes had to find a place to hide.

The children were gathered all around him in one of the beds. Nuala hiding all her furry toys under Coyne's arm, as if to act out the story. Jennifer holding her eyes open with her index fingers.

And even though the underwater man had no ears, he could hear everything. Every tiny sound. He could hear a bubble bursting a hundred miles away. So he could hear the shark coming back.

Coyne almost fell asleep himself when the story was over. Coyne the real father, tucking them in, rubbing his hand over his son's forehead, stalling to pick up a sock near the door, walking down the stairs lightly. Coyne eating his dried-out dinner. Coyne stealing biscuits in his own home.

Relaxing in front of the TV, he was still wearing his uniform, tie undone, watching the men of Papua New Guinea re-enact old tribal rituals. Above all else, he was concerned with extinction; the disappearance of legendary people. Last men belonging to ancient and pure civilisations which had clashed with modernity. Men and women like the Blasket Islanders.

Half-lying across the opulent floral sofa which Carmel had picked out on the advice of Mrs Gogarty, he watched the warriors jumping around, preparing for battle. He was almost asleep again when he saw one of the men running towards him with a hatchet. He jumped up. Kicked the dinner plate on the floor with his foot thinking he was dealing with Perry again. He found the remote control and played it back again and again. The warrior wore nothing but a purple jacket and a felt hat. Chest bare. White curly hair. The braided jacket looked like part of a hotel porter's uniform which had somehow become separated from the trousers. Maybe it came from some famous American Hotel, like the Waldorf Astoria, and made its way right out to Port Moresby, sold and resold, only to be worn in ceremonious battle with a painted face and bare painted legs underneath. The warrior's white teeth bared as though he was smiling, waiting for a tip. The hatchet came up in the right hand, just like Perry.

Suddenly Coyne thought everything he had done and said that

day was entirely unbalanced. Out of control. The volume turned up too high. He had overdone it with Perry. Coyne had to get smart. He should try to be more cool. A balanced cop, calmly tracing the shite back to the arsehole it came from.

It was Gordon Sitwell who held the door open for Carmel when she was going home. Her painting rolled up like a precious scroll in her hand, smiling like a child. But he was laughing to himself and shaking his head.

Got a dash of paint on your nose, he said.

Oh really, she said. But when she tried to wipe it off, he held up his hand as though she was about to rub away a secret sign.

No, no. Leave it there, love. It's proof that you were at your art classes and not in the pub.

Adieu, he said, and then walked off briskly in the direction of the car park.

When she got home, Coyne was already in bed, sitting up reading a magazine. Bare hairy arms outside the duvet. There was an explosion of talk; so much to catch up with. He exaggerated the chase, and the hatchet. Vowed he would get his revenge as though it was Carmel herself who had been placed in danger and he was expected to uphold a bond of chivalry on her behalf.

She pinned her painting up on the dressing table and asked: what do you think?

Good, he said.

But Coyne was absolutely amazed. It was the sky he had come home with earlier on; the fading, yellow and red furnace which hung over the city that evening when he drove out along the coast road. The end of Coyne's day, looking like an old bruise over Dublin Bay. Her painting contained such honesty, such complete understanding of Coyne's mind that he felt he was looking into some kind of new mirror through which he could look back along the day and see everything radiating with burning violence, down to the wine-red glow along the side of the trees. Coyne was afraid to say it was brilliant. Angry that she could be so accurate. You didn't fucking do that yourself; no way, he wanted to say.

She got undressed, talking about the art class, still watching as if to make sure nobody would steal her painting. Slipped a giant T-shirt over her head and stood before him for a moment, a headless, naked woman struggling to come to the surface. Then she drew lines of white cream on her face and her elbows like a female warrior about to take part in a fertility ritual.

Do you think the tree is muscular enough, she asked?

Muscular. Yeah, I suppose so.

But Carmel was unhappy that he could so easily dismiss her work.

God bless you, Pat. You're such a headbanger.

I said it was muscular, didn't I?

You're a philistine. She smiled cheerfully.

Coyne mistrusted this new language. He stared at her until she got into bed and kissed him. He dutifully kissed her back, like a man tiptoeing around the intimacy of words. For a while they sat up in bed, Coyne reading, Carmel squinting at her own masterpiece. The voices from next door drifting softly in through the wall. Light switches being flicked. Water running. The Gillespies moving around and speaking to each other, asking final questions, offering final assurances, perhaps sitting up right there on the other side of the wall, in the same position, back to back, like a mirror image of Pat and Carmel Coyne in their bed.

Come on, Pat.

Come on what?

You never headbutt me any more.

So Coyne got up and switched off the main light, while she turned over on her hands and knees. He pulled back the duvet, though he could see nothing and stumbled against the end of the bed. It was pitch black, and in that moment of blindness, the unspoken aim was that she would keep shifting around like a moving target, while he would score by crashing his head against her bottom. Again and again, bashing his skull like a young buffalo into her soft rump while her shrieks went out the window.

Drummer Cunningham drove the Range Rover up to a small Corporation estate in the north of the city. He had left the dogs at home. There was a bit of business to settle with Brannigan. Like Coyne, he was dedicated to his work, beyond the call of duty. He had never once been out of the country and boasted about it as though it pointed to some extreme loyalty towards his own piece of turf. Leaving even for a short holiday to Ibiza would be a major act of betrayal, surrendering the sovereignty of his ground to others. He'd come back to find his territory and his followers subsumed into some other gang.

Drummer usually wore a gold bracelet with his suit. He occasionally brought a set of rosary beads, just to mock his victims. Praying over them and blessing them before they were done in. The nickname, Drummer, had stuck to him from a long time back so that nobody really knew its origins, except his victims, who said they heard drums whenever they faced him. Otherwise, Berti Cunningham was ordinary in his taste for nightclubs and let on he was the king, holding a mobile phone, surrounded by a whole load of other boneheads in suits. Now Drummer had even bought a nightclub of his own.

Coyne's ex-Garda friend and mentor, Fred, had given him a lot of these details on the gang. All the stuff the Special Branch knew but could not prove in court. Fred was close to the source and in a position to pass on sensitive information to Coyne. Two men had been shot or beaten to death in Dublin in the past six weeks, both of them attributed to Drummer. It was clear that Drummer was trying to transform himself into a respectable nightclub owner while at the same time reasserting his authority over the underworld. There was nothing the law could do about it. But wait till Coyne started dealing with him. One of these days, Coyne would wipe the floor with that bum-fucking primate – stick him back in the serious offenders wing of Mountjoy zoo.

Outside Dermot Brannigan's home, two rookies from the Serious Crime Squad were keeping a vigil when Naomi Keegan came walking towards them. Her gold skirt, leather jacket and long legs drew their attention. She appeared to be dancing down along the pavement almost, and just as she got past the two detectives, she screamed. When they looked around they could see that she was being assaulted. A youth trying to take her bag. They jumped out of the car and ran towards her, but the youth had already disappeared without the bag, leaving the men there to try and comfort her.

Around the back of Brannigan's house, Drummer and his chief accountant were already dragging their victim down a laneway towards the blue Range Rover. Brannigan was trying desperately to shout for help but uttering no more than a minimal squeak under his gag. It was no use. He had been delivered up to Drummer's court of justice. Brannigan was shittin' bricks. Nervous as an albino rabbit staring into the eyes of a starving ferret. Obediently got into the Range Rover and found himself going for a little drive out to Brittas Bay, after they drove around to pick up Naomi and Mick again.

She sat in the front seat listening to a Walkman all the way, occasionally slapping her hands on the dashboard in time to the music. Mick had taken over the wheel while Drummer and the Chief sat on either side of Brannigan in the back. Berti making the sign of the cross and taking out a luminous set of rosary beads. *In nomine Patris et Filii et Spiritus Sancti.*

Amen, said the Chief Accountant, laughing.

Moments later, Berti almost broke his mobile phone, jabbing it into Brannigan's groin because he wouldn't answer his question. By the time they got out to Brittas Bay, Brannigan had sweated a gallon of crude oil out through his forehead and there was condensation all over the windows.

At a boathouse, Drummer kicked his pleading victim around for a while until he got tired. Brannigan inhaled and tasted the sweet terror of his own blood as he swallowed. With the headlights of the car shining on him, they began to staple Brannigan to the door by his jacket. In crucified formation he hung in his clothes as the Chief Accountant whispered into his ear, telling him he was going to heaven and he would be well looked after up there, speaking with the gravitas of a liquidator to one of his doomed shareholders.

You're surplus to requirement, pal.

And Brannigan kept looking at Drummer as though he hadn't even heard Chief. Please, Berti, Jesus, please, he repeated, grimacing through his pink teeth like he'd been eating loads of raspberries. But Drummer just got tired of listening to this whining and told Chief to replace the piece of packing tape over his mouth. Then he went over to put some music on the car stereo.

Come out and do your thing, he commanded. Naomi had hardly seen anything of what was going on because she was lost in her own narcotic fantasy.

Berti, don't ask me to do this, she said.

But there was no way of refusing, so she got out and began to perform a sort of liturgical dance in front of Dermot Brannigan. Right there with the waves crashing in on the shore and the sand dunes all round shaped into smooth bellies and thighs behind them. A light breeze stirred the bristle of reeds. The car stereo blasted out across the deserted landscape with Chris de Burgh: *Don't pay the fucking ferryman* – the most appropriate musical murder to emphasise the tackiness of life and death. Brannigan stared with open eyes at the girl swinging her hips with wonderful accuracy, pointing all the fluid narrative of her physical attributes at him in order to take away the pain of his imminent departure. He felt the self-pity of a dying man. Duped by desire. Legs, hips, breasts and smiles; the supreme icons of compassion, warmth and self-preservation dancing in front of him. A dance of mercy in which she began to uncover herself, bit by bit, turning to show glimpses of her body that made Brannigan wish he was already gone. It was like sex had become a rehearsal for death. She danced until he could see a strip of black pubic fur, which seemed to be stuck on at the top of her legs with velcro. Her discreet tattoo looked like she had Taiwan stamped on her right buttock. It entered Brannigan's eyes and slipped into his unlocked mind along the secret passages of desire, sitting like a silent cat beside the furnace of his fear.

That's all they allowed him to see. He had tears in his eyes when they put a black refuse sack over his head. They stood around smoking and watching the sack moving in and out with his breath.

Naomi pulled on her clothes again, but instead of getting back into the car, she walked out towards the sea as though she had done her life's work and was now ready to depart herself. Chief had to run out and drag her back to the car at the last minute.

You didn't say you were going to kill him, she kept pleading on behalf of Brannigan as though the dance had turned her into a carnal companion.

Drummer was ready for this and gave her a syringe. Put on the light inside the Range Rover and helped her to send the cool blast of smack into her arm. All the venom of Berti Cunningham's law flooding into her veins. She slammed her head back against the side of the car. Her eyes rolled around her head.

She'll remember nothing, Drummer muttered and then went over to make sure his victim was nailed up properly. With a hammer and two large nails he crucified Brannigan one last time. Blood rolled down from the palms of his hands in long red lines along the flaky, light-blue door of the boathouse. There was no sound of pain, just Brannigan looking like a monk and a martyr, bowing his head all the time under the black plastic hood.

Fuckin' mouth, Chief said as though he was speaking for Drummer. As though the silence was too much and something had to be said in the presence of such violence. He won't fucking talk again, that's for sure. The next time he'll talk is when he's begging to be let into the big nightclub in the sky.

Drummer laughed but said nothing.

The words were surplus. They stood back and watched the bag moving in and out. Chief looking at Drummer and waiting to see if he should take the bag off again. But Drummer remained silent. The victim's hooded head sank forward and the breathing stopped. Then they left.

Brannigan's body was found early in the morning. The Special Branch were all over the beach, combing the sand for clues, erecting Garda crime scene tape to keep possible onlookers away from the location of the murder. The discovery had been made by a group of early morning pony trekkers. A woman had to be sedated on account of the shock.

Superintendent Molloy was pacing up and down, knowing that he had not only lost a valuable witness but that he was also, in a way, responsible for it. His personal war with the Drummer gang had come to a pitch. An incident room had already been set up at his own station at Irishtown. They were following a definite line of enquiry, they announced, but that was all bullshit. What they really needed was somebody tough like Coyne. Somebody who would sort out Drummer and his followers once and for all. People like Molloy and the Special Branch would be too scared even to put a parking ticket on his car, for fucksake.

Coyne played with the children after breakfast, letting them jump down from tables and cupboards, catching them in his arms all morning. It was like bungee jumping for kids. Nuala was absolutely fearless. Threw herself off any surface down into the safety of Coyne's embrace. They all trusted him, but Nuala went a step further and liked to throw herself backwards, with her eyes closed.

Carmel didn't like it. To her, the game was childish and dangerous. She was afraid they would throw themselves off somewhere when he was not there.

He's teaching them to commit suicide, was Mrs Gogarty's attitude.

But Coyne urged his kids to go higher and higher, to find new peaks of fearlessness, and to hurl themselves off the roof of the car, right in front of the neighbours. Carmel inside trying to draw her mother, who was looking out through the window and shaking her head all the time with shock and horror.

He's showing them how to kill themselves. That little grimace around her nose as though she was constantly caught fighting back a bad smell.

You're such a headbanger, Pat, Carmel said when he finally stopped and came inside. Why don't you build them a swing instead? That would be useful. More normal too.

You call that useful, Coyne responded, looking at the half-finished painting of Mrs Gogarty looking all flushed and red in the face, like she was asphyxiating.

Coyne went into the kitchen. Underneath that instant surge of aggression, he reflected on his role as a father. Felt that he'd failed his kids. Of course they should have a swing. It wasn't a lot to ask for, and maybe he was desensitizing them to feelings of fear with his games. They were deprived kids and he vowed he would build the swing. A really good one. But he wasn't going to do it on orders from Carmel. He wasn't going to do it for Mrs Gogarty, the voice of righteousness. No way. So he sat in the kitchen and stared with contempt at the pictures of Chagall and all the others on the wall.

Shag off, Chagall, he muttered.

Maybe it was the way Coyne was brought up. Maybe it was the passionate severity of his father that made him the way he was. His father had come to Dublin from West Cork to claim his part in the making of a new Ireland. An Irish, Catholic Ireland. With his job in the Civil Service, Coyne's father began to involve his family in a personal crusade for the language. He would shape the new Ireland through his own kids, turning them into native Irish speakers. Making them speak Irish on the buses, like aliens in their own land. Coyne could see that his father was right, but too late. By the time Coyne was growing up, rock 'n' roll had already taken a grip of his intellect. The Irish language could never work in neon. It was unsuited to the electric guitar. Unsuited to commerce. It was like jumping off the roofs of cars.

Coyne was sent to the Gaeltacht in Connemara at the age of nine where he learned how to smoke. The old woman in the house gave him Sweet Afton for his sweet asthma. *Puffail siar air sin,* she said. That will make you cough it up, and it took him twenty years to give it up again. He could still hear the song of her voice calling out on the wind, the chickens proclaiming newly laid eggs, and the sound of enamel buckets, slopping with milk. Coyne loved Irish Ireland, the warmth and non-judgemental nobility of the west. At Colaiste Mhuire, the all-Irish secondary school where Coyne was educated in the city centre, the Christian Brother idea of education was nothing but decolonization, lash by lash. The panic of a young nation. They had nothing in common with the Blasket Islanders, or the famine cottages of West Cork.

Now it was Coyne's turn to shape the nation. Only that it was changing again and all the old historical landmarks would be eclipsed by new outrageous shrines of crime. As a Garda, he saw it all coming. Murder at the Rock of Cashel. Armed robbery in Enniscorthy. A paedophile priest at a summer camp in Glendalough. The old Yeats poem, 'Come away, O human child...', took on a whole new meaning. The sacred places of Irish history defiled by new atrocities. And now it was murder in Brittas. Crime was the nation's biggest growth industry.

Back in the squad car that afternoon, Coyne was casually telling McGuinness what he had read in one of his nature magazines the night before. They were crossing back over the toll bridge at the time. The green river backing up into the city, bridge by bridge.

Come 'ere, Larry. You know something I found out about scorpions last night.

What?

You know they have a sting in the tail and all that.

Yeah!

Well that's not all they have. Did you know they have a disposable penis?

McGuinness laughed. But Coyne remained serious, looking for some sense in his own words, some new allegory he could pin on to his fellow humans.

I'm not joking you, Larry. One shot. Then they grow a new one.

Coming back into Ringsend, they passed by a convoy of police vehicles. In the back of one of them sat Drummer Cunningham, who was being taken in for questioning. Molloy sat in another vehicle waiting to extract a confession from his man. But Berti Cunningham had a special grin on his face as though he was enjoying the journey. Behaved like somebody on a state visit.

Somebody should impale that fucker, Coyne remarked.

He's the real Teflon criminal, McGuinness responded with the usual lethargy. No evidence will ever stick to him.

I wish his mickey would fall off, Coyne said, waiting for his turn to deal with Drummer.

But Coyne's life revolved instead around petty crime and they were soon called to the scene of a mugging, where an old woman stood bewildered at the side of the street, outside some shops, holding a strap in her hand.

I seen them do it, a bystander kept saying, as Coyne got out of the squad car and went over to them. I seen her holding on, the poor thing. Dragged her along the pavement so they did.

It was this kind of situation that Coyne had to deal with. Some junkie out of his mind taking the price of a fix off an old woman and nearly putting her into the grave in the process. There she was, lost and shocked, just passing the strap of her bag along in her hand like a set of rosary beads. Shaking and crying.

We'll run her up to the cemetery, McGuinness said, and they led her gently towards the car. Drove up along the canal to see if there were any new bags floating along the surface. Then stopped at a place under a railway bridge which they called the handbag graveyard. A place full of handbags and other rubbish. They brought the old woman out to see if she could identify her own.

What colour was your handbag, Mam?

Tomorrow, she answered.

What colour, Coyne tried again.

Wednesday, she said. My appointment is Wednesday, isn't it?

Animals, Coyne muttered to McGuinness.

Come on, we'll take you home, he said, leading the old woman back to the car. And as he placed her in the back seat, Coyne began to think of his own mother. He should review the security arrangements before anything could happen to her.

Coyne saw it all. He saw the pigeons pecking at dried vomit and discarded chips. He saw the victims, culprits – the lucky and the unlucky. Coyne could tell you more about the nature of society than anyone else. The kids sleeping rough. Boys for sale. It was difficult not to be whipped by compassion. But that was Moleshaver Molloy's golden rule to all Gardai – you couldn't allow it to get to you. Never entertain your emotions.

Coyne had witnessed everything. The amount of people he brought to Focus Point; women with their entire families on the move in the middle of the night. Whole families of junkies. Beatings, muggings, suicides. Shopkeepers held up with syringes. The distress of a woman after rape. They dragged a man in his pyjamas out of the canal one night. Found a well known politician in a car with a young boy. Once helped to contain a riot near the British Embassy. Yobbos. Paedophiles. Alcoholics going downhill year by year. Rich kids acting the fool as though they owned the city. And the endless succession of car crimes. Road accidents.

Coyne saw the filth and the funny side of the city. In broad daylight, he once had to restrain an old traveller woman standing in the middle of a busy intersection with an oar, beating the cars and buses as they went by. A boy who had accidentally shot an arrow into his mother's neck. A burglary where the criminal called the Gardai to save him from a snake. A car parked suspiciously, only to reveal a woman's naked arse in the windscreen. And all of this had to be interpreted for the larger public audience. Each incident had to be put in official words, for the records, and for the press. Gardai at Irishtown received reports of a man interfering with himself on the canal bank. Drunk and disorderly youth, barking at the punters in Shelbourne Park. There was a lot of repetition. Lots that Coyne didn't even remember offhand. Or care to. The foreign tabloids across the water frequently had more spectacular stories, but this was

Dublin. And Dublin had everything. He tried not to make a political judgement. He had his own ideas on how the society should be run, but he was only concerned with justice and fair play. Coyne's Justice.

Mick Cunningham was arrested in the snooker hall. When members of the Special Crime Squad walked up to table number five, he looked around and said: wait till I take this shot. The Gardai ran and lunged forward to prevent him potting the last red. Under interrogation, he got them back, however, by making total fools of them. One detective after another went in to listen to Mick talk like a cross between a garrulous DJ and a pro-life spokesperson, droning on in a kind of pseudo-legal gibberish, The term 'You have the right to remain silent' took on an entirely different meaning. We beg you to remain silent and stop fucking going on about article this and article that of the constitution.

Chief was arrested at his home. He was sitting there with a two-day stubble on his face, trying to get his girlfriend's cat drunk. Devising new sources of delicious cat food that could be marinated in alcohol to deceive the suspicious animal. But the feline hangover must have rated among the world's worst. And when Chief answered the door to two detectives in plain clothes, the cat made a dash for it.

Drummer Cunningham and his gang were finally sitting in various interview rooms at Irishtown Garda station. Drummer surrounded by Superintendent Molloy and top members of a special unit that had been set up to deal with this case alone. In the yard of another station, the Range Rover was being examined carefully by forensic experts, sweeping little bits of dust and sand particles into plastic bags. Moleshaver Molloy, with his jacket off, was there leading the enquiry, asking lots of questions and getting no answers. Like his brother and understudy, Mick, Drummer put into effect his strict policy of obfuscation, saying something utterly daft back to them – something domestic, something philosophical that would demonstrate clearly what a waste of time it was. Then Molloy would start all over again.

OK, Cunningham. That's all very interesting, but let me ask you a simple question. You filled the Range Rover with petrol in the afternoon. Next morning it's empty. That's a lot of mileage, Drummer. Can you explain that?

You went for a drive, isn't that so? one of the other detectives added. A midnight beach party maybe.

Who was with you, Berti?

But Drummer just smiled. You could see that it was all very amusing to him. They were trying to get into the select VIP lounge at the back of his head again, so he just stared at the wall.

Gentlemen, is all he would say. Because even trivial answers would help them. He rarely gratified them with anything. It was only when Superintendent Molloy seemed to lose his temper and start shouting the same question at him again and again that Berti Cunningham decided it was time to give them something.

All right. I'm going to tell you something. Just to keep yous happy.

Cunningham began to talk to them about his new nightclub, offering invitations to the stunned detectives. They had to hold themselves back. And secretly, they were also curious, as though there might be some hidden clue for which they dutifully had to listen.

My club, Drummer said. Opening up next weekend. Bring the missus.

Molloy glared back. Refused to entertain the joke and remained serious. In order not to lose face, he immediately lashed back with another question. A crucial one that would get Drummer worried. Looked like he was going to beat the living daylights out of him. Came right up close to him, breathing mint and black pudding breath over his face, staring straight into the whites of his eyes and speaking in a quiet, eerie tone of voice.

What's the sand doing all over your car, Cunningham?

Drummer seemed to be caught out by the question. He was smiling with pride, and suddenly went serious. Looked up with a kind of new-born innocence and came up with the most straightforward answer.

The dogs, he said. I walk the dogs on the beach every day. They need the exercise.

Coyne was on duty that night. There was hardly any action except the usual complaints: dogs barking and drunk driving. A youth pissing against the railings of the American Embassy; somebody puking right up against the window of Pizza Hut, like an action replay for the diners inside; break-ins, car thefts and loads of domestic stuff. It was not until the early hours of the morning, just before they went off duty, that they received an unusual call. A girl on the railway line. Tightrope walking along the tracks in some kind of death wish. With the first DART due any minute, she was impervious, treading along one of the silver rails in her bare feet like some angel of commuter despair.

Coyne parked at the level crossing. And while McGuinness stayed with the car, he ran down along the sleepers, behind the terraces of the Lansdowne Road grounds. Coyne had begun to see certain moments like this in sharp relief, like a symbol of what had become of his life, running along the railway line wheezing. This is where he had ended up, his friend Vinnie Foley would say.

He shouted but the girl didn't hear him. When he got closer, he discovered that she was humming, or moaning. She wore starry purple shorts and a loose belly top, holding her shoes in her hand. Some young one dancing as though she had lost control of her intellect altogether.

What are you trying to do, kill yourself, he shouted.

A glazed blue trance occupied her eyes and she was shivering, mouthing a frantic, silent refrain that reminded Coyne of Lady Macbeth. Fucked-up on smack or something. He then realised that she was trying to top herself.

What's wrong, love. Why don't you come with us. Everything will be all right.

He took hold of her bare arm, feeling the soft, creamy white flesh in his hand. He was miles away from the squad car and had to walk her all the way back along the line. She didn't even realise that he was guiding her, she was so stoned out of her mind. Trembling with the chemical imbalance in her blood. Deeply unhappy, stopping every now and again to fret and clutch her shoes to her chest.

Not far to go now, love, Coyne said, coaxing her along like a father bringing a child to the bathroom in the middle of the night. But then she suddenly pulled away and ran towards some railway huts. He followed her, calling after her until she stopped in the shadow of one of the huts. And when he moved towards her, she pulled up her jumper exposing her breasts to him. He stalled a moment to look at them. The nipples and their dark aureoles were staring at him. Challenging him. Women like that gave him a fundamental feeling of inadequacy, because he felt a duty to go after them. It brought out all the hard man talk at the back of his mind. I'd love to drink your bathwater, missus. *Suas do Guna, Una.* She lunged forward to embrace him, kissing and crying at the same time, trying to make him place his hand on one of her breasts. But Coyne jumped back.

Pull yourself together, he said almost to himself as much as to her. He drew her top back down again.

What's your name?

Naomi, she said in a melancholy voice, as though to indicate that he was another failure.

Well look, Naomi. We've got to go home now. Come on.

Lights were coming on in the nearby houses. Silhouettes in bathrooms. Kettles boiling in kitchens with built-in pine cupboards. You could see right down into the houses, and through one window he saw a duvet pulled back on a bed. Somewhere else just a naked bulb lighting up a bare room. Dawn seeping across the city like a great sadness. It crept along the railway line, all the way from Wexford, emptying out a steady blue-white flood of solitude on to the dewy sleepers. Dublin-lonely. The night was dying and a blanket of cold reality claimed back the illusion, bit by bit, reaching in under bridges, along the empty streets and down the long narrow gardens below. Dogs were barking somewhere. Soon there would be people everywhere.

He had brought junkies to the methadone dispensary before, but this was like his own daughter. When he got back to the squad car, he opened the rear door and placed her in the back seat.

Jesus – she's like Madonna on oysters and Guinness, he whispered to his colleague.

By morning, Moleshaver Molloy had been forced to release the Cunningham gang. There was no evidence, nothing they could pin on them. Drummer emerged from the Garda station triumphant, shaking hands with his solicitor, thanking the forensic experts for cleaning all the sand out of his Range Rover.

Coyne was there to see Mick Cunningham and Chief being released some time later. Made the Gardai look like a whole bunch of flowerpots. The law was an asshole. And on the way home, Coyne dropped in on Fred Metcalf, his older, ex-Garda friend who now worked as a security guard at premises in Dublin Port. Fred kept saying it was time to get tough. Somebody was going to have to get dirty. Rules had to be broken.

What do you expect, Pat? Criminals have taken on designer status. No question about it. It's Kilkenny Design. Look at this place here. Gurriers coming in here every night to see what they can rob or smash up. It's the dogs of illusion, Pat.

The dogs of illusion, Coyne said, puzzled.

Fred had guru qualities. He knew the city like the back of his hand. He was an encyclopaedia on crime and Dublin anthropology. Knew the background circumstances on every court case and every personality involved. Fred had taken early retirement from the force, though Coyne never found out why. There were various excuses, but it was too late to ask. And Coyne was his protégé, in a sense; destined to succeed where Fred had failed.

It was to Fred Metcalf that Coyne looked for real guidance. With his grey moustache and his slow, deliberate movements, he provided great encouragement. Coyne admired the way Fred could follow a line of enquiry by simply going in and talking to local newsagents, butchers, car mechanics. He just talked for no reason about the weather, football, the government; anything that could sustain a subtle little question here and there about the local suspects. Fred was a natural born local, no matter where he went.

Whenever Coyne tried to make some of his own discreet investigations, the result was always uneven; either he got on too well and revealed more about himself than he gathered, or else the conversation got stuck on the weather. An old woman in the local shop just going on about the wind, saying it was penetrating, and Coyne just walking off thinking about the choice of word: penetrating.

Fred was such a talented investigator, he could only have been hounded out of the Gardai by some injustice. Lack of promotion perhaps. Fred had a way of being invisible. A good listener who offered little titbits as bait. The great Irish trade of information – give a little, take a little. Somebody's always dying to talk, he'd say. Fred and Coyne had already built up quite a dossier on many of the top criminals.

How's Carmel? Fred asked over tea and Kerry Cream biscuits.

She's gone mad on this art business, Coyne replied.

Fred also played a role in Coyne's moral and intellectual well-being. Liked to listen to Coyne talking about his kids. Took an interest in Carmel's latest craze.

Won't last, Fred pronounced. I can tell you that straight off.

That reflexology thing lasted long enough, Coyne insisted. I'm telling you, Fred: she's gone nuts about this painting business. She's at it all the time now. Day and night. All over the kitchen she's got this calendar of Chagall, or whatever his shaggin' name is.

Won't last. There's too many at it. All that self-expression lark. There's too much expression and too little understanding, Fred thought.

Not Carmel. She's hooked.

Have you thought of taking her away? Fred asked.

Away?

Coyne considered it. Since when had they been away together like a couple, without their kids? In fact, Coyne was afraid of that. Afraid in a way that they would have to face each other, some kind of imaginary family court where everything would come up in evidence between them. He was afraid of the honesty of a weekend trip with Carmel.

Think about it. A weekend in the west. Be good for you, Fred said.

Inevitably, however, the conversation would return to crime. And as Coyne accompanied his mentor on his tour of the compound, shining his torch under parked trucks, lighting up the deadly shadows behind containers and checking the razor-wire-topped walls of his fortress, Fred came up with a theory.

Will I tell you what's causing all this crime, Pat?

What?

Cars! That's what. The private car is what's doing it. You see, all that privacy is no good for people. Alienates everybody. Makes them unfriendly. A sick society. There should be no such thing as private cars.

We'd be walking around in the rain otherwise, Coyne remarked.

What's wrong with taxis? There should be nothing but taxis and trains. Far more sociable. It would give people things to do. And reduce the crime. A nation of taxi drivers and delivery men.

And squad cars, Coyne added.

It's the dogs of illusion, Pat.

Drummer Cunningham was a man of few words. Within hours of his release he was walking around his new nightclub on Leeson Street as though nothing had happened. He wasn't even being triumphant, or celebrating his release like a primitive criminal. He just got on with his business and nodded quietly as the builder, Brendan Barry, explained how they would be finished in a day or two.

We're just putting in the spots, then we're ready to roll.

Rock 'n' Roll, Drummer echoed.

The workers were busy carrying out the last minute renovations. A DJ was already trying out the new sound system and two go-go dancers were shifting around on the dance floor with mechanical movements.

Chief was there too, looking busy with a little pocket calculator. And Mick Cunningham leaning up against the new oval-shaped bar. Drummer looked a little concerned as he stood back and squinted at the dance floor. Liked everything to be dead on. Felt he knew something about architecture since he had a former student of architecture as a girlfriend. With his new-found talent for interior design he gave the builder some minimal instructions. Then started looking around in a suspicious way as though something was wrong.

There's something missing here, he said, and Builder Brendan instantly became a ball of nerves.

What, Berti? There's nothing missing.

Something isn't right here, Cunningham insisted.

I swear. There's nothing gone out of here, boss. You can search us.

No, I don't mean missing, Drummer said. I mean, there should be something else here, like a fountain.

A fountain? The builder smiled with relief.

Yeah. A fountain would be nice.

Where?

There, you know, Berti said, waving his hands in the general direction of the dance floor and then moving on to inspect the lights and the mirrors, leaving the builder to ponder the sheer lunacy of erecting a fountain at such short notice. A fountain would require a water supply. That meant pipework, ripping up the floor again; a nightmare. And while Drummer was walking towards the DJ, Chief whispered discreetly into the builder's ear.

Put in a fuckin' fountain, he commanded. I don't care where you get it. I want to see a bleedin' fountain there by tomorrow.

Some days later, Coyne found an opportunity to deal directly with the Cunninghams. Just to let them know that even if the Special Branch had given up on them, the whole business with Brannigan wasn't over yet. They hadn't come across Coyne yet. Be afraid, was the message he was trying to get across.

Coming around the corner towards the canal at Percy Place, Mick Cunningham drove the Range Rover through the city, showing the world and his mother what an excellent driver he was. Should have been a stunt man, doing wheelies maybe. Except that Coyne happened to be driving the squad car from the other direction. A conversation with McGuinness about why he didn't go to the cinema had to be postponed. Coyne felt there was far too much escapism. The streets of Dublin were like one big movie anyway, something that was borne out like an instant illustration by Mick Cunningham, lashing around the corner at high speed.

Coyne was just in time to switch on the blue light and pull out to stop the oncoming car. Got out and discovered he had stopped Mr Big Time's brother Mick. Should have known not to proceed any further because it was a sensitive case. But Coyne was beginning to see it as his own personal crusade, a kind of tacit competition with Moleshaver Molloy to see who would put these boys behind bars first. The Cunning brothers, he called them.

Out, he shouted, McGuinness standing right behind him with a torch.

Mick Cunningham was the calmest person you could ever meet on a dark night. Thought he was being arrested again, so he didn't put up any struggle. He was like the Pope, waving his hands up and down in slow motion like a wind-up doll. Wearing his reversed baseball cap, and bomber jacket with a mobile phone in the pocket. Clean shaven, number one haircut, with highlights. Coyne was staring into Mick Cunningham's eyes, just to make him understand who was who around here. The air laden with silent aggression.

You think you can get away with the Brannigan murder, Coyne said. Well, wait till you start dealing with me.

Coyne lifted up his baton as though he was going to beat Mick

Cunningham to a pulp in the street. McGuinness anxiously shifting around in the background, hoping this would go off peacefully.

You can't touch me, Mick Cunningham said.

That's what you think, Coyne said, instinctively throwing Cunningham up against the car, showing him the baton.

Have you ever shat one of these before?

You'll have to ask my solicitor, was Cunningham's slick reply.

Coyne laughed. McGuinness coughed in the background as though he wanted to pass on some urgent message to Coyne but was afraid to interrupt.

Are you in the VHI? Coyne asked, holding Cunningham by the throat. The voluntary health?

He got no answer, just a stunned look. Coyne released his grip and turned away, satisfied that he had delivered his message. He knew he had gone too far. It was not the right time yet. That day would come soon. But Cunningham was even more amazed that he was being let go. Looked at Coyne with great surprise.

You better be in the VHI when I deal with you, you *glick* bastard. Plan fucking D.

Coyne began to walk back towards the squad car. He turned again at the last minute to add a final warning, pointing his baton at Cunningham once more.

'Cause, I'm going to get medieval on your arse, boy.

Back in the squad car, McGuinness was uneasy about the incident.

Take it easy, Pat. You're shittin' yourself.

But Coyne was still furious, as though everything had broken loose inside him. He was all over the place. These Cunningham brothers had it coming. Coyne's Justice was on the way.

That was mild, Larry. They're going to get it. They'll wish they were born scorpions.

I don't like it. We've nothing on Mick Cunningham. It's not our case.

You have to connect the shite back to the arsehole it came from, Coyne announced.

But McGuinness was starting to act the psychologist, telling Coyne he should relax. Had he ever thought of taking up golf?

Piss off, Larry. Golf is for emotionally disturbed whackoes.

Even before the shift was over, Superintendent Molloy sent out a message over the radio asking Coyne to come back to base. Molloy was hopping.

For Jesussake, Coyne. What are you up to? he barked. Threatening a suspect in the middle of a murder enquiry.

I was keeping an eye on him, Coyne offered.

Keeping an eye on him? Do you fancy him or something?

Molloy looked like he was going to start foaming at the mouth like a wounded horse. Yellow teeth all biting the dust. He was squinting up as though he was going through a particularly difficult gastric experience. Mouth curled up into an O of incomprehension. His hair-flap all out of place.

Look, Coyne. You lay off these guys. Ignore them. They don't exist. Are you watching too much feckin' television or something? You're a plain and simple Garda on the beat, no more. This is Special Branch stuff, stay out of it. Got that?

Yes, Coyne agreed.

Molloy was staring up at him as though he'd had his stomach lanced by a pike, horse intestines spilled out all over the place. Moleshaver Molloy crawling away from the agony of his own bowels.

What the hell has got into you, Pat? Relax. You should take up golf. It would calm you down a bit.

Coyne stared back with great indignation. Golf? Coming from Moleshaver, that was a good one. You think you can solve Dublin's crime with golf. Coyne was no ordinary cop. They would see. Coyne's Justice was coming. He had nailed down some of these bastards and was keeping an open mind on a lot more. He had solved a few minor mysteries and put a certain Brian Quinn behind bars. And Sergeant Moran had become the station's best-known alcoholic, leaving Coyne directly in line for promotion. All he needed was one big case. One big crap which he could bring back in a plastic evidence bag and put on Superintendent Molloy's desk.

Coyne's Justice referred to an incident at school. A concept of fair play that wasn't without regret, as though justice was always accompanied by a certain guilt and compassion for those who were condemned. Even as a child, Coyne had wondered about the cruelty of Divine justice. I mean, how the fuck could God get away with burning people for ever. Bet there were a whole load of innocent people in hell too, people stitched up on spurious confessions. Coyne knew all about the innocents. And Coyne's Justice referred to Brother O Maolbheannaigh, and his little dog Bran, who came to a bad end on behalf of his master. O Maolbheannaigh's innocent little terrier took the rap for all the beatings dished out to the pupils over the years in school.

Every Wednesday, Coyne went out to the playing fields along the Liffey in Chapelizod for hurling. Next to the Garda rowing club as it happened. Health of body, purity of mind. There was no way out of it. Hurling was compulsory, even if you were an utter gobshite with no sense of direction, wielding the hurling stick like a sword or a *Claimh Solais* around your head as though you were after a wasp. The fastest game in the world. The first time Coyne ever tried to hit a ball he nearly decapitated Proinsias De Barra, otherwise known as 'Spunk', with an almighty blow to the back of the head.

O Maolbheannaigh was always there on Wednesdays, extolling the virtues of the air. Seagulls everywhere, waiting for a new delivery at the dump on the far side of the river. Flocks of them milling and screeching as the bulldozer turned over the city's rubbish for them. And the playing fields were usually covered in sheepshite. The Brothers let out the fields to a sheep farmer through the week, and on Wednesdays the lads were lifting *sliotars* of dried black dung and whacking them into the air. Boys stuffing great lumps of it into each other's nicks, forcing each other's faces down on to the grass to eat it. Oh you boyo. Flying sheepshite everywhere until O Maolbheannaigh came out with the real ball and his little dog, Bran. Sometimes he would send some of the goodie boys down to get a bar of Aero for the dog.

There was always a smell too, Coyne remembered. From the river. From the dump. From the Guinness brewery. A mixture of rot and ferment drifting across the playing fields, like O Maolbheannaigh's breath, shouting at everyone all the time: go, boy. Go, you moke, or else I'll take a big *sceilp* out of you with my bare hands. It was never clear whether the players were inspired by the ball or by the fear of O Maolbheannaigh, who sometimes chased after a player and gave him a clout for not doing what Christy Ring or Jack Lynch would have done. He treated the little leather *sliotar* like a museum piece, holding it up in the air as though it was the one used on the grassy slopes of ancient Ireland by the fucking Fianna.

And one day, Coyne's Justice took over. Coyne took his revenge for all the casual beatings that O Maolbheannaigh had given out. Struck a blow back on behalf of his friends and all the other pupils. He got O Maolbheannaigh's dog. Bran was always there on the sidelines, looking for rats, everybody dying to use him as a *sliotar*. Coyne could not recall ever hitting the ball, except for one day when he was required to take a seventy-yard puck. Ten minutes whacking the clear daylight with the stick until O Maolbheannaigh came over and said: Right, me bucko. In fear, Coyne attempted one last time, throwing the ball up gently and finally making contact, sending it into infinity like a legendary puck from the Ulster Cycle. The impact of the ball shuddering back through the ash and stinging his fingers, all the way back through his arms, down to his groin. The ball went sailing out over the perimeter fence towards the river and O Maolbheannaigh instantly rained clouts and punches.

You clod, O Maolbheannaigh shouted, giving Coyne an almighty kick in the arse that almost sent him over the perimeter fence as well.

They carried on with a tattered back-up *sliotar* while Coyne searched in the reeds and bushes along the banks of the Liffey. Bran searching too, and before he knew it, the dog was somersaulting through the air down into the green water. Bran surfaced and tried to swim, even though the chocolate was holding him back. He got to the shore, but Coyne was there throwing stones at him, pushing him back out again with his hurley, running along the bank to make sure. And then Bran started going down, Coyne watching from the side, feeling a new sense of compassion for the innocent dog. Maybe for O Maolbheannaigh too, who was going to be the loneliest bastard in Ireland without his partner. Coyne felt awful. Tried to rescue the dog, wading out into the muddy water and almost drowning himself, but it was too late and the limp, upturned corpse floated down the river, mouth open, teeth bared in the agony of defeat. Coyne's Justice.

Carmel was sitting up in bed sketching, the noise of the pencil on the paper scratching at Coyne's brain. He stood by the window, looking out over the gardens, and saw Mr Gillespie next door playing golf in darkness. There was only the light from the kitchen illuminating the tiny garden in which the neighbour was swinging his iron. Each swish followed by a small pock of the plastic golf ball against the back wall.

Gillespie, you're a sad case altogether. What's this, the Irish Open or something? You wanker. Who do think you are, Bernard Langer?

Carmel continued sketching. The time on the digital clock was 12:12. It always came back to those even numbers again and Coyne thought he was going mad, surrounded by all the tiny signals of suburban melancholia. Swish, pock, scratch, flush is what his life amounted to. It was at moments like this that Coyne became aware how trapped you could be by noise. The trademarks of his home. It was this shaggin' art business. She was as bad as the nocturnal golfer next door. Every night she sat up in bed with her sketch pad, scratching away like a chicken while Coyne drifted off into sleep. Fruit bowls, baskets of flowers, trees, children's faces – the whole house was already infested with drawings. Everything had to be recorded in art as though it was in danger of evaporating. And how many times in the past month had Coyne heard her repeat the story about Matisse, how Matisse could not afford to eat the fruit he painted. How he would work away in a cold studio because he was afraid the heat would make the fruit go bad. Again he saw Mr Gillespie placing the plastic golf ball on the grass and shuffling up, getting ready to tee off in his little suburban dog pound of a garden.

Everybody's gone golf mad, Coyne muttered, and Carmel ignored him because she had just had a brilliant idea.

Pat, why don't you let me paint you?

Give me a break, Carmel.

Please, Pat. As a special favour?

What, like this? He almost conceded. He was standing in his boxer shorts and a vest.

No, silly.

You mean in my uniform?

No, Pat. In your nude. With no clothes on.

No way, Coyne retorted immediately, turning around towards her. She could put that out of her head immediately. No way was he going to become part of this running archive in art. He wouldn't be trapped on canvas. And certainly not in the nude. Whatever about living in reality, he was sure as hell not going to allow himself to be immortalised in fucking art.

And you better give up those ideas, Carmel. You've gone far enough. This art business has gone to your head, love.

The art teacher, Gordon Sitwell, said Carmel was very good. Week by week he watched her making great progress.

You're coming on very nicely, Carmel. I think you've got real talent.

At the end of the class, when most of the other students had already drifted on home and Carmel was gathering up her materials, Sitwell leaned on a table and said he had been meaning to talk to her.

I'm impressed with your work.

Thanks, she said. But she wasn't going to allow herself to be flattered too much. She was a married woman with three children, afraid of letting the whole art thing get out of perspective.

And you're not getting quite so much paint on your nose any more, he joked. Carmel instinctively ran the back of her hand over her nose to check.

Only joking, Sitwell said. I seriously think you've got what it takes. Look at the skies you paint. They're really quite... visceral.

I've never really done this kind of thing seriously before, she said. Only with the children at home. You know, crayons and stuff.

Sitwell was disappointed. Didn't like her downgrading her own talent like that. Wanted his students to think big. To let go of all the emotional domestic traps that held her back from real self-expression.

You speak the language of colour, he said. I run a workshop from time to time. Only for the really talented, mind you. I think you would be good on portraits and human form.

A workshop, Carmel stammered.

Think it over. I think you could make a career of it.

Oh no, Mr Sitwell. It's only for pleasure.

Maybe they were right. Coyne needed a break. Over the next few weeks he tried to take things easy. Tried to get closer to his family. He wanted to get back to basics with them. He got a call from one of his old drinking companions, Vinnie Foley, but he put the binge on the long finger. Most of Coyne's friends had disappeared or moved out of reach somehow. He went for pints occasionally, but he was more inclined to devote his life to his work and his family. Vinnie Foley was an advertising executive now. Look where we've all ended up, Vinnie would say, before he went on his own public relations monologue. And you couldn't talk to somebody who was constantly reviewing life like it was a comparative study.

Coyne had too much to do. He had to look after his mother, who lived on the outskirts of the city. Make sure she was safe. His sister was in England. His brother Jim lived down the country, so it was up to Coyne to protect her. He drove out there to erect wire grids on the downstairs windows at the back of the house. He had the sudden feeling that his mother was in great danger and prone to attack. She stayed indoors all the time now, just watching TV. He put a massive, ugly bolt on the back door and felt better after that. It eased his conscience as he walked away from his old home with the feeling that he had left his mother locked in safely behind him, like the *Sean Bhean Bhocht* – the old woman of Ireland besieged and incarcerated by wire grids of immobility.

Coyne felt he was on top of things. He achieved moments of deep intimacy with his family. One day, he just told everyone to get into the car. He was going to buy them all chips. Jennifer and Nuala giggling in the back of the Escort, touching tongues until Carmel told them it was disgusting. The local chipper was closed, so Coyne just drove on as though he was going to drive for ever.

Left or right, he said at each junction, and they all said different things until they eventually arrived far away in Bray, at the amusement arcade on the seafront. They bought chips and went on the dodgems. Carmel and Jennifer versus Coyne and Nuala. Jimmy in a car of his own. There was nobody else around and they had the whole place to themselves. Jimmy drove in a figure of eight, looking up at the sparks on the electric cage, colliding with everyone. Nuala's bag of chips hopping up in the air out of her hand, making her cry. Flattened chips all over the dodgem track. Carmel laughing like she'd never laughed before, head jolting back, hair bouncing up around her head like she was in some shampoo ad.

For once, Coyne heard nothing but the sound around him of the dodgems and the video machines and the camel race. No inner voices telling him to carry out some impossible goal. He smiled at the woman in a cardigan inside the glass office with the towers of tenpenny coins. The sound of a pop song was hanging over everything like a soft duvet, eliminating the past as well as the future, pinpointing just one feeling of warmth, love and utter joy. *Can't live, if livin' is without you – Can't live, can't live any more.* Coyne had lost consciousness. He was entertaining his emotions, afflicted by a great longing to be swallowed up in this comic bubble of happiness for ever.

Then they moved on to play the Tin Can Alley, where the whole family threw coloured balls into a red dustbin from which a woolly cat peeked out every few seconds. Coyne with all the remaining chips stuffed in his jacket pocket, lifting up handfulls of balls to bring the score up so that they would win a free game and be able to stay there for ever, game after game. Jimmy like his dad, serious and determined. Jennifer and Nuala throwing one ball every minute between them. And Carmel just leaning on the rail in weakness, unable to breathe with the pain of laughter.

Do you want to go away? he said to her that evening when they got home again. He had eventually built up the courage to ask her, and she looked up to see what he was getting at. What possessed him?

Away to the west. A break. Just the two of us.

Like lovers? She laughed.

An autumn break, like. I just thought we should try and get away together more often.

Out to the west. Brilliant, she said.

Carmel had already begun to imagine the trip as a great art excursion, giving her a chance to do some outdoor work. Mountains, coastline, bogs; provided it wasn't raining. He let her make all the plans. She phoned up the tourist board looking for a cheap hotel. Bought an easel so she could stand and paint the sun going down over Galway Bay.

And so they were off. Late one Friday morning, Mrs Gogarty waved goodbye from the door as Carmel and Pat drove away. The children had been bribed with sweets and promises of new toys. The last beep of the horn seemed so final.

They drove through Ireland with the blues on the car stereo. It was the first time in ages that Coyne and Carmel had actually listened to music together. My God, why hadn't they thought of doing this before? How green everything was. They had been out of touch with nature. Carmel thought she was looking at cardboard cut-out cows. All the familiar landmarks from the hitch-hiking days – Newland's Cross, Newbridge, Kinnegad. They were heading west, into the sun. Subliminal blue flashes of the Atlantic already appearing in their minds like holograms of past journeys. They stopped for lunch in Athlone and on the last part of the journey Carmel changed into a teenager. Sang along with the songs on the car radio, giggling. It was as though the glass of wine at lunch had gone to her head and she tried to dance in the front seat, moving her shoulders; embarrassingly happy; happy beyond any of her wildest dreams.

At the hotel in Galway, the receptionist apologised for the renovations. There was dust all over the place and dirty footprints of workmen on the carpets where the plastic sheeting had shifted. Walls had been broken through in some places. In others, new plasterboard walls had gone up. But the bar was still in business as usual. The dining-room had a massive sheet of plyboard over the window holding out the wind.

They were led through a maze of corridors and little steps going up, down, then back up again into an extension which was not finished. In some places, the roof had not even gone up yet. Smell of paint and bitumen everywhere. Men hammering and whistling all around. A sign in the hallway apologised for the inconvenience on behalf of the management. Right beside it, an attempt to restore the sense of hospitality with a gilded print of a child playing with a kitten. All covered in dust. At the end of the corridor, they were shown into a room overlooking the Corrib river. The smell of fresh paint was intoxicating and a new picture of horses galloping through canyons at night hung on the wall. The bathroom was all in pink. And Coyne's Garda obsession with time noticed that the ever-present digital clock stood at 4:44. Enjoy your stay.

It's a shagging building site, Carmel.

It doesn't matter, Pat. We got twenty-five per cent off.

Carmel threw herself across the bed. There were men passing by the window, clanking down the steel emergency staircase outside in their boots. Coyne closed the curtains and threw the room into a tropical yellow and green forest interior. The duvet had apple blossoms and red apples at the same time. Above them, the men were hammering, shifting pieces of felt and plyboard, whistling and laughing. Soon they would be knocking off for pints, which increased the urgency in their work.

Come on, Cowboy, Carmel said.

Coyne pointed at the ceiling. Indicating the audience above. But she pulled him down on the bed beside her. Unzipped his trousers in such a hurry that he thought she was looking for money or something. Pulled up her dress to show him that she was wearing no underwear, and had come all the way from Dublin like that, arriving in Galway with the Atlantic breeze whistling around her thighs. What if a gust of wind had blown her dress up? At the hotel as she got out of the car? Was she going to walk around like that all weekend? Until she met an almighty squall up on Eyre Square and ended up looking like an inverted umbrella, exposed to the entire western world. But there was no sense in trying to talk because somebody had started using a drill outside and plunged the whole place into a sound-shadow. She began to kiss him. With the noise of the hammering and sawing and shouting, they made love. She drew him on top of herself, on the apple duvet. Smothered him with her tongue and pinned his buttocks down with her hands. In front of all those workmen, you could say. All that violence and passion on a Friday afternoon. The noise around them urging on the fury of love. His breathing like that of a labourer. Her shouts merging with the shouts of men outside, beating the last Friday afternoon nails into the timber planks above.

They fell asleep with all that clamour in their ears. A deep afternoon sleep from which they would never wake up. They might as well have been dead. No amount of noise could raise them out of the torpor of this love-drugged sleep. It was only after the men had gone away that Coyne eventually roused himself out of the coma in a great panic, sweating, as though he'd been left behind in utter emptiness. He had never experienced such absolute silence before.

When Carmel woke up, she found Coyne naked at the foot of the bed, his hair all wet, rubbing his back with a towel. He had just come out of the shower and she reached up to slap his buttocks.

There was a naked man in my room, your honour, she laughed and ran away into the bathroom before he could lash back with his towel.

Pat Coyne was the most complicated man in Ireland. He bore that slightly troubled expression of a man with an indeterminate mission. He was no messer. He was waiting for a crisis, some apocalyptic occasion when he could really come into his own. 1916 might have been a good year for him, but he was born half a century too late, looking ahead to the next major event and resenting the complacency around him, as though all that humour and laughter in the country was denying the presence of real disaster underneath. Right from the beginning, Carmel could see that he was devoted to sorting out the world.

Stubborn as hell too, he was. And full of contradictions. Always coming out with his own notions on the way things should be done, even down to the small details like whether to go for wooden or plastic clothes pegs. The kind of man who would remind you of what gear you were in, and give you firm instructions on the most direct way from A to B. The kind of man who could fix the washing machine as if he was dealing with a broken heart, and interfere with the buttons of your blouse with the detachment of a gynaecologist. Stopping to admire the design features of the bra strap.

He was no pain in the arse, though. And there was a soft side to him as well. A gentleman, who occasionally allowed people to talk him into things. Her man, protective and courteous, drawing on chivalry from a bygone age.

He was afraid of affection, however. As though affection was always something progressive, leading up to a goal. Making love was one thing, but affection was really scary. Ireland was not a very tactile country. It was a place where people touched each other with words. Songs. Jokes. The kind of verbal intimacy of islanders. And Coyne was not a groper, or a poser, or some kind of bedroom hero. His advances came in the shape of ideas. Thoughts. Observations. Pronouncements on the environment. Projections about the future. He touched her with words and silent spaces between words.

In a way, you didn't marry one person, Carmel always said. You married a place, an era, a set of pop songs and world events that all merged into a general drift towards one person. You were in love with a gang. In love with the pubs you drank in, the cafés, the arch at Stephen's Green, the taxi driver who once let you off with half the fare. It was group consciousness. She recalled the clothes, the way she wore her hair, the clumpy high heels, the expressions everyone used at the time. The jokes, the repetition, and Vinnie Foley's stories in which they all appeared like characters in a soap opera. Billy Burke's enigmatic laugh. Deirdre Claffey's father's car. All the other friends who had now emigrated. And Pat.

She had come away with Pat. She had married a Garda. A good man. Could have been more ambitious and ended up in a right mess with Vinnie Foley. It was only later on that you realised your luck. Even though she remained loyal as ever to that collective feeling, to whatever song was in her head at that time, to the Lakes of Ponchartrain, to the Rolling Stones, or even the Bee Gees, she had now become an individual. Somebody with biography. Only years later, with three children and a unique memory, had she thought of doing something for herself. And she would not allow that moment of individuality to be consumed by her family. She was determined to become an artist.

That night they sat over dinner in a Galway restaurant as though they had gone right back to the beginning, the first moment alone together. A dangerous moment. With the silence left behind by workmen still ringing in their ears.

She had the Chicken Butler Yeats, with its golden, crisp breadcrumbs. Coyne almost exploded when he saw the T-bone Bernard Shaw on the menu; wanted to rant at the factual sloppiness of the management until she told him to calm down. They were on holidays. And who cared if Shaw was a vegeterian.

Later, Carmel was shifting the last crumbs of chocolate gateau around on her plate, listening to Pat talking about consumerism. He hit her with a wave of statistics. Did she know how much Coke they drank per capita in Iceland. Did she know that they drank more Coke in Northern Ireland than they did in the south. He was about to come to his conclusion, his vision of the future. It all culminated in cataclysm, in pollution – the end of the world. But he was so enthusiastic about it, so committed to that vision of miasmal disaster, that it came across the table to Carmel like words of love. If the universe came to an end that moment, Pat Coyne would say: what did I tell you, Carmel?

Do you realise what they pump into the lakes, he went on, with light radiating from his eyes. And the sea. Look at the Irish Sea, full of nuclear crap.

Pat, don't start getting worked up on the ecology again, she said.

Coyne poured more wine.

Look at the Black Sea, he said. A cauldron of filth and gunge, like a thick soup with all these big lumps. Dead horses and that kind of thing. Islands of floating ordure.

Come on, Pat. We're eating.

The world is shagged, Carmel. I'm telling you.

Carmel looked wonderful. She was wearing a pearl necklace borrowed from her mother. Her hair was clamped up at the back with a spangle the children were afraid of, because she called it jaws and chased them around the bedroom with it, like teeth going up and down. In the light of the candle, her face was illuminated by a kind of Mediterranean warmth.

But Coyne talked as if he had a big cardboard box around his head. Massive boulders of ice had come loose in the Arctic, he cautioned. Something was happening. The depth of the permafrost was shrinking each year. And did she want to know what was going to become of the melting ice caps? Rain. More clouds and more shagging rain. It was all going to be dumped on Ireland, that's what. I'm telling you, Carmel, he said, holding her under a spell of doom with the power of his forecast, there's going to be another flood soon. Wait till the water starts coming up to our front door.

In a feckless, end-of-the-world decision Coyne ordered two brandies. A sign of abandoned hope.

Come a day very soon though, he continued without a hitch in his delivery, when water will mean everything. Everywhere else will be suffering the biggest drought in history. The world will have its tongue hanging out and water will become as expensive as oil. Then we'll have the last laugh. Us here in Ireland and all the rain.

With a triumphant look in his eyes, he sat back, sniffing the exotic liquid in his glass as though he could measure it for toxic waste. He was thinking wooden barrels collecting rainwater at the gable end of each house. Rain-money. Water-sheiks. Selling bottled clouds from Croagh Patrick to the tourists. He was drunk on a distant notion of future prosperity. Carmel looking across the table at him in solid agreement. Waiting for a moment where she could speak.

Pat, she whispered. I've never been so happy.

Yes, he said, as though she concurred with his predictions of chaos.

I really don't have words to say how I feel.

He reached over and held her hand: steady on there, Carmel. Don't entertain your emotions in the restaurant. He had to lean sideways to look beyond the candle. Couldn't take it if she cried, because it would make him all soft and pathetic.

I've found something really worthwhile, she uttered through moist eyes.

Sure.

My art, she said at last. Doing something creative has given me something to live for, something to look forward to. I feel really fulfilled.

Coyne could not hide his disappointment. He was looking across the table of betrayal. Withdrew his hand and folded his arms to register his surprise. It was as though she had said something about the universe that disproved his forecast, some amazing revelation that meant he had been staring into a blind alley. The world was safe and he didn't know it.

What's wrong, Pat. I thought you'd be happy about it.

Carmel, there's far too much creativity in the world already. That's what's wrong with the place. Too much junk. It's only going to lead to trouble, believe me.

You don't understand, Pat. I need to do something with myself. I'm not the type to stay at home and make puff pastry and soufflés. Can't waste my talent on that.

Coyne took the opportunity to pay the bill. A climax of romantic illusion, shattered in an instant.

You're afraid I might improve myself, she said in an outburst of absolute lucidity, but Coyne wasn't listening any more. He was already planning a great future. A world without improvement where people could be themselves and not keep trying to be creative or paint pictures of each other.

Back at the hotel, he came to a peak of new ideas and suddenly asked an absurd question. Suggested they should move down to the west altogether, to the Gaeltacht, where the children would speak Irish, where they would be a part of the real Ireland. He would get promotion easily and become a celebrated Connemara cop; famous far and wide among the ordinary people; a kind of nobleman of the west. Out there with all that raw nature she wouldn't need any of that art lark. They would be content on the beauty of the rocky land, living an uncomplicated life between the bog and the sky. Nothing else. Maybe they would learn a few songs. And there was that business in water. They would start something with water, that's for sure.

But Carmel stared at him. Like he had made some outrageous sexual demand on her.

You must be out of your Vulcan mind, Pat, if you think I'm going to live down here and speak the *cupla focail*.

Then she started laughing again and calling him a teddy bear. Giggling hysterically while he remained utterly serious. As if something in her mirth pointed the finger straight at something in his doomed vision. As if her laughter was bringing the world to an end more rapidly than he had expected. And he could not see what was funny about it. His proclamation was in shreds.

Carmel jumped on the bed, bouncing up and down. Behaving like a child, not a mother. She put on the bedside radio – Daniel O Donnell singing *Whatever happened to old-fashioned love*. She danced on the spring-harvest duvet like she was in a field, running with her hair blowing back in the wind. Looked up at the painting with the white frame above the bed and felt she was galloping across the blue moonlit canyons with the horses. Coyne was the horse on his own, heading in the wrong direction. Inspired by a magnetic signal that nobody else was willing to answer.

Catch on to yourself, Carmel, he said.

But there was no point in talking to her. She was drunk and disorderly. He had chosen the worst moment to put his daft dream of relocation forward because she had begun to perform a mildly erotic floor-show, laughing defiantly, showing him her new bottle-green knickers with white lace edging. He stared at them as if they were some kind of plastic carrier bag from Dunnes Stores. Refused to enter into the spirit of shopping, denying his instinct, cantering off towards a different moon.

You can take nothing seriously, can you, he said in pure Garda-speak.

Her hips moved at angles that contradicted any musical logic. She pouted and pulled the dress down off her shoulder, gazing at him with mock shyness like a calendar girl. A deadly sex kitten. Eyes radiating a comic impression of lust; something between deep trust and deep suspicion, between hatred and love, barely holding back the next burst of helpless laughter.

Coyne wasn't going to wait for it. He'd had enough and opened the door suddenly. Said he was going out because he needed to clear his head, leaving her behind with a look on her face like the moment the track begins to fade away on the radio. She had gone too far and it seemed he was about to set off right away to find himself a bothy or a disused cottage to spend the rest of his days in.

Had she misunderstood him? Had she not acknowledged his stark vision? Such consummate pessimism was like an act of faith, an act of obstinate loyalty to their love. All that talk of imminent catastrophe, all that irrational longing for a simple life in the west was just a way of stopping the drift away from the night they first kissed in public, at the bottom of Grafton Street, while everyone else was running for the last bus. One of her feet off the ground, toe pointing. Coyne had become obsessed with endings, with the futility of things carrying on and being repeated into infinity. Once was enough of everything on his fevered plane of understanding. Things needed to come to a conclusion.

It had begun to rain. Buckets of rain. He was soaked already, walking through the narrow streets of Galway in his good jacket. To go back to the hotel for his coat would have seemed like an expression of immense hope and reconciliation. His hair was already plastered down on his skull. Rain in his eyes. Cool water running off his face, in around the back of his neck. He blew sprinkles upwards from his nose. Kicked water forward with his shoes. Jumped back in fright when he saw a couple huddled together in the shelter of a doorway. The rain drove people in Ireland into each other's arms, while back at the hotel, Carmel was already lying on the bed, face downwards, crying.

Coyne was right about the rain. The streets were like rivers and there was a sense that things had adopted the appropriate tone of emergency. Everyone had fled the deluge, and the sheer fury of the rain bouncing on the pavement had proved him right. Everything about rain was moving downwards to a glorious end. He saw the herring-bone pattern along the gutter as the water rushed away into the shores. A saturated welcome mat. A car hissing along the street with the driver leaning forward and the windscreen wipers dancing. Rain sloping across headlights and street lights and small upstairs windows. Across the plains of Connemara and across the islands. The Corrib was in spate and he stood on the bridge of despair, looking down into that wild, single-minded frenzy as though it was his salvation.

Drummer Cunningham got his picture in the paper. On the same page as the headline – Farmers attack Taoiseach – he was smiling at the people of Ireland from some charity function where he'd won the prize as best-dressed man. Coyne saw it the day he got back from Galway. It made the Irish legal system look like it had crashed into the side of a mountain in thick fog. One of its greatest adversaries on the loose, wearing the double-breasted suit of respectability. The benevolent face of Berti J. Cunningham: philanthropist; supporter of the blind; man of substance and owner of the Fountain nightclub, his new laundry operation. He had become an overnight celebrity, laughing at the law with a grin that looked more like a slashed bus seat.

Whoever took the Drummer out of circulation was going to make legendary status. A real modern-day patriot. Superintendent Molloy's methods were no use. All Moleshaver could do was dance around his office in a great fury, like some new rap king, moving his arms up and down in a steady rhythm and repeating: The Gardai have their hands tied. Moleshaver, you're so funky.

There was little Coyne could do either. He was trapped in his squad car again like a shaggin' astronaut, listening to McGuinness giving him the membership rates on all the different golf clubs, still trying his best to persuade him to join. The Garda club at Stackstown wasn't a bad spot. What they needed, however, was a floodlit club for people on shift work. Fair play to the first person who runs a twenty-four-hour golf course.

Trust a Kerryman to think of that.

Give it a chance, McGuinness urged. You'd love it.

But Coyne dismissed it. His views on golf were well known; it was for failed psychopaths. He had already made up his mind to go for strength and speed. He had booked an appointment at the chest clinic. He was going to join up in some local gym and get into serious shape. There was going to be a showdown and he would be ready.

In his new role as businessman, benefactor and best-dressed man, Drummer seemed to be getting a taste for funerals and charity functions. The man who had sold smack to kids on the streets, robbed banks, snuffed out the lives of anyone who threatened his empire, was now transforming himself into a regular statesman. He knew the way to the hearts of the people. Go to the funeral. Offer your condolences. Shake hands. Put some money in the fund and turn up at a benefit concert for the young widow of Dermot Brannigan. How fucking cynical can you get? Front-row table for Berti and Naomi, Chief and Mick, drinking pints and buying all colours of raffle tickets, maybe hoping to win back the satellite dish Drummer had donated for the first prize. Drummer could be generous when the time came to demonstrate that he had a heart.

A hundred pounds' worth of satellite dish, the master of ceremonies announced every ten minutes. Kindly donated by Berti Cunningham. A hundred pounds' worth of satellite dish, ladies and gentlemen.

That's cause I couldn't get the rest of it off the roof, Drummer whispered discreetly to his friends, and they all chuckled.

He liked simple pleasures, and though he remained mostly serious and aloof, speaking only whenever he had to, he loved a bit of clean fun. He smiled and tapped his foot to the music. Enjoyed the sound of laughter. Felt the warmth of the community around him as they clapped and danced in their seats, singing along with the band: *Knock three times on the ceiling if you want me*. What a night! Drummer even danced with some of the girls from Crazy Prices. Invited them all to the new nightclub. Then he laid into more egg sandwiches and Smithwicks, and watched a stripogram dressed in black leather and fishnet tights, cracking a whip and hauling two very embarrassed local men up on the stage for a double birthday celebration.

I'm gonna whip yous to death, she threatened, as the men dutifully knelt down on the stage to remove her red garter with their teeth.

It would be a brave woman who would get Drummer Cunningham to do that, because he was such a deeply private individual at heart. You wouldn't make a show of him. Only at your own peril. It would be like breaking and entering the VIP lounge in his head. People knew not to try that kind of thing on him, like you wouldn't try it on a priest, or a doctor, or a politician. Berti Cunningham was in a position of power, with influence over people's lives. He was too well respected.

Even the Special Branch had learned to respect him. They never troubled his ex-wife, Eileen, for instance. For security reasons, she and her two sons lived in an apartment in Ballsbridge, where Berti could play happy families whenever he wanted to. Christmas, Easter, birthdays and the occasional football international. Or whenever he felt like being the head of the family, and using his wife for a punch bag, leaving her with a few marks to remember him by. The two little Cunningham boys were going to a good school and Berti was obviously intending to break the cycle of crime that he had inherited from his own father. They were going to grow up like decent citizens.

Two senior detectives who once went around to the apartment to check it out got the surprise of their lives. Eileen rang her husband and Drummer got so angry that he sent a squad of young lads round to deal with the situation. That's not your car, is it? she then asked them, and the detectives looked out through the window to see their car engulfed in flames.

That taught them to respect Eileen's privacy. The family flat was out of bounds for detectives. Just as Berti's house in Sandymount was out of bounds for his wife. Only his brother Mick slept there occasionally, as well as special guests and the most prominent members of the gang like Chief, and their women friends.

Fred was of the opinion that Drummer had insulated himself so well, there was nothing the Special Branch could do at this stage. He was in the process of going clean. Had some new friends in high places.

The whole thing needs to be tackled in a different way altogether, Fred said.

Yeah, like joining them.

It's time to get tough. That's the bottom line. I tried some innovations when I was in the Force, but it was all ahead of my time.

Coyne was waiting to see what Fred might suggest. Watched him pour milk into his tea in the small night-watchman's room. Then waited a while further as Fred dunked a Mikado biscuit and chewed as though he could extract some great new plan from its soft pink flesh.

Pat, somebody with your abilities should be actively beavering away. The person who nails that bastard will shoot up the ranks. You should be out there preparing your own dossier on these guys.

What do you mean?

Surveillance, Pat. In your spare time. Just keep an eye on them. Take away some of his privacy. You'll come up with something in the end, wait till you see.

What about the rookies from the CDU, and the drug squad?

Don't worry about them, Fred said. I have the contacts in there. I know for a fact that they've been ordered to drop the stake-out.

If the Super finds out, he'll go bananas.

Forget Molloy. He's got his head up his arse. You'll get the results, Pat. It'll take time, but you'll win if you persevere. Check out his new nightclub.

Ah Jesus, Fred. My clubbing days are over.

Coyne could see it already. Girls in hot pants – men with mobile phones and wedding bands in their pockets. Spiderwoman getting into the car and asking what the baby seat was doing in the back. Oh fuck.

Be worth having a look around some night, Fred urged. Keep a low profile, though. Stay incognito.

But instead, Coyne began a special surveillance of Cunningham's swanky home in Sandymount. Kept walking up and down Hawthorn Avenue in the early hours of the morning, staring into the window of Cunningham's cosy front room with its lampshades and floral wallpaper, all deluxe and delightful. Until he eventually saw Drummer coming out with his dogs. An overcoat slung over his shoulders, like he was fucking Napoleon or somebody, leading two Rottweilers up the pavement. The dogs were larger than life, straining on their leads, almost pulling Drummer up the street with them, as though they could smell the local Abrakebabra about half a mile away. Berti all cool and aggressive, smoking a cigarette and jerking the leads back violently.

Wait, ye fuckers.

Coyne had come up behind them, walking at a slightly faster pace, feeling the edginess of being on the same street as his enemy, posing as an ordinary suburban resident. He wanted to get a good look at his man, stare into the whites of his eyes. Get a sense of his stature.

But as he caught up with them, Coyne was surprised at how small Drummer really was. He was tough looking. But he expected a much larger man. And Drummer's hair seemed a little bit laughable; cut short at the sides and long at the back, like one of those really stupid haircuts that *Wrestlemania* stars wore.

As Coyne approached, Drummer stopped on the street to undo his fly. While the dogs were lifting a leg against one of the hawthorn trees, Drummer joined them, pissing in public to mark his territory. A gesture of contempt towards the people of Sandymount.

Like a normal, disgusted neighbour, Coyne took the opportunity to cross the street to avoid him. But he had made eye contact at last. Under cover he had managed to come face to face with Cunningham. You'll be pissing in hell soon, Berti. You'll be passing boiling urine with the dogs of the underworld to keep you company. Burning and barking into infinity. Just you wait.

In a new sense of reform, Coyne decided he was going to be more of a brick. The new Coyne would be all muscle and speed. He was going to get in touch with his body, so to speak. All he had to do was get his health cleared first. The lungs had been acting up quite a bit recently, so he found himself in Vincents, lining up for another chest X-ray. Felt he was back in short trousers with his mother, endlessly shifting from one bench to another to see the consultant and talk about the dinosaur in his chest. How is the bronchitis? Coyne with his indigenous lungs, rasping and coughing with the hollow bark of a seal until the tears stung his eyes. Lungs like a damp Irish cottage with the wind whistling and the half-door banging.

Once more he found himself walking along the polished corridors with a new pink card and big folder containing his skeletal upper half; humble ribs and air bags that had acquired their own medical fame over the years. It was like a homecoming for the nostrils – the disinfectant, the stuffiness, the heavy smell of hospital food rushing towards him like an old uncle, urging contrition and humility. The alarming clang of kidney bowls. Nurses squeaking along the lino in their white shoes, and the patients everywhere infecting each other with a deep sense of mortality.

Hard man? He felt about as hard as a globule of phlegm in a plastic beaker. Waiting outside the pulmonary lab, he listened as the others went ahead – could you please spit into this cup, like a good man. Who needs a tennis racket? An old man serving a high-speed green ace and Nurse Proctor saying: excellent, well done. Oh my God, call the Ghostbusters, what's this? Then they were proud of themselves, thinking of their record-breaking sputum being rushed away to a research centre where it was going to be tested for radioactivity, for fucksake.

Coyne observed fellow patients like the ghosts of his own future. Some of them were inmates from the wards. A thin man sat opposite him in his pyjamas, ribcage showing and his whole frame heaving and droning like a set of human *uileann* pipes. Ivory feet stuck into a pair of tartan slippers and a bony hand holding on to a sort of metal staff on wheels, with a suspended see-through bag and a tube that disappeared up one nostril. His face was more like the Tolund Man they found preserved in the bog with a thin leather gauze pulled over the skull.

They were all so desperate to live on. Old women talking all the time about how long they had to wait. As though they had something urgent to do somewhere else. One of them urged Coyne to read something in *Hello!* magazine.

See how the other half live, she said. There's Burt Reynolds. He's coming to collect me after I'm finished here. Then she threw back her head like a young girl, closing over the dusty pink dressing-gown and shaking with laughter; Jesus, you'd think she was holding back a chainsaw.

Coyne found no soul mates in *Hello!* Healthy bastards. You'll be coughing up daiquiris, you'll be spitting up Bailey's on ice one of these days, you fuckers. Burt, you big dickhead. Who do you think you're codding? You and your missus will be in for tests any day now.

Then St Patrick got up and shuffled in with his mobile crozier and there was a kind of hypnotic peace attached to the sound of his forerunner wheezing away to the chant of Nurse Proctor's voice. Proctor? Who Proct her?

Put your mouth around the nozzle for me, like a good man, and blow out all the way. Now take in a deep breath and blast it out – all the way, all the way, all the way, all the way. Excellent. When it came to Coyne's turn, he blasted all the way like a bricked camel. He was showing off, sending the indicator crazy, numbers on the computer spinning out of control trying to keep up with his carbon output.

But in the end he still came up with no more than a sixty per cent capacity. How did things get so out of hand? There was a lot of bronchial scarring on the lungs, the consultant tried to explain, pointing to pathetic white shadows on the X-ray. We're going to have to put you on an inhaler, and Coyne felt the elation of imminent death. I'm dying, he said to himself like a celebrity who had gained instant recognition.

There is no need to panic, the consultant said. Nobody is a hundred per cent. And people function perfectly on much less than sixty per cent. However, you'll need the inhaler to reduce the inflammation.

For fucksake. Coyne felt he had been cheated. He was going to live after all. Whereas he wanted to go out in glory. Wanted to have something really serious, something that would make them all look up and take notice. Something terminal that would make his audience hiss. Not the same old half-arsed lung ailment that he would carry around for the rest of his life until he was walking around in pyjamas with a tube up his fucking nostril. In the middle of the action, Coyne would be stopping to puff on his little blue pipe. Vlad the inhaler.

Then he joined the gym. He was going to be as fit as a raver. He was going to be Keanu Reeves from the neck down. Carmel had been echoing his concern for his health, saying it was about time he started getting into shape. And there was nothing more irritating than somebody telling you what you've already made up your mind to do.

Do you want me to go down with you? she asked, maybe just to give him a bit of moral support.

Yeah, hold my hand.

I'm only asking. Just thought you'd like the company.

What's this, the first day at school or something? Come on, Carmel.

There were odd moments like this when Coyne became so embarrassed of his own family that he disowned them completely. As though they might blow his cover. Wanted only to be an individual, a lone ranger with a clean slate and an unquantifiable past. Even wondered if he had suddenly ended up just like his father and would one day overlook his own son in the street. As though his family was in danger of destroying any slender sense of mystery that might have been attached to him. Coyne the family man, they'd be saying. Whereas Coyne was a much more complex figure. A man of many permutations. Didn't even want anyone to know he was a Garda, and let on to the girl with the orange face at the desk that he was in advertising, like Vinnie Foley.

Done any trainin' before? the instructor asked bluntly.

Sure. I'm just out of the habit.

I thought so.

But it was obvious he hadn't a clue. Made the mistake of pointing to his chest when the talk was of deltoids. Got the biceps right and luckily didn't say anything about forceps. But from the way he eyed the gym equipment it was clear that Coyne anticipated some kind of human mousetrap that would fold up on top of him as soon as he touched it.

We're going to have to develop that chest, the trainer said after measuring him. He'd already used his first name about seven times. And Coyne kept looking down with a sense of awe at the trainer's industrial-size build.

Good job Coyne had chosen a quiet time of the day. There was a man at the end of the gym, letting out a terrible grunt every now and again. Agony beyond human endurance. He wasn't even doing very much, just looking at these barbells and flexing his fingers like he was going to get metaphysical on them. There were two more men working themselves to death on the machines. One of them suddenly began to beat the shite out of an invisible enemy in front of a mirror. The other walked around in circles shaking a leg. *Girl I'm going to make you sweat* on the sound system. Smell of armpits everywhere.

Punch my chest, the trainer commanded.

But Coyne was far too much of a gentleman. Didn't see what the point was.

Go on, Pat. Punch me. Like, hard as you can.

Coyne slapped a gentle fist against a faded picture of James Dean and dutifully pretended he had hurt his hand.

Know what I'm sayin'?

What?

This is you in four weeks. Guaranteed. On this machine alone. It's called the Pec Deck, Pat.

Coyne sat into the machine and couldn't help a little self-conscious smile. Here's me on the Pec Deck. Wondered what it would sound like if his name was Declan – here's Deck on the Pec Deck.

He looked at the poster of a girl on a similar machine, except that she was smiling and making it look like it had suddenly inflated her breasts. Coyne was out of breath within seconds. Broke into an instant sweat. Wanted to grunt like the man at the end of the gym but wouldn't let go of his dignity. He furtively puffed on his blue pipe and it took no less than twenty minutes before he was completely exhausted and sat slumped on a bench.

The trainer had talked about a high. Coyne felt nothing but low and inadequate looking at one of the other men pulling himself up on a chinning bar, issuing a kind of abbreviated Fu... every time his body was hauled up. Afterwards, Coyne saw him walking towards the Pec Deck, keeping his legs apart as though the exertion had forced a little accident in his track suit pants. Then he started using the Pec Deck on his neck.

Strange, Coyne thought, and secretly called him Neck Deck. That machine is meant for the chest, you thick fucking Neck Deck.

Coyne didn't last long. He gave it four weeks and felt nothing but intense claustrophobia each time he went there. It was clear that exercise in a confined space caused a delirium of sorts, along with an unexplained hatred for people he hardly knew. The same kind of irrational hatred he felt at school when he stared at the pronounced twin barrels at the back of O Ceallaigh's neck in front of him. Always had a passionate desire to chop the side of his hand down on that neck for no reason.

Carmel tried to persuade him that it was only a matter of getting used to the place. You'll soon be grunting like the rest of them, she said, laughing hysterically.

I'm sorry, Pat, she said, trying to calm down. It's just the idea of you on the machines, grunting. Then she collapsed again, out of control. Breaking her shite laughing at nothing.

Coyne gave it up. It wasn't the exercise that got to him at all, but the other shapers. What made up his mind finally was the night he walked into the changing rooms, totally exhausted, and found none other than Neck Deck, carrying on with his exercise in the nude. The last few toe-touchers, with his hole staring up at everyone coming in the door. Coyne's timing was all wrong and he ended up having to sit in the sauna with him. Even having a nice conversation, talking about the new ferry, until some of the other lads started coming in and the place was suddenly packed out. Then it came, just as Moleshaver had forecast: some bastard farted.

I wouldn't put it past you, Neck Deck, you sly bollocks.

Oh Jesus, they all said, fleeing through the narrow door. The smell was like superglue at boiling point. If it had a colour, this was deep aquamarine with curling yellow streaks. The problem was that Coyne was the last out and so, inadvertently, became the culprit, stared at by all the others. It was the story of his life – always got away with the ones he did, always got blamed for the ones he didn't.

Coyne did make one more attempt to get fit. Cross-country running. At least he wouldn't have to put up with a pack of grunters with rubber buttocks. So he took the whole family with him out to the Phoenix Park for a picnic. The children could go to the zoo while he was doing a long distance around the fifteen acres.

Oh no, he said in the car. We forgot to bring Gran. Wasn't she meant to go back today?

What's that supposed to mean? Carmel huffed.

And Coyne was playing to the gallery again. Hoping his children were on his side at least. Turned round and told them that Gran Gogarty came from the zoo. She was let out on parole. Coyne had to go into the zoo and sign a document saying that he would be responsible for her.

Very funny, Carmel said. That's Garda humour, is it?

Coyne ran like a maniac around the Phoenix Park, staring down at the grass and the mud and chestnut leaves. Whenever he looked up he saw the Pope's Cross, stuck like an ugly big stake through the heart of Dublin, and the voice of the Pope echoing in his ears. People of Ireland – I loff you. Let us pray together for *piss*.

Coyne ran back to his family as though they were all he had. He joined them sitting on the grass near the Wellington spike eating sandwiches and apple boats. Little bars of Crunchie and KitKat. Zoo shrieks in the distance and a giant bottle of Fanta standing like a monument on the chequered green rug surrounded by white plastic beakers. He was thirsty as a dog. And Jennifer kept looking at his steaming forehead, tracing a line through the beads of sweat with her finger, saying: I like the smell of Dad.

You could never really be a hard man in Ireland anyway, because sooner or later somebody close to you would give the game away. Coyne would remember his own father and succumb to some hereditary softness, some underlying regret which tugged away at the heart, pulling the rug from underneath. You could act the brick all you liked until somebody started singing 'Dirty Old Town'. Then you were fucked.

And you could not avoid a little self-irony too. Get a bell for that bike, and all that. Do you think I'm not a fool? Third Policeman stuff. You had to pre-empt derision and be aware of the vulnerability of your own country and its people. As a Garda, Coyne knew he was an open book, so he had to play it cool: eager but calm. Tough, but not outside the humour of the moment. Surfing somewhere between commitment and contempt.

The Rod Steiger–Gene Hackman school of authority, chewing the same piece of gum into eternity, didn't come off right in Ireland at all. Not enough heat. You could hardly wear those big, steel-rimmed reflector sunglasses in the rain. And you couldn't stand with your legs apart because people would only be asking themselves if you had nappy rash or something. A truly hard man had a way of reflecting great anger, yet would still be ready to look a woman up and down. Don't fuck with me, chiselled into the frown. All it took was one more pestering fly to change the delicate balance. You had to be able to stop chewing suddenly, grimace, blink twice in rapid succession like a series of warning signals. One false move, pal.

A truly hard man turned his back on Ireland, buried his tragic past, slapped his fist and said something like: OK, any blood donors here? Do you like hospital food? They'll be reconstructing your face from old photographs. Coyne had developed his own brick qualities, like showing sudden curiosity for minute details. He could pretend he was highly interested in knowing where the underground drainage ran. Measure distances between blades of grass, between knuckles. He had a look that made people remember their prayers.

Moved with slow precision, as though each blink was being recorded contemporaneously. Sweet suffering Jesus, hold me back.

But ultimately, the mask was flawed. The hard-man image would turn porous because he would remember his father, whom he had never really been able to get close to. Never managed to communicate with him or build up any real warmth until it was too late. When Coyne got married to Carmel, he finally became an equal, inviting his father to the christening of his son Jimmy. And shortly after that, just when they began to like each other, he died. Killed by his own bees. Every weekend, Coyne's father went out to check his beehives. Dressed with a square cage around his head, he was out there with his smoker calming the bees, taking out the frames, clipping the queen's wings. He had taught Coyne all about bees and chosen him to take over. But it was no way to get close to your father, with that lethal humming all around. And over the years, the bees had turned vicious through inbreeding.

The neighbours hated the bees even more than the Irish language. And every once in a while, when Coyne was a boy, there would be a scream from the garden as his mother or his sister, or one of the kids next door, ran wildly into the house with a tormented bee buzzing in their hair. Coyne was the one who would usually take the tea towel and crush the bee with a soft little crack, before it managed to get as far as the skull. Coyne remembered nights with bees all over the house, buzzing up and down the window frames. Bees coming alive again out of nowhere at night and flying madly with intoxicated light-fury around the naked bulb in the middle of the room.

And one Saturday morning, they got his father. Got under his protection. Stung him in the ear so that, when he dropped the frame full of bees to stop the immediate pain with his hand, he inadvertently allowed more and more of them to get in. All over his neck. Under his arms. All the children had left. Only Coyne's mother was in the house at the time, and in the panic of their lonely marriage, they battled with bees, aggravating everything, running out into the street shouting, until one of the neighbours eventually came to help and brought him to the hospital.

At crucial moments Coyne was exposed to memory. And guilt. There was nothing you could do about that.

Carmel announced that she had been invited to Sitwell's studio. Sitwell had been urging her to come and join his workshops. He had been full of adulation for her work, telling her she had exceptional talent.

Pat, I've been asked to take part in a workshop, she said.

A what?

A workshop. You know, artists getting together and painting.

Ah, here we go again, Coyne muttered. What, like all painting each other, is that it?

It's just a few of us, she said, rubbing cream on herself. The art teacher is giving us a chance to use his studio. The ones with any talent.

Coyne looked her up and down. Once again she had turned herself into an artwork with white markings under her eyes. Two white blobs of cream clinging to her elbows waiting to be distributed. Against premature ageing, she had explained once. The elbows get older faster than any other part of the body.

Talent? Coyne questioned a little maliciously.

Don't look so surprised, Pat.

But he had reverted once again to his own fatalism, reading disaster into everything. He sat up reading *The Great Rivers of the World* and heard the noises coming from next door. Click, flush, mumble, bump. Then silence; the echo of Coyne's own mute intransigence. While outside, the wind was pushing against the glass and shaking the life out of the trees.

Bum, bum, bum, Carmel said, staring up at the ceiling for a moment while she rubbed cream into her neck. Coyne looked at her with horror. What was this *bum, bum, bum* business all about, he wanted to know. She had the kids repeating it all the time around the house. Even Mrs Gogarty was cracking up laughing as though they were inventing some arcane gypsy language that Coyne wouldn't understand.

Bum, bum, bum, what? Coyne demanded.

Bum, bum, bum, nothing, she said. It's only what Mr Sitwell says all the time. He's got this real Anglo-Irish accent and keeps saying things like that. It doesn't mean anything. It's just like saying 'now' for no reason. Or you know when people are trying to think of something and they say, 'well – eh'. He just says '*bum, bum, bum*'.

Big fool.

Everybody laughs at him, Carmel went on. Do you want to know what he says at the end of each class? *Boom-she-boogie*. That's how everybody knows the time is up.

Boom-she-boogie, Coyne repeated, squinting at her.

Yeah. *Boom-she-boogie*, Carmel said once more in a Royal tone. Then she laughed and Coyne stared at the great green flow of the Amazon pulsing by silently through his hands.

Carmel arrived at Gordon Sitwell's house on Saturday morning, full of apprehension. Even going in through the gate, she hesitated, but then forced herself onwards, like a friend was pushing her in the back. Go on, what are you scared of. You're bursting with talent.

Darling, so glad you could make it, Sitwell gushed.

She found herself being led through the hallway, through a dining-room and into a large extension at the rear of the house.

Welcome to my studio, he said, ushering Carmel into a tall, spacious room which had sunlight streaming in through the skylights. Other people were busily painting away and hardly stopped to look up at Carmel, concentrating only on the slightly obese model, stretched out naked on a *chaise-longue* at the end of the room.

Natasha has kindly agreed to model for us today, Sitwell said. A medieval beauty.

Natasha smiled and shifted to contain the ache of immobility, setting off a chain reaction of movement along her body. She was a perfect subject, with lots of folds. Full of generous shadows and contours to work on. She seemed to be constructed in shimmering rings – double chin, neck, voluminous breasts as well as two or three stomachs, under which the pubic area seemed to disappear gracefully without any effort at modesty. Hard to say where it was under all those layers. Androgynous almost. Like Thelma and Derek rolled together into one big human waterbed of undulating flesh, legs and arms wobbling like buttermilk.

Would you like to set yourself up there, Sitwell urged. Have you done much life-drawing before?

No, she said. But I'll give it a go.

That's the spirit, he whispered. It's the greatest of all art forms. You'll see.

Carmel got herself ready in the most clumsy fashion, dropping things, clattering her easel around so that she drew some hostile glances from other artists. Hardly started working when a big blob of green paint shot out of a tube on to her knee. Tried to wipe it off with her hand at first, which only spread the paint around. She found a little cloth and rubbed at it, but it seemed to distribute it even further so that, when Sitwell looked over at her, she appeared to be trying to conceal some intimate signal which had begun to spread around her knee and thigh like a green blush.

Boom-she-fucking-boogie.

Coyne was at home picking the debris out of the washing machine. Must have left a tissue in one of the pockets because all the clothes had white flecks of fluff attached to them. While the children ran around the house, he attempted to bring the washing from the kitchen out to the garden, getting distracted by other things all the time. Remembered that he still hadn't started building a swing for his kids. Read an old *Southside Advertiser* to see if anyone was selling any.

Neighbours then saw Mr Coyne running like a maniac out through the back door and into the garden, barking and growling like a cross between an Airedale terrier and a bloody inferno victim. A black and white cat on the back wall waited for a moment to see if this was for real then jumped down casually on the far side just before a colander clattered against the bricks. Coyne walked back into the house trying to straighten out the dent, and then answered a ring on the doorbell. A man stood behind a massive bunch of flowers and said there was no answer from No. 5. Could he accept them and pass them on later? So Coyne was left standing in the hallway with a bent colander and Mrs Gillespie's shaggin' bouquet, for Jaysussake.

Finally he managed to hang the clothes out on the revolving tree in the garden, stopping to examine the engineering design of Carmel's Wonderbra, like a frilly harness. Lucky that Mr Gillespie was out, because Coyne didn't want to be seen hanging out her tiny little string knickers.

There was nothing on TV except a programme on tropical fish, which Coyne decided to watch with Nuala sitting in his lap brushing his hair. He began to explain to her why the fish had such exotic colours. There were artists who dived down with a paint brush and a box of paints. It was a big job. They had to catch them in a net first and then give them their colours. It took years and years to get around to them all. And then they had to start again on the babies.

Jimmy looked up at the ceiling and Coyne smiled. But Nuala and Jennifer believed the story and wanted him to go on, so he went on to tell them that their mother was doing that kind of work, right at that very moment.

She's down under the sea painting baby fishes, he said, and after a while Coyne felt he was inside a big blue fish tank with his family, dozing away with a stream of fantastic bubbles going up from his mouth. Algae waving, surrounded by coral and the underwater plinking sounds of Nuala's constant snivelling in his ear as she combed his hair down to the front like a monk. Then Jimmy began to speak bubbles.

Dad, I think it's starting to rain.

Shit, he said, jumping up.

He ran out the back door once more, regretting the bad language, knowing that Jennifer would only repeat it to Mrs Gogarty. Do you know what Dad said today? Do you know that Dad once did a peepee in the sink? And Mrs Gogarty would believe anything because she was like the Stasi, or the KGB, with her omnipresent portrait commanding its place in the kitchen, the heart of the home, like a face that had third-degree burns.

He was too late. It was lashing already, so he simply lifted the whole clothes tree out of the ground by the roots and ran inside with it. Decided to erect it in the living-room, between two armchairs, so the children could play house underneath. And soon the windows began to steam up. He went to open a window and noticed that Mr Gillespie's car was back. At least the rain had done one good thing. It had prevented Gillespie from playing golf. Coyne ran out with the bunch of flowers, getting wet as he climbed over the wall just to get rid of the damn bouquet at last.

Through the front window next door he saw Mr Gillespie, playing pitch and putt on the living-room carpet. God's teeth. Am I seeing things, Coyne said to himself. And there followed a mime performance between the two men, as though neither of them could bear to make contact through language. It looked as though Coyne had suddenly contracted BSE and was dancing like a madman with a bouquet of flowers, warning Gillespie to give up this indoor golf lark immediately or else he'd stick that putter up his arse. Just you wait, Gillespie. I'll make a black banana sandwich out of your langer.

Flowers, he mouthed like a big fish outside in the rain. Flowers for your wife.

With a great deal of suspicion, Mr Gillespie finally came out like a man who had been caught in some deeply solitary, broad-daylight sexual perversion, with the golf club hidden behind his back and his mouth open in astonishment.

They're not from me, Coyne said, in case Gillespie got the wrong impression. You were out earlier when the van came.

Oh, Gillespie uttered.

Then Coyne disappeared back into his own aquarium. And when Carmel returned later on, she found them all asleep on the couch, except Jimmy, who was playing his computer games and producing sounds like a submarine. The clothes tree had fallen over on top of the TV.

Then there was a further tip-off from Fred. Apparently Fred had learned from a very good source that detectives were now connecting Drummer with a butcher shop in Sallynoggin. Fennellys had already come under suspicion recently as a laundry operation.

From smack to sausages, Coyne remarked.

Tender loin chops to tender advances in the nightclub, Fred added.

So where's the connection?

Meat is murder, Fred proclaimed as he was slowly opening a new packet of biscuits. There's more to that butcher shop than black and white pudding, if you get my drift.

Coyne waited to see if Fred would give him any more details. But Fred just kept nodding and tapping a Gingernut off the rim of his cup, as though he was some kind of cult leader, preparing his flock for the big doomsday. Coyne waiting for him to dip the biscuit as a signal for collective suicide.

Remember the black plastic bag, Fred asked.

Yeah, Coyne said, trying to remain cool.

Brannigan's death hood?

Sure.

Looks like it came from that butcher shop. Forensics found traces of animal blood and sawdust inside. They only released that information to me the other day after a lot of pressure. Check it out.

Coyne was off like a champagne cork. This was a real lead for him to follow. He decided to investigate the butcher shop under cover, as a family. Told Carmel he had found a place where they could get cheap lamb chops. Lamb in October? Brought the whole family with him as a kind of smokescreen, so that he could ask some discreet questions. Where was the lamb from? Wicklow, the owner said with butcher's pride. And the beef all came from another farm near Trim, Co. Meath. We make our own sausages too.

And what do you do with your black plastic bags?

I'll take a half-pound of sausages, Carmel said.

Anything else I can get you, Madam?

And I know what goes into those sausages. Dirty smack money. Ecstasy sausages. Crack pudding.

Coyne found the right moment to ask if he could bring the kids up to the farm one day. Said he wanted to show them the sheep, and the pigsties. Where milk came from and all that. The butcher was only too glad to draw a map. Two maps, stained with blood. So Coyne first drove up one Saturday morning, to a small farm near Roundwood. Carmel with her sketch pad, like she was some kind of scene of the crime expert gathering together all the geographical features on the location. Doing Identikit drawings. The suspect had brown eyes and a long nose. He was wearing a sheepskin coat and spoke with a Wicklow accent: maaaah.

Coyne was going to be one of these thorough policemen, leaving no stone unturned. Kicked a few *sliotars* of sheep shite with the toe of his shoe. Eliminating them from his enquiries.

He found nothing at the farm near Trim either. Nothing but copious cow flops. Cows with their large faces and their little curly hairdos between the ears. Big grey tongues licking and clicking and a hollow sound echoing in their large round stomachs. Carmel did a cow's face that looked half human, smiling, with intelligent eyes. *La vache qui fucking rit.* A suspect with a bovine grin. Jennifer wanted to know why cows were so dirty and Coyne said it was the farmer who stuck all those bits on at the back. Flies were landing on cow dung one minute and on Nuala's face the next. And the highlight of the investigation was in the milking parlour when the Coyne family all stood behind a cow, watching the tail rise up and a stream of hot, green-brown liquid cascading on to the concrete. Splat. Splutter. Nuala screamed. Oh my God, stand back, Carmel exclaimed. And Coyne was amazed how a cow could chew, give milk and crap at the same time. Splash. Flop. It was like a whole pile of Telecom bills coming in through the letter box at once. Steam rising. Carmel blessing herself.

The family that prays together, stays together. The family that drinks together, stinks together. The family that laughs together at the sight of a cow's arse will be blessed for ever in the eyes of the Lord. He was connecting the shite back to the arsehole all right. Make a note of that in your sketch pad, Carmel. Take a sample of that down to the Garda Technical Bureau for identification.

As an investigation, the whole thing was laughable. But Coyne had covered himself. Of course, there was more to the trip than watching grass turn to shite. Mystery man Coyne always had another reason for the outing up his sleeve. There was a place along the road to Trim called Echo Gate where he was told you could stand and hear your own echo perfectly. The most legendary echo that's existed since ancient Ireland. Since the Celtic Dawn. Where Fionn MacCumhaill once heard his own voice as clear as a modern tape recording and thought his soul had left him behind. All along the road, Coyne kept stopping the car and getting out, shouting over gates into the green fields, like an eejit. Hello. Hello. Hello yourself. But no echo. Nothing but dogs barking into infinity across the evening landscape, and the sun going down, stabbing through the clouds and casting long shadows, lighting up patches of raised land in the distance like a stage.

Carmel was laughing her head off. There's another gate. Try that one. Hello. Hey. Hey. Cattle stopped chewing for a moment to look up and see what the problem was. Until at last he found the right one and they all stood there shouting and howling and barking. The Coynes at the gate. Each voice clearly piercing the dusk. Then silence while they listened to their own echoes coming back from the monastic ruins on the far side of the valley like a strange, marooned family calling out to be rescued.

Carmel was always laughing. There was nothing to laugh at, but she would just suddenly crack up on the sofa. The only time she was serious was when she was painting. For the most indecipherable reasons, she would just go into stitches, holding her stomach, in tears. Jesus, Carmel, don't go into labour on me. And then she'd attempt to tell some story that would take for ever to finish because she'd break up on every second word. And in the end it wasn't even funny.

Coyne sometimes suspected that she was laughing at him, but agreed that it was just a paranoia he'd picked up as a boy. The paranoia of an islander. The same old fear of mockery in a small demographic pool with the rictus of derision on everybody's face.

He had come across an explanation for laughter once in one of his anthropological magazines. 'Laughter began with the apes and is first thought to have been used as a weapon of self-defence, long before it became recreational. Its effects were to suspend warfare and contrive a false surrender which offered a degree of superiority over other species.'

No wonder people in Ireland were laughing all the time.

But Carmel wasn't having any of it.

That was total rubbish, she responded. Why analyse fun? I'm only laughing because I can't help it, she said. And no matter how much Coyne tried to persuade her, she didn't want to understand the politics of fun.

If you stop to think about it, everything ceases to be funny, she concluded.

That's what I'm saying. There's a hidden agenda. *In risu veritas,* it says here. Every joke has its own truth.

Come on, Pat. It's just a laugh, for God's sake.

But there was more to it than that. And Coyne eventually realised that he had picked up the notion in the Aran Islands, where he was sent when he was fifteen, to brush up on his Irish. From the beginning, they called him Donkey-shite, and the way they pronounced it seemed like they wanted to say *Don Quixote* each time but ended up saying *Don Quix-shite* instead. After some time, when he started hunting rabbits with them, he realised that it was a form of inverse admiration. In Ireland, the insult was a truly intimate term of endearment in which you graced your friends with mock expressions of contempt. Only by hurling abuse could you allow people to enter your space and become your friend. If people ever stopped calling you Donkey-shite you had something to worry about. Politeness was a sign that somebody was about to violate your arse.

Maybe it was impossible to be close to anyone in Ireland without feeling suffocated. You could only have friends or enemies, nothing in between.

In the Aran Islands, Coyne felt like he had joined a noble race. As they allowed him to slit the rabbits open and throw the livers to the dogs, he knew he had become an equal. A hard man who drank his first pint and called them gobshites and puffing holes as good as he got.

There was always somebody laughing though. Animal laughter. Each time they caught a rabbit the islanders would yelp and laugh. Each time the rabbit escaped they would say: the bastard is laughin' at us now, hiding deep down in one of the fissures of the rock, with the sea crashing against the base of the cliffs, and white balls of foam lifting up into the air across the Glasen Rocks. It was the edge of the world, where all other sound was obliterated by the violent thump of the waves and the wind humming like flutes across the openings in the rocks. The rim of the cliff luring Coyne to his death with a kind of vertiginous madness. And the dogs staring down into the gap in the rocks where the rabbit had disappeared. Tongues hanging out, whining with indignation. The lads poking their sticks down, but the rabbit safely out of reach, laughing his heart out, in Irish.

It was the same with the donkeys, roaming around the airstrip. They behaved a bit like a herd of wild mustangs, belonging to nobody and obeying no law but their own. By night, they stood in the middle of the road like solitary phantoms in the pitch black, trying to get into somebody's potato field. By day, they sniggered to themselves at the hoof damage left behind. And if you tried to catch them, they threw you off their backs and galloped away with their ears down, kicking out behind them and farting, stopping a hundred yards away to laugh.

On an island, there was always somebody laughing. Burglars, pimps, child abusers, dealers, beef barons. The Bank of Ireland was breaking its shite laughing. Cats. Dogs. Moleshaver Molloy, Mrs

Gogarty, Chagall; all laughing themselves sick. These days, it was Drummer Cunningham who was doing all the laughing.

But we'll have the last laugh, Coyne vowed to his colleagues at the station one evening at the end of his shift. We'll have the last laugh. That's for sure.

Coyne made up his mind to take a look at Drummer's nightclub. He needed to invent some excuse, however, so he got in touch with his friend Vinnie Foley. A little disingenuous, perhaps, but Vinnie was always ready for a binge with an old pal. They were sure to end up doing a trawl of the nightclubs, offering a perfect undercover approach. Foley never talked for long on the phone. Just gave the name of a pub and a time, like orders for a bombing campaign.

We're going to murder a few pints, he said.

They met in Conways. Foley had already planned out the whole night, like the old days. Let's do some damage, he kept repeating like the slogan of an underground army. Talked about women, past girlfriends, past drinking sessions. Quickly ran through some of the major events that they had experienced together, just to set the record straight, so they could carry on from where they had left off. And when Coyne tried to talk about a few things like the Amazon basin he found his friend looking at him as though he'd lost touch with the real world altogether.

Things are getting desperate, Foley complained. All my friends are happily married and talking about the Amazon.

I'd love to do it, Coyne said. I'd love to take an old beat-up ferry and sail down the Amazon. That's where it's at, Vinnie. Everywhere else is fucked.

You're reading too many nature magazines, Coyne.

Just put me down on a raft and let me go.

Look, why are we talking about rivers when we could be talking about women, Foley wanted to know.

Coyne was already drifting helplessly off course. He had lost the ability to communicate with other men. Beyond redemption.

Rivers are like women, he said.

And for once Foley stared at Coyne as though he was a prophet. At last he had come back to reality. His pronouncement had such depth and truth that it instantly made a new bond between them. As though men together drinking pints had a sworn duty towards glory and gloom.

Look at me, Foley said, as if to put himself forward as an example. I've been trying to stop the river for years. He described the women he had met in the past ten years. Couldn't count them all. I'm telling you, man, my career is a brilliant success, but my social life is a brilliant disaster. Rode the arse off them all and what have I got to show for it?

A smoking mickey, Coyne offered. But there was a suggestion of offside because Vinnie Foley was being serious.

What I admire about you, Coyne, is how you can hang on to one woman, he said, as though he was referring to some extreme form of brand loyalty.

The conversation with Foley was always more like one-way traffic and it was clear he didn't really want to know anything about Coyne. It was like answering back to the TV. Foley just took over, rearranging the world in his own advertising vocabulary.

Carmel! She is beautiful, he said. That's all I can say. She's a fucking lady.

Ah, come on, Foley. You can't hold your drink any more.

I'm serious, Coyne. She is a real person. No question about it.

And Foley took a hold of Coyne's shirt to indicate that he meant every word he was saying. With the sincerity of a Toyota ad, he looked into Coyne's eyes, holding on to him in a fierce grip of white-knuckle friendship.

You are one lucky bastard, Coyne. Carmel and three lovely children.

Coyne was still indebted to Vinnie Foley for many things. He had got him a job at the harbour with Jack Tansey when they were growing up, selling mackerel and crabs and lobsters; working at the boats, hiring them out to people who came to the harbour for pleasure trips in the bay. Men who came to fish in groups. Families with all their children in lifejackets. Lovers sailing off to get shipwrecked on Dalkey Island.

Whenever Coyne and Vinnie wanted to get close, they would recall this time. They talked about the schoolteacher from Loreto Abbey who came down to swim at the harbour. All the lads working at the harbour knew Miss Larrissey's body intimately because Jack's shed had a small window at the end, through which they could watch women undress and perform a kind of Houdini act under the towel. The Irish striptease. Until the schoolteacher looked around one day and noticed a half-dozen faces crammed into that little window staring at her naked arse. And of course it was Coyne's face she remembered. And Coyne who had to get the lobsters for her the following evening, when she arrived down all dressed up with earrings and high heels and *Failte Romhat* written across her plunging neckline. Coyne who hauled the lobster storage box up from the water and sold her three of the biggest lobsters, knowing that they would soon blush and boil in the pot. And Coyne who forgot to tie the storage box properly so that the lid opened on the way down and all the remaining lobsters fell out into the harbour, splashing into the water one by one. Crawling helplessly backwards out to sea with rubber bands tied around their claws, defenceless and doomed.

They were quite drunk by the time they moved on to the nightclubs. But at last Coyne was back to his mission, sizing up the bouncers on the way in. Boneheads stinking of aftershave and with faces like hub-caps. Necks as thick as sewer pipes. Wearing tuxedos or double-breasted suits, like double glazing, making everybody feel honoured to be let in.

The Fountain! Coyne looked at the sign outside. Blue neon handwriting, with a small palm tree and a pathetic pink sprinkle of water pissing upwards and flashing on and off. Underneath, the words 'Nite Club'.

Inside, the methodical thud and the usual cast of frozen intellects that you found in any nightclub. Stale basement air, laden with sweat, smoke and perfume. More men with big jackets and greased-back hair throwing deadly looks around as though they were going to mutilate all the women. And the women wore hunted expressions, dancing with packets of cigarettes and throwaway lighters in their hands as though the men were only after their cigarettes. Maybe they were all really nice, decent people at home, but the club brought out a cold killer instinct. Hot pants and cold hands. *You Sexy Motherfucker – shakin' that ass, shakin' that ass.* One man allowing a young woman to lead him around the dance floor by his tie, turning him into some

kind of farm animal out for the night. A couple dancing back to b
like Balloo scratching himself on a tree trunk, and one guy on hi
own as though he was working out to a time trial on an invisible Pec
Deck.

There was an oval-shaped bar with a bald barman and backless
barmaids. Customers were perched on high stools and there was a
fountain with green and occasionally pink water gushing upwards.
At the end of the dance floor there were two elevated cages with
railings, like raised corrals, in each of which a young woman did
a kind of marathon breast-stroke in a silky miniskirt. Coloured
spotlights flashing down on them and dry ice coming up under their
legs.

Coyne approached the bar like a serious law enforcement agent,
ordering a bottle of wine, acting like he was Nick Nolte with a brain
implant. Vinnie right behind him, already drawing up a short list
from the dancers on the floor.

But you had to get all the talkin' off your chest first before you
got to the shakin'. So Coyne and Vinnie had a further existential yak
over a lousy bottle of wine, served by a waitress who refused to look
at what she was doing. They stood facing each other, Coyne listening
avidly to the healing power of his friend's proclamations.

I want you to know one thing, Foley said. We'll always be best
mates.

Sure, Coyne agreed.

They had reached a level of friendship that could never be
surpassed. It was like the old days. You couldn't go any higher. You
couldn't become closer than they were at that moment, with Vinnie's
arm around his shoulder.

No matter where I am in the world, you can count on me, Foley
swore. No matter what happens, I'll be there.

The same goes for me, Coyne said after a moment's hesitation.

It was what Vinnie wanted to hear. Like a soul brother, he stared
silently into Coyne's eyes for a long time as though he was close to
tears. Tears of unbreakable friendship. Embracing him, then punching
him in the chest.

You fucking bastard, Coyne.

Then he leaped on to the dance floor as though he was imitating a
rooster recently aroused from his sleep. Elbows flapping to the music

aggeresque rings around the woman in fur-rimmed
is shakin' that ass alright. Coyne could see the bum-
Then he found his view blocked by a woman with
Georgian backside and conservatory who was slightly
overdoing the hip movements, like she was making a point, doing a
new Lil-Lets ad. There was condensation running down the mirrors.
Some total gobshite was doing air-guitar in the background with his
head down like he was Rod Stewart or Aerosmith or something. And
the dance floor was momentarily packed for *Let's talk about sex,
baby,* as though it was a new national anthem, for a United Ireland.
Exploratory talks that everybody could agree on.

Vinnie danced back over to the bar and told Coyne to come join
them.

I'll say you're an accountant, he said, and dragged Coyne out on
to the floor. The big Coyne comeback. But Coyne moved around a
bit like a shaggin' knee-cap victim, lifting each leg alternately to see
if it still worked, with the imprint of his inhaler clearly visible in his
trouser pocket. Trying to look cool, noting details about the décor
and the lights. Scanning every shadow in the place for suspicious
signs.

At one point Vinnie came over and reminded Coyne how he had
once saved his life. When they were out on the sea at night in one of
Jack's boats, rowing across the smooth black water until they got to a
cast of lobster pots. The plan was to steal a few lobsters and then call
on two girls they knew who would cook them up. Food of love. The
lights all along the shore like a necklace behind them. The lighthouse
casting a flash across the surface and Coyne lifting one pot after
another up to the boat. It was too dark out there to see into the pots,
so Coyne had to stand up and hold each one up against the lights
on the shore. Until he lost his balance and fell backwards, going all
the way down into the deep black sea with the lobster pot strapped
across his chest. Coyne would have drowned if Vinnie hadn't caught
the rope just in time with his oar.

Started pulling the pot back up so that Coyne eventually surfaced
again, coughing up mouthfuls of sea water.

Remember! I saved your life, Vinnie said as he danced a circle
around Coyne, giving him a drunken kiss on the cheek before going
back to dancing belly to belly with the fur-rimmed goddess of the

sea. Coyne had the impression she had silver mackerel scales all over her body. As though they were on the floor of the ocean, surrounded by lobsters and waving seaweed.

Except that there wasn't a lobster in sight nowadays. Everywhere was overfished to bejaysus. Two or three hundred pots out waiting for the one poor unfortunate creature that was left, searching around for his mates. All emigrated. It was Armageddon for lobsters. The rest of his clan crammed into a glass holding centre in some bastard's sea-food restaurant. People coming in to look them in the eye and say: I'm going to eat you. Lobsters once had the whole bay to themselves. Now it was all over. And because Coyne was such a bad dancer, he found himself trying to talk to the woman with the conservatory at the rear, telling her about destruction, boring her to death with his endangered lobster statistics.

Don't tell me – you do the accounts for fishermen, she said, and looked at him as though she had detected the smell of mackerel coming from his crotch.

Coyne left the dance floor and sat alone at the bar, drunk, watching Vinnie Foley doing hip collisions with the mermaid. Some time later, Vinnie came over and said he was leaving. The woman with fur-rimmed hot pants, smiling on his arm, with Vinnie's leather jacket thrown over her shoulders.

I'll be fine, Coyne insisted.

Give me a shout, Vinnie said, winking.

They were like warriors parting, locking arms and vowing to reunite again in battle soon. Then Vinnie walked towards the exit and their friendship became suspended again. It would lie preserved in ice until the next time they met, who knows when. In a way Coyne was glad because he could now begin to search the place for anything that might be relevant to his investigation. He ordered another bottle of plonk and the waitress gave him a white plastic beaker as though he could not be trusted with a glass. Drank the best part of it until he suddenly saw a young woman he recognised on the far side of the bar.

I've seen that woman before, he thought, but where? He liked the way she looked. Dressed in the most provocative tight-fitting ribbed top that magnified every detail of her breasts. I'd eat broken glass out of your knickers, he muttered to himself in a drunken way.

It was only when the young woman spoke up and ordered an orange juice that Coyne's memory finally clicked into gear. It was Madonna on oysters and Guinness. Coyne was amazed to realise how close he had already come to the Cunningham gang.

He kept looking at her. Making mental notes. The real detective. He could teach Moleshaver a thing or two about the nature of crime detection. Wait and see, he repeated. Knocked back his beaker, grabbed the bottle and walked around casually to the other side of the oval counter.

Naomi, isn't it?

She looked up at him with a wasted expression. There seemed to be nothing behind the focus of her eyes but a series of interlinking empty rooms.

Do you remember, we met on the railway tracks, Coyne blurted. It was such a stupid thing to say. Blowing his cover right away. But she appeared to remember nothing. Just stared at him as though she had to pick him out of an identity parade of men in her memory. Coyne took the liberty of sitting down beside her, pouring the last of his wine into a plastic beaker for her. But she stared at that too as though all human gestures were alien to her.

What's your name, she asked suddenly, and Coyne was put on the spot, hesitating.

Vinnie, he said. Vinnie Foley.

But that was another mistake. Subconsciously he had always wanted to be like Vinnie. Now he was losing his cool altogether. Too drunk to be a cop.

Vinnie Foley, she repeated a number of times, then swivelled around as if to indicate that she had an announcement to make.

Well, listen carefully, Vinnie, she said, pointing at the door of a VIP lounge, with brown leather upholstery. You better not be sitting there when he comes back. That's all I'm saying.

Who?

Drummer, she said, speaking in such an exhausted tone of voice that it meant she was perfectly serious. Coyne felt rejected. Wanted to tell her how concerned he was for her. He could help her. He would look after her. Get her away from that gang.

Coyne had reached such a suicidal drunken pitch and was ready to have the showdown with the Drummer, right there and then in his nightclub, vowing to protect her honour at all costs, when she suddenly showed him her wrists.

Look, she said, like a final warning, and Coyne stared down at the scars where she had allowed the hot blood to rush out. The taut, almost see-through skin draped over the thin blue rods of her arteries had been disfigured by a violent design. Gashes like melted wax. Healing over like white latex cloth which had been held to the flame. Coyne recoiled from the aesthetics of this mutilation, but also perceived it as an expression of intimacy. She was showing him where she had poured out her life into a blood-red bath. He took it personally. He was entertaining his emotions.

Do you need help? he asked.

She looked puzzled by that. And before she could even react, Coyne tore off a tiny piece of beermat and wrote out a telephone number. She refused to accept it in her hand, so he placed it in an empty beaker.

The man's name is Fred. He's a nightwatchman. He'll get in touch with me.

Moments later, Coyne was picked off the chair from behind by a large, beefy companion of Drummer. It was the Chief Accountant, pulling him up by the collar.

Are you giving trouble, mate?

And Coyne became instantly aggressive. Instead of leaving it alone and walking out, pretending that the whole thing was a mistake, he began to argue with Drummer's right-hand man. Trying to stand up for Madonna with the slashed wrists.

I'm having a conversation here, right.

Is this man hassling you? Chief asked her.

But Naomi didn't even look up, delivering Coyne up to his own fate.

Piss off and mind your own business, Coyne said, but there was a halting slur in his speech which lacked conviction. Perhaps he felt the security of Vinnie's companionship around him like a protective charm. Tried to shake the Chief's vice grip off his shoulders. Pushed him away with his elbow and tried to engage Madonna's eyes to show that she had a free choice to decide whether or not she wanted to talk to him. But Coyne was wasted. Couldn't even stand up properly, let alone fight back.

Out, Chief shouted, dragging Coyne away.

For a moment, Coyne felt it was quite funny to be hauled away like a limp statue, with his feet sliding along the floor behind him, and the dancers turning round to look at the cartoon simplicity with which he was being ejected from the club. The barman was already clearing away his beaker and wiping the counter. Naomi didn't look up. And outside, things were not quite so funny. The two bouncers took over from Chief, hauling Coyne up the cast-iron stairs on to the pavement with a punch in the ribs.

Before Coyne could retaliate or begin to speak out with righteous indignation at these men in tuxedos, he received a boot in the crotch. He didn't know where it came from, but the pain spread like a vicious stain right up through his stomach and stopped him from wanting anything. He doubled over obediently. Received a few more punches here and there, but they seemed only like minor pats on the back in comparison to the great purple ache in his groin. He sank down. Hand on the railings, face on the cool pavement, feeling the full ignominy of his expulsion.

Now fuck off home, he heard one of them shout through a cloud of sickness which had begun to churn around inside. His whole mind was white. Thought people in the street were looking at him, but could see nothing apart from the polished shoes of a bouncer, and the white socks, inches away from his eyes. He was vaguely aware of the men standing over him, folding their arms. His ears were whining with nausea. He dragged himself away by the railings, but stopped again, puking up all he had, holding the agony of his manhood in his hand.

Back in his humble Ford Escort, Coyne sat for a long time by the canal feeling huge anger. Then he went back to feeling stupid, knowing that it was his own fault. He felt self-pity. Felt there was no fair play left in the world and came full circle again with a growing fury that he had never dealt with before.

He drove around, knowing that he was too drunk. He was just the kind of man he would have been arresting if he was on duty. Drove past the nightclub a number of times wishing he could do something, trying to find some way of getting back at the men who beat him before he went home and before sleep would rob him of all the resentment. He held an image of the girl in his mind. Felt he had suffered everything for her.

In a side-street he spotted Berti Cunningham's Range Rover, parked neatly under a street light. He knew the registration number by heart. He couldn't believe his luck. What if he just slashed the tyres. That would give them a taste of their own shite. That would teach them not to mess with Coyne.

He parked near a small laneway and waited for a while to survey the street. He had one concern, that a patrol car from Irishtown or Donnybrook might cruise past and one of the lads would recognise his car. They would stop and say hello, maybe. And he'd have to abandon the plan. When the street seemed quiet, he faced his car into the opening of the laneway, giving him direct access on to another street. Left the engine running and got out.

He walked up and down past the target car. When he was satisfied that there was nobody around, he first of all decided to urinate on the door of the Range Rover, looking around him all the time. A symbolic piss, transferring ownership to himself, like some common canine law where the property belonged to the individual who last urinated on it.

After that, Coyne had to act fast because it would all become very noisy and spectacular. He had no Stanley knife in the car. So he took the spare petrol can from the boot, along with the wheel brace. Went back along the pavement, calm as anything. Not a single nerve twitching. Broke the windscreen with one smack of the brace, setting off the agonised wail of the car alarm. There was no breeze and no danger of doing lateral damage to any other property. Precision bombing. Coyne threw the contents of the can on to the front seat and set the vehicle alight with one match. Coyne the car terrorist! Felt the air being sucked violently towards the flames from all around him. He didn't even need to look back and see it. Burn, you bastards. It was like 1916. Flames reflected in the Georgian windows all around the city.

That will teach them, he said to himself as he got back into the car with the adrenalin foaming around his brain. He raced down through the lane, crossed a main street and raced along another lane. Such intimate knowledge of the city enabled Coyne to put a considerable distance between himself and the scene of the fire. Within minutes he was driving back along Leeson Street just in time to see the men in suits bounding up the cast-iron steps of the Fountain, leaping out through the gate and lashing down the street like they just had a chilli pepper inserted up their hole. A positive indicator if ever there was one.

Coyne's Justice.

On the way home, Coyne found a hedgehog on the road. Jammed on the brakes and ran along the pavement as though he was possessed by some haunting guilt from which he needed to escape. Looked like he had been struck by some nauseating premonition. Drivers along the dual carriageway caught a glimpse of him bending down, picking a good spot along the granite wall to get sick on, it seemed. Christy Moore blasting out through the open door of the car as though it caused his stomach to turn. Looked like he just puked up a ball of brown needles. Oh Lisdoonvarna.

Running after a fecking hedgehog, for Jesussake. What he intended to do was to catch it and bring it home to the children. They would be amazed to see a hedgehog in their garden in the morning. But there was a practical side too. He had been looking for a permanent and humane way of dealing with the snails who invaded his garden every year, preventing anything from growing. Liberation from snails. The hedgehog and the fight for Irish freedom, he thought, as he took his coat from the car, gently picked up the heaving creature from the street and placed it into the boot. How was he to know that the Irish hedgehog carried twenty-six different kinds of fleas? Coyne was thinking storybook hedgehogs here.

By the time he got home, however, the hedgehog had disappeared. He searched the whole car, under the seats, everywhere. Coyne eventually figured out that it must have escaped through one of the holes where the rust had begun to eat away under the spare wheel in the boot. The night of the escaped hedgehog. He dreamed of missing hedgehogs. Felt a sense of immeasurable loss. Something deeper that he could hardly define. Something that could never be recovered. He'd lost far more than a hedgehog.

Carmel was going mad in the morning. Told him how she had been up half the night worrying. Nearly had to phone the Guards.

I was with Vinnie Foley, Coyne said, as though that was sufficient explanation in itself.

I should have known.

The children watched Coyne attempting to make porridge. They found a black rim all along his lips and Jennifer said there was a smell of petrol coming from his mouth. He stared back at them with cinder eyes, as red as Dracula's. Everything was too bright for him. They wouldn't eat the poisoned porridge, so he made a stab at the lumpy lava himself, gave them sugar puffs instead and returned to his crypt, where he slept all day.

In a coma of the undead, he was unable to tell whether he was dealing with dreams or reality. Occasionally he woke up in a panic and remembered the burning car. Saw for the first time with any clarity what he had done. He had broken through the thin membrane between good and evil, on to the criminal side of society. In a half-sleep, he understood the dangers of his borderland excursion, crossing into Drummer's world, perhaps never finding a way back. Sometimes saw himself back in the nightclub, fighting, kicking the duvet from his bed with a great burst of unconscious violence. He heard Nuala banging a spoon against a toy wheelbarrow in the garden outside and dreamed she was hammering on the outside of his coffin. Voices came and went throughout the morning and afternoon, like muttering mourners. He was aware of Jennifer and Nuala's presence in the room at one point, whispering and giggling, but his eyelids were too heavy to open. From the kitchen he heard the cutlery being thrown back item by item into their separate compartments, like the bells of disapproval in the distance.

Drummer held a conference at his home in Sandymount. By lunchtime he had selected a team of seven men to comb the city for a guy named Vinnie Foley. He wanted the whole of Dublin to suffer until he found out who did his car. Hadn't even gone to see the damage himself because it would be too hurtful. Held on to his dignity and just allowed Chief to present him with a picture of the Fire Brigade hosing down the charred brown wreck of his Range Rover hissing and tinkling, with smoke rising up over the streets like a Benetton poster. Took the news in silence, fists clenched, eyes staring into the distance like cigarette burns on the sofa.

All he did was question Naomi. Pinched one of her nipples in his fingers as if he was picking a cherry from a tree, until she squirmed with pain and gave him the name.

And what did you say to him? Drummer demanded.

Nothing. I swear, Berti. He just tried to chat me up.

I don't like you talking to people like that. Could be the law.

Let go of me, for fucksake. I swear to God, Berti, you're paranoid.

If I find out he's a cop, you're fucking dead, he said, finally releasing her nipple.

Berti Cunningham was the kind of guy with a high metabolic rate who would get up in the morning and think, who do I need to whack today? Now he had a real reason to feel he was under-achieving. He commanded such absolute allegiance that his gang of executive dickheads in suits hung around outside the downstairs luxury bathroom of his swanky home, waiting for instructions while Berti was inside, battling with a serious bowel blockage. It was just like the tribe of communal crappers, except that Berti was the only one who actually engaged in the ritual. The acrid stink imposed a sense of realism on to the proceedings.

Drummer even took his lunch into the bathroom with him, in the hope that it would shift his furious condition. Never ate enough fibre. He would start and end his day with fast food, and the more tense he was, the more he needed to eat. Even as a baby, his nappies used to smell like Big Macs.

I feel my allocation of mercy has run out this month. I want every mother's son in this city to scream until I find out. I'll knock long-lasting briquettes out of him, whoever did it.

The Cunningham gang spent the next three days extracting information by brute force from everybody they knew around the city. The Chief Accountant's trade mark was to hold a lighted cigarette butt up to a person's eye. Mick Cunningham preferred to let his boot do the talking while Berti had his own subtle techniques that would make his victims sing. He understood pain best of all and knew how to maximise the effects of sleep deprivation. They burst into a service garage at Dublin Bus and slapped some of the mechanics around, threatening them with spanners. At a snooker hall in the north of the city, the Chief Accountant tried to impale a man on a billiard cue. They even slapped Joe Perry around in an alleyway at one point, asking him out of desperation if he had anything against cars. A lot of people would have been cursing Coyne for the mayhem he had unleashed on the underworld.

The widespread investigation yielded nothing. Drummer's men-in-tights were flit-arsing around the city, cross-examining all kinds of innocent people, kicking rashers and eggs out of harmless junkies and coming up with fuck all. In the agony of his rage, Berti called on a second-rate, ageing dope dealer from Leitrim by the name of Noel Smyth who owed him some money from a long time back. They burst into his Ranelagh flat and slapped him around, going through all his possessions while Drummer stared silently out the window at a stained mattress dumped in the back yard.

You greasy fucking dopehead, Chief shouted. You still owe us some dosh.

Chill out, lads. What money?

There's a lot of interest due on that, Chief demanded.

I've no bread, lads. Take anything you want. You can have Mick Jagger's underpants. Go on, take them. And Marianne Faithfull's Mars bar. Take the lot. Take Jimmy's roach too, that I shared with him in Marrakesh – there on the mantelpiece in the Woodstock ashtray.

Mick Cunningham started force-feeding him a bag of coke which they had come across. Chief looked through the CD collection and found *The Chieftains in China*.

The Chieftains in fucking China, he laughed. But Drummer wasn't amused. He continued to stare at the melancholy landscape of rainy back gardens, working everything out in his head. Didn't enjoy the idea of mindless violence. There had to be a purpose. He had to have the right man. So he told the lads to lay off Smyth. Allowed the Leitrim man to gather himself together, thank them for his life and shake his hand. Then they left again.

Carmel started going on these autumn painting workshops, organised by Mr Sitwell. Boom, boom. Off they went, drawing the halfpenny bridge, the Customs House, reflections in the canal. They did a whole series of harbour locations. Then they were off to Enniskerry to draw autumnal landscapes and mountains. Sitwell wearing a tweed jacket and a woolly scarf wrapped around his neck like one of the magnificent men in their flying machines. On top, he usually wore a navy sea captain's hat and he smoked a cheroot with a filter, leading his troupe of artists up the slopes of Wicklow. He was indiscriminate in his quest for beauty. Undeterred by flocks of sheep and fertiliser bags stuck in hedges, he trekked across the landscape like an explorer with a pack of converts carrying their easels and picnic baskets. All red in the face and sweating like cheese in a greenhouse, they stopped when Sitwell suddenly held out his arms, struck dumb by inspiration.

Splendid, he would say. Bum, bum, bum! But the words were a mere insult to such a vision of magnificent creation. It was breathtaking. Stupendous. Sitwell would take a moment or two to reflect. The artists all humming in agreement, eagerly putting down their gear, before he spoke again.

This place has been touched by divine inspiration, ladies. It's got everything an artist could ever want in nature – a green patchwork of fields in the valley, a mountain slope of deciduous trees and a sky that was left behind by Michelangelo. The earth is on fire. An inferno of red and yellow shades, flaming along the hills and disappearing into an awesome darkness at the base of the valley.

He would get really exercised about light and darkness for a while. Puffing on his cheroot, pretending to draw a little sketch with it in the air. Then point out the awesome darkness again and say it was the key to genius, to be able to capture that absence of light at the end of the valley.

If you forgive me, ladies. But the artist's eye is drawn to that absence of light in the same way that a man is drawn to those intriguing, shadowy qualities in the cut of a woman's blouse.

Some of the women laughed or sniggered in complicity at his jokes. As though you were admitting you had had a mastectomy if you didn't join in. Some of them gave him more than he bargained for with a string of Wonderbra jokes. The valley of darkness. Twin peaks. Lift and separate. Schtoppem-floppen.

But everything settled down and his troupe was won over by the new purity of artistic invention. Everyone painting away quietly. A mixture of smells, ranging from Sitwell's cigar, his aftershave, along with the smell of cut hay, lingering in the air. In the distance, the crows arguing in the tops of the trees. At times an unseen car or a truck in the valley. And the landscape shifting with the angle of the sun, the shape of clouds, and the progress of sheep, swinging their jaws endlessly in a silent musical rhythm.

Coyne had left messages for Vinnie Foley. Wanted to warn him. Kept on phoning and speaking to these sweet advertising voices, telling him that Vinnie was not available. Or else he was at a presentation. And when Coyne hadn't heard from him a week later, he marched into the offices of Cordawl, O'Carroll, Beatty and fucking Banim to make sure he spoke to him. Yes, it was a matter of life and death, in a way. The woman at the reception greeted Coyne like she knew everything about him in advance.

Hi, she said, ushering him into an oak-panelled reception room, leaning over to show Coyne her lace bra. Blinking at him and gesturing towards a seat by the marble fireplace. There was a massive sculpture like a knotted penis by the window.

Have a look at the mags for a sec, she urged, with a laconic smile as though everything had to be abbreviated into a sexual endearment. Vinnie will be with you in three shakes.

Three shakes of an archbishop's mickey.

Coyne was then brought upstairs by a chubby young woman wearing a big sweater and a ring in her nose. Took him by the elbow and led him into an open-plan office where people hung around talking in a sort of party atmosphere even though it was before lunch. The place was like a big crèche with a basketball net on the wall. A woman in black leather trousers was physically acting out the punchline of some anecdote, after which she turned and walked away with her arm in the air, waving without looking back, leaving two chuckling men behind her. In another part of the office, an old man with a crew cut started fencing a duel of rulers against a younger executive, while a woman with large pink horn-rimmed glasses was silently staring out the window, thinking up some new super-catchphrase like 'Shaws, almost nationwide'. I mean what the fuck was almost nationwide – Dublin, Cork, Borris in Ossary?

All over the place, there were posters and silly messages – Vin, I want to share my last Rolo with you, Viv. Memo to Moll from Mike: cough up the Fisherman's Friend ad before the big storm. Memo to Fran from Dan: The Ancient Mariner wants the Fish Fingers poster by Friday. Alfie: the sex was great but the coffee was lousy. Everything paired, everything rhymed. Gary Larson humour had spread like a virus throughout the office and people spoke in cryptic one-liners which recalled the latest TV commercials. Somebody held up a three-day-old doughnut with yellowed cream and said: nothing added but time.

Coyne held them in contempt, even worse than artists or golfers, or even motorists. They thought they were all really clever and creative. But their language was just a series of semi-poetic, post-coital hints. They sounded like men on the make. Madame Bovary in leather. They were all living on an endless paradigm shift, like an infinite flat escalator at an airport.

Coyne, what are you doing here? Vinnie said. He was working on a Kerrygold presentation and was pressed for time.

I had to contact you, Coyne said, looking around, indicating that they needed privacy. But there was no such thing as privacy in an ad agency. It was all egalitarian. An open society with no secrets. And Vinnie thought Coyne had come to him with a marital problem.

Did you empty the tanks, Coyne? Vinnie asked, and Coyne looked startled. What tanks was he referring to?

No, I filled them, he replied.

So what's the problem?

Your life is in danger, Vinnie. I've come to warn you.

Foley laughed as though his friend was reading out a script for a new insurance commercial. Coyne explained that he had spoken to a girl by the name of Naomi who was linked to the crime world, but Vinnie took him by the arm and led him back towards the stairs again.

Relax, Coyne. You're sleepwalking.

I'm serious, Vinnie. These heavies at the club will come after you.

Why? What have I done?

I'm sorry, Vinnie. It was all a big mistake, but I gave her your name. Just for the crack. Then this situation developed. Vinnie, you better not stay at home for a few days. Stay somewhere else for a while.

Vinnie thought the whole thing was a practical joke. Felt his privacy had been invaded. He was ten minutes away from making an all-important presentation to Kerrygold and his brain was like rancid butter.

Jesus, Coyne, you don't even look like me.

Carmel was complaining about a terrible smell in the car. A really evil stink of something rotten. It was so bad that Mrs Gogarty had been forced to anoint the vehicle with Lancôme.

Carmel didn't drive the car very often. But when she did, it was a spectacle. She never hit anything, but the sight of her leaning forward, driving in a high gear and turning her whole body around to look behind, was enough to make Coyne nervous. He didn't have to witness her driving, of course.

Except on that one occasion, when she picked up one of those luminous yellow Garda cones. Somehow she had chosen to park in a restricted area, thinking that she was immune from the law, and while reversing out, managed to run over and lift up one of the plastic bollards on the fender without hearing the crunch. There she was, driving across Dublin, people waving at her from bus stops and Carmel thinking they were all being terrible friendly or terribly hostile that day. Thought the man in the blue Mercedes was making a pass at her, so Mrs Gogarty beside her kept telling her to ignore him – the dirty scoundrel. Three young children in the back of the car and all. And what had to happen of course was that a squad car from the Clontarf district eventually flagged her down. And she explained that she was married to Garda Pat Coyne from Irishtown, so the news went around double quick – Coyne's missus dragged a No-Parking cone all the way from Blackrock to Clontarf.

The journey was undertaken on those rare occasions when Carmel's mother felt the need to go back across to the Northside to visit old friends, look at the old house and chat with the neighbours. A journey of triumph. Behaving like a returned lottery winner. With the Brown Thomas walk, and the scent of Lancôme marching ten paces ahead of her. I'm living in Dun Laoghaire now, near my daughter Carmel. It's nice over there. Very convenient. But Mrs Gogarty still could not help being curious about her origins and the place she had lived in for so long with her husband. Couldn't help noticing the improvements around the neighbourhood – a new porch here, a new fence there, an attic converted, and the fact that a certain Mr Donore had finally died so that his pigeons weren't a nuisance any more. She could not resist the secret feeling of envy, knowing she had betrayed her real friends and was therefore banished for ever across the city to the Southside and a life of imagined superiority.

The tea was better on the Northside, she had to admit on the way home. Back into exile, where her only friends were Carmel and the kids, and another widowed lady by the name of Bronwyn Heron. Brownwind, as Coyne called her. And maybe the perfume was wearing off on the way back over the toll bridge, because Carmel and her mother both agreed that there was a foul smell in the car. Mrs Gogarty of course thought it was the smell of her son-in-law, the way she held her nose up and looked around the car. They had to drive with the windows open. Such a vicious stench that Mrs Gogarty insisted on dousing the whole vehicle with Lancôme as though it was holy water.

So much that nobody could smell a thing after that. Coyne gathered it must have been the hedgehog. May have left behind a few little trophies in the boot before escaping. Found nothing when he examined the boot, however, except three little black marbles. And now he had to drive around the shagging place in what smelled like a beauty salon on wheels. Pong all over his uniform. Such a slagging he got from the lads.

The trouble was that Coyne was seriously indebted to Mrs Gogarty. Mrs Gocart, as he sometimes called her, had given them the deposit for the house. Otherwise they'd still be renting. When her husband died, the life insurance, along with a very good offer on her house in Drumcondra, enabled Mrs Gocart to set up a nice little empire on the Southside. Bought her own house, put down a substantial deposit on Pat and Carmel's house nearby, as well as retaining more than enough money in the bank to live comfortably for the rest of her days, yacking to Carmel over tea and spelling things out in letters so that the kids couldn't hear.

Coyne was compromised by the deal. She owned him. The clothes the children wore were practically all bought by her. And still Coyne never had any money. Carmel had gone into debt just to buy curtains and fittings, just to keep up with her mother's image of her daughter's lifestyle. And because of Mrs Gogarty's constant presence, Coyne's own mother refused to come over to the house any more. She'd rather sit on her own watching TV than have a posh conversation with Mrs

Gocart. Instead, Carmel and the children went to visit Mrs Coyne once in a while. Coyne's mother never tried the self-appointed role of special adviser to the new family, telling Carmel that Coyne shouldn't be seen coming and going from the house in his uniform.

You don't want the neighbours knowing what he does.

Wait till they needed him next, that's all Coyne would say. It was all right to look down on a Garda and call him a pig and a redneck and all that. Until the time came when you needed him. Coyne to the rescue. Like the time he had to get a ladder and climb up into a bedroom on the estate, because a three-year-old boy had locked his mother into the bathroom and Coyne found the bedroom destroyed, lipstick marks on the walls, jewellery all over the place, like a break-in. It was all fine until Madam Gocart needed to have her hedge cut back. It was all right to laugh until the next little domestic crisis turned up and Coyne would be called in to fix a hoover, or just explain that the trip switch had gone on the fuse board. Where would you be without Coyne?

In fact he had a reputation for his eco-friendly inventions. Carmel had once told him that the only ecological disaster to get upset about was the toast burning. So he had come up with some great domestic innovations. Like the wooden clothes peg he had screwed up against the kitchen window to hold the rubber gloves. And the wooden tray he invented with spare door handles at both ends.

But as usual, Coyne took his inventor status too far. Like the time he gathered his whole family around the kitchen table, asking them all if they could find a way of standing a raw egg up. And everyone kept trying it and laughing at their own inadequacy, Coyne watching them with his arms folded and a smirk of absolute wisdom on his face, until they all said they were giving up and Coyne just simply took the egg and cracked it on to the table so that it stood on its head. Ah but that was cheating. We all could have done that, Mrs Gogarty said.

Then why didn't you do it, Coyne said, full of triumphant glee, while Carmel started cleaning up the mess and muttering that he was getting a bit too silly.

Mrs Gogarty was beginning to get on Pat Coyne's nerves. Sitting around the house all the time, always giving advice, indoctrinating the kids and holding Carmel under a spell of moral superiority.

I always pick the number seven, Mrs Gogarty was saying to the children one evening before Coyne went out to work on the late shift. He was in his uniform, reading the paper. He looked up and saw Mrs Gogarty filling in the Lotto numbers.

Seven or any number that has a seven in it, she said. Like seven, fourteen, twenty-one, twenty-seven and so forth. If I run out of numbers then I pick a number and add seven to it.

Coyne gazed in amazement at this new Gogarty rationale. Could not concentrate on his newspaper any more.

Is seven your favourite number, Gran? Jennifer asked.

Seven was the number on my hall door when I was a little girl like you.

Coyne threw his eyes up to the ceiling.

I like seven too, Nuala said.

It's my lucky number, Mrs Gogarty continued, and Coyne was ready to contest this new arithmetic ritual. She went on about seventh heaven, and the seven-year itch and all the other superstitions that revolved around the number. Some say you get seven years bad luck if you crack a mirror.

What about Seven-Up, Coyne burst in. And Seven Brides for Seven Brothers.

Absolutely, Mrs Gogarty argued back with great venom. For your information, Pat Coyne, the number seven happens to be the most vital number in the human cycle. The basis of all mathematics.

007, Secret agent James Bond.

Ignore it if you like. But seven is the number of goodness, she said. Seven is kindness, righteousness, love of God.

Yeah, like seven shades of shite, Coyne concluded as he got up to leave the kitchen. He was having the last laugh and Mrs Gogarty looked like she had swallowed seven barrels of Seven Seas cod liver oil.

In the squad car with McGuinness, Coyne's patience was ready to snap. All he needed was one little trigger, some small incident to set the fuse.

At a set of traffic lights they pulled up beside a red BMW which McGuinness began to admire.

Nice machine, he said.

Heap of shite, Coyne returned. He had been going on a serious ticketing binge recently, as though he was conducting a personal crusade against the private car. He had taken Fred's words to heart. Cars had the effect of alienating him.

What are you talking about, McGuinness insisted. That's a work of art, that car. Beautiful.

Wouldn't be seen dead in it, Coyne said, and before McGuinness could say another word they noticed that the driver of the BMW seemed very young. With a shaven head and a bomber jacket. It was none other than Joe Perry.

Bejaysus! It's fucking hatchet-man.

Coyne had had enough of these joyriders hooring through the streets of Dublin like it was Los Angeles or someplace. He would teach them. There will be one less car on the streets tonight.

We'll see who's laughing now.

Take it easy, Pat, McGuinness kept saying. We're not meant to give chase.

The BMW shot off and Coyne was pleased to get a chance to prove what the squad car was made of. They caught up with the BMW again on its way out towards the power station. Chased it all the way, in through a number of side-streets, doing handbrake turns outside front windows. Coyne felt a crisis dose of adrenalin rushing into his already boiling bloodstream. Nothing came close to the roar of engines, the squeal of the tyres and the wailing siren, howling like yobbos through people's dreams. Coyne and Perry communicating through burning rubber.

You should be back in your pram, Perry.

Where's your L plate, Garda?

Go back to your toy cars, Perry, you little sparrowfart.

You thick Garda gobshite. You couldn't drive a fucking wheelchair.

Life seemed to accelerate here. It was touch and go as Coyne put the squad car up on two wheels, falling back with a thump and a jerk, leaping forward again with new determination like a super-horse.

Jesus, McGuinness prayed, and then phoned for a backup vehicle. He was all white in the face. This is going too far. Don't do a Mr Suicide on me, Pat.

But Coyne had saved time with the wheely and saw an opportunity to trap the stolen vehicle this time. He was thinking ahead, trying to corner Perry in a dead end as though everything else in life had suddenly become irrelevant.

McGuinness was putting his foot down on an imaginary brake pedal, trying to persuade him it wasn't worth it. Coyne laughed: you've got nothing to worry about, mate. I've got a wife and three kids. Which didn't sound very reassuring, because Coyne raced up through the gears again, and McGuinness felt he was suddenly changing from golf to Russian Roulette. Mice to men. McGuinness saw an image of the great floodlit golf course in the sky.

A small crowd of youths had gathered to watch and McGuinness said it was all a set-up. They had been drawn on to some kind of race-track, for a laugh. We're doing exactly what they want us to do, he said. But the idea of being laughed at urged Coyne on even further. There was no way that Perry's new BMW was going to get out of the trap. He was in a duel, racing at his opponent with McGuinness fast forwarding through his prayers.

Hail Mary – fucking hell, Amen he said, but Coyne had no religion left, just an icy devotion to victory in this contest of wills.

The headlights of both cars had picked each other out in a high-speed stare. Coyne was racing straight at death. Who will blink first and run back to the safety of life? Coyne experienced the manic passion of his choice. Kept his nerve, even had time to look right into Perry's eyes before swerving away at the last moment, just as the tail of the squad car was clipped by a searing screech of metal. He lost control and could do nothing to stop the squad car going into a spin, tumbling over on its roof three times before it crashed into a wall. Nobody was hurt, but the steam of defeat hissed from the engine while the red BMW raced on, laughing. By the time Coyne and McGuinness got out, a small group of boys and children stood around the overturned wreck.

All right now. Stand back, Coyne said.

Moleshaver was crapping himself, of course. By the end of the shift, Coyne had to face him in his office again. Red West Cork ears flapping with incomprehension.

Mr Suicide is absolutely correct. It's a complete fucking write-off, Molloy was saying.

Molloy was even trying to be dignified about this. Trying to cling to the Garda ethic of standing by your own. But that ethic was eroding each time Molloy looked down at the caption underneath the wrecked squad car in the morning paper. Midnight duel. Gardai and joyriders in deadly showdown at the Pidgeon House.

You must have paid off Saint Christopher, that's all I can say.

I had him cornered, Coyne offered. It's that bastard Perry again.

But that just sent Molloy into paroxysms of rage. He was like a kettle that somebody forgot to switch off in 1922, boiling off all its water and going into the initial stages of meltdown. The hair flap lifting off his head with the steam.

Look, I've had head office on to me about this already. You're like a crazy shorthorn. Worse than any joyrider. This is the last warning.

Moleshaver had no bloody idea. He was locked into his own tiny universe. Part of the problem of this city, just pretending to enforce the law without any concept of where society was going. Moleshaver, you're as thick as the rest of them, you dense briquette brain.

But Coyne was thinking about more global issues. He was thinking about the whole nature of society and predicting the decline of the car culture.

There are too many cars on the road, he said.

What? Molloy stood back as though he'd just been called a horse's bollocks.

There should be no such thing as private cars, Coyne insisted. There's too much privacy. It's the dogs of illusion. The wheels of destruction.

Molloy had difficulty breathing. But instead of finding his rage, he was completely baffled by this outburst of sociological wisdom and could think of no response except a disintegrating cough and splutter.

You need your fucking head examined, Coyne.

Carmel and Coyne had been invited to a dinner party by some of her new artistic companions. All that Saturday she had been going on about art, so that Coyne was half threatening not to go with her. He hated dinner parties anyway. All that empty talk. Watching people buttering water biscuits and pecking at cheese and de-seeding grapes like an assembly line.

In the kitchen, while Carmel was feeding the children, she seemed to be struck at one moment by a vision. Looking out through the back window, she saw some kind of apparition, like the Blessed Sacrament exposing itself to her outside in the back garden. Coyne was getting worried about her.

Isn't the light really amazing, she said. So strange. So mystical.

Coyne half got up from his seat to see what she was on about.

That's what all these artists and film makers are coming to Ireland for. It's the quality of the light. The Irish skies. So atmospheric. So magical.

Magical my arse, Coyne said. He got up from his seat again and gazed out the window properly.

What light? he said.

Can't you see the sky. The sunset illuminating the walls. It's like candlelight. Like one of those ancient oil lanterns in the sky somewhere.

That's the floodlights, Coyne remarked. He had never heard her talking like this before. It was most probably the light from the football field at the back of the houses, he explained. On Wednesdays and Saturdays, he could hear the anguished shouts and roars of men's voices. You'd think they were killing each other. Re-enacting Vinegar Hill on a floodlit battlefield. Agony and torture echoing through canyons of semi-Ds. Pass the ball – Aaargh. You Saxon foes. Croppy, croppy, croppy. Maybe the Battle of the Boyne – Billy, Billy, Billy. Then the unified roar whenever there was a goal, followed by deadly, lingering silence when everybody was gone home again.

You're as blind as a bat, Pat. That's the reflection of the sunlight.

It's the lights from the football field you're looking at.

Carmel ignored him. Went upstairs to have a bath and get ready for the dinner party. Jennifer and Nuala went up with her. Jennifer playing shop with all the bottles of talcum powder and conditioner and hair spray, while Nuala was washing Carmel's knees with a sponge.

Will you wash my back, love, Carmel said, and Nuala dipped the sponge down deep to get lots of bubbles and soap.

Were you painting fishes, Mammy, she asked, and Carmel looked up smiling.

No, lovey. Why?

Dad says you go down under the sea with the colours.
Did he say that, really?
He said you have to paint the little baby fishes.
Well, don't mind him, love. He's only joking.

The dinner party was everything that Coyne had predicted. Lipstick marks on wineglasses. People talking shite. Coyne ended up sitting beside a hypochondriac by the name of Mary Donoghue, talking about homeopathy and rebirthing in every detail.

What line of business are you in yourself? she eventually asked, and Carmel on the far side of the table tried to pass Coyne off as a barrister.

Law, she said. But that backfired because Coyne overdid the legal terminology. Without prejudice, this soup is really excellent.

Would have been better off just to say you were in the Force. Except that somebody would be thick enough to pursue it and say: what force? Star Trek? Oh, a Garda; that must be a fascinating job these days. Or else they would ask him how much more they could drink, taking into account that they'd already had two gin and tonics and four glasses of wine approximately. And every time he tried to make conversation, he would say something stupid, something nobody understood. Like something about the environment. People looked at him like he had a slice of lemon up his nose.

Coyne could see that Carmel was drinking like a fish. She had the capacity of a water biscuit and he knew by the volume of her laughter that she was well on the way to getting plastered. By the end of the dinner she was arseholes, talking about the healing power of art.

I just think people have become blind to beauty, she announced. Beauty can heal us.

Sweet Jesus, Mary and Joseph and the donkey. Where's my inhaler?

There's beauty all around us that we don't see. Every object has its own healing personality.

Then Carmel picked up some lettuce. Look at this leaf of lettuce, she said. Everybody takes it for granted.

Thanks a lot, the host, Deirdre, said with a smile.

But Carmel was talking aesthetics here, holding up the leaf of lettuce like she was starting a new religious cult.

Will you just eat it and shut up, Coyne interrupted.

But Carmel was hurt. Threw him a dirty look across the table and prepared to get her own back. Heat-transferring currents making their way across the table.

Excuse my husband, she said. He doesn't know a thing about culture. He's a complete philistine.

Coyne shrugged his shoulders. Other couples sometimes slagged each other too, as long as it didn't go too far. He saw Carmel knock back her wine and look at him in defiance.

When it comes to aesthetics, zilch, she said. Forget it. It's like showing a Goya to a goat.

Well, at least I can make up my mind about lettuce.

Silence followed. Everyone looked at Carmel, then at Coyne, to see who was going to back down. Deirdre cleared the air a little by saying she took it as a compliment to her salad. But then Coyne felt he needed to put the record straight – people took art far too seriously – while Carmel argued back from the opposite end of the table saying that people had become immune to it. Somebody joked about goat's cheese and Mary Donoghue tried to change the subject back to vitamin supplements. They were all too eager to brush everything under the carpet. There was a point to be made here, Coyne felt. People were afraid to say it.

Why is everybody getting so worked up about art these days? There's too much bloody art, if you ask me. We're all going to suffocate in culture.

Coyne talked far too fast. Tried to cram all his ideas into one argument and make it sound prophetic. He said that culture was the next form of totalitarianism. Look at MTV. The beat goes on like a dripping tap. It's war on the senses. Forget the cold war, this is the fun war.

Everyone stopped eating. He didn't know if they were interested in what he was saying or completely dumbstruck. Or were they going to start laughing?

Listen to him, Carmel said. Mr Philosophy.

The host tried to force more wine on everyone and Coyne blocked his glass with his hand, like a karate blow. Carmel was the only person to hold out her glass, as Coyne stared in horror.

It's called civilisation, Pat. In case you never heard of it.

Well, we need a bit less civilisation, if you ask me. Like, we've got to stop interfering with nature. Art is pollution.

Carmel laughed out loud. Do you hear him? That's complete and utter bullshit, Pat Coyne. Culture is part of human nature. It's art for art's sake.

Art for fucksake, is more like it.

An awkward silence descended over the table. Coyne and Carmel stared at each other as the host went to get the water biscuits. Carmel reached a pitch of fury and hurled the piece of lettuce across the table at Coyne. But then she could no longer hold on to her anger and started laughing at him. She was hysterical. Absolutely skuttered, pointing at him and breaking her heart laughing until Coyne announced that they were going home.

It was true. On the way home in the car there was a terrible smell. And it wasn't Lancôme either. They had to drive with all the windows open. Carmel was still laughing, trying to sing the Cranberries song – *did you have to let it linger?*

Coyne was furious. Then he eventually had to pull up suddenly and let Carmel out to get sick. It started with a giant hiccup. Then came the unmistakable splash on the pavement. Puking with her fancy underwear on. Stomach heaving. Coyne holding on to her from behind.

Come on, Carmel. Pull yourself together.

But she was starting to sing again and a new stream of gazpacho lyrics came rushing forward like the first gush of water through the spout of a rusty roadside pump. He gave her tissues. Wiped her face. Pulled matted hair away from her mouth and asked if she was all right now. He never said a word about the vomit on his shoes. Such a gentleman. And she flung her arms around him and said she was sorry. Drivers thought they were snogging in the street in answer to some spontaneous passion. Love sick. Carmel's lips all slack. Eyes drained of sight. Spittle shining on her white cleavage and the legs collapsing from underneath her so that Coyne had to drag her back into the car like he was abducting her.

She had to keep her head out the window until they got home, the stench was so bad in the car. And then it dawned on Coyne at last. Christ. He was driving around with a dead hedgehog.

During the night Vinnie Foley paid the price for ignoring Coyne's warning. Returning home to his Ballsbridge apartment after the clubs, looking forward to a night alone in his own bed, a car pulled up beside him. The window rolled down and a man casually called his name, to which Vinnie automatically responded with a smile. He was living in the positive reality of the TV ad, where everything turns out right and where he was immune from the real world. He was buying the right cars, eating the right chocolate bars and using the right deodorant.

In spite of all that, two guys in bomber jackets just got out and slapped him around. Vinnie didn't even have time to look at their faces. Received a few crunch kicks that made him regret the last half-dozen sexual encounters as he dropped to the pavement moaning. He issued a long-drawn-out whine that sounded like an old door hinge. One of them gave him a going over with a rustic fence post from the boot and Vinnie was ready to do a deal with them. Anything so that his punishment squad would finally leave him alone and drive away again. He was spitting blood on the pavement and cursing Coyne.

I swear, I had nothing to do with it.

Who's your mate then? Chief wanted to know.

I don't know who he is. I just met him that night.

Vinnie suffered a few more blows of the fence post and surrendered all.

Coyne, he said. His name is Coyne.

Come again, Chief urged.

Coyne. He's a Garda at Irishtown. Garda Pat Coyne.

Sunday morning, Coyne's house was like a mortuary. Carmel had such a hangover that she was crying all the time. Stayed in bed with the curtains closed, moaning like a dirge. I am stretched on your grave. Children silent as in church.

Coyne gave them all crunchies and set them up with jigsaws. Got them started and told them he was thinking up a big story for them, about ships and treasure while he slipped out quietly and began searching through the car with a handkerchief tied over his face. He searched all around the boot, under the seat, in the engine. Finally, he took off the side panel on the driver's side and had to jump back from the assault of the stench. He got his torch out and found the creature at the bottom, trying to get out through the tiny air vent, a victim of his own ideals.

Leaning over the vicious fumes, Coyne could see the shape of the hedgehog lit up by the beam of his torch, like a corpse at the bottom of an elevator shaft. The needles gleaming with rage. Screaming thirst and starvation. He felt the hair standing up on his back. Heard Carmel upstairs getting sick again, with her head leaning over the stainless-steel bowl, spitting as if she was paying back all the kisses of her life until there was nothing left but a dry, velvety mouth. With a long set of pliers Coyne reached down into the narrow cavity and pinched at the needles, dislodged the dead animal and dragged it up slowly: a spiky brown bag of rotting entrails, dripping from the nose. Big black drops splashed on the driveway as he carried it over to the side of the garden.

With both hands clamped around the pliers, face held as far back as he could, he brought it to a place beside the new tamarisk bush where he quickly dug a hole. Then he rolled the hedgehog over so that it fell down into its grave, feet up. Settled the clay back again, stamped his foot and then stood back in shock. All three of the children were at the window, staring out at the burial.

Drummer treated the news about Garda Coyne with extreme respect. Didn't like it at all. The fact that he was dealing with a cop gave him a sinister feeling. He could not work out whether the arson attack on his car was some kind of new departure, some official Special Branch action designed to flush him out, or whether this Coyne character was some kind of maverick. He hated the possibility of being drawn into a trap, having to fight an all-out war with the Gardai. He preferred to keep them at a distance.

Of course, somebody was going to have to pay for burning the Range Rover. Though he had already bought himself a brand-new, spiffing red Nissan Pajero, and the insurance would soon cough up for the damage. He wanted to find the most suitable way of getting his revenge. He would not be rushed into anything. This was delicate.

Whack the fucker, his brother Mick urged.

He'll do it again, Chief added.

But Drummer was uneasy about killing a Garda. All hell would break loose if you did that.

They'd be on to us like flies on horse's shite, he said absently, because he was no fool, and would not just lash out indiscriminately. He was a quick-thinking individual, but also had the capacity to give a measured and calm response. That's why Drummer was still in business so long. In fact, the flies usually had to pay landing fees.

At the same time he knew that this new menace had to be dealt with. On a cold November morning they were walking along Sandymount Strand discussing the matter without fear of being overheard. The Rottweilers were bounding way out near the water's edge raising flocks of gannets and seagulls into the air, forcing them to fly off and settle again at the far end of the strand. The tide had retreated away from the city like a lover. A man digging for lugworm left a trail of gashes behind him along the smooth surface of the sand, giving it the appearance of an unmade bed. In the distance, one of the Pigeon House stacks was smoking.

The fucker has to cough up, Chief insisted.

Give him an offer he can't understand, said Mick.

Drummer had no intention of letting Coyne off the hook. He stepped on little spiral mounds of sand. Red and brown shore cockroaches fled. His Nike runners left wet prints where they sank into the moist surface and slowly dried up again as he moved on. A DART train drew a line along the rim of the city, clattering far behind them from the edge of civilisation.

The guy must have a wife and kids, Drummer said, looking out to another thin blue line ahead of him where the sea met the sky. The dogs came back briefly seeking encouragement before they ran away again to chase more birds.

His missus, Mick echoed.

Drummer stopped walking. Sat down on his heels for a moment to pick up a shell. Examined it for a while like a natural scientist. Then stood up again, tossing the shell like a coin in his hand. Heads or tails.

Everybody has a vulnerable side, he said. You can find a man's flaws in his wife.

Carmel's paintings were everywhere: on the landing, in the hallway and in the living-room. Every square inch of wall space was occupied by her work as though it would soon obscure the real world altogether. Another painting of Mrs Gogarty hung outside the bathroom door looking like she had severe eczema. And when Carmel could not paint Coyne, she decided to begin a replica of their wedding photograph, transcribing their marriage on to a voodoo canvas which changed every day according to the way they spoke to each other. Work in progress, she called it. She kept talking about an exhibition that Sitwell was organising for her and wanted Coyne to help her select the best paintings. But Coyne came to a road block at the mere notion of praise. He was so shocked by the accuracy she had achieved in her art that he feared and despised it. The paintings of the harbour were so vivid that they exposed him to the memory of working with Vinnie Foley as a boy. He was afraid to compliment her, afraid of being positive in case it might backfire on him like some islandman's curse.

Coyne went to visit Vinnie in hospital, where he lay bandaged up like a pharaoh's mummy. He brought grapes and Lucozade as though it would repair their friendship. If there were peaks and troughs in every kind of relationship, this was the lowest they had ever reached. This was beyond salvaging.

What the hell did you do, Coyne?

Vinnie could hardly speak without triggering off some pain or discomfort somewhere. Even the sight of Coyne's pathetic grapes on the little bedside locker was enough to make him weep.

Don't worry. They'll pay for this, Coyne said.

Get well cards hung on a line at the back of Vinnie's bed. Most of them had come from his colleagues in the advertising world, from another country it seemed almost, the country of health and fun where life was being lived to the full. Coyne glanced through some greeting cards on the locker. Ready to donate my DNA for you, love Viv. Survive, Tom. Nurse on call, any time any place, Gillian. At work, his desk had been turned into a shrine with flowers and speedy recovery messages. The switchboard was jammed with calls.

Coyne asked some questions about the attack, but Vinnie wouldn't go into it. He had already told the Gardai all he knew. And he had about as much faith in the Gardai as he had in the concept of loyalty.

You fucked me up, Coyne. Vinnie spoke on a great wave of self-pity. I should never have had anything to do with you.

I'll get them, Coyne vowed.

They'll get you, you mean. I had to give them your name, Vinnie said.

Coyne remained silent. Just stared at Vinnie while a great cloud of fear and emptiness came across him. Everyone was deserting him. Coyne would soon be alone in the world. An orphan with nowhere to go and nobody he could talk to any more. Looked like a man on a sinking ship, not knowing how to say goodbye.

What could I do, Coyne? I had to. They were going to kill me.

Inevitably, Coyne had to explain to the children what happened to the hedgehog. They were asking so many questions that he could not side-step it any longer. Brought them out and had them all standing around the front garden while he placed a wooden cross on the grave. They said a prayer and he allowed them to pick a posthumous name: Here lies Robert. Robert, the hunger-striking hedgehog. They hung a black flag up and held a minute's silence, and afterwards the children asked lots more questions like: how many spikes has a hedghog? How long does it take for a hedgehog to die without food and water? Or, why didn't he just go into hibernation? Would it be better to die of starvation or thirst? Would you rather be nearly drowned or nearly saved?

Nuala subsequently locked herself into the bathroom and refused to come out. While Carmel was off on one of her art excursions, Coyne spent an hour gently coaxing Nuala to pull the little brass bolt back, only to find that she had gone on a dirty protest all over the walls and the floor. She had smeared herself and the tiles and stared at him when he came in as though he would admonish her. But Coyne wasn't angry because he understood the naus-eating smell which clung to the air like a sweet, pungent self-accusation. Just said they'd have to clean this up quickly before Mrs Gogarty came, changed her clothes and then went downstairs to give her biscuits and milk and read her stories from books so that she'd forget.

Coyne felt sorry for his kids. With a hurt love in his eyes, he began to embrace them with a kind of dangerous and exuberant affection. He covered them with a paternal cloak which they craved and feared simultaneously. He wanted to bind his family together against all threats from the outside so that he almost suffocated them with love and warmth, like an overheated room. The smell in the car had been replaced by a strong whiff of detergent and he began to drive them all over the place, up to the mountains, out to Newgrange. Sometimes he came back from his shift bringing home presents for them and flowers for Carmel. He would hug everyone, not even wait to have his dinner and just say: come on, let's go, taking them all off for chips again, or ice cream. Carmel would have to drop what she was doing and just go with the sheer passion of the moment, get into the car with the children already in their pyjamas. He would mindlessly fill them up with Fanta and crisps and park on the hill overlooking Dublin Bay so they could look down over the world and see a million sparkling lights below them like the reflection of infinite stars in a black pool. Howth glittering in the distance like the sequined arm of a tango dancer stretched out along the sofa. Coyne re-invented the world. With the smell of crisps and alcohol on his breath he turned it into a city under the sea, giving them fables and great new mythologies of strong, honourable men on horseback and beautiful women who could put whole armies under their spell with a song. With his stories, everything could be put right in the little republic of Coynes.

Ultimately, however, that spell of elation and hope was followed by an equally ardent phase of despair in which Coyne returned to the genius of gloom. He abandoned the car. Told his family that they would walk everywhere from now on. Began to warn them about imminent disaster again and went on endlessly about things like the ecology and global warming and biodiversity, which nobody understood except Jennifer and Nuala, because they were spellbound by the fatalistic tone in his voice. He made European cereal growing sound like a wicked-witch story. Told them about featherless chickens being held hostage for life in battery chicken farms. Had them all scared out of their wits of the Colorado beetle, so they would no longer eat potatoes in any shape or form, not even chips. And at night they began to dream of giant unstoppable bugs, the size of Alsatians – immune to all pesticides, until Carmel came and sprayed her special Christian Dior twenty-four-hour protection all over the bedrooms so they would calm down and go to sleep.

Have you nothing better to do than to terrify the living daylights out of your own children, she accused.

I'm informing them about the world.

Well, go and inform somebody else, she said, because the kids had already begun to hoard their sweets, thinking there was another famine coming.

Invaded by doom and paranoia, Coyne visited his mother on the outskirts of the city and decided to put in a proper three-levered mortice lock in the front door this time. Checked the security arrangements all over the house again, got rid of all the stale bread and took his mother out shopping. With her arm on his he walked through the nearest shopping centre at a shockingly slow pace. Her handbag dangling loosely from her arm with 'Go on – snatch me' written all over it. Coyne daring every young passer-by to come within a yard of her. Even allowed her to walk around some of the shops alone, keeping an eye on her from a distance, ready to leap over trolleys, hurl himself down the escalator, crash through all kinds of news-stands and flower arrangements and absolutely clobber the living shite out of the assailant who should attempt to take her handbag. Pat the protector.

It was around this time, too, that Coyne discovered his son Jimmy was being bullied at school and felt it was a direct affront to himself. Thrown back on his own memory of school, Coyne flew into an instant rage and vowed to deal with the bullies for ever.

I know which shoes belong to which face, Jimmy claimed, and after Coyne first admired his son's powers of observation, he wanted to know why Jimmy would be standing at the wall, memorising all the other boys' shoes.

I just know the shoes that kick, that's all, Jimmy said, already regretting that he had brought the subject up, because he was developing other ways of counteracting the bullies, through humour. Carmel said he should let Jimmy fight his own battles, but Coyne was going to do something about this and the following afternoon, in uniform, he collected Jimmy from school and sat in the car waiting until one of the Fitzmaurice brothers came out through the gate. Jimmy tried to talk his father out of it; not knowing that there was an ancient battle to be fought here and ancient debts to be repaid. Coyne was dealing with all the bullies in history.

A few boys stood outside the school gates, chopping the air, kicking each other's schoolbags, when Gabriel Fitzmaurice eventually came out. Coyne was amazed that such a fat, red-faced little punk could strike fear into his son. But he understood the dynamics of terror and school-yard sectarianism. He was determined to resolve it and told Jimmy to wait in the car while he got out, adjusted his cap and stood blocking the schoolboy's path, the way he would one day block Berti Cunningham's path.

Hold it right there, Coyne said, and the schoolboy stood back. Jimmy in the back of the car with his head down.

Are you Gabriel Fitzmaurice?

Yes.

We've had a complaint about you. You've been bullying some of the other pupils in the school.

The boy's mouth was open, denying everything until he eventually burst out in a wail of self-pity and tears.

We're going to let you off with a warning this time. But the next time we'll arrest you. And what's more, I'll twist your ear around a hundred and fifty times and then let it go – whizz, have you got that? Fitz-whizz. Now move along.

But it was no triumph. Ridiculous. Just kid's stuff. And on the way home, Jimmy was completely silent. Coyne felt it was like being with his own father. Three generations of taciturn Coynes.

Then came the letter from the bank. Carmel had gone bananas on the oil paints, so they had to go and see the manager, Mr Killmurphy – Mr Killjoy, as they called him. It wasn't the first letter either.

Carmel went to the meeting with him and they walked through Dun Laoghaire, on the sunny side of the street. Coyne blinded by the sun reflecting off the bonnet of a car. Wintry breeze piercing through his shirt.

They were brought up the stairs, along a corridor to a room at the back of the building and invited to sit down. Killjoy glared at the Coyne file on his desk. A small barred window behind him had not been washed in years. Encrusted with dusty grey rain marks. Because nobody ever needed to look out there. There was no view. Only a granite wall with glass and razor wire on the top.

We're going to have to add this overdraft to the existing loan, Killjoy said.

Carmel tried to explain that she had become an artist. Her art teacher said that she would soon be in a position to sell her paintings. That would solve everything and Coyne thought it was a stroke of genius. Fair juice to you, Carmel.

Let's get this in order first, will we. Killjoy smiled. You'll just have to learn to budget a little better. You'll have to stop shopping in Brown Thomas.

Coyne looked at the plastic Brown Thomas bag beside Carmel. It wasn't even hers. It was Mrs Gogarty who had been out shopping, for fucksake.

The bank manager did a sort of cavalry imitation on the calculator with his fingers. He was trying to look grave and sincere, like he was just about to tell Carmel she had breast cancer. Carmel and Pat still trying to look respectable and nice. We like you, Mr Killmurphy. You're a decent man.

Who's in charge of the finances? Killmurphy asked, so Carmel and Pat looked at each other.

Look, you've got to run your home like a business. This feckless spending has to stop. You've got to have a balance sheet – your income has to match your expenditure, simple as that. And if you can't afford Brown Thomas, then you'll just have to go to Dunnes Stores like everybody else.

Coyne saw that Carmel had tears of artistic rejection in her eyes.

You've no right to say that to her, he said.

Mr Coyne, I have every right to keep the bank's finances in order. If you can't control your spending, then I'm afraid I've got to do it.

Coyne sat forward, furious and helpless at the same time. As though he was going to put his fist through the bank manager's face. You bastard, Killjoy, you made her cry. But Carmel put her hand on Coyne's arm to restrain him.

Killjoy watched Carmel take out a tissue. He was trying to show compassion and understanding. But he wouldn't give you the steam off his piss. He had as much regard for human feelings as a dead badger's back passage.

We all have to shrink our expectations, he said gently, nodding his head like a social worker.

I'll shrink your goolies, pal, is what Coyne wanted to say to him. But ultimately, it was all bark and no bite. Carmel was blowing her nose quietly and her eyes were red. She was entertaining her emotions. As a last resort, Coyne pulled out his inhaler, as though he was suddenly short of air. Appealing for mercy with his little blue sympathy pipe.

It was no use. Killjoy didn't flinch. His brain was in formaldehyde. He had turned them into criminals, turfed out of the Garden of Eden. He drew up the new repayment schedule and pushed the contract towards them like a confession. Sign here – unless you'd rather go for suicide counselling. The bank offers a very attractive package whereby you can solve the whole problem with no strain on your domestic budget. Why not avail yourselves of our friendly advice? Take a long walk off the short pier, Coyne.

And Killjoy had a recent suntan, the bastard. Off roasting his arse in Gran Canaria or some place. Brown hands, immaculate pink shirtsleeves and grey suit. It's a wonder you wouldn't clean that fuckin' window some day and let a bit of sunlight into your office. Coyne stared at the confession and Killjoy handed him his own special blue fountain pen. What – you want me to kill myself with this shaggin' pen?

Carmel had decided she was taking over control of the finances from now on. Nothing new in that, except that she had become more price conscious than ever before. She would budget like Michelangelo. Art before food. Yellow-pack, no-name brands all the way, even if she wouldn't stoop so low as Dunnes Stores.

On Saturday morning, Coyne was making none of the shopping decisions. His role from now on was to do nothing but push the trolley, like a horse and cart, waiting for the click of the tongue so as to move on. Leaning forward over the handle, pushing with his elbows, while Carmel was rushing around with the list, and the children were chasing each other through the aisles. In the background, the omnipresent sound of Phil Bleeding Collins, or Chris De Shagging Burgh, or somebody else who would happen to be Princess tacky-heart Di's favourite too. Shoppers high on emotion. Interrupted every now and again by the voice over the loudspeakers calling for assistance. 'Staff call!' 'Spillage!'

Occasionally, Coyne abandoned the trolley to investigate certain items. Wanted to take part in the new fiscal rectitude. Had his own views on economy.

Look at the feckin' price of that, he said, picking out a jar of marmalade and turning around to Carmel, only to find that she had moved on and he was suddenly speaking to a startled old woman wearing a sort of pastel-green turban on her head. Found himself apologising and putting the jar back sheepishly. And because he hadn't realised that Carmel had gone ahead with the trolley, he then started pushing the old woman's trolley away by mistake.

That's not yours, the woman squealed in horror as though he was a madman. A crazed supermarket fiend.

I beg your pardon.

Carmel sniggering as always. Shoppers mistaking her effort to contain the laughter for some kind of neuralgia or facial paralysis. And Coyne back to leaning on his own trolley, drifting through the aisles after his family; arse imperviously stuck out behind him as though nobody could see him. As though people in supermarkets were blind.

And who should they see at the check-out only Mr Killjoy, of all people. As though he had been following them to see if they were acting on his advice. Not at all; they were spending like bedamned as soon as he, Killjoy, turned his back. Coyne tried to shield the trolley from view; like a shoplifter, hiding the bottle of wine with a family-sized packet of cornflakes. But he had made eye contact with his basilisk-eyed bank manager who greeted him with a minimal smile like he was giving him a last warning: I said Dunnes Stores, Coyne.

And look at all the junk that Killjoy had in his trolley. No way he was sticking to the Marietta biscuits. And there was Nora Killjoy walking along beside him like she was his colostomy bag or something. Fellatio face. Skin like a crumpled brown envelope, you'd think she rubbed herself down with French polish every morning. And him trying to look forever young beside her, in a yellow and blue Battenberg jumper. I hope you get coronary thrombosis, hardening of the arteries, angina, the lot. I hope they give you a pig's heart, you bastard. Killjoy – the Wank of Ireland.

Late on a Friday afternoon, Chief drove the new Pajero slowly along the street. Even though they were travelling at walking pace, there was a new sense of purpose. Mick Cunningham was sitting in the passenger seat while Drummer sat in the back. They were watching Carmel Coyne walking along the pavement with a black portfolio under her arm. It was tied together with a red ribbon.

Looks like a big Valentine card to me, Chief remarked.

More like a Mass card, Mick laughed. She's going to a funeral.

She was, in fact, going to see Gordon Sitwell at his house. He had promised to look over her paintings and help her make a selection for an exhibition.

That's a portfolio, you ignorant pack of dickheads, Drummer finally informed his gang. She's into art.

The men examined her in a new light. A walking work of art. They tried to remember the names of famous artists, as though they were having an impromptu table quiz in the car. Michelangelo. Van Gogh. Vermicelli.

That's pasta, you prick, Chief said. It's Vermeer.

Picasso!

Pick your own asso, mate.

But Drummer didn't like the idea of his men acting out Beavis and Butthead while they were out on a reconnaissance job. So they all shut up and watched. Carmel walked up to a redbricked house and rang the bell. Chief pulled up across the street and they waited until Sitwell came out and let her in.

Hang on. Is she plugging your man here? Chief asked. They fell silent again until Mick had an idea that it would be a good thing for Berti to get his portrait done.

It might be a good way of getting paid back for the burned-out car, Drummer was thinking quietly to himself.

Do you reckon she's any good at dancing? he wanted to know.

Chief was puzzled. Turned around and looked at the shadow of a grin widening on Drummer's face, trying to read his mind.

You mean Irish dancing. Diddli-eye stuff, Chief answered with a big laugh.

Brilliant. Extraordinary. *Shama-Lama-ding-dong*, is what Sitwell thought of Carmel's paintings, smacking his lips as though they could be consumed. He talked about her harbours with all the emotional slither of an emigrant returning to his birthplace after years abroad. Her work was so evocative that he was frequently moved to tears of artistic joy and wanted to hug his protégée. Carmel found him gazing at her body to see if it matched the undiscovered genius of her art. He was falling over himself as they poured over canals and forests and halfpenny bridges, churning up intense excitement.

You will be discovered very soon, Carmel, he said with a tremor.

Then he changed gear and started moving around Carmel as though she had suddenly been covered in a silver web. Stared closely at her hair, her eyes, her face – standing back and squinting as though he was struck by a new creative ailment that would kill him if he didn't instantly take to the brush.

Shhsssssssh... he said. Don't say a word.

He pushed her gently backwards and forced her to sit down under the fading autumn sunset coming through the skylight, standing back to follow an aura of pale light around her with his outstretched hand. Feeling her face and hair and body from a distance with his brush, narrowing his eyes and inhaling deeply.

Shsshhh... it's the light, he said. An occasion of sheer benediction. One must seize the moment.

Carmel was pinned down in the chair while Sitwell ran back and forward, getting a new canvas ready, mixing paints and occasionally coming towards her to arrange her hands, one lying over the other, like a Royal portrait.

Sheer benediction, he repeated. The illumination is unique.

He brushed vehemently at the new canvas and Carmel was unable to move. The light was fading fast and Sitwell worked in a race against time before they were both almost in darkness, unable to see each other across the fog of inspiration.

Coyne decided it was time for action. From now on he was taking a more holistic view of things. Society could only be brought back from the brink of insanity by direct intervention. Before going to work that evening he made up his mind to start taking the shite back to the arsehole in a more general sense, with the duty sheet in one hand and the flame thrower in the other.

He would start with Killjoy, the bank manager. Somebody needed to fix the man for all seasons with his pink shirts and his year-round suntan. He should be squashed into a sunbed and frazzled like a burned sausage sandwich. Coyne first contemplated a little surgical strike on the bank itself; but the staff there were all a pack of smiling fish heads and the person he needed to get was Killjoy.

So Coyne planned a little job on his home in Killiney – Dublin's Beverly Hills. Cruised by the house in the early evening just after dark and waited until he saw the Killjoys leaving for the weekend. A little autumn break in the west of Ireland perhaps. Dinner out in Bunratty Castle, stuffing yourselves with duck and pheasant, like chieftains before the Flight of the Earls was even thought of. Then up to the Cliffs of Moher to buy the postcard of a dog lying across the donkey's back smoking a pipe. Maybe out to Lahinch for a round of fucking golf, what?

Killjoy's house was a dead easy target. Wide open. No need to disturb the alarm. All Coyne had to do was walk right in through the side gate of this delightfully detached residence overlooking Dublin Bay. Where the fuck did you get the planning permission to build an eyesore like this, Killjoy? And everything so neat and tidy. All the garden tools neatly stacked in the little wooden shed. Hose rolled up perfectly. And the garden furniture all beautifully arranged on the patio.

Coyne casually opened the tin of bitumen and began to pour it across the Liscannor slates. Coyne, the patio terrorist, strikes his first blow, turning the thick tar out over the pristine white deckchairs. Over the beautifully pointed granite barbecue in the shape of a miniature Norman castle. Over the replicated Burren rockery. Lovely thick black blood dripping all over the crazy paving halfway down the garden until it ran out and Coyne was so pleased with his work that he regretted he hadn't brought a camera. Now there's a nice little surprise for you, Killjoy, when you comeback from your dirty weekend. That'll teach you not to insult people in your office.

When the light had disappeared, Sitwell put on a small lamp beside Carmel. Another one had already been lit over his easel, shining down on the nascent masterpiece like a beam of inspiration. It was warm in the studio and Carmel had taken off her jacket. She was leaning back now across the *chaise-longue* offering herself to art by holding forward a naked shoulder and a naked arm, looking out with a natural expression of self-awareness. She was no longer shy because she was communicating her body to an enlightened public. Nor did she pout or try and look vampish, but rather understated her own sexual presence by looking confidently out across the room, not so much at Sitwell, who had become the intermediary, but at the people who would file past her in a gallery and say: there is a woman at ease with herself.

It would have been difficult to establish the precise chronology of events that afternoon, but it seemed that Carmel was now obeying each decision that Sitwell made on canvas. He had begun with her face and her hair and the vague outlines of her body reclining along the seat. But as he worked silently, it became clear that he was crafting an image of Carmel with less and less clothes on. She fully understood this creative progression and responded by discreetly removing her shoes, her dress, her underwear until she lay back in the pose of a classical nude, liberated by each brushstroke, a thin scarf draped across her stomach.

Sitwell waved his brush about with excitement. Came forward for a moment and said he needed to get a more precise idea of scale and take some rough optical measurements. He closed one eye and held the brush up vertically. Then stood over Carmel holding the brush across her body like a spirit level. Took in all the details of her skin, the little folds in her elbows, the shadows under her arms, the slight burr of goosepimples along her hip and the hint of natural gravity in her breasts. Her chest and stomach were moving in and out on each breath like the sea, and one of her legs was half crossed over the other so that her pubic hair looked like fine, dark-brown seaweed, swept into a cleft by a receding wave.

Sitwell felt his subject was beginning to make the subtle, indefinable leap from the earthly world into the imagination. One more delicate touch and he could elevate her from life into art. He churned up some light-blue paint on his pallet and drew a line beginning at her shoulder and continuing down along her arm. He covered her thighs and her breasts with light-blue markings that made her look like a bedouin queen.

Coyne called around to Fred for a cup of tea before going on duty. It occurred to him to tell Fred about everything that had happened, but he decided not to. The news of Drummer's car burning had been greeted by the Special Branch as though they were a pack of sniggering schoolboys. They put it down to some gangland feud. Some reprisal for a drug deal that had gone wrong. Coyne decided to keep the real facts under his hat, only informing Fred on a need-to-know basis so as not to incriminate his mentor.

Fred was about to have something to eat and brought out his lunch box.

Blasted chicken legs again, he complained. You'd swear they were breeding chickens with ten legs.

Have some of mine, Coyne offered, going out to his car and coming back in with his own lunch. He had gone off food. Eating had become one of his lesser priorities. Fred loved Carmel's sandwiches and said each one was a masterpiece.

She's up to something, Coyne said.

What?

There's something going on. I know it.

Who, Carmel?

The whole art workshop thing is just a front for something else. It's art for fucksake. I know it.

But Fred would not believe him. Said it was all just in his imagination. He would never allow himself to think for one instant that Carmel was like that. She's got a heart of gold.

She's messing, Coyne insisted.

You'll have to talk to her.

I'll do more than talk to her. I'll kill the bastard, whoever he is. I swear. Either that or I'll kill myself.

Ah now relax, Pat, Fred said, offering him a drumstick. Here, have one of these.

When Carmel had almost reached home, walking along a tree-lined avenue, the Nissan Pajero pulled up beside her. She thought somebody was looking for directions when they rolled down the window. She stopped and got ready to help, but in that same instant two men jumped out from the back and grabbed her round the waist. One of them held a gloved hand over her mouth. She could smell leather.

The portfolio dropped out of her hand as though it had suddenly become too heavy to hold. She tried to scream, but managed only a tiny squeak. She was powerless. Within seconds she had been bundled into the car and was being driven away from her home again. She thought of her children and her husband Pat. A man wearing a suit spoke in a very polite tone, holding a gun to one of her knees, telling her not to make a fuss. The other man slowly released his hand from her mouth and she was in such a state of shock, she could do nothing but stare at the metal mouth making the print of a capital O on her skin.

Drummer untied the red bow of her portfolio as though he was undoing a dressing-gown. With a glance at Carmel, he seemed to ask for permission to take a look at the paintings. Examined them with great respect and awe.

They're brilliant, he said. You're very talented.

Where are you taking me?

Are you any good at dancing, Drummer asked.

Back in the squad car, Coyne decided to go and investigate Sitwell for himself. Found his redbricked house in Blackrock and rang on the doorbell. There was nobody in, so he began to keep the house under surveillance, getting to the source of the problem at last. They were a long distance off their beat and McGuinness became apprehensive.

What are we doing here, Pat?

Just need to check out something. Won't take long.

But McGuinness was very agitated.

Come on, Pat. This is over the top. You can't just watch somebody's house like this.

I need to verify something, Coyne replied. Wait.

By then, they could see the shape of a stout man coming down the street towards them. It was Gordon Sitwell. The man with the artistic touch. Coyne got out of the car and met Sitwell just as he reached the gate.

Are you the owner of this property? he asked.

Yes, I am, Garda. What's the matter?

Coyne wanted to tell him straight out to keep his visual arts mickey out of other people's marriages. But he kept his cool and looked like a concerned Garda.

We have reason to believe that there may be an intruder on the premises, Coyne revealed. We have been keeping your house under surveillance for the past twenty minutes.

Good God.

If you'll allow me to accompany you into the house Mr...

Sitwell. Gordon Sitwell.

Mr Sitwell, Coyne said in a whisper. Perhaps you'd better let me have the key. For your own protection. I would like to satisfy myself that the house is safe.

Sitwell thanked him and Coyne opened the front door of the

house, signalling to Sitwell to stay outside for the moment. Walked into the iniquitous mansion with his torch shining ahead of him, lighting up the interior art world which he had held under suspicion for so long. He soon found the extension at the side of the house where Sitwell had his workshop.

Even as Coyne shone the torch into the studio, he felt the nauseating shift of betrayal rise through his body like a fever. He saw the little podium and the props used by the models. Then like a kick in the stomach, the beam of his torch fell across a painting on the easel. It was Carmel, reclining on a gold green *chaise-longue* with nothing on except a loose *crêpe de Chine* shawl draped over one of her breasts and along her stomach. She was absolutely naked otherwise and her auburn triangle seemed to be darker than he'd ever seen it before. Her nipples redder. Her skin pink and glowing, like it was after a hot bath. The painter had given her a slightly masculine nose. But they were Carmel's eyes. No fucking mistake about that, Coyne thought.

He stood over the painting, admiring her with a helpless feeling of betrayal. He had never known her to look so beautiful, as though seeing her through another man's eyes was like a critical revelation. Here, pinned on to Sitwell's canvas, she was stunning. For the first time in his life he could watch her like a voyeur, without having to make conversation. He loved the blue markings along her body with a flood of passionate jealousy. Beside her stood an Irish harp. In the grassy background landscape, a round tower.

The Pajero drove through the Phoenix Park, pulling off the main artery on to a side-road towards a more remote area of the fifteen acres. It progressed slowly, then stopped at a quiet intersection close to a stand of trees. In the distance, the orange glow of the city had discoloured the sky, steam from the Guinness brewery adding a touch of grey. The headlights of cars continued to pass up and down along the main road through the park, and it struck Carmel how far away civilisation could be, even if she was staring straight at it, only three hundred yards away. The only thing that separated her and those people in their cars were some trees.

The doors of the Pajero opened and she was pulled out. There was nothing rough about the way they were handling her, which increased the sense of fear. It might only make things worse if she started screaming now. Nobody would hear anything out here.

Chief took her by the arm and walked her a few paces towards the trees so that she stood directly in the beams of the Pajero. Light shining through her legs, giving her a luminous appearance. She felt cold and could only think the worst. Maybe she should try and run.

Drummer put some music on the tape deck in the car. Irish music. A reel ripping through the night air with fiddle and accordion, flute and bodhran, belting the living daylights out of a simple melody. Suddenly it felt very homely in the park, and Drummer looked at Carmel as though he expected her to know what he wanted her to do.

Go on, dance, he ordered with a hint of impatience. Waving the gun at her legs.

Give us Riverdance, Chief added.

She stared at the three men and slowly began to obey. Made an attempt to hop and kick out her legs. Kept her arms stiffly by her sides. Her hair bouncing off her head. But in doing this, she realised that her knees were so weak with terror that she was ready to collapse. She danced like a marionette, with rubbery legs and rigid upper body. Stopping and starting again to show that her heart wasn't in it.

A h-aon, do, tri agus h'aon, do, tri... one of them shouted. But there was nothing fluid about her movement. It was the worst humiliation she had ever felt. The dance of fear. The dance of servility and introversion. Of chastity and repressed liberty. They watched her with great amusement for a few minutes, then got back into the car and drove away. Before the Pajero had gone very far, however, it stopped and reversed all the way back to where she stood on the grass, petrified. The door opened and her portfolio came flying out, landing at her feet.

If you talk to the Gardai about this, we'll come back and kill you, Chief shouted.

The Pajero disappeared and she stood for a long time, crying and staring at the leaves which had begun to blow across her portfolio.

Coyne could not look at the painting any more. He switched the torch off and made his way back outside. He wanted to say nothing, go straight home and talk to Carmel. But when he emerged from the house he found Sitwell standing on the granite step with his arms folded, anxious to see what the Garda had to report.

Mona Lisa lost her clothes, Coyne said.

I beg your pardon?

You're a painter of some sort, aren't you? Coyne asked, indicating that the danger of intruders had passed.

Yes I am, actually, Sitwell was proud to announce. I teach night classes at the VEC – Painting for Pleasure.

Well, there's too much pleasure and not enough clothes, if you ask my opinion. Coyne pointed back into the house. There's too much nudity in this painting business.

What are you suggesting, Garda?

Boom-she-boogie. That's what. You're nothing but a fucking piss-artist, Mr Sitwell. Coyne knew that he had broken through the barrier again. He'd lost his cool. Sitwell gazed back with enlarged eyes, neck throbbing with indignation.

This is outrageous, he said. Get off my property.

Coyne watched Sitwell getting worked up, moving towards him, as if to whoosh Coyne down the path off the premises. And Coyne just couldn't allow himself to be expelled like this, so he put out his hand to stop Sitwell. Coyne had lost all respect for his own uniform.

You couldn't paint shite in a basket, he delivered as a final blow.

There was hardly any physical contact at all. It was more like a rapid gust of wind between them giving Sitwell enormous problems with his own centre of gravity. His body lost its sense of balance, as though he was being sucked back into a vacuum behind him. In a slightly ungainly fashion he began to flap his arms backwards to try and regain his upright integrity, while attempting to cross his legs at the same time. What the fuck? Coyne thought, as he observed this strange acrobatic performance. But then he understood what Sitwell was attempting to do. There was a low box hedge running along the path and Sitwell looked like he had decided it was a good idea to sit down on its flat, perfectly sculpted surface. Be seated, Mr Sitwell. Still flapping and already looking comfortable with his legs crossed, he lowered himself down on the green wall, which supported him for a moment, but then gave way with a multiple crack of little twigs. It sounded more like the rip of an involuntary fart as the hedge parted to allow his weight to take its natural course. Sitwell disappeared and his legs went up in the air. Feet with slip-on shoes sticking up out of the wrecked hedge.

Coyne could not stay on duty that night. He drove the squad car straight back to the station and said he felt ill. Drove home and found that Carmel wasn't home yet. Mrs Gogarty gave him a dirty look as though she was going to accuse him of being a cat killer or of some other asocial misdeed. Said she was mildly worried that Carmel wasn't back, but didn't want their mutual concern to lead to anything closer than that.

As soon as she left, Coyne began to search through stacks of Carmel's sketches to see if he could find anything incriminating. There they were; a half-dozen drawings of nude men. Sitwell, no doubt. Large as life and bollock naked, grinning back with his lascivious half-shut eyes. Well, Coyne admitted, it was the head of Sitwell all right, but the body a hulk, with massive pectorals and brawny arms. It was Sitwell with superhuman genitals. Not the fat specimen of a man he had just knocked over the hedge.

Coyne paced up and down the kitchen. Every now and again he went back to take a look at the paintings, just to keep his sense of betrayal at its peak. Just to gaze at the sheer obscenity of Sitwell's oversized genitals, allowing himself to descend into a deep depression.

When Carmel eventually returned home she walked into the kitchen to find Coyne standing there in his uniform, with his arms folded. She looked pale, dropped her portfolio on the floor and sat down, exhausted. Before she could say a word, she met a tirade of accusations.

I need to have a word with you, he said, talking to her like a child.
What?
I have reason to believe you are fooling around, Carmel.
Carmel placed her chin in her hands and gave Coyne a look of weary disbelief, followed by a sort of laconic half-laugh.
I don't think I heard that, she said.
Is it true? Are you messing?
Pat, what is wrong with you? she said, looking at the male nudes spread out on the kitchen table. Are you going to take me down to the station for questioning or what?
It's true, isn't it. All this art business is just a cover-up. Isn't that so? You're up to something.
Jesus, I don't deserve this, she sighed. You've got this all wrong, Pat.

If it's true, Carmel, I swear I'll kill myself. If you don't stop all this painting for pleasure, I'm serious, it's the end. I'll do myself in.

Carmel's head sank down. Her shoulders began to shudder and it took Coyne a moment to realise that she was crying, not laughing. He looked at her quite helplessly. Then went over and sat beside her, taking her hand. She was shaking. Tears rolling down her face as she looked up.

These men attacked me in the street, she finally said. Three men just jumped on me and took me away in a car.

Coyne put his arm around her, as if to offer some belated protection. He felt miserable. Could not believe how cruel he was to accuse her.

Where? What happened?

I couldn't scream for help or anything, she explained. They just drove me to the Phoenix Park. I thought they were going to do something. Jesus, I was really scared, Pat.

She burst into tears again and he pulled her close. His face wet on one side from contact with hers.

Are you all right, Carmel? What did they do, love?

They got me to do Irish dancing. They made me get out and told me to do Riverdance. It was horrible, Pat. Right in the middle of the Phoenix Park, near the Pope's Cross. They told me not to go to the Guards.

What did they look like? Coyne wanted to know. Did you get the registration?

No, she said. One of them was big and fat, with braces, and a shaved head. And a young guy with a baseball cap. I've never been so afraid in all my life.

Coyne held her in a fierce grip of remorse.

You're all right now, he said, pushing the male nudes away with his elbow.

From then on it was war. He would have to deal with the Drummer direct. Back on duty the following night, the whole city looked like it was going to commit suicide. Saturday night mayhem. Coyne and McGuinness came across a teenager who had died from a drug overdose. They went to a flat where the occupants were so stoned they were trying to pretend the victim had merely dozed off, when it was clear that he was as dead as a mouse with a hatchet in the back. Then they came across an old man, staggering in the middle of the road outside the New Jury's hotel with a limp hand held out, just in case some motorist might accidentally stop, or money came falling out of the sky. So blind drunk, the hoor couldn't even see a coin in his hand. Reeling all over the street with the cars dodging him left and right, as though it was some kind of rugby international in which everybody denied they had the ball. Until he did a late tackle and half attempted to grab a Saab by the aerial, spun around like a whizzing turnstile and fell down flat on his back, blood pumping from the back of his head, like a broken jug.

What was going on? Coyne no longer understood the logic of ordinary life. Where he had once been reassured by his role in protecting the nation from itself, he now felt subjected to a new wave of cynicism. Somebody sprinting across the toll bridge with a car stereo. Some students banging like shite on the door of the Hare Krishna Temple, saying they had a message for Harry. A bunch of girls waiting for the Nightlink bus, singing their heads off and screeching *I want you back for good*. Some gobshite *extraordinaire* trying to conduct a moral campaign against prostitutes, and a bunch of kids trying to make a horse swim across the canal like it was the wild west, with the animal's head out of the water, grinning with fear.

Coyne went ballistic. He spewed Exocet lyrics, effing and blinding as he drove the squad car around the city. In his head there emerged a new obsession with the idea of operating outside the law like a real extremist. Where Coyne had once derived his sense of belonging from his uniform, he now felt it to be the principal barrier in his internecine war with Cunningham. From now on Coyne felt he would have to operate outside the nation.

Later on that night, they got a call to a house in Ballsbridge where somebody had committed suicide. Walked around to the back of a semi-detached house and found a man hanging from one of the trees. The bright security lights shone down, giving him a gaunt, agonised appearance, swinging on the axis of the rope, head leaning to one side and the feet searching for solid ground. His beige trousers soiled with a spreading stain around the crotch. Self-murder.

Jesus, Coyne said, involuntarily taking his cap off. But in the same instant, just as McGuinness was about to say a brief prayer, the deceased man suddenly spoke up.

Jesus, Billy, it's the Guards.

Coyne and McGuinness jumped back. It was only then that Coyne realised there were other young men in the garden too, standing behind a video camera on a tripod. Another seemed to have his face covered in blood.

What the hell is going on here, Coyne shouted.

Get down from there, McGuinness said to the dead man, lifting a step-ladder that was lying on the grass.

He's OK, one of the men behind the camera said. He's in no danger. He's got a harness around his neck. We're just making a film.

Well, you can't be doing this kind of thing in the middle of the night, Coyne announced. We've had a complaint from the neighbours.

This is obscene, McGuinness echoed.

Coyne took a moment to put the scene into perspective. With a nickname like Garda Suicide, he felt he had been picked out specially for derision. Was this some kind of practical joke? Were these people trying to give him a message?

What are we going to do, Coyne roared. Start dancing around like we're in some shaggin' margarine ad? Come on, get him down out of there.

The step-ladder was placed under the dead man's feet and he rejoined the world the way he had left. Found his footing on the top step, slipped the rope over his head and descended the ladder like a ghost helped back to life. Coyne's attention was then drawn to the man who appeared to have shot himself, with half his head blown off. Blood spilling from his mouth and a gun hanging loosely in his hand.

What's wrong with him, Coyne demanded.

That's just a wig, the director explained, showing the flap on the man's skull, a bit like what Moleshaver had on his head. You see there's a built-in hinge and it just explodes.

Do you have a licence for that firearm?

It's decommissioned.

Coyne took possession of the gun. Said he would have to confiscate the weapon and have it examined. Told them to put an end to these antics. Couldn't understand the logic of these aesthetics. Did they not think there was enough of this kind of thing happening around the city?

It's the only sub-culture left, the director said.

Snuff movies, Coyne muttered to McGuinness. But the whole incident seemed to have a depressing effect on him. He turned back to the director and raised his voice again, menacingly. Do you want us to charge you with disturbing the peace?

And wasting Garda time, McGuinness added.

Gordon Sitwell went to Irishtown Garda station and lodged a complaint against Coyne. Said he had been attacked. Verbally abused and assaulted on his own doorstep. When Coyne arrived for work next evening, he could see by the look on Larry McGuinness's face that something was wrong. Before he could find out anything, Superintendent Molloy said he wanted to see Coyne in his office. Moleshaver could hardly wait for Coyne to close the door before he hissed at him in a kind of half-scream, half-whisper about a serious breach of Garda rules.

What the hell were you doing at that man's home in Blackrock, Coyne?

I was investigating a suspected burglary, Coyne replied.

Investigating your arse, you were. It's way off your beat. And I don't see it on the duty report. We've had a serious complaint from a gentleman by the name of Sitwell. Said he was assaulted outside his own home by a Garda with a description that bears a remarkable resemblance to you.

Coyne feigned a sort of puzzled expression. As though the gentleman in question must be out of his mind to make such an outrageous complaint. He stared at Molloy and got the impression that the mole on his face was flashing on and off in warning, like a little pilot light. Do not exceed recommended temperatures.

He's a crank, Frank, Coyne tried to say.

I'm near disbelief, Moleshaver uttered with a shake of the head. You better have a good explanation for this. I don't know what you have against this man, but you can tell it to the enquiry. In the meantime, you've left me with no option but to suspend you from your duties until further notice.

Somebody else had already replaced Coyne on the beat in the

squad car. And Superintendent Molloy was strangely dignified about the whole thing to demonstrate that it had gone out of his hands.

This man Sitwell is pressing charges, Moleshaver added in an official tone, shifting documents on his desk. Suspension without pay, that is.

I need protection, Coyne suddenly said.

Moleshaver was dumbstruck.

I need protection for my wife and family. She was abducted by Drummer and his gang. They assaulted her and threatened her.

Don't start entertaining your emotions, Coyne. What's that got to do with this?

She needs Garda protection. Her life has come under threat from the Cunningham gang.

Molloy smiled to indicate how ridiculous this request was. He looked at Coyne as though he had gone soft in the head. Living in some kind of fantasy.

Look, if you need protection for your wife, then you go home and protect her. Is there something going on between you and the Drummer gang?

No way. Coyne hesitated. They just abducted her and took her to the Phoenix Park. Subjected her to inhuman and degrading treatment.

Like what? Molloy demanded. The story had become too far-fetched and he was already picking up the phone and dialling a number, as though Coyne didn't matter any more.

They made her perform Riverdance. She needs protection, Frank. Who knows what they might do next.

You can tell that to the enquiry, Molloy finally said in the hope of dismissing Coyne out of his office. He didn't want to listen to any more extracts from Coyne's imagination. He was too busy.

But...

Stop looking for sympathy, Coyne. You know where you can find sympathy, he said, holding his hand over the phone. In the fucking dictionary, between shite and syphilis. You're suspended.

On the way home again, Coyne called in to Fred and explained the whole Sitwell situation to him.

It was all the art stuff that got to me. I went out to investigate his house and what do I find, a nude painting of my wife. I'm telling you.

A nude painting of Carmel, he has. Then he has the nerve to report me, the bastard.

You'll have to talk to her, Fred advised. Just tell her the whole story. She'll sort it out. Maybe she can get him to withdraw the charges.

There's going to be an enquiry.

Fred thought long and hard. Drawing inspiration from the soggy brown corpse of a marshmallow he was pulling up from his tea.

I've never heard of a door closing without another one opening at the same time, he said.

Coyne tried to work that one out. As far as he was concerned, there were too many doors opening and closing. It was all too much like a revolving door for his liking.

It's an exit I'm looking for, he said in despair.

Ah, now take it easy, Pat. Don't be talking like that. Explain the situation to Carmel. She'll go and sort this Sitwell fellow out for you.

By the way, Fred said, changing the subject. That girl was on the phone looking for you.

Who?

Naomi, the one you told me about. Hangs around with Drummer. Said she was looking for Vinnie Foley. That's a pal of yours, isn't it?

Sure. He's my friend.

Fred got up from his seat and went over to Coyne, placing his hand on his shoulder. He stood staring at the yard outside the dusty blinds. One of the arc lights was shaking on a pole in the breeze, throwing unstable shadows around the parked trucks. Making them look like they were beginning to reverse slowly.

You'll have the last laugh, Fred said after a while. The doors are beginning to open. Go home and talk to Carmel.

But Coyne could not go home. He drove back through the city aimlessly, merging with the lights of night-time traffic, drifting around slowly in his own car as though he was still driving the squad car. For once he had changed out of his uniform at the station, but he was still vigilantly looking at people on the pavement, taking in all the tiny details. He was still a cop, and the fact that he had been suspended had not yet sunk in. He stopped at a pub and drank aimlessly, one pint after another. Moved on to another pub and drank till closing time, then bought a small bottle of whiskey and went back to the car. He couldn't face the questioning from Carmel, so he parked by the river for a while to consider his position. Drinking down the whiskey, he watched the lights on the far side reflected on the red-brown water, until he became mesmerised by the flow and felt the river had stopped and he was travelling back up into the city.

His life was finished. He would be dismissed from the Guards and have to take up some job as nightwatchman, like Fred. There was no future for him. He would be a disaster in the eyes of his children. He threw the empty bottle into the river and contemplated going in after it himself, driving straight over the edge. It seemed like a perfect ending. He had always had that passion for endings.

Instead he drove back into the city, feeling a new anger growing. He wasn't finished yet. If he was going to be hounded out of the Guards, then maybe he should go out with a bang and make one big, final, heroic act. Something that might even save the day and make the whole Sitwell thing look like a plastic bag in the wind; one of those tattered bags stuck in the trees. He would show the bastards what it was all about. Coyne would be remembered as the man who took on the Drummer. This was the showdown he was waiting for.

Coyne stopped at a petrol station, one with an all-night shop, where he bought an assortment of odd items. A bizzare shopping list. Sunglasses, packets of steak, chewing gum, pliers, screwdriver, a holdall bag, as well as a T-shirt and one of those baseball caps. All the things he needed on his final mission. Driven by a new mood of optimism and complete fearlessness, he placed them in the boot, all except the items of clothing, which he put on. He needed a new image to go with his make-or-break role. Wearing red sunglasses and baseball cap, along with a brand-new T-shirt with Madonna staring lasciviously at an angle out from his chest, he drove up towards Leeson Street and parked in a quiet street close to the Fountain nightclub. He calmly peeled back the wrapper on a piece of chewing gum, allowed it to fold over neatly in his mouth and got out of the car. He was chewing vigorously as he walked towards the club.

Drummer was having a slight problem with the builder, Brendan Barry. All the work that had been done on renovating the club had not been paid for. Builder Brendan was coming to the club every night hassling Drummer about some kind of instalment plan. But Drummer never liked to part with cash and was trying to encourage the builder to invest in the nightclub business. He was buying champagne and telling him he could have shares in the Fountain instead of payment.

Look at the place, Bren. You'd be doing the right thing, investing.

I need the money, Builder Brendan kept saying.

Don't worry so much about money, Drummer said, pouring out more champagne. We have different ways of settling our bills.

He looked away towards the dance floor where Naomi was dancing in one of the elevated corrals. She was wearing a short blue skirt and a belly top that was hardly more than a bra. She had retreated into her own internal world, rocking herself like a baby.

Builder Brendan had a face like a dartboard. Looked like he was into sailing, wearing a blue blazer with gold buttons and a matching red, pockmarked face. He had the mentality of a mechanical digger but he also had all the attributes of respectability that Berti Cunningham admired. Lived in a white mansion in the foothills of the Dublin Mountains that had a Doric porch and a tennis court out at the back. Drummer wanted him as a silent partner. Some true redneck gobshite who was as clean as the Pope's underpants and would keep his mouth shut at the right time.

Let me guess, Drummer said at one point. You do a bit of sailing.

But Builder Brendan said he was more into flying. Looked up as though he'd spotted a Cessna tracing across the ceiling of the night-club. Said he already had hundreds of flying hours behind him.

When you're up there, man, it's like holding Sharon Stone by the hips, he said. From behind.

Into the aeronautics, are we?

I'm just waiting for the day when I get a young one up there for a bit of in-flight service at two thousand feet over Glendalough, the builder bragged.

I think I've got somebody in mind for that, Drummer said, looking away towards Naomi again.

Coyne entered the Fountain by stealth, linking up with a group at the door, shifting around, hopping a little on one foot, and blending in with the real clubbers as though he couldn't wait to get inside and start dancing his head off. Are you buzzing, they all kept saying to each other. The usual bouncers in tuxedos were standing outside, and Coyne recognised the men who had beaten him up. He felt quite drunk and didn't care. But he was only interested in getting past them so that he could hit his real target. The disguise was perfect and he was sluiced through the entrance with the flow of the crowd.

The dance floor inside was packed. A spawning mass of arms and legs shifting and jerking to a never-ending beat. At first it looked like a heaving jar of tadpoles, bursting to live and give life again. *Get your rocks off, Honey, get your rocks off...* flashes of coloured lightning illuminating individuals for one or two seconds at a time in a thunderstorm. What was it in music that caused such democratic epilepsy? Some electrical interference with the human pulse that made the nervous system jump. Coyne jittered through the crowd, manoeuvring his way towards the far corner of the dance floor from where he could see the whole nightclub virtually. Through the shifting mass he could catch glimpses of Naomi at the bar. She was there with Drummer and some of the other men, dressed in a provocative skirt. Coyne couldn't take his eyes off her. The shape of her nipples was printed out through the little belly top and her legs beamed mercilessly at him like a flashing WIN sign in an amusement arcade.

Drummer was introducing her to Builder Brendan at that moment, letting them shake hands and get to know each other. He was like a matchmaker, a one-man dating service.

Have you ever been up in a small plane, he asked her. He explained that Builder Brendan with the red neck and the Pope's underpants and the stupid, South Country grin on his face was an expert in the air.

She gave Drummer a forced smile. The dual meaning of his words was not lost on her. She read them like a threat, looking the builder up and down with a mixture of contempt and nausea. Pass the bucket.

Naomi would love a trip, Bren. All around Wicklow. Show her the round tower.

But Naomi was happier to stay on the ground. She said she had a lifelong problem with altitude. Anything higher than the third floor was tricky, unless it was something injected. So Drummer put his arm around her and promised he'd provide her with a parachute. Then he squeezed her in his vice grip to give her a subtle, sub-verbal message. You're a natural air hostess. Then he dragged Builder Brendan out on the dance floor and set them both afloat among the sea of dancers.

The perfect couple. Builder Brendan in his navy blazer with a little flap at the back that looked a bit like a cat door when he put his hands in his pockets. And Naomi with a belly button that swivelled and swung like a hypnotist's watch.

The builder was already drunk on the champagne. His sense of rhythm wasn't bad, but he moved as though he was lifting breeze blocks in his arms. His feet were stuck in concrete. Arse like a swinging sandbag. And it was only when he tried to introduce the aeronautics theme into dancing that he really took off, flying around her in a drunken figure of eight, arms stretched out like a fucking cement mixer that had been converted into a glider.

Coyne watched all this from a discreet distance. He waited a while until he saw Cunningham and Chief retreating to the VIP lounge. And when he spotted the builder futt-futting around her again with his tie flung back over his shoulder in the wind, Coyne decided his moment had arrived. It was time for action.

He took off his baseball cap and danced over towards them. Stood before Naomi and took off his sunglasses. She seemed to recognise him through a myopic stare.

Let's go, he commanded, taking her by the hand.

He began to pull her away and she said something that he didn't hear. She didn't offer any resistance. It was only the builder who thought of putting up a struggle, trying to hold on to Naomi by the shoulders. But Coyne turned back quite lazily, bringing the builder down to earth with a neat punch in the stomach. He doubled over and swayed back into the crowd vowing horrific ramifications. Everyone looked on in amazement as though they were watching a trailer from a movie. Coyne pulling her towards the exit. Naomi tottering on her high platform shoes behind him.

Outside, the pack of Neck Decks were only concerned with people getting in and seemed to ignore those who were leaving. Coyne did it with great chivalry, escorting her out silently on his arm, but then, when he saw a look of suspicion in one of the bouncer's eyes, he began to push her up the cast-iron stairs towards the street. Somewhere close to the top, she lost one of her shoes and it fell all the way back down into the den of dickheads below, just as they started to come up the stairs after him.

Where do you think you're going, mister?

Coyne managed to get her out on to the pavement. Fuck the shoe, he thought. The men were bounding up the steps, holding the hand rail in one hand and their chicken curries in the other, keeping the jackets tucked in neatly around the stomach to maintain their dignity. Coyne had time to notice their dickie bows and the dainty buckles on one of the men's shoes. Then whack! Just as Coyne was getting ready to say he was a Garda from the Special Branch, taking this girl away for her own safety, he realised there was no point and simply stuck the boot into the first groin that came up the steps, followed by a smart crack of the fist on the nose. He felt his hand had turned into a packet of sausages with the impact. Tit for tat. It had the desired effect of sending the bouncer back into the arms of his companion and both of them crumbled down the steps under their own weight as though it was all choreographed in advance. The first man laying his cheek softly against the railing, loosening his dickie bow and moaning to his friend to go after Coyne.

But Coyne was halfway around the block by then, pulling the limping beauty behind him. He got to his car and bundled her inside. Left the lights off as he drove away, just in case they might get his number plate. He had struck deep at the heart of Dublin's crime empire.

Coyne drove around in circles. Now that Naomi was in the car with him, he had no idea what he should say or do. He was drunk, and as the tension of the escape wore off, he tried to think of his next move. Stopped the car by the canal and left the engine running. Asked her where she lived, but she gave a cynical grin to indicate that it would be suicidal. The first place Cunningham's men would go looking. Coyne had got her out of a potentially nasty situation at two thousand feet over Glendalough. She was expecting him to take her somewhere interesting. Her legs were stretched out in the car, recently rescued written all over them.

You're in trouble, he said, talking like a priest. You're entertaining some very bad company.

Yeah, she said with laconic resignation. What a creep. Wanted to teach me flying, for fucksake.

Not him, the Drummer.

What about him? she asked suspiciously.

You know he's killed somebody. Murder, Naomi. That's what.

You're a cop, aren't you, she said, looking him in the eyes. I knew it.

Coyne gave a little affected laugh.

What makes you think that? I work in advertising. I'm only trying to help you out of this mess, Naomi. You're a nice girl. You shouldn't be hanging around with those guys.

In fact, he sounded just like an archbishop. Really in touch, like. There she was, with her legs all over his car and he was starting to speak like a concerned parent. Giving her a load of paternal advice that she didn't want to hear.

If you're a cop, then I'm dead, she said.

Don't worry, I'll take care of you. You need treatment. I can help you.

Chief and two of the bouncers who could recognise Coyne got into the Pajero and drove around the area searching in the alleyways, checking all the side-streets. Mick went out on foot while Drummer stayed behind in the nightclub trying to calm Builder Brendan down a bit. He was more interested than ever in making sure that the builder was enjoying himself and saw the potential of a neat little sex scandal which he could hold over him. Gave him some explanation about a jealous former boyfriend. Got two of the silky girls down from the elevated corrals and asked them to dance with him instead. Drummer ordered lots more champagne and persuaded the builder he was still having the time of his life. That plane trip over Wicklow was still on schedule, with a new cabin crew.

Coyne left the engine running. He felt uneasy by the canal. It was too close to the nightclub scene and he should have driven away to some other part of the city. But where? He had no game plan. Thought of driving up to Fred's lock-up compound. That was the safest thing to do. Fred would have some things to say.

What do you do for a living? Coyne asked.

I'm a dancer, she said. I dance people to death.

Come on, Naomi. I'm trying to help you. Where are your parents?

Fuck my parents. They should have used a fucking condom, she said. Now look at the result.

You need them, Coyne argued. They're the people you can turn to.

Like fuck. Are you trying to rescue me or something, Vinnie?

I'm on your side, that's all, he said.

Coyne was just about to drive off again. He had finally decided to take her to Fred. Perhaps she would start drinking tea and eating lots of Mikado biscuits. See the light of justice and tell the whole truth about Drummer and his gang. It was worth a try. There was nowhere else.

But in that moment, Naomi began to embrace him. Threw her long bare arms around him and kissed his cheek. Coyne froze. Looked all around him as though the people of Dublin were watching him, even though the street was silent and empty, with nothing stirring except a few leaves being blown along the canal bank walk. She rubbed the back of his neck with her fingers and he felt a warm, erotic shiver. He denied it and began to push her gently back into her seat.

Look, you must be cold, he said, reaching into the back for a jacket, which he placed around her shoulders. He was treating her like a daughter again. And she stared out at the canal silently. Disappointed.

You're married, aren't you?

She leaned forward and picked up a child's furry rabbit from the floor of the car. Played with it in her hands as though it was one that she had owned not long ago as a small girl. Her childhood flooded back, and for a moment she was like Coyne's daughter, grown by almost twenty years in the space of one night.

You need protection, Coyne tried again. I can get you protection. Trust me.

Protection, she said, puzzled. You're married and you're a cop.

She sat looking at the soft toy in her hand. Tickled it under the chin as if it was her baby. Held it to her chest and then started crying. The sudden exposure to such family warmth had overwhelmed her. She opened the car door, threw off Coyne's jacket and stepped outside, running away along the street.

Wait, he shouted.

He took the jacket and followed her, leaving the doors of the car open. It was sure to attract attention. So he ran back and switched the engine off and closed the doors. Then went to where Naomi had stopped in the mouth of a small alleyway, back against the wall, staring up at the yellow street light through her watery eyes. All around her, the junk which people had thrown out into the lane. He reached her and put the jacket back around her shoulders again, trying to take her hand and coax her back to the car.

Let's go and see Fred, he said. He's a good pal of mine. He'll help.

Love me, Vinnie, she pleaded, throwing her arms around him once more. I swear I want to go clean. I'll get off junk. I'll go for treatment. I'll do anything for you, if you love me. Just once, Vinnie. Go on.

She looked different in that laneway, in a jaundiced twilight, with an upturned couch and an old electric cooker dumped a few feet away from her. Coyne had been asking her to make a choice and realised that she had been so whipped by authority, so subservient to the demands of her addiction, that he would have to employ a more commanding tone. For her own sake, he would have to drag her forcibly back to the car. But when he took her arm and allowed the soft, milky flesh to enter his imagination, his conviction slipped.

Coyne was drunk and did what Vinnie Foley would do in this moment; took hold of her hands and kissed the mutilated wrists, to which she responded by looking into his eyes as though they were in a suicide pact together. Their faces were green, almost, under the yellow light, and he was struck by a great spontaneous urge to fuck her brains out. He was being honest about his desire. More than ever before, with the graffiti and the scorch marks of old fires along the walls of the lane, where men pissed on their way home from the pubs and where cats howled their tortured songs at night, he wanted to follow his instinct. In the gap between her top and her skirt, he watched her navel moving in and out gently on her breath. He placed his mouth on hers and pushed himself up against her so that he was no longer sure how tall she was. As he began to examine her body with his hands, each part of her took on such an immense significance that she seemed to be completely out of proportion with any other earthly or material measurement.

For once, Coyne did not ask questions. Under this gold-grey reality of the yellow street light, his mind stopped triggering off a running commentary to his audience. Her eyes and her mouth looked black, with a wet, liquorice tongue and sweet liquorice breath. His lobster-blue lips sucked her nipple as if it was a dark-green cough drop. Even her knickers looked black when she pulled them down and stepped out of them like she would step out of a *currach*, holding on to his arm. She placed them in the pocket of his jacket for safe keeping and he held one of her legs, the one with no shoe on, by the knee underneath. His feet crunched on broken glass and he pushed her against the wall with such ferocity that he was in danger of breaking her bones. He was doing it now. What he had never fully been able to imagine. Unprotected. Unforeseen. Irreversible. He had become Vinnie Foley. He was sailing down the Amazon. The fact that he was striking at the Cunninghams increased the intensity of his desire and he squeezed her slender jaw in his hand to extract a contorted expression of pain on her face. The Pajero passed right by them.

You should have told me that's what you meant by treatment, Naomi said afterwards when they got back into the car. Coyne wanted to tell her all about himself but couldn't risk such a compromise. He would never let her go again, he vowed to himself. He wanted to bring her back to where she lived and repeat the whole thing, but she suddenly had an idea. She was starving and wanted chips, so he drove off to find a chipper on Baggot Street and got out while she sat in the car with her feet up on the dashboard, inhaling the glory of her recent sexual encounter with a Garda, knowing that she would never be the same again. When he came out, however, carrying two bags of chips, she had disappeared.

Chief and the bouncers returned to the nightclub. Mick was already back there talking to his brother. Chief was worried, saying the girl could no longer be trusted. Something should be done with her, he was suggesting. But Drummer was far more relaxed about the whole situation. They underestimated his power over women. He knew exactly how to deal with Naomi. And besides, there was no point in making a fuss right there and then. He didn't want Builder Brendan with the redbrick face to get the impression that something was going wrong. He had plans for him and had invited him back to his house in Sandymount for a private party.

Coyne threw the chips into the canal where the rats would swim out in due course and claim the salvage rights. Sat in the car waiting to see if she'd come back. Then it was his turn to cruise around like a returned emigrant and search for her like a distant first love in his memory. He should have gone home and stored it in the vaults of his mind, but he drove back to the laneway and stopped to look at the place where they had stood together, staring at this love shrine of casual sex. He was soon filled with such longing and fury that he decided to move straight on to the real mission. He had planned to target Cunningham's house that night and the self-destructive aftermath of sex with Naomi forced him into action.

As Coyne drove out to Sandymount, he began to think about Carmel too, feeling a new guilt which could only be avenged by war and attrition. He ripped the luminous green statue of Our Lady from the dashboard of the car and put it in his pocket. He had already spent long enough surveying the house to know that there were two dogs at the back waiting for Drummer to come back and feed them. The house seemed impenetrable. There was an alarm and wire meshes on the back windows. In any case the two ugly-looking Rottweilers in the back garden went into hysterics as soon as Coyne glanced over the wall with a Man United holdall bag under his arm. They snarled and barked as though they hadn't been fed in months. There was a sign saying: 'dog bites first, then asks questions later'. Rottweiler number one was consistently showing his dentures to Coyne, while Rottweiler number two kept turning around and coming back again. Like a man in a stetson hat renewing the pleasure of seeing himself in the mirror, the dogs kept running back and then attacking all over again from the beginning, as though they wanted to relive the darkest experience of their lives, the first sight of Coyne's face coming over the back wall. Imagine the neighbours having to put up with the barking and the pungent stink coming at them from the next garden, like a burning hamburger, Coyne thought. Not to mention the sight of Berti Cunningham every now and again in his jock strap feeding them scraps of his kebab and petting them like he was St Francis of Assisi or something.

Coyne had come prepared. He threw them a piece of meat: nice fillet steak for you, lads. They ignored it at first because they were just too angry and disgusted. Who the fuck do you think we are? Mind you, we'd settle for the prime hindquarters of a live Garda through a seven-foot concrete wall with razor wire on top, they seemed to be saying. But eventually the glistening red piece of fillet steak became too tempting, flashing at them like a neon sign in the grass, so that each dog was inspired by subliminal jealousy at the thought of the other dog getting it. Even if it wasn't Garda loin chop, one of them just inhaled it between barks, before you could say succulent.

Coyne had his gloves on. From the bag under his arm he took out some more pieces of mildly tranquillising meat, giving the less fortunate of the two Rottweilers the chance to get his own bit as well. Very soon the barking stopped and the dogs dropped down where they were standing. Lie down, ye dogs of illusion.

Quickly Coyne took the opportunity to snip the razor wire and climb across the wall. He had to negotiate his way among the landmines of dogshite all over the lawn until he got to the back door of the house. It was locked. But then he found the patio door unlocked so that he could walk straight in. Berti hadn't even switched on the alarm. Or maybe he didn't have an alarm, just put the box on the wall like everyone else. Probably thought he was immune to crime. And what about all this neighbourhood watch? Some neighbours you have, Berti.

Coyne's first concern was to find some evidence which would put Berti behind bars. Even though the house had been searched in vain many times before by the Guards, Coyne tried to locate secret lockers.

The twin reception room was furnished with a white Louis XIV sideboard and a white piano, for God's sake, with Richard Clayderman open on the stand to show the level of refinement in the Cunningham home. There were two suites, a leather one and a pristine white one on which there were two long brown stains. Coyne worked them out to be the fake tan stains left behind by one of Berti's women. As though everything in the man's life was fake. Coyne threw a few cushions around. Ripped the leather sofa in order to stick his hand right down and feel for hardware. He searched the whole room and came up with nothing more than a few Bryan fucking Adams CDs. Whitney dentures Houston, and the fucking 'Woman's Heart' album. Berti, you sad bastard, there's more musical taste in a donkey's fart. If ever the courts needed evidence of a complete bone-brain moron, here it was.

Coyne took a quick blast of his inhaler, holding it up in this strangely tacky and elegant palace like a symbol of demonic vengeance. He had decided that gathering evidence was too much trouble at this late stage and resolved to deliver justice right into the heart of Drummer Cunningham's home. There was no point in acting like gentlemen any more, Coyne thought as he pushed the Waterford glass cabinet over until it rocked and fell into the room like an office block collapsing into the street. There was glass everywhere and Coyne thought the noise would have been heard right across the street. The dogs outside had heard it and he was taken by surprise when they were up again so soon, barking like never before, knowing how easily they had been duped. They could see Coyne inside the house, smiling at them, kicking over the TV set, which fizzled as it imploded. No more MTV, for you, Berti Butthead.

On the way home, Drummer decided to call into Abrakebabra for some kebabs for the dogs. Brendan Barry and the two silky girls on either side of him were in the back of the Pajero, while Mick and Chief were stopped right behind them in the Chief's Mazda 626. What a service! Drummer offered his creditors only the best of everything. They would even phone his wife in Stepaside for him and tell her he was detained at an official function. And food too. Drummer came out carrying a bag of kebabs, offering them around.

Anybody want some of this dogfood? he asked, placing them on the dashboard, where they steamed up the windscreen.

Coyne wandered around Drummer's house, ate a chocolate chip cookie in the kitchen and found the study full of Berti's law books. The constitution. The one and only *Bunreacht na hEireann*. But what did Cunningham care about Ireland or the Irish people. He was only interested in his own rights and what was in the constitution for him. He had other books on case history since the foundation of the state. Extradition law, the lot. Jesus, the guy knew more about the law than a Supreme Court judge. No wonder he was impossible to pin down. The latest government white paper on legal reform lay open on a small Victorian desk. A notepad beside it on which Coyne hastily wrote his guiding slogan – The law is an asshole.

Coyne went upstairs and took a small petrol can from his bag, placing it on the landing. He laughed when he saw the master bedroom and thought Mrs Gogarty would appreciate the pink, two-inch-deep, furry carpet, heaving with house mites. Pink bedside lamps held up by brass snakes coming out of the wall. Brass bed posts for Drummer to tie up his women, and mirrored wardrobes so he could watch his own arse as though he was in a porn movie.

Outside the dogs continued barking again and Coyne stared down at them, knowing that his escape out the back was blocked off. He felt he had already spent too much time in the house and intended to leave again, giving his enemy a slightly religious message to reflect on. Took out the luminous Virgin Mary that Mrs Gogarty had once stuck on to the dashboard of the car and placed her in Berti's bed, tucking her in under the duvet. In bed with Madonna. Sleeping with the BVM – the immaculate contraception.

Coyne heard the car outside. Then the voices coming towards the house, followed by the key in the hall door. He was trapped, and it was too late to start pouring petrol.

Drummer Cunningham came in and dropped the keys of the car on the hall stand, ushering Brendan Barry and the two silky girls inside. Mick Cunningham was there too and they stood in the hall for a moment where Coyne could see them from the landing. Berti with his blond hair; short on the sides and long at the back like some kind of helmet. Whenever he moved his head, the helmet of hair moved with it. Any minute, all hell would break loose, and Coyne took the decommissioned gun from the Man United bag. He had kept possession of it instead of handing it in, initially with the intention of threatening Mr Sitwell. Now he stood in Cunningham's home with a useless weapon. It was all he had.

Ah fuck, he heard Berti shout downstairs. The bastards. We've been done.

Drummer came rushing back out into the hallway, just as Coyne ran down the stairs, pointing the gun straight at his head.

OK, hold it right there, Coyne shouted, stopping halfway down.

Just give me a reason to paint your brains all over that wall, Cunningham. Come on.

But Berti kept his cool and said nothing. A lot of things could go wrong, so he just stared at Coyne, memorising his face. Brendan Barry was the first to put his arms up in the air. You could say what you liked, but no amount of aeronautics with the silky girls was worth having to look straight at the foreskin of a gun. There was peace at any price written all over his Stepaside façade. The Pope's underpants were not so pristine perhaps.

Get down on the floor, all of you, Coyne shouted, and when they obeyed him he was amazed at the power of the weapon.

You won't get away with this, Chief said. We'll get your wife and kids.

Like fuck you will, Coyne said more quietly. If you go near her again, I'll come and kill you all. I'll do the same as I did to your car, Drummer. I'll burn down your house and your club and everything you own. Nobody will even remember who you were.

Let's rush him, Mick Cunningham whispered.

Go ahead, Coyne shouted in response. If you want to increase the number of holes in your arse.

Coyne roared so loud that it echoed all over the house. Drummer Cunningham held his brother back and nodded reassuringly to the builder.

Relax! Nobody's moving.

Go on, lie down and put your arms out over your head, Coyne commanded. He remembered that the gun was useless and began shaking, eyes wide like a possessed man who was capable of anything. Then he walked down the stairs, took the key-ring from the hall table and made his way to the front door.

We'll get you, Chief said in a burst of injured pride. This is not the end.

Make my day, you gobshite, Coyne said as he retreated towards the door, pointing the trembling gun at the mass of bodies on the floor of the hallway. He laughed in a state of self-induced shock as he opened the door, slammed it shut and locked them inside.

Coyne could hear the shouts coming from inside the house as he ran.

Get the dogs, Drummer roared as Coyne fled past the cars in the driveway, out on to the pavement. He threw the keys into a nearby hedge. Then sprinted back towards his car, parked around the corner in the next street. He was only halfway there, however, when the dogs came shooting out of Drummer's house with the full velocity of diarrhoea. The hounds of illusion, ready to rip Coyne's arse into shreds for playing such a dirty trick on them with the meat.

There was a lot of shouting going on. The neighbourhood watch had finally been brought into action. Lights went on everywhere and residents looked out through their bedroom windows at the cold street outside. Mick Cunningham was running down the drive with a hammer in his hand, ready to use it as a mace and make a bloody pudding of Coyne's head. But Chief held him back, waiting for Drummer to come out with the gun.

In the meantime, Drummer had been upstairs, ripped a firearm from the mattress in the bedroom and found the Virgin Mary sticking out from under the bedclothes. It freaked the shite out of him all right, like seeing his own mother in the bed, holding her teeth in her hand. He also saw the petrol can sitting on the landing. But he put his fears on hold and was already hurling himself down the stairs again carrying the gun in one hand and the mobile phone in the other.

Get the Pajero out, he shouted, throwing the phone to his brother. We're going after this cunt until he bleeds.

Then he ran down the street after the dogs in the hope that they would catch up with Coyne and drag him back like some unfortunate Jock-of-the-Bushveld victim. Drummer Cunningham unleashed his hydrochloric invective across the prim hedges as he ran. You'll die with fish hooks in your eyes. Rats crawling up your arsehole. Don't worry, Naomi is going to dance for you, my friend.

He was a hurt man, with one hell of a bee sting in the crotch. So sore that he stopped, out of breath, just a hundred yards short of the corner, whistled at the dogs to come back and steadied himself in order to take aim. Bewildered neighbours withdrew their faces again in case his indiscriminate wrath might turn on them instead. It wouldn't be vomit on the hedges this time. Or empty Strongbow flagons on the lawns. It would be more than slashed tyres and broken windows from now on. They jumped back from their windows as if they had seen lightning with the naked eye – some of them hiding behind sofas, like they were going to be watching the TV with their backsides from now on.

A shot whipped through the street, hitting nothing but the trunk of a hawthorn sapling. The dogs kept on running after Coyne. And Berti sprinted down the pavement after them, his body passing along the hedges at a steady elevation and his legs fast-forwarding in multiple small steps underneath him. He was holding the gun across his balls, helmet of hair lifting up at the back, nose flaring, and his thin, minimalist lips puckered into a raging arsehole as he ran. A late-night pedestrian stopped to look at this extraordinary athlete.

Coyne had taken the corner faster than he intended. Mr Suicide was right. He had lost his footing along the kerb and fallen down. Now there was a huge pain in his chest as he got up again. He could feel the asthma attack coming and thought he was crawling out of his own nightmare, unable to move. The whole idea of fear came to him like a charge of lucidity, a great rush of mental energy in the face of death.

He managed to get up and half run or limp away towards his car. His knee screaming with new pain. He had dropped the decommissioned gun on the pavement. But the more immediate concern was the sight of the dogs hooring around the corner after him, so that his legs felt like Pedigree Chum by the time he reached his car. He was in a palsy of terror. Like a rabbit in the headlights, he was overcome by a powerful weakness as he fiddled with the key and watched the Rottweilers' eyes and teeth lurching towards him in great bounds along the street. Finally he opened the door and only just slammed it shut again behind him as the dogs leaped up on to the side window, paws scratching the paintwork, saliva all over the glass.

Piss off, you savages. Go back and give your owner a blow job.

Then Berti came belting around the corner with a face on him that would do for a haemorrhoid in a medical journal. Saw the dogs trying to mount the little Escort and ran across the street towards them.

Coyne's chest was killing him. Don't fail me now, Vlad, he muttered, as he took out the inhaler like a gun, preparing for a final shoot-out. He puffed and kept trying to start the car, or start his lungs, whichever of them would stop coughing their shaggin' rings up first. Felt he was trying to pull fuel in through a tiny pin-hole. Face turning blue with the effort, and wishing he could just pass out like the prey of a grizzly bear and let Cunningham do what he had to do. Rip Coyne's entire face off with a downward strike of his paw. At least he didn't have his back to the enemy.

As Berti ran towards him, Coyne could see the gun in his hand.

Their eyes met, white with rage, just as the car started and surged forward like an unexpected ejaculation. He heard the crack of bones against the fender, along with the involuntary wail as the Drummer was lifted into the air. His legs were all floppy, as though he was practising Irish dancing horizontally on the bonnet. Face sliding along the windscreen for a moment in some bizarre attempt to kiss Coyne goodbye before he disappeared. The force of the acceleration felt like a hand pressing into the small of Coyne's back. Back to the future. The car shot forward so fast that the dogs were left barking at an empty parking place, until they saw their owner sitting on his arse in the street, feeling his legs, repeating the registration number over and over as though it was going to kill the pain.

Coyne woke up in the car and tried to piece together his last movements. It was almost dawn and the light was coming up over the sea. He had parked at the harbour and now found himself looking out over the water at full tide. His head was in a vice; massive hands were gripping the side of his neck and it seemed as though he was carrying a dead hedgehog in his stomach. He was like Major Tom, lost in space. The record he had played for his kids, ever since Jimmy was small, was now Coyne's own reality. He had told them endless stories so that they believed Major Tom was still adrift in space, floating into infinity, arriving at an unending succession of planets, searching for ways to get back home to earth. The planet of laughs. The planet of bad memories. The planet of sudden holes in the ground and the planet of colours. Jennifer and Nuala wanted him back to tell them more planets and explain things like infinity. He had a great one in his head about the planet of friends and enemies.

The events of the night paraded around his head in a procession of detached and incomprehensible images. He got out and stood on the pier, staring into the water. There was a slight breeze blowing from the shore and he felt the absurd urge to go fishing. He listened to the sounds of the harbour and caught the smells of seaweed, oil, paint, tar and the fish skeletons dumped at the end of the pier. In the pocket of his jacket he felt Naomi's knickers in his hand. A souvenir or a trophy which he had been given inadvertently, recalling the overwhelming meeting of their bodies. Holding this frail proof in his hand at first light, he noticed that they were not black. The details of her body evoked by the sight of her wine-red knickers would be buried in his memory like a hidden icon. He put the tiny garment up to his face and inhaled deeply before throwing it out on to the water, where it floated on the surface, as though Naomi was dancing and swaying her hips, swimming languorously on her back. He longed for her with such a sad, guilty desire that he wanted to join her and die. There was nobody around and Coyne could easily have plucked one of the boats from the moorings and rowed out, like Major Tom of the sea. All the islands he would get to. He would drift across the ocean beds, banqueting in the realm of lobsters, swimming with shoals of mackerel, talking to men with fins and lidless eyes as he passed through their extraordinary underwater kingdoms. Some stories he would get out of that. It would take months to tell them all. It would be an epic voyage. Coyne of the sea.

He turned his back and walked up the hill, away from the harbour. There was a great fury in the way his feet marched forward. He had never experienced this level of emptiness before, as though he had lost everything now, his friend Vinnie Foley, his wife, his family. Coyne had become an individual. A grown-up. Abandoned. An islandman, with a blue glimmer of dawn in the sky at the end of the street, increasing the panic in his soul. He began to notice dogshite everywhere. He had had hangovers before, but this one beat them all. This was revisionist. The dogs of illusion had been let out during the night and left their columns everywhere along the pavement. Dirty big craps of every denomination. Chalky versions, fossilised on granite kerbstones. Some trodden on already and carried on along the pavement like a piece of abstract art. It was like the aftermath of a war. Faeces clinging to his brain. Every shade of shite, from black to brown, littered all over like battle debris under the street lights. With great revulsion, his intellect became unstuck with guilt.

He kept walking uphill. As long as he was moving, there was a feeling of going somewhere, until he reached higher ground and saw that the dawn sky over Bray Head had turned blue. He turned back in shock and remembered suddenly that he had still not begun building the swing for his kids. He was hit by a great swell of love and self-loathing. He wanted to be with Carmel and his kids again, feel their chubby arms, hold their dimpled hands or pretend to bite their toes. Tell them of his great adventures under the sea. He was going to start building the swing for them at last.

Drummer and Chief caught up with Naomi in the early hours of the morning at her flat. After Drummer went to hospital to get his fractured arm seen to, he found her at home, fretting and crying. With one arm in a sling, he slapped her around a bit with his good arm, saying that he had no mercy left in him at all any more.

You didn't put up much fuckin' resistance, he shouted at her, but she swore she had been abducted and made her escape as soon as she could. Explained that she had tricked him into buying chips and then slipped away. Drummer looked deep into her eyes. He engaged in a little foreplay with a kitchen knife, just enough to hurt her and make her see the colour of her own blood again. But he needed her for a dance of revenge with Coyne and let her go at last, when she was pale with fear.

I wouldn't trust her any more, Chief whispered.

But Drummer was clearheaded. Prepared a little fix for her. Knew that all he needed in order to get her absolute allegiance was to find a vein in which he could deliver the full force of his chemical cocktail.

I want this done right, he said, cleaning a spot on her outstretched arm with a swab of gin. I want to get this fucker myself. He'll be coughing up his goolies. I want to see the wax shooting out of his ears. Then I want to see him dying, slowly. Psychedelic, like.

He's probably got Garda protection by now, Chief warned.

Didn't fuckin' help Brannigan very much, did it?

The weather had turned very cold overnight, and by afternoon, when Coyne got up, the children stood around outside with their scarves and their hats on, pretending to puff smoke while he measured the garden. It was an odd time of the year to start erecting a swing, but Coyne set about the task like a farewell act – ordering the cast-iron frame, and the concrete blocks, and the bolts. It was going to be a decent swing, not like those useless contraptions he saw in the DIY Centre, with a hollow frame that lost balance and hopped up each time somebody swung out. It became a major project which absorbed him completely, spending hours in the garden hacking back the hedges in order to clear enough space. Standing back to look and imagine it when it was finished. Holding an image of his smiling and excited kids in his head all the time.

He thought of it as an essential last minute deed before Drummer Cunningham would come and eliminate him. As long as they left him enough time for that. If it was the last thing he would do, he would see Nuala swinging back and forth, with one sock up and one sock down. But he was not giving them any clues and kept them guessing.

It's a big secret, he said to them. Not even Carmel knew.

Carmel was worried about other things. She was still reeling from the shock of her abduction. Felt she should have reported the attack to the Gardai, for the record. But Coyne said he had dealt with it at the highest level already.

I'd hate to think they knew where I lived, she said.

You can put that out of your head, he assured her. The lads are on to them. The Super even asked me if I wanted protection, but I said it wasn't necessary. Nothing will happen.

Are you sure?

I'll protect you, love, Coyne said with a big smile.

That evening he went to the Garda club for a drink. He had the longing to be with his colleagues in the Force. McGuinness came to meet him, along with some of the other members. He also needed to be out of the house so that he could pretend for the time being that he was still at work. He hadn't told Carmel anything about the suspension.

At the Garda club, Coyne was excited. Talked as though he hadn't seen them in months. Telling them about things he had read, people who had survived mauling by lions and Bengal tigers.

The Elixir of Prey, he announced, holding them spellbound with the facts while he drank back his pint.

This guy was mauled on the ice by a polar bear, Coyne went on. Said it was like an orgasm. Stronger than anything he'd ever experienced before in his life. His companion managed to shoot the bear just in time.

Was the polar bear wearing a condom? That's what I want to know, one of them asked.

I'm not messing, Coyne insisted. They did a big survey on people close to death. They all said it was a sexual experience.

Would you fuck off, Coyne.

You mean to tell me that dying is the same as riding? somebody questioned sceptically.

They were laughing at him. Coyne ignored them, trying to drive his point home. They were chuckling away like the rabbits on the Aran Islands, but they would soon see that he was right all along. Laughing out of uneasy acknowledgement, they were. Reflecting on the times when they were most recently lying with their partners, heaving and struggling in a furious sexual contest, bucking in the throes of death. Recalling the encounters when they expired on a wave of pleasure, edging closer and closer to the moment when the soul parts company with the body.

No shit, lads, Coyne continued. They're not denying it frightened the shite out of them. These people knew they were fucked. They were staring death in the face. They were halfway to heaven. But after they were rescued, they said it was like a climax. There's a close link between sex and death, that's all I'm saying. Same snowfall of endorphins.

I'm dying in your arms tonight, one of the men started singing.

Coyne took it as a signal that somebody understood him at last. Sex is a form of epilepsy, he said, bursting forth with all his anarchic thoughts about men who had been tricked into death and thrown from helicopters at three feet. Bank clerks who felt an orgasm of fear during an armed raid. Victims of failed assassination plots who recalled the smell of the beast in their nostrils. And then there were the sexual proclivities that involved suffocation. The last ejaculation of a hanged man. Until they stared at Coyne like a new Freud, or Fromm, informing them that they underwent a death rehearsal each time they made love.

Think about it, Coyne said. But they had all begun to laugh again. The whole country was laughing at him and Coyne got up to go to the bar with his pint. McGuinness was the only disciple to follow him, keeping the faith where other men had lost their way.

Sheep shaggin' is probably all they know about, Coyne muttered.

But McGuinness wanted to talk to him about other things. The forthcoming enquiry. What he was going to do in his spare time. And there was another matter that troubled him about Coyne.

Pat, can I ask you something? What did you do with the gun?

Coyne looked at him and hesitated. Drank down an enormous gulp of his pint and ordered a new one with a nod.

The gun you confiscated. Molloy has been asking about it.

Coyne was drunk again. Walking back towards his car he stumbled across none other than Joe Perry. Hatchet-man Perry. The small-time criminal who had caused Coyne so much trouble with the post office job and the joyriding incident. Perry had just hopped across the gate of a building site through which he had taken a short cut and was unfortunate enough to run straight into his worst enemy. Coyne caught him and pushed him up against the hoarding.

You little sparrowfart, Perry, he said.

I done nothing, Garda.

You little bastard. If I catch you near any cars again, I'll put your lights out. Do you hear me? Keep away from cars.

And Perry was even more surprised when Coyne let him go and walked away, turning back only to give him a last warning over his shoulder.

Stick to public transport, Perry. You hear.

Next thing, Coyne's mother got broken into. He immediately thought it was a reprisal. His world was falling apart, bit by bit.

She's had a mild stroke, Carmel said. It was the neighbours who found her. She's been taken to Tallaght.

Bastards, Coyne shouted, as though they had been waiting for the moment when he was off guard. He drove straight out to the hospital. His chest was tight and he took a blast of the inhaler. He rasped and coughed as he ran across the carpark, spitting out a priceless golden globule on to the tarmac, where it seemed to bounce forward before coming to rest. Bastards, bastards, bastards, he kept repeating.

The nurses said his mother would be fine. She'd only had a very mild stroke and was as tough as old boots, they assured him. But his anger had already changed to remorse. He sat beside her and looked out the window at the tops of trees. Staring through a fine drizzle he realised that he had let his own mother down in the end.

He drove down to the local Garda station to speak to the lads before going up to the house. No fingerprints had been found, apparently. But they were following a definite line of enquiry all the same. Of course, it wasn't the Cunninghams, but Coyne felt he had lost the whole battle. The intruders had removed the entire back door, including the door frame. All those security measures that Coyne had taken had been less than useless. It was only a joke. And all they had stolen was her television set. All she ever did in the last few years was watch the *Late Late Show*. Tele and Mass. Mass and Tele. And then they came and almost killed her for it. At least she was safe now in hospital.

Coyne stood in his old home and tried not to get worked up. He left again and didn't even put the back door up again. Left it open with the breeze blowing the wet garden debris right on to the floor of the kitchen. Spiders, wasps, all the creatures of Ireland could come in now. It was all after the fact. His mother would probably move straight to a nursing home from there. They were welcome to take whatever they wanted. There was nothing left of his home, only a gaunt set of memories. Rapacious cats could come in and wander around the whole house. There was nothing to protect.

While Carmel was selecting paintings for her exhibition, Coyne started digging away passionately in the garden on Friday morning, making dirty big holes in the lawn without anyone having any idea what they were for. Four black gashes in the little patch of green, so that even Mr Gillespie from next door took a furtive look out the bedroom window. Must have thought Coyne was erecting another one of those white pagodas that they had in number fifteen. The whole nation was in suspense. The final act in Coyne's life.

He was digging to beat the clock, trying to get the project finished before the rain came, before the kids came home from school, before the Cunninghams arrived to execute him. Carmel inside with her mother, trying to choose between two identical harbours. Spot the difference kind of thing. She couldn't ask Pat because he would say nothing. In the end, every artist had to manufacture his or her own confidence, Sitwell always said. You couldn't rely on other people. You had to be your own supporter.

And then they saw Coyne with a steel arm crossing the front window. The leg of a giant steel spider maybe. Holy Mary, Mother of God, Mrs Gogarty exclaimed. So they ran out to see Coyne struggling to get a big metal frame over the side gate of the house. Scraping half the pebbledash off the side wall and not saying a word, just puffing like a set of *uileann* pipes on the run from a pack of greyhounds.

He ignored them completely, and when he shoved the frame into the four holes in the back garden, Mrs Gogarty and Carmel were standing at the kitchen window like commentators in a press gallery, reporting silently on every little development. Chuckling and arguing among themselves as to what it could be.

Looks a bit like a gallows to me, said Mrs Gogarty.

Coyne laboured all afternoon with the swing, missing one deadline after another. First it rained. Then the kids all came home from school and saw him trying to bolt down the steel frame and having no luck at all, cursing and blasting because he discovered the bolts were too small.

It was too late on Friday afternoon to replace the bolts. The kids were already getting excited about the swing, begging to be given the first go, until Coyne drove them all inside and he sat in the kitchen like a condemned man, jumping up at every knock on the door. The milkman came like a cool assassin to collect the money, so he told the kids to say they would pay next week, which he had already said for three weeks running. Next week: no problem. A milkman's mercy, smiling a sinister reprieve. Nobody knew if Coyne would even be there next week.

Coyne stayed awake all night, thinking he would die leaving behind an unfinished swing. First thing on Saturday morning, he drove around to the DIY centre to see if he could get some bigger bolts, only to find that he had to buy a set of eight bolts plus a set of steel brackets, all in a pre-wrapped packet. The man in a mauve uniform and a teak Rustin's Wood Dye suntan shrugged his shoulders and Coyne went bananas again. Wanted to wreck the shop, spill chemicals all over the floor, rip big holes in bags of cement, maybe even pour adhesive all over the new tools. What kind of a fucking DIY centre is this, when you can't even buy a few bolts, Coyne raged. Next thing they'll be selling you a shaggin' barbecue or a wheelbarrow every time you want a few pozidrive screws. Special offer: get this power drill free with every six-inch nail.

And the amount of DIY dickheads hanging around on Saturday morning was unbelievable. People all over the place couldn't stop the urge to improve things. Can't you just leave the world alone, you pack of demented dipsticks? Nothing better to do than to start taking apart your sad little semis. Guys deciding to build shelves every

Saturday morning of the year until they had drilled an almighty hole in one of their plasterboard walls. Women looking at new wooden toilet seats with adulterous glints. A man wobbling a saw in his hand like a diviner, as if that was going to tell him something. Some absolute wanker asking one of the men in mauve how you put up the self-assembly pagoda, while his family sat down inside one that was already assembled to see if they'd all fit. And what about the attic stairs with the picture of a woman halfway up like Dracula's bride smiling and handing a mug of coffee to a terrified man trapped in the attic with his hammer. Maybe he had just put his foot through the bedroom ceiling, the fucking eejit.

In the end, Coyne decided to rip open the packet and put the bolts he wanted in his pocket. Bought a 60-watt screw-in light bulb instead. God knows, he had bought enough stuff off these guys before. What about all the tar he bought for Killjoy's patio?

Then he lashed back home to screw the bolts on to the concrete blocks he had already sunk in the garden holes. While the rain held off, he mixed the cement and poured it across the blocks, then covered it with sheets of plastic. Nuala doing everything in miniature somewhere else in the garden, mixing mud with a spoon.

In the afternoon, he gave Carmel a lift into town to her art exhibition. The kids all piled into the back seat, separated from their parents by a massive black portfolio with its red ribbon, all wrapped up in anoraks and woollen hats, fighting among themselves behind this opaque membrane of their mother's art. Coyne couldn't see through the rearview mirror, so he was unable to confirm the constant feeling that the car was being followed.

He pulled up in Merrion Square, where Carmel had arranged to meet Sitwell. Coyne was going to have to play this one very cool, so as not to be recognised. Quite possible too that he would simply get the urge to step out of the car and knock flying shite out of Sitwell as soon as he laid eyes on him. But there was something else to think about when they both saw the rows of paintings hanging along the railings of Merrion Square. So this was the gallery. For amateurs and enthusiasts who drew nice pictures of Irish life with no rubbish in the streets, no puke and no poverty. Trinity College without the kids holding out the empty Coke cups. People who drew the faces of Joyce and Beckett five hundred times a week. Liffey paintings with the severed heads of Swift and Wilde floating along the water. Halfpenny bridges with pink, candy-floss skies. Where was the statue of Daniel O Connell with the white wig of seagull shite?

Is this what you call an exhibition, he said maliciously.

Carmel and Coyne exchanged a look. He could see the moment of naked disappointment in her eyes. He was ready to say to her that she was much better than this. This is beneath you, Carmel. Your stuff is too good for here. But she misread the silent allegiance in his eyes for hostility and got out of the car, dragging her portfolio out violently after her. She kissed the children goodbye and stood waiting on the cold, windy corner, within a stone's throw of the National Gallery, assailed by an inward shock of deep artistic defeat.

Coyne drove away, but he stopped again at the traffic lights, where they all looked back at her for what seemed like the last time. He was struck by an overwhelming pity. She was exposed to the wind of betrayal, on the coldest corner in Dublin, in her black coat and her blue scarf, waiting for the gobshite who had duped her into thinking he was going to offer her a future in the arts. Coyne saw Carmel the way he had once seen her waiting for him long ago when he was late for a date. He was stunned by her spontaneous anger. Her sense of independence. He secretly admired her from this distance until she saw him and all the kids staring at her and waved them away. Get lost and stop embarrassing me. Because Sitwell came sauntering along the pavement with his arms out, wearing a sheepskin coat.

Darling, he said.

But Carmel wouldn't allow herself to be kissed or welcomed. Showed resentment.

You call this an exhibition?

It's the best start you'll get, Carmel. Cheer up, for Godsake. You'll be discovered here. Merrion Square. Many a true artist has had their humble beginnings here and gone on to great things. Wait till you see.

And then he put his arm around her and led her to a small space along the railings where she was to put up her precious work. If Coyne had not already driven off, she would have asked him to take her away immediately. But then she decided to make a go of it. Hung up some of her paintings, refusing to speak a word to Sitwell or any of the other artists. Frozen with fury, waiting to be discovered.

There was no point in going home because the cement around the swing had not dried yet. So Coyne decided to take his children for a walk around town. Showed them Trinity College with its cobbled courtyard and its green railings. The railings of exclusion, he called them. Stood outside the gates holding their hands and staring at the Saturday afternoon traffic crossing College Green.

Some day there will be no traffic at all here, he told them. No cars or buses or anything. Just a big square with fountains and benches. Wait till you see.

Then he brought them to the zoo. Got them all chips and cheerful cartons of orange juice with twisted straws. He was happy to be in public places. Drove through the streets, looking at the wind pushing people along the pavements. There was always wind in Dublin, hurling everything with contempt along the street – plastic bags, cans, dead umbrellas. He saw trees beyond garden walls where all the leaves had been blown off and some of the red apples still remained.

At the zoo, they would be protected by crowds. And Coyne felt like a real father again, talking to them about all the different animals and how cruel it was to keep them behind bars. Explained to them what it was like for each animal to be in its natural habitat. Spoke to them like David Attenborough. Told them how leopards teach their children to taunt lions so that they would learn to run faster. Told them about the owls who eat the eyes of mice, like sweets. Watched the motionless crocodile for twenty minutes, and finally announced that all nature had been turned into a zoo.

When they came to the elephant enclosure, he began another speech. Here we have a great example of the African elephant, he said. In his native habitat, he feeds on grass and leaves, eating up to…

He stopped abruptly. Reading straight off the information plaque, he suddenly found something wrong.

Hang on a minute. The elephant's tusks are made of ivory.

Coyne gave a sort of manic laugh and looked at the other people all around him. Sleepy families trudging around, exhibiting their ill-fitting teeth and their little domestic whines and squabbles to the animals. Another chance for the zoo's inhabitants to see some typical families of greasy-head Hibernians on a Saturday afternoon outing.

The elephant's tusks are made of ivory – Jimmy, tell me what's wrong with that.

I don't know, Dad.

The elephant's tusks are not made of ivory, Coyne said with great indignation. The elephant's tusks are ivory. It's the other way around. Ivory is taken from elephants' tusks. That's outrageous.

It was the final straw. The ultimate insult life could throw at him. Robbing this great animal of his dignity, even if the elephant didn't look like he cared very much.

The elephant's tusks are made of ivory. I've never heard such bullshit.

He had a duty to inform the superior race of Irish families around him and shouted his message out a few more times like a possessed idealist, just like his own father would have done on the subject of Ireland and the Civil War, and the Irish language. Until Coyne realised that his children got distinctly embarrassed and dragged him away, followed by the shocked gaze of the small crowd, who must have looked on him as a dangerous, unbalanced psychopath. Far more deadly than any of the docile animals in their cages.

In the background, two men were leaning on the rail of the seal enclosure, watching him.

Carmel's humiliation reached a pitch. Her feet hurt with the cold. She might as well have been barefoot on the concrete pavement. Other artists had all worn boots, double pairs of socks, long johns, double tights. Not a soul had come even to look at her work. She was in a bad spot, she told herself. If only she were up closer to the National Gallery, people would already be buying her stuff. But the likelihood was that her precious paintings would end up in grotty B&Bs, along with the pictures of stallions in the moonlight, tall ships on raging seas and toddlers in pyjamas with tears in their eyes. Paintings that people didn't bother screwing into the wall because nobody would steal them. Thatched cottages and country roads, bought by the dozen for approved, dirty-weekend guest houses. It was all like a fucking Bank of Ireland calendar.

Nobody was interested in looking at her art. Nobody except Drummer Cunningham. He was there, strolling among the general public, wearing sunglasses, looking as though he was a very keen art collector with his arm in a sling. He didn't come too close, however. Stopped at a selection of dog paintings some distance away. He was bewildered by art. Took a great interest in the little puppy drawings as though they tugged at his heart.

Sitwell dropped around to check on her. What was he expecting? Big-lip Sylvester Stallone to come along and rescue her with his testosterone talk: I'll take every last goddamn one of these things. I love 'em. Got any more, honey? Sitwell even had the audacity to ask her to come for a drink later on, to celebrate.

Celebrate what?

Your first exhibition, dear.

You must be joking, she said.

And one of the women next to her heard this rebuff and began to talk to her as soon as Sitwell disappeared again.

I've been here two hours and nobody's discovered me yet, Carmel said.

The only people who'll discover you here is the St Vincent de Paul or Focus Point. Your stuff is too good, that's why. You shouldn't be in outdoor galleries, the woman felt.

Thanks, Carmel said.

Just rubbish around here, really. It's like background music.

Carmel had a quick look at her neighbour's paintings and, sure enough, it was nothing but cottages with a grey curl of smoke rising away from the chimney. Lots of nude women with harps and round towers in the background. The woman admitted she was only there for the money.

I don't even paint these myself, she said. Any thick eejit could do them. I'd never bring my own stuff here.

And the two of them conspired to find ways in which they could get a place in a joint exhibition, maybe. The woman had some addresses. And perhaps because of the cold, the two of them started laughing and giggling, watching Sitwell throwing his arms around himself to keep out the wind, chatting up more women with weather talk. Winking at one of his old girlfriends and turning to one of them who had just tried to tickle him and saying: you devil woman.

Carmel collected her paintings from the railing, put them back in her portfolio and left without even saying goodbye to Sitwell. *Boom-she-boogie.* She was happy walking away and in many ways it felt like a new start. She had made a new friend. And with a stack of gallery contacts in her diary, she got on the bus back out to Dun Laoghaire. When Sitwell came back later on to check on his most gifted protégée, he was surprised and disappointed that she could have left so suddenly without saying adieu.

Sugar puffs, he said.

When she got home there was a car waiting across the road with a man sitting inside. She got a fright when somebody called her name, but it turned out to be Coyne's colleague, Larry McGuinness.

Can I talk to you for a moment, he said, so she brought him inside and offered him a cup of tea.

It's Pat, McGuinness said nervously. I'm a bit concerned about him, you know, since he got suspended.

Suspended? Why? He never told me anything.

Maybe I shouldn't be telling you this. I don't want to interfere, like.

That's all right, Carmel said.

I was just a bit worried about him. I'm trying to get him to play a bit of golf.

Carmel stood in the living-room with McGuinness. It was like the schoolteacher coming to the house to talk about a problem child.

Has this got something to do with the abduction, she asked. But McGuinness was equally stunned.

What abduction?

The men who took me up to the Phoenix Park.

What men?

So Carmel had to explain the whole thing to him until McGuinness became nervous and thought Coyne would arrive back any moment and find them having a secret meeting about him. Afraid that he might have to reveal everything, he left before Carmel could ask any more questions. Told her he would have a word with Superintendent Molloy about the whole thing. Assured her that there was nothing to worry about. But Molloy was showing no interest in the matter. He was up to his neck in work and wasn't in a mood to deal with any more trouble from Coyne. What he was interested in was another round of golf. Suggested they might try Straffan again some weekend.

It wasn't till late that night that Carmel got a chance to speak to Coyne about the whole thing. He was standing at the bedroom window in his boxer shorts, barricaded behind his folded arms, looking out with great disdain at the golfer next door. He asked her if she had sold any paintings. She shook her head and seemed very quiet until she finally asked him about the suspension, dragging it out of him like a sexual secret.

You must have done something to get suspended, she said, when he tried to get out of it with a minimal explanation.

Somebody lodged a complaint against me, that's all, he said.

There was a pause and Carmel sat up on the bed looking at him, waiting for the story to emerge in its own time. He would have to tell her in the end. And suddenly he had a great urge to give her bad news. The worse the better.

I'm in the right, Carmel. I was just checking a suspected break-in when the owner came back. Claims I assaulted him where, in actual fact, he just fell over himself.

How can he just fall over?

He tried to push me off the premises and I just reacted and he fell over his own shaggin' hedge.

Carmel laughed in disbelief. As though the whole thing was too childish to belong to the real world of Gardai. Her reaction seemed so flippant that Coyne felt he needed to shock with more information. The bridge of truth.

It was your art teacher, if you want to know.

What? Gordon Sitwell?

Yes.

I don't believe it, Pat. Why didn't you tell me? Carmel's eyes were wide open. Coyne was expecting her to go mad and start punching him around the head.

You pushed him over the hedge, she said. There was no burglary. You went to his house because of me.

He's going to make trouble, Carmel.

That little box hedge in the front garden? You threw him over it? That's deadly, Pat. What made you do it?

He had become a hero. He had demonstrated his desire to defend her at all costs. She began to laugh her head off and Coyne wanted to know what was so funny. He was about to tell her about the painting he had found of her. Couldn't understand how she had suddenly converted to his side and wanted a full description of Sitwell's legs up in the air. And when she had finally got the whole incident out of him, she got up and went over to embrace him.

Shag me, Pat, she said. I want you to shag me, right now.

Coyne stood back as if he was being assaulted. She had broken through the shield of melancholia and hailed him like a hero in his own bedroom. Coyne leaned awkwardly against the window, unable to reverse any further, staring down at her kneeling below him, pulling his boxer shorts down. She found his testicles, like precious copper artefacts rediscovered after a millennium in the bog, hidden on the retreat from some battle. Celtic spirals on his scrotum. Monastic messages along his penis recording sacred, mythological moments long ago. He almost fell over at one point, spancelled by his own shorts.

But then Coyne pulled back from her. Pulled his shorts up again and moved away. She was left kneeling like she was Bernadette of Lourdes or somebody in her knickers. Looking up at him in shock. Rejected.

What's wrong?

Nothing, he said. It's just all this...

Forget about it, she said, trying to reassure him. I'll sort out that fool Sitwell. God's clown, that's who he is. He'll withdraw his complaint. Wait till you see.

Carmel jumped up again and went over to the wardrobe. She found one of Coyne's Garda caps and put it on. Stood in the room with her breasts standing to attention. Bangarda Carmel Coyne in her cap and her white underwear, posing for him again like a pin-up.

You won't be needing this for a while, will you? she said provocatively.

Coyne seemed to be uneasy with her antics. Something was holding him back. He just turned and stared out the window again.

Look, will you stop worrying about Sitwell. I'll sort him out for you.

It's not that, Coyne finally said. It's other things. Things that I can't put right again. Things nobody can put right again.

Is there something you want to tell me?

She went over and sat down on the bed again, knees up, waiting for Coyne to speak. But he wasn't able to say anything. He wanted to be honest with her and tell her everything. All about Naomi, all about Drummer, the whole lot. But he stood silently at the window as if words had not been invented for what he needed to say. The gap between his mind and the simplest methods of communication was too large.

There are things I can never talk about, he said. Things I regret too much that I can't even speak about them.

Like what? What are you saying, Pat? Is there something else you haven't told me?

Coyne looked at the floor. He remained silent, as though language had betrayed him. Carmel waited and waited, looking at his eyes, encouraging him to reveal whatever it was that was on his mind, showing great patience with him. She feared what he was going to tell her. She scanned all the bad news that she had ever imagined. Betrayal was undoubtedly the worst. She hoped it wasn't that. She hoped it wasn't him being unfaithful, because that was the worst.

I can't speak, he said at last. I never learned to talk. I never learned to say what was on my mind. It was my father. We never really spoke to each other.

Carmel kept listening to him. She saw that he was struggling with words. Sitting on the bed, she rested her chin on her knees and gave Coyne all the time in the world. She was relieved, and took off her Garda cap again.

I never got to know my father, he said. He was always very distant. Things like that you can never put right.

You don't say much about him, do you, she said.

He didn't recognise me in the street. Just passed me by.

Maybe he didn't see you, Pat.

I was coming home from school one time and I met him, but he didn't recognise me.

What do you mean?

I was standing at one of these news-vendors on O Connell Street, looking at the papers and the magazines, you know. He came right up beside me. I didn't see him approaching. I just looked up and saw him, because I recognised his voice asking for the *Evening Press*. I knew it was his hand holding out the money. It was his briefcase, so I smiled up at him and waited for him to see me.

Coyne searched deep in the lonely memory of his Dublin schooldays to come up with the right words for this day. It was Dublin lonely. Unlike the loneliness of a foreign land, it was more private, more exclusive. As a boy, Coyne walked home from his city centre school alone, past Parnell, the Gresham, the Savoy, and Daniel O Connell, past the news-vendors with their lurid racks of crime books, daggers and stilettos. Press-ah-Heral', somebody was always shouting. And Coyne remembered how, one day, the familiar voice of his father spoke softly in his Cork accent beside him. He was seeing him for the first time as an ordinary person, an ordinary Irishman in Dublin. Beard. Glasses. The briefcase with its flask, morning paper, comb and a book on the bombing of Dresden. Or was it the new book on bee keeping. That was Sean Coyne's life. A private person – an idealist.

I was literally as close as you are now, Coyne recalled. I said, Dad, it's me, Pat. But he didn't hear me.

He was about to tug his father gently at the sleeve. I'm here. It's me. But then what? What would they have said to each other after that? They would have spoken in Irish, forced to go home together on the train, stared at by everyone. Father and son: the last silent survivors of the Irish language war.

He saw his father hand over the money. Knew each vein. Knew each knuckle and the white tufts of hair between them. Admired him like nobody else, and wished there could be a truce for a day so they could laugh and just be like ordinary Dubliners. Wished, above all other people in the world, he could talk to his own father like a friend. The vendor folded over the newspaper and accepted the money in his blackened hand. Coyne smiled and waited to be noticed, but then watched his father walking away – newspaper under his arm, not very tall, limping a little from polio as a child, merging with the ordinary people of Dublin.

I just stood there watching him until he disappeared in the crowd.

You never told me this before, Carmel said.

I should have run after him, he said.

There was a long silence and Carmel came over to him. She put her arm around him, his only friend. Kissed the side of his face. Rubbed the back of his neck and said nothing for a moment, just to let him know that she understood him. Everything would be fine in the republic of Coynes.

I still wish I could run after him. I'd talk to him now. I'd have things to say to him now, he said.

She knew that he had tears in his eyes, but was too proud to let her see them. Tried to turn away again, towards the nocturnal golfer outside in the moonlight. She continued to kiss his face and his chest so that he felt the warm healing sirocco of her breath on his skin. Carmel was the only person who would stand by him. He was not alone.

Come on. Lie down, she said, drawing him away from the window, and pushing him towards the bed.

She switched off the light so that only the moon shone across the bedroom, turning his body blue. At intervals of twenty seconds or so, the neat smack of the golf club was heard outside lifting the plastic golf ball, followed by the echo of a hollow click against the back wall. She kneeled beside him on the bed and kissed him silently all over his chest. There was no need to speak any more, because they had finished with language. They had reached the intimacy of islanders where nothing needed to be said. She threw herself across him like a surf and made love. Gave him such a complete understanding of drowning and submission that he thought he had sunk down into a deep, blue underwater room where he heard nothing except that violent kiss of the golf club and the plastic ball, and the pleading response against the concrete. Coyne reached the floor of the sea and heard the last of the sounds outside, confirmed some time later by the Gillespies' back door closing, and a few more indoor sounds, like water running, a drawer being shut, muttering, an elbow accidentally punched against the wall and a flick of the light switch, followed by the utter silence. It was the end of language.

During the night, Coyne woke up in a terrible panic. It was 3:33 and his body snapped up into a sitting position, like a bear trap. He was ready, listening out for tiny hints of intrusion. There was a sound of glass, so he jumped out of bed and ran to the window. But he could see nothing whatsoever at first with sleep-blindness. The Cunninghams, he thought. The day of reckoning had come. So he picked up the hammer from under the bed and ran out to the landing, looking down the stairs and then calculating from the nature of the sound still in his ears that it must have come from outside.

It was the crash of car glass. Coyne ran into Jimmy's room and looked out, only to see a young man breaking the window of his car with a large rock.

For fucksake, Coyne whispered. Hatchet-man Joe Perry had finally come to claim his share of vengeance, and Coyne watched the destruction of his car for a moment before he ran back to his bedroom and put his shoes on. Flung himself down the stairs. Threw his Garda overcoat on over his bare chest and boxer shorts. Opened the door to see that Perry had already gone. The fucker had taken off and was hooring away along the pavement like a cat on E. With the hammer in his hand and his bare legs showing under his Garda coat, Coyne ran along after him, but his lungs were seized.

You slimy bastard, Perry.

In despair, he threw the hammer wildly at the shape of Perry in the distance, climbing over a wall and disappearing. Coyne walked back. It was freezing outside and he could hardly move with the sudden shock of cold air in his lungs. Must have looked a right sight too – in his Garda coat, with no socks and no trousers.

He examined the car and found that Perry had smashed the front window on the driver's side. It was as though the damage Coyne had caused to Berti Cunningham's car was returning to him inadvertently by instalments. Though Perry could hardly be working for them. Breaking windows wouldn't be their style. Too mild. In a great burst of resentment and emotion, Coyne began to formulate soft plans for killing. He would have to eliminate his enemies or be eliminated himself.

In his shocked and dreamy insomnia, he saw himself dealing with the obstacles in the world like a benevolent dictator, saving the nation and saving the planet. Not like an eco-fascist, but a saviour kicking the ass of the globe back into shape. Coyne's revolution was coming. But when he climbed back up the stairs of his house, the scale of his plans was reduced by a feeling of utter despair and helplessness. The whole world was committing suicide.

Carmel had not even woken up. She was fast asleep, with one arm hanging over the side getting cold. He covered it up, treating her like a child. Then he put on his clothes. Went in to the children and stood there, just watching them for a while, sleeping out their tiny dreams of wild animals and elephants and, of course, the swing. He stood another ten minutes over Jimmy's bed, silently saying goodbye to them all.

He walked out of the house with some vague idea that he would drive around the streets and find Joe Perry. But it had already just become a minor detail in a grand disaster. He brushed the glass off the driver's seat with his arm and drove off with no clear idea where to go, just relying on the motion of the car to convince him that there was some sense of direction left in his life.

In the meantime, Fred had received another call from Naomi. This time she wanted to tell everything, so Fred told her to get into a taxi and gave his address in Dublin Port.

She arrived and made the taxi driver wait for her outside. Told Fred she didn't have much time, so he sat listening carefully, nodding his head at every word as she told him the story of her life. About the big drug deals, about the killings. Mentioned the crucifixion of Dermot Brannigan and said he died with a plastic bag over his head.

I danced him to death. They made me. And they're going to kill Vinnie Foley too. They'll make me dance for him.

Are you willing to testify to all of this in court? Fred asked.

But that scared her. That was too much to ask.

I don't want the Gardai, she said, afraid she had already gone too far. I just want to save Vinnie's life.

Think it over, Fred urged, speaking like an oracle. You have the power to change the world. In your grasp is the key to a new destiny.

But Naomi wasn't taking any of it in. She had been preached out for one lifetime by her parents and all kinds of counsellors who had lined up to have a go at her over the years. She was seen as a social worker's dream. A challenge of a lifetime to the person who could convert her from rags back to riches.

I'm not going to the cops, if that's what you're after.

Who said anything about the cops? All I'm saying is that you're standing on the bridge of no return. Get the Cunninghams off the streets and you can start a new life.

Fred asked her where she came from. She started talking about her childhood and where she grew up in Churchtown. Said she could never go back to her family. But she wanted to go back to college. She was nervous and kept looking back out the window to see if the taxi was still there.

You'll have to start listening out for the dogs, Naomi.

What dogs?

The dogs of illusion, Naomi. They're after you. If you cross the river, you can escape them. If you don't, they'll be howling after you all your life. The dogs of illusion, can you hear them?

She looked at Fred as though he had gone insane. She feared this kind of talk more than anything else, as though he'd been trying to hypnotise her and open up a huge new vista in her drugged intellect. Wide open prairies of game flashed across her mind. Shallow lakes with thousands of pink Mikado biscuits flapping their wings like flamingos. Her eyes were strangely bright and empty, as though she was already looking at packs of dogs coming after her.

He'll kill me, she said, beginning to shiver. Then she got up suddenly and went out to the waiting taxi. She asked to be brought back to the Fountain.

Drummer Cunningham was at the club waiting for her. He had sent Mick and two of the bouncers out to Dun Laoghaire to take Coyne from his home. Carmel woke up with a terrible noise coming from downstairs as the front door was pushed in and bounced back off the hall table with the force. Heavy footsteps came rushing up the stairs. She reached for Pat and was horrified that he could be missing from the bed. It was after four, and in the muddle of half-sleep she thought he was on night shift again.

Two men, wearing balaclavas, came bursting into the bedroom. It was all like radio reports, and Carmel heard herself giving a small inaudible gasp of shock. The terrifying presence of strangers in the house. The feeling that all the windows and doors were open to the elements.

Where the fuck is he? a man shouted.

He's out, Carmel said instinctively.

But then one of the men reached into the room towards the bed to drag her on to the floor by the hair. The sudden pain made her want to scream: leave us alone. But she was too frightened. Or maybe she had made an important calculation, that any sign of her fear would impact on her children and send them into hysterics. She was hoping that Mr Gillespie next door would have woken up with the noise.

Then the phone rang and nobody would go to pick it up, even though it was ringing for ages. It was Fred, trying to contact Coyne.

The man standing over Carmel in the bedroom was wearing thin pink rubber gloves. She had heard a squeak as he pulled her hair. His mate was quickly going through the jewellery case on the dressing-table but was obviously disappointed because he threw it on the floor along with all her underwear.

The man with the gloves pinned her back to the wall and showed her the gun, with its matt black gleam along the side. Moved it slowly from her face down along her body. She had fallen awkwardly, naked from the waist down, and felt the gun making its way swiftly along her thigh, between her legs, seeking out a place of invasion. She tried to move away and prevent it. Sitting up straight in order to assert her decency, keeping in mind that she must not scream. Must not frighten her assailants either, even as the cold tip of the gun entered her. He stared into her eyes, then drew away the weapon and sniffed it. He took out his mobile phone and made a call.

He's fucked off somewhere, he said, and waited for instructions.

We're going to wait here, he then said to her. If we don't find him, we'll get you and your kids. You'll get my bullets, missus.

Jimmy stood silently in the doorway, as though he was there to replace his father. Ready to protect her.

Coyne was already driving towards Leeson Street. He had decided he was not going to let them come to him. He would have the showdown on his own terms. He had driven around the streets of Dublin aimlessly until one side of his face was cold from the broken window, until he was hardly in touch with the physical elements any more, like an amphibian whose body didn't matter. He had stopped twice for coffee. Hardly talked to anyone, except for one man who recognised him and said: Goodnight, Guard. Then he drove up to Fred's place, but failed to get inside. Found it strange that Fred was not there, as though he wasn't letting him in any more. His old world had suddenly become out of bounds. Coyne was in exile.

He had no alternative but to bring the battle back to the Cunninghams. He drove past the house in Sandymount and found it empty and moved on to the nightclub, where he left the engine running and stepped out. From the street, he shouted down at the bouncer below in the den of dickheads. Get that bastard Cunningham out here.

Realising that it was over his head, the bouncer obediently decided to refer this personal message directly on to the boss, who was inside in the VIP lounge at the time, idly pushing the stem of a broken champagne class into Naomi's breast, asking her where she'd just been to.

I was starving, I went for chips, she said.

Chips, me arse, Chief said. You can't trust her, Berti.

They were waiting for Mick and the men to come back with Coyne. But Coyne had come to them instead, like a fool surrendering himself voluntarily. Coyne the noble islander, giving himself up and presenting himself for due punishment when told to.

But when Drummer and Chief came out to the door of the nightclub and looked up the cast-iron stairs, Coyne was raging like a possessed cleric from the railings above. Cunningham would love to have had a gun in his hand at that moment, but it would not have done justice to the hatred he felt for Coyne. He held Chief back with his hand and waited to see what Coyne would say.

Berti Cunningham, you're the greatest piece of dried-out, calcified shite that was ever shat on the streets of Dublin, Coyne shouted down from his pulpit. So lyrical and full of passion, it was like a bard's curse, like something Seanchan would have roared at the woman who stole his socks.

You're nothing but a donkey shite and a puffing hole, Coyne added, so that it almost sounded like he wanted to be Cunningham's friend. Look, you can't even spell. Nightclub. It's N-I-G-H-T, night.

Coyne had said all that in front of some late-night customers going along the street and then added the further libel of an ignominious spit which landed like a cheap demoralising coin at Drummer's feet. Then Coyne got back into his car and drove away again.

Dried piece of calcified shite. Drummer Cunningham, the archetype of all Irish waste, had been called many things in his life before, but the graphic eloquence of this defamation made him feel like so small, so basic. This was tribal. He had been slandered on a sectarian scale and could not rest until he had put an end to the author of such abuse.

They pulled Naomi out of the VIP lounge and got into a Mazda 626 parked on the street. Mick had taken the Pajero. Drummer didn't have to go far, however, because Coyne was waiting for him at the end of the street, revving the engine of the Ford Escort, throwing his arm out the window as though he had some kind of death-wish. With the Mazda in pursuit, Coyne drove through the back streets, down laneways, across car parks, showing off his command of Dublin cartography. He led them on a chase through the least travelled arteries of the city, even managed to pass the laneway where he had made love to Naomi, hooting his horn in three short barks like a coded signal to her as she sat in the back seat beside Drummer. Coyne was leading his killers down to the river. The two cars raced along the docks past the cranes and containers, with the river flowing like a slit wrist out of the city, red and yellow lights reflected along the surface.

Coyne considered another duel along the docks, like the one he had conducted with Joe Perry. He was sure to win this time. But the thought of Naomi in the car made him think again. In any case, it was impossible to put enough distance between the two cars, they were right up on his tail all the time. He drove along the quays, giving a kind of farewell speech to his audience.

Telling his inner public what he would like to be remembered for. The warnings which nobody took seriously. His prophecies.

Drummer Cunningham considered firing his gun at the car in front, but felt it would attract too much attention. And Coyne had already done a handbrake turn and driven into a sort of corral, where he found himself trapped. A fatal choice. He had half expected to find another opening at the other end of the quay but discovered only chains and bollards blocking his exit. Coyne had given himself up.

Amid shouts and commands from the back, Chief took the opportunity to drive across the opening of the corral with the Mazda. Coyne was cornered at last. He had reached the terminus, parked the car in a dignified and orderly way along the quay and switched off the engine. He got out of the car and thought of making a run for it, but Drummer and Chief were already stepping out of the Mazda. So he got back into his car and sat looking out at the river, pulsing by beneath him. At least he had made the swing for his kids.

The men walked as if there was no hurry, approaching Coyne's

car with all the time in the world from two separate angles. Berti
Cunningham with a gun in one hand and the other arm in a sling.
Now we have the bastard. Come here, fuckhead. Come here and feel
pain.

Naomi was left behind in the car watching this final show-down
and waiting for the order to come out and dance. The dance of
dockland is what it would be, in among the containers. Or maybe
Berti had somewhere else in mind, like the VIP lounge back at the
club. She lifted up a mobile phone left on the front seat of the Mazda
and quickly dialled a number.

Drummer opened the passenger side door of the Ford Escort
and found Coyne sitting inside, looking up passively. He seemed to
have surrendered everything now, just waiting for death. Drummer
pointed the gun in at Coyne, looking him over cautiously to make
sure that he was unarmed.

Watch her, he said to Chief, and then got into the car beside
Coyne. Chief walked back towards the Mazda.

So you want to talk to me about spelling, Drummer said to Coyne.

Coyne sat motionless in the car, hands on the steering wheel as
if he was waiting to be told where to go. Like he was going to be
Drummer's chauffeur from now on. Drummer hit him across the
side of the head with his gun, then slammed the butt into Coyne's
stomach so that he let out an involuntary grunt. He was winded.

OK, you have two choices, my friend, Drummer said. We can
settle this here and now by the river. Or you can come back to the
club and settle it there in comfort.

Coyne looked back at him with a stoic expression, defying the
pain in his eye from the blow he'd received. Ready to demonstrate his
hatred for Cunningham.

That's one choice, he said. You've got it wrong. Two choices would
mean three different things to choose from at least.

Well, that said everything! That summed up human existence all
right! It was clear that Coyne had given up any respect for his own
life at this point, because there was no choice. He had been cheated
out of his extra choice, so he would accept nothing. Drummer just
laughed at him. Thanked him for the information and told him he
might like to know something else.

We've got your wife and kids, Coyne. Come on. Let's go, he

said, and Coyne obediently started the car with the point of the gun sticking into his heart.

Outside Coyne's home, there was a large force of Gardai. Several squad cars parked at angles across the street and three men were being led away from the house, among them Mick Cunningham.

Inside, Carmel was sitting in her dressing-gown in the front room, with her three children around her like refugees. A number of uniformed Gardai and detectives were in the room with her. And Fred was there too, holding her hand, trying to assure her that everything would be fine. The Gardai were taking care of it. But their presence in the house and the shock of her ordeal left her pale and frightened.

He's in trouble, she said.

It will all be right in the end, Mrs Coyne, Fred kept saying. The Gardai will sort these people out. Wait till you see. Fred was the fountain of authority and reassurance. Offered to make tea.

I'm afraid Pat will do something, Carmel said.

He'll do no such thing, Fred insisted. Pat is a good lad. He'll be all right.

Naomi saw Chief coming back and dropped the phone. She was talking to the Gardai. She had that look of betrayal on her face.

You fucking bitch, Chief shouted as he reached the car. But in the same moment, he turned around and looked behind him at the Escort. Heard the engine racing with an angry whine. Coyne had reversed back, but instead of coming towards the Mazda, he put the car in first gear and raced straight towards the edge of the quay, rushing forward with a desperate grin on his face. Drummer had no time to react and sat in the car like a helpless passenger as Coyne's car went over the side into the river. Mr Suicide, bejaysus. Chief ran back to the edge just in time to see the roof of the Escort sloping forward at an angle in the water, headlights shining down through the thick, green-brown river. The engine acted like a plumb weight, pulling the front of the car down. There was a dull gunshot from inside the car as the red wounds of the brake lights began to disappear. It was all over within seconds, it seemed. Bags of air escaping to the surface containing the echoes of Drummer Cunningham's final curses.

Coyne felt the impact of the water. First like a concrete wall. Then like a soft pillow on which the car sank down swiftly. Berti Cunningham shouted beside him, holding the gun up towards Coyne's head. But Coyne ducked instinctively and in the moment of crisis judgement, the shot fired aimlessly out to sea, smashing through the windscreen, bringing the river right in on top of them. Drummer then tried to free himself from his sling, certain that he wouldn't need it any more in the water. Tried to open the door but was prevented from doing so by the pressure of the water which rushed in all around them like a cold bath. Pockets of air remained trapped in Coyne's clothes. His foot was still on the accelerator and his hands were on the steering wheel as though he was going to carry on driving wherever Cunningham wanted him to go, as soon as the car settled on the bottom of the river. He felt the cold water reach his armpits.

The engine cut out. So did the lights. It was utterly silent and Coyne could only think of Carmel right then. There was an extraordinary moment when his body began to panic and fight against the invasion of water, releasing his mind into a strange state of tranquillity where he thought back to when they were making love, only hours ago. He could see it clearly as the water rushed around his head and up his nostrils – Carmel's presence, the unforgettable absence of words, the lucid feeling of eternity as he felt her belly against his. I love you, Carmel. The words he had never been able to say before, the words he had substituted in a million different ways with a million other gestures, hurried up in tiny urgent bubbles to the surface.

The force of the tide turned the car over. Even before it crashed into the slimy silt floor of the river, it had drifted some distance seawards, finally coming to rest on the bottom, lying upside down on its roof. Coyne felt Cunningham's hand on his arm in a dead man's grip, like they were going to be the best of friends from now on and into eternity. He struggled in the sheer darkness to get away from this new companion. His legs kicked involuntarily and he reached out through the window, clutching at the door. The priority for air had eliminated any other thought at this stage.

Coyne felt the water churning around him. He was unable to move, surrounded by millions of beige bubbles, like the ascension in a pint of Guinness. He was escaping from this world into another, floating up into a higher state of being – a creamy head. His soul was leaving his body, swallowing black mouthfuls of the river. Carmel, I love you.

Chief ran to find a lifebelt and came back to the rim of the quay. A head had surfaced on the river like an unsinkable water rat. He heard the hoarse shout of Drummer in the water, a hollow, desperate sound, which echoed back from the far quay and lodged in the tall corridors between ships and wharf. He threw the lifebelt out and began to rescue his leader. Had to drag him along in the water to the next set of steps where Drummer could come back out again.

By then, however, the blue lights of squad cars were already flashing across the surface of the river, racing along the docks to where Naomi stood on the quay beside the Mazda, waving.

Drummer appeared over the edge, wet and exhausted, only to find the Gardai waiting for him. The river and the whole of dockland had become festive with the amount of lights. Squad cars everywhere. Drummer told himself not to panic. He'd survived worse scrapes than this. Gave himself up, knowing that his grasp of the constitution would save him again.

But then he saw Naomi being escorted away by a Bangarda. He looked back at her, just as they placed the handcuffs on him and pushed him into the back of a squad car. Their eyes met and he knew that he had been betrayed by her in the end. Shivering and coughing up the oily water from his lungs, he understood the depth of her infidelity. He knew that she had made love to the law.

At dawn, with the grey light seeping up from the mouth of the river, the Garda subaqua team located the vehicle on its roof, already half submerged by silt. Mobile cranes were brought to the quay and the car was eventually dragged towards the bank. Carmel was there, waiting. She had left the children with her mother. Fred and McGuinness stood by her for support.

Other people had gathered there too. People on their way to work stopped to see what was going on. Two young men with a video camera set on a tripod, waiting for the crane to start lifting. And as the chains tightened and the wheels began to emerge, Carmel first thought this was the wrong car because it looked so dirty and discoloured. Plastic bags and slimy, grey debris clung on, making it look like an ancient wreck. The roof was dented and crushed down so that she could hardly see anything. Expected to see the shape of her husband upside down inside, slumped over the steering wheel. But as the water gushed out through the windows and the doors, she saw nobody. She could identify the registration number alright. But Coyne was missing.

He had managed to climb up a steel ladder along the wall of the river. He had hidden himself among some of the containers, saw the lifebelt going out to Berti Cunningham and ran through some of the side-streets leading back towards the inner city. He had coughed up so much salty water and spit that he felt light-headed. Felt as though he had swallowed black washing-up liquid. A bad pint maybe. Thought he was already in the afterlife as he dragged himself along the deserted streets, all wet and dripping. Trousers clinging heavily to his legs as he walked. Frozen with the cold.

He had shed his old persona. As he wandered through the early-morning streets with the commuters flooding in to work, he was absorbed by a feeling of personal triumph. Coyne was a new man. He had survived. He had abandoned the one possession which had troubled him most. He had shed his private car like a shell. He could now make a new beginning.

At a men's shelter in the city, he was given a change of clothes. Nobody recognised him out of his uniform, even though he had often delivered homeless men to the door. He was given breakfast and stood there surrounded by these familiar faces, drinking his tea with them and talking to them about the river. He was one of them now and they were listening to his story, how he had dragged himself up the ladder, how he had been washed clean. Told them he had abandoned his car. In the river he had become a new man, because he had got rid of that burden. There was too much privacy, he told them. We are all victims of somebody else's privacy.

They were dumbfounded. Each of them chewing quietly or muttering to himself in agreement. Somebody hummed *The Rocks 'a Bawn*, then stopped again. Each man preoccupied with his own troubles, deep in his own exclusive thoughts. Coyne's message washed over them like the words of a prophet. He was saying what they had all discovered for themselves many times over, but were no longer able to express, because it was so long since anyone wanted to listen to them. They were a silent bunch of people, not used to saying much to anyone any more, except to ask for the price of a drink, or a cigarette. They watched Coyne, the voice of the new homeless, talking about laughter. It was all about who was laughing at whom. They sat or stood around gazing at him in such silent agreement. Some shuffled around, thinking about that. Laughter! None of them was laughing. One man stood with a stack of newspapers under his arm, eyes wide open in complete amazement, waiting for him to say more. Coyne had found his audience at last.

There was a quiet sense of euphoria too in walking through the streets again. The fact that he was travelling on foot in another man's clothes made him feel light-headed. He should not be alive at all. And perhaps he wasn't. He was existing in a kind of twilight, a life after life, or some kind of angel state beyond death, marching with great Gulliver steps in the opposite direction to the general flow of commuters. He seemed to be heading into the wind, moving like an unseen ghost while the traffic rushed past him. He saw faces peering out through the windows of a bus as if they were blind and could not see him. He thought of waving at them but then moved on, heading out along the railings of Trinity College, along Merrion Square, stopping briefly outside a shop to watch people coming and going, buying newspapers, Kleenex, Polo mints for the office. People rushed up granite steps and disappeared into Georgian buildings. Drivers fought over the last parking places while Coyne slipped quietly out of the city. Further out he found himself waiting for a bus, facing out over an endless stream of cars. It was almost silent. As though the sound of the traffic all around him had stopped or been substituted by the crashing of waves and he was standing on the last outcrop of rock, facing out to sea. This was the afterlife. Coyne standing at the bus stop, raising his arms into the air, blessing the rush-hour tide. When his bus came at last, he went upstairs, a solitary passenger on the upper deck.

Fred told Carmel they normally find the body within ten days. As he drove her home, he asked her if there was anything he could do to help. He said he would stay at the house for a while to keep her company in her grief. This was a great tragedy. A moment when the whole nation stood behind her, he said. Carmel collected her children from her mother's house and went home. The house was empty when she got there. Detectives had already taken fingerprints and left. One unmarked Garda car was still outside, keeping vigil. And as soon as they got inside, Superintendent Molloy phoned to offer his condolences, insisting that the Gardai would make all the arrangements for the funeral. Coyne was a contemporary hero, as far as he was concerned. He had fought the worst enemies of the city. There would be posthumous medals. Molloy said he was coming over to pay his respects, personally.

Mrs Gogarty sat down in the kitchen and began to cry. The children wanted to know why. What was wrong? And Carmel was preparing to tell them – your father had to go away for a while. But how could she explain that he would never come back? They measured his absence in shifts until they saw the dark blue shape of his uniform through the front door. Words like forever and never were concepts that only Coyne could explain.

Carmel gathered the children around her by the kitchen table. Your Dad, she said. He won't be coming back.

Mrs Gogarty looked at them all red-eyed, waiting for the shock of the news to appear in their eyes. Carmel had to hold all their hands. They looked puzzled. What did she mean, he wasn't coming back. They looked around at the solemn faces, Carmel, Mrs Gogarty, Fred, waiting for somebody to tell them what was going on.

And then Nuala looked out through the glass in the back door and saw her father on the swing outside. He was rocking back and forth, staring at the sky. Unaware that they had returned.

He's out in the garden, she said, laughing. He's hiding outside, on the swing.

Everone stood up and saw Coyne sitting on the swing in his ill-fitting clothes. Tears instantly sprang to Carmel's eyes as she opened the back door. Then she couldn't help laughing. This was ridiculous, she thought, as they all stood looking out at Coyne wearing another man's suit. He was smiling at them. Testing the strength of the ropes. Making signs at her to come out and sit on his lap.

So she ran out and sat on his knee, holding on to him.

Why don't you draw me on the swing? he said, putting his arms around her.

What, in those clothes? she answered, looking him up and down, feeling the bristle on his face and running her hand through his matted hair.

Jimmy came out and began to push them, rocking his parents back and forth slowly. Nuala and Jennifer ran over to help him, all three of them pushing as though they could never allow the swing to stop. As though they had to keep the swing going for ever to make sure that Coyne and Carmel would never get off. To make sure they remained locked in their embrace for ever. To make sure Carmel would never stop kissing Coyne's face. At the window of the kitchen Fred and Mrs Gogarty looked out in amazement. They were joined in the same moment by Superintendent Molloy, who stood aghast at the back door, holding an enormous bouquet of flowers in his hand. Next door, Mr Gillespie watched these new antics with great concern. Sad bastard, he muttered to himself, as he leaned down to pick a ball out of a hole in the ground.

Sad Bastard

Sad Bastard

HUGO HAMILTON

NOEXIT2

This edition published in 2017 by No Exit Press,
an imprint of Oldcastle Books Ltd, PO Box 394,
Harpenden, AL5 1XJ
noexit.co.uk

ISBN
978-1-84344-901-0 (print)
978-1-84344-902-7 (epub)
978-1-84344-903-4 (kindle)
978-1-84344-904-1 (pdf)

2 4 6 8 10 9 7 5 3 1

Typeset in 11.65pt Sabon
by Avocet Typeset, Somerton, Somerset TA11 6RT

Printed in Great Britain by Clays Ltd, St Ives plc

FOR MY SISTERS, MÁIRE, ITA AND BRÍD

Coyne sat drinking his pint. Minding his own business. Like many other men alone at bar counters throughout the city of Dublin, he looked like he was driving something big. Sitting on a high stool, steering a crane, or a truck, or a bus full of half-drunk passengers. He was leaning forward a little and staring straight ahead at the inverted spirit bottles – Hussar, Paddy, Napoleon, Cork Dry. As always, his wheatfield hair was standing up on his head. As always, he looked like he'd just had an idea.

He called over the barman and ordered a gin and tonic.

Behind him in the background, there was a click of pool and the wash of voices from the back bar. The TV was like a grotto in the top corner with the faithful flock staring up in blind devotion. Traffic rocked the bar as it passed by outside. And from the lounge next door, the nasal lament of a band howling through bathroom acoustics: *You don't know what it's like.* Dragging through the words, like red fingernails down along the spine.

What on earth did Pat Coyne think he was up to? Gin and tonic was not his kind of drink. It was an odd decision all right, and the barman did a quick double-check with his eyes, announcing the name of the drink in bold to make sure he hadn't got it wrong before he mechanically dropped ice and lemon into a glass, pushed it under the Cork Dry teat and sent clear air bubbles floating up through the bottle. Turned and whisked the cap from the tonic.

Coyne nodded. The symbolic gin and tonic sitting beside his solitary pint. It was for Carmel. Coyne's estranged wife, Carmel. Some distant hope that she would walk into the Anchor Bar and sit down beside him.

As always, Coyne was talking to himself. Explaining every move he made. Justifying his contorted logic to the inner audience in his

head. If somebody was to draw a map of Coyne's mind, some kind of three-dimensional elevation of his intellect, it would look something like the Burren landscape of County Clare – full of shale and fissures and layered escarpments, full of complicated underground channels of water and all kinds of exotic plant life surviving in the most unlikely places. In matters of the head, this temporarily off-duty, perhaps soon to be ex-Garda, was an enigma even to himself at times. Damaged, some might say.

The Anchor Bar was full of familiar faces. Some of the ferry workers were playing pool in the back. McCurtain from the Port and Docks board was there, talking his head off to some of the fishing people from the harbour, while in the snug as usual, the poet was sifting through a manuscript, mouthing words to himself. One of the barmen was acting as a kind of quiz master, asking some of the men how many airports there were in Ireland. Think about it, he said, and the men pondered over their pints, knowing that there had to be some kind of catch.

It was a quiet sort of place, with wooden compartments for separation and lots of nautical artefacts such as a copper beacon, Admiralty charts of the Irish Sea, pictures of Galway hookers and bottles of Finest Sea Dog rum that nobody ever drank. There was a brass clock and a brass bell which they rang in desperation at closing time as if they were on a sinking ship. After which all the drowning people would desert the vessel and stand outside on the pavement talking. It was the kind of place that left the Christmas decorations up all year long – a furry red, tinsel boa draped all around the top of the bar along with a set of fairy lights. It was a place for all types. A ferryport refuge at the back end of Dun Laoghaire. And Dun Laoghaire was the back door of Dublin city. And Ireland was the snug of Europe.

Coyne ordered a further gin and tonic. And later on another, even though he knew she wasn't coming. It made no sense. Would have been a true miracle. An apparition. Three untouched gins and three full bottles of tonic stood lined up on the bar counter alongside his own pint on the highly improbable, more than impossible odds that she might stride in through the door. Coyne even looked around from time to time whenever he heard the squeak of hinges. No chance. He was a sad bastard.

Coyne had been off work for five months now since the fire. Injured in the line of duty. His wounds had healed to a greater degree, but the acid lick of flames had left its marks, like embossed hieroglyphics on his back. His lungs too had suffered smoke damage, and water damage, like blackened walls and waterlogged carpets. Occasionally, he was forced to stop in the street to cough uncontrollably. Traffic coming to a halt as he rasped and dregged up some magnificent verdigris trophies. Jesus, some of the stuff Coyne had uncovered in his chest since the fire should have been exhibited.

But these were only minor problems in comparison to the subliminal damage. No amount of compensation could make up for the unquantifiable psychological scars. He was jumpy and unreasonable. Sometimes angry and uncontrollably moody. Potentially violent, even. Suffering from a range of emotional problems and currently undergoing a series of psychiatric assessments to determine whether he was fit for work. He was regularly attending a therapist, though with great reluctance. He didn't believe in that sort of thing.

Coyne was refusing to co-operate. He resented the interference and hated the sound of encouraging words. Turned down all medication and mistrusted every prognosis. He would have preferred a good ending – the nobility of things coming to a close. He wanted to go out in glory. And this was perhaps the key to the hidden backlands of Coyne's unfathomable psyche. He didn't want to be healed.

Coyne – the man they could not cure. The code they could not break.

Tommy Nolan came into the Anchor Bar towards the end of the night. The last pub on his odyssey. He came in the back door and drifted around the bar greeting the regulars one by one. He was everybody's friend. Did odd jobs for people at the harbour, like a grown-up child or an orphan that everybody took under their wing; a harmless, good-willed man with a limp and a stammer who still lived with his older sister Marlene in a small corporation flat nearby.

Coyne bought him a pint.

I have to tell you something, Tommy said.

Tommy sometimes repaid the pints with bits of information. He had a serious speech impediment, with saliva spilling from his mouth, like a tap that could not be fully switched off. Lips soft and glistening.

Coyne looked up and tried to read Tommy's lips. Then watched him opening his mouth wide to drink from his pint. Black liquid sloshing back and forth between the glass and his mouth. An exchange of fluids in which it was hard to establish if there was more of it rushing in or more saliva rushing back out, until the whole lot finally drained down and Tommy Nolan smiled at Coyne with his red face, and a brown dribble running down from the corner of his mouth. Ready to start the next pint.

The *Lolita*, Tommy spluttered.

He was showering Coyne with a spray of diluted Guinness and local gossip. Hosing down the whole place with droplet infection, trying to tell Coyne about the illegal imports. Right here at the harbour. The *Lolita* had just come in an hour ago. No cargo of fish. No ice-boxes. No trailing flag of seagulls.

Coyne looked around uneasily. Not here, he thought, putting up his hand. He didn't want people to think that Tommy was a scout or an informer of some kind. Once a cop always a cop in the eyes of the public at large.

Besides, Coyne was preoccupied by his own internal world these days. He had no real interest in crime any more. He was looking for broader solutions, something more global than the ordinary day-to-day activity around this coastal suburb of Dublin.

By then they had started ringing the bell and the Anchor Bar was going down fast. The band next door had finished at last with an almighty crescendo that went on like a five-minute orgasm at the end of every night. End after end, amen. McCurtain from the Port and Docks board was furtively receiving a no-cover, porn video from one of the ferry workers. And Coyne was still sitting at the bar with his three gin and tonics in front of him, beaming out like beacons of love and betrayal. He might as well have been looking at the emptiness of the Irish Sea by night. Lines of latitude; streaks of foam; wave after wave rolling unrelentingly towards him across the wide open counter on a black night. Another lonely bell clanging furiously next door and men shouting 'time'.

He began to pour the tonics into the gins. Then shared the lot into two equal glasses, and handed one over to Tommy.

Here you are, Tommy. Knock it back.

Put it this way, it was a waste of time trying to bring Coyne back to normal. He had never been normal in the first place, and was hardly going to fit into the parameters of textbook sanity at this point. His psychologist, Ms Clare Dunford, kept encouraging him to try and put the past behind him and to seek personal satisfaction. Not to feel so guilty about peace and pleasure. She talked about happiness as if it was the ultimate goal. As though everybody had a moral duty to be content and make the most of life. And nobody was ever allowed to be sad, or unfulfilled, or maladjusted ever again.

Coyne's ex-wife, Carmel, was the same, trying to arrange appointments for Coyne to go to all kinds of healers and alternative practitioners. Even though they had been separated for over a year now and Coyne was exiled from the family home in his own two-roomed flat, she was still devoted to fixing him up. He presented a real challenge. Anyone who met Coyne thought to themselves – I could repair him. Christ, that man needs help. He should be on medication. But Coyne had developed the protective coat of a hedgehog, balling himself up into an untouchable mass against the society around him, with a shield of cynicism and indifference. He had become a solitary creature. A dissident on the Happy Block.

Don't take away my pain, is what he bawled at his psychologist on the first encounter, when she spoke about the properties of Prozac.

I mean, what else would a man have to hold on to. If he was cured and normal, then he was as good as dead. They would take away his roar and leave him like a defenceless creature. A certain amount of chaos and insanity was vital to his existence. Rage and insanity were national characteristics. There was mayhem and derangement in his blood, which couldn't be erased that simply without turning Coyne into some kind of benevolent Frankenstein.

Coyne had been told already on numerous occasions that he had a fixation with the past. He was unable to move forward. The clock had stopped with the symmetry of a significant ending, somewhere around 5:55. The calendar hadn't moved on since the day of the fire and he was holding on to history. He had no current story for his life except the old one. I only listen to songs that evoke memories, he revealed under psychoanalysis. He kept getting into arguments, and generally behaving badly, complaining about things that nobody took seriously but him. Unfit for work. Unfit for society.

The Anchor Bar was closed. Barstools placed upside down on the counter. The barman was sweeping the cigarette butts into a corner and the lounge next door was silent and empty, except for the musicians packing up their gear. The pool table at the back was in darkness and the bar was deserted, with a high blue cloud of smoke and conversation still hanging in the air. Somebody counting the till.

Coyne was the last to leave. He went home along the seafront, feeling the breeze blowing in off the sea. He saw the black water of the harbour and the row of trawlers berthed along the quay. He saw the sleazy, orange-pink glow coming across the water from the city. The yellow lights of Dublin Bay lit up like a tinted crystal bowl. The twin stacks of the Pigeon House with its red beacon lights and the flag of dusty-pink smoke drifting inland.

He walked home along streets of B&Bs and guesthouses. Past all the names like Stella Maris and Belleview. Santander or Casablanca. With tacky palm trees outside casting a subtropical illusion, and leatherette leaves whispering on the breeze. Gardens with stones and rocks pillaged from the coast and placed in neat decorative lines on the edges of grass lawns; around flowerbeds and benches. Suburbia's last line of defence. The whole borough had barricaded itself in behind these stones. Streets named Tivoli, Adelaide and Villarea. Maretimo Terrace. Sefton and Grafton. Houses that sounded like they came from a shaggin' Yeats poem, like Ben Bulben, Lissadel. Where did these people think they were? Where was Phil Lynott Avenue?

Coyne lived on Crosthwaite Park, or Cross-eyed Park as they called it. This was the flat where he had spent the past twelve months or so with his son, Jimmy. These were the separation terms – Coyne looked after Jimmy, while Carmel kept home and looked after Jennifer and Nuala. It was not a final, end of all communication, separation, and there were still a lot of common areas of concern that allowed the marriage to linger on at a distance.

Coyne still talked to Carmel in his head.

It's not the way you think, he said, indirectly giving her a report on his life as he climbed the stairs and entered his flat. She was the inner audience to whom he offered his querulous commentary.

Look, the place is tidy, he pleaded. It's not a health hazard, you know. Look at the tea-towel neatly hung up on the stove. Look at the

crockery all washed and put away. I know I'm a useless cook, but I do my best. I look after him, Carmel. I swear! Jimmy's a good lad.

But there was something reductive about this one-way conversation. He sat down in despair, as though people had stopped listening to him. His audience had gone to sleep again. He watched a *National Geographic* video on spiders. A male spider was plucking the web of a female. Serenading spiders! Web harpists! Would Coyne ever be reunited with Carmel? seemed to be the question all nature was asking.

Coyne woke up in his armchair some time later, stiff and numb along his left arm. He got up and switched off the TV, went over to the phone and dialled a number. He waited a while until the phone was picked up at the other end and a sleepy male voice answered. It was the voice of his old bank manager, Mr Killmurphy.

Hello, Killjoy, Coyne said.

The voice on the other end was stunned. Hello! Hello! Who is this?

Remember the patio, Killjoy. Remember the bitumen all over your crazy paving. And the granite barbecue in the shape of a miniature Norman castle. Remember the garden terrorist.

Who is this?

I'm coming back Killjoy. I hope you haven't forgotten, you bastard.

I'm going to call the Guards!

The phone went dead and Coyne smiled. This was part of a new campaign of remembrance. What was the point in letting Mr Killmurphy walk away from the past? Coyne was playing the role of civic conscience here, meting out punishment and retribution to an old enemy. Coyne, the sad bastard, standing by the phone with the grin of a sick deviant on his face, carrying the mother of all grudges in his heart.

Coyne's son, Jimmy, was pissed out of his head that night. Rat arsed! Maybe even off his face on some other substances. How Coyne had missed running into him was remarkable. They practically crossed each other's paths as Jimmy and his friend Gussy made their way towards the harbour. His son was a headbanger, following in his father's footsteps. Except that Jimmy had no declared idealism other than getting out of his head.

He was insane in the membrane, as the song went, with little sense

of self-respect. He and Gussy were on their way to do damage. They had their minds fixed on getting into one of the yachts on the marina.

They were not looking for anything in particular. It was more like a general quest for the crack. A bit of harmless sport. Or maybe Jimmy had lost it, somehow, since Coyne and Carmel broke up. Perhaps he was the real victim, acting out the fracture of his parents' marriage in a more dramatic form, for all to see. He and Gussy made their way on to a yacht and kicked in the cabin door. Opened the fridge and found it stocked with champagne and sausages. Started celebrating right away so that Jimmy got twice as drunk again and couldn't even stand up. Sat on a mound of sausages and laughed uncontrollably as he opened up a tube of Pringles.

Once you start, you can't stop, he said, as it rained Pringles all over the cabin floor.

Jimmy didn't even have the sense to leave the flare gun alone. While the champagne corks were popping and Gus started spraying the stuff around like a rally winner, Jimmy struck back with a flare which suddenly ripped through the cabin like a red meteor. Almost took Gussy's face off and sent him back, dribbling champagne over himself in shock while the flare continued to spin and fizzle around on the floor, burning a crest in the navy carpet. Big black Cyrillic script. The whole cabin lit up pink like a love boat. Pink portholes throbbing until Gus covered it with a jacket and snuffed out the brief comet's life.

How they weren't spotted by the harbour police was a miracle.

Jesus Christ, Gussy said, and within minutes they were back on the pier again. Jimmy getting sick into an empty Pringles tin, as though it had been specially provided for seasickness. Hanging over the blue railings like a puking pilgrim, retching up his ancestors.

Gussy made a run for it. But Jimmy didn't see the point. He found himself a sheltered place along the pier and sat down. Watched the swell of the tide lapping against the steps in the harbour. Tried to focus on the swirling red beam of the lighthouse for a while until he laid his head down on the cool granite stone and fell asleep. The sea was calm. A heron stood on the steps close by, like a silent witness.

Around that time, two men were driving along the coast road towards the harbour in a red van. The man at the wheel was the skipper of the

Lolita, a chubby, forty-year-old man by the name of Martin Davis. Bald with a full-blown, bushy brown beard, he carried an extensive bit of freight out front, like a beanbag paunch hanging over the belt of his trousers. He was convinced that women liked a big belly with soft black fleece. It could be massaged and slapped. A convex sign of prosperity, fun and formidable appetite.

In the passenger seat, with his legs stretched out, sat a wiry man by the name of Mongi O Doherty who interpreted the bulging shape of the skipper's stomach as a sign of weakness. The exploitable, soft underbelly of a man devoted to pleasure.

Mongi was younger than the skipper, with a shaven head and a different temperament entirely. He saw pleasure as something you stole from others. He had been brought up in an environment where pleasure was something you grabbed while you had the chance, something that was normally associated with another person experiencing pain and dispossession.

As everyone knew, pain and pleasure were the same thing, only on opposite ends of the scale. Understanding this was the basis of capitalism; if you didn't grasp the barometer of human longing, then you were fucked as far as making money was concerned. At the point of a knife, or a dirty needle, it was surprising, for example, how quickly people despised their own material belongings. Moneylending and drug sales had also proved this point beyond any doubt. And a gun, well that was the true revolution. At the point of a gun, you had people begging you to take their money. Fear and pain altered everything.

With these elementary rules of commerce, Mongi had developed true leadership qualities.

The name Mongi had various sources. One of them is thought to have had something to do with his protruding teeth. People recognised an uncomfortable combination of the benign Bee Gees smile and a savage horse-bite of yellow neglect. His smile was a kuru grin of cannibal revenge, and his laughter produced a kind of echo over the city of Dublin. The hollow laugh! The millennial laugh of progress. The great capitalist laugh of eternal growth and incessant innovation.

It was rumoured that Mongi had once bitten a Garda in the face. Leading people to believe that the origins of his name had more to do with the style of the mongoose, darting in and out rapidly to bite its prey. But the irony only fully ripened when you discovered that his

nickname Mongi actually came from the word *mangach* in the Irish language, meaning toothless. His real name was Richard O Doherty.

To hell with fishing, he was saying to his new associate, Martin Davis. Fishing had become an extinguished way of life belonging to the last century.

You're dead right, skipper Martin Davis agreed.

Everywhere around the Irish coast had been fished to bejaysus. Mackerel-crowded seas, my arse. You had to compete with a massive fleet. Every factory ship in Europe was out there grabbing the same statistical slice of fish pie, fighting like a bunch of cut-throat pirates over the Atlantic fish-finger quota. Nobody would eat the glow-in-the-dark radioactive plaice from the Irish Sea any more. And what was the point in braving all kinds of inclement conditions, getting your hands raw like the Man of Aran and risking your life for a bit of stinking turbot. Every piece of fresh cod was marked and numbered on a radar screen; caught, gang-raped, cooked and consumed before you had a chance to slip the mooring.

Fishing is a cold and smelly business, Mongi said gravely.

Don't be talking, Martin Davis said, a grimace of disgust on his face.

You probably spent more money on fucking talcum powder than you earned on the catch.

Old Spice!

The skipper couldn't agree more. He was nodding like a rear-window travel dog. I hate the fish trade, he was saying. I hate all those biblical innuendoes. Casting out nets. Gathering souls and all that stuff. Look, Mongi – I know what you're saying here. I've seen the movie.

But Mongi continued to place his own philosophical spin on the new dawn of opportunity. He was putting forward a vision for his people. The Irish were through with subsistence economics. He was the right man to be talking, with a name like Mongi. As they sped towards the harbour in the skipper's new van, he sounded like a fishmonger, glorifying the new enterprise of loaves and fishes. Sudden abundance! Economic miracles! All that had changed was the nature of the catch.

Wet-backs!

Fish-backs!

Wet-backs and fish-backs, Mongi echoed with his hollow cackle.

They could see the lights of the harbour below them. Two piers reaching out into the sea, embracing the visitor. Grabbing trade from the outside world.

Can you believe it? Mongi said. People paying money to get into Ireland. Remember when all we ever did was send out emigrants through that harbour. Every story ended with a man or a woman taking the boat to England. Remember the sign on the old mail boat as you walked across the gangplank: *Mind Your Step!* The last word of advice to the Irish exile.

Who woulda thought? Skipper echoed.

That's the new frontier, Mongi pointed, lighting up a cheroot in celebration.

If I woulda-hada known it was going to be like this, I woulda-never-hada busted my balls on the fishing for so long, the skipper said.

Fucking frontier is what I'm saying.

Mongi liked to repeat catchphrases to great literary effect. It gave things profundity. Added a cheap metaphysical lacquer to his words. Made him an innovator. He liked to remind people that there was such a thing as original thought, and it came from him. Out there in the future, the face of Mongi O Doherty would some day appear on the Ecu banknote.

Without me, you'd be nowhere, captain.

Martin Davis kept his humble mouth shut; just nodded in compliance. They had gone through all of this before. But since there was so much money involved, perhaps it was necessary to define the roles again. Who was the boss, in other words. Who was the creative genius behind this new enterprise.

Without me and my European connections, you'd still have fish scales on your mickey, Mongi continued. Without me, you'd be out there near Rockall with a floppy herring in your hand, like some prehistoric islandman. Spanking the mackerel! Jesus, Mongi laughed. No wonder people in Ireland hate fish.

Bud asail, the skipper muttered in Gaelic through his beard. The peasant revenge.

Mongi's grasp of the Irish language wasn't so hot. But he knew enough to understand that the word *bud* referred to the male prosthetic supplement. Mickey. Mackerel. He looked around angrily,

demanding to know what the skipper was unhappy about. He had left fishing behind and was making serious money. All he had to do was bring in a consignment of illegal immigrants, hand over the money to Mongi, take his share and then go and get bricked out of his head. Eat food, get drunk and get laid for a few weeks until the next lot was to be brought in.

It was the new frontier all right. The *Lolita* rose and fell gently on the tide, with its human cargo of East Europeans still below deck, waiting to disembark. They were stiff from sitting on the cramped bunks of the two small cabins, looking out through a porthole at the bilge pump gushing rhythmically through the side of the next boat. Some of them were pale with seasickness and still vomiting into plastic bags. They couldn't wait to see Ireland. They had paid good money to get this far.

The journey was not over yet, though, and according to plan they would have to spend some more time in the back of the van, until the skipper saw fit to release them on to the streets of the capital. Drop them at some labour exchange. Or just show them where to get the 46A into town.

The van reversed along the quay and the men got out. Martin Davis did what all truck drivers and van drivers do at this point; he adjusted his trousers and put everything back in place. He hopped out of the cab, stood with his legs apart and briefly performed that obligatory freedom jiggle, giving his trousers a little shake and pulling them up over his hips again before moving on. Then he followed Mongi and stepped on board the *Lolita* like an immigration officer.

For Jesus sake, Mongi hissed through his horse-teeth as he heard the singing below deck. The immigrants had been in those cabins too long and were trying to keep their spirits up, dancing and singing to combat poverty and loneliness and homesickness.

They're as bad as the Irish, Mongi roared. Can't go anywhere without starting a party. Drinking plum brandy and enjoying themselves. Singing sad songs.

Martin Davis hammered his fist on the door of the cabin and everything fell silent. Then he rooted under a seat and handed Mongi a red sportsbag.

Jesus, man. I said Irish or sterling!

What could I do? the skipper pleaded. I could hardly send them back.

What am I supposed to do with this stuff? Mongi held up a bundle of dollars, threw it back into the bag and zipped it up. It's awkward.

What was far more awkward was the presence of Tommy Nolan on the pier. He was on to this reverse emigration business. Already he had witnessed one consignment arriving a few weeks back. He had gone to the harbour after the pub and concealed himself on the quay, behind a stack of fish boxes and a mound of damaged blue nets. Behind him some tyres and ropes to sit on; and the smell of diesel and paint and piss all round. The lighting was poor and some of the lamps on the pier were missing. Tommy kept his eye on the trawlers shifting on the tide. Listening to the wood squeaking and groaning, so that he nearly fell asleep himself.

Until he saw the van arriving and the men getting out. Exhaust fumes drifting towards him.

After a while, Mongi came up on deck again carrying the holdall bag. Stepped off the boat and threw the bag into the front of the van and shut the door again. He stood around, smoking. The smell of cigar smoke blending with the smell of exhaust as he began to pace up and down beside the van.

Fuck this, Mongi muttered impatiently and jumped back on to the boat, down below to speed up the immigration procedure. He was demanding expediency that nobody could ever get used to. His people had been brought up on a spiritual sense of hope that ran counter to crass, wash-and-go, Euro-efficiency. They had lived on the imagination for so long that they didn't know how to grasp the material urgency of the moment. They still thrived on the accident, the casual diversion, the gift of surprise. The twist out of nowhere!

At this precise moment, Jimmy Coyne walked down the quay. Refreshed from his sleep, he walked straight towards the red van as though he had just parked it there himself. His face was disfigured with the imprint of granite on his cheek. His mind was disfigured with drink and sleep. But he seemed to walk straight with a great air of purpose. Assumed that the new van on the pier had been placed there for him, with the engine running and all.

People were driving all kinds of new vehicles in Dublin these days.

He opened the door of the cab and got in. Didn't even notice the holdall bag on the passenger seat and just started playing with the clutch and grinning to himself like a halfwit, getting ready to drive away when the door opened.

Beside him on the pier stood Tommy Nolan, mouthing at him like a guardian angel, begging him to stop. This is unconstitutional, he was trying to point out, with saliva streaming from his mouth. Trouble is close behind. Think about this – get out and walk away slowly before it becomes irreversible.

Jimmy pushed Tommy away. Slammed the door and got ready to drive.

In the meantime, Mongi had come up on deck with Martin Davis behind him. The immigrants with their bags down below at the bottom of the steps, eagerly waiting to be told to come up and breathe the misty night air. Mongi leaped on to the pier in disbelief and grabbed Tommy Nolan by the neck.

You dirtbird bastard! Mongi shouted, dragging him over to the edge of the pier. I fucking warned you.

Jimmy Coyne considered hiding, or escaping out the far door of the van. He looked out and saw Mongi turning around. Made eye contact with him, just before the van leaped forward with a terrible gear-grinding sound of agony.

Mongi was left standing on the pier, looking into the harbour. Then he tried to run after the van, tripping over a rusted brown mooring ring as he went. But Jimmy had managed to put the van in second gear and was already driving away up the hill towards the main road.

This was Black Monday for Mongi O Doherty. This was share freefall. He looked into the harbour and then back up to the main road where the van now disappeared. Nothing on the pain/pleasure scale was more agonising than being ripped off due to your own carelessness. This was like biting your own tongue. This was like catching your foreskin in the zip. Like mistaking your own mickey for a mackerel.

Coyne made another phone call before he went to bed that night. It was something that had to be done with systematic dedication. Some things could not be dropped and forgotten. No way! Terrorism was

an exact science that had to be consistent, unrelenting.

Killjoy, there is something I have to tell you, Coyne said into the phone as soon as it was answered.

If you don't stop this I'll call the Guards! I'll get this call traced.

Killjoy, you stupid bastard. You intransigent fucking moron. I hope that taught you a lesson. You'll live to regret the day. Killjoy, I hope they give you a pig's heart.

Tommy Nolan's body had no obvious marks when it was taken from the water the following morning. There was a lot of activity around the harbour, with blue lights flashing across the side of yachts and reflected in portholes. A sense of shock had already spread through the borough. Shopkeepers were talking. People stopped their cars along the main road overlooking the seafront. A crowd had gathered behind the yellow crime scene tape, looking down into the harbour. Into the gap between the trawlers and the pier where the debris normally collected into a compilation of styrofoam boxes, plastic litre bottles of Bulmers and Sprite, bits of saturated wood and usually a condom, floating in a greasy film of rainbow coloured diesel.

Tommy's body was discovered by one of the fishermen. The skipper of the *Lolita*, Martin Davis. Sergeant Corrigan from the local Garda station took a statement. Apart from some rope burn marks around Tommy's chest and a single bruise on the head which might also have occurred when he fell into the water, there was nothing to indicate foul play as such. These marks could have been consistent with a fall across the mooring ropes, and while the state pathologist was still going through his examination, the whole thing was explained as a tragedy. Gardai were of the opinion that Tommy Nolan might have been knocked unconscious by a fall against the hull of a boat after which he had become entangled in the mooring ropes. They were keeping an open mind – waiting for witnesses to come forward.

Coyne was down at the harbour himself that morning. As it happened, he was half keeping an eye out for Tommy Nolan and only became aware of his death some time later. Coyne was wandering around the area as though his life was one big Bloomsday, getting in touch with the real world, discovering all the extraneous, non-essential details he had been deprived of while working with the Gardai. Like water slapping against the steps. The echoes of the

harbour. The sheen of sunlight on the surface of the water and the sound of bells everywhere, warped on the breeze. Coiling like oval rings across the tide.

He saw Garda activity on the far side of the harbour and went over. Stood on the edge of the crowd and finally heard the news. He started blaming himself immediately, spiralling into another bout of guilt and self-effacing torment. He should have listened to Tommy while he had the chance. He had failed him. A further instance of Coyne's inability to deal with the world.

Jimmy Coyne and Gus Mangan were arrested just before lunchtime.

Coyne received a call from Carmel in the early afternoon. There was a touch of bitterness in her voice that he had never heard before. A plaintive tone. As though all of this was Coyne's fault. As though he had instructed Jimmy to create havoc in order to provoke her. Coyne was doing all of this on purpose.

You better go down and straighten things out, she said.

It was no surprise that Jimmy had ended up in some kind of trouble. He was starting to drift. And Coyne had no way of being firm with him. Jimmy often stayed out all night. The eldest son of a broken home, at liberty to come and go as he pleased. Whenever Coyne's atrocious cooking got too much for him, he went home for a meal in the family home with Carmel. Barely nineteen and in custody already.

Leave it to me, Coyne reassured her. He would have a word with the lads.

Coyne knew most of the Gardai at the local station. He had met them at one point or another in the course of his work, but he hated the humiliation of having to intercede on behalf of his own son. The worst thing was having to sit on the public bench. Coyne the temporary off-duty Garda, robbed of his status and told to sit and wait. The ignominy of it. Instead of ushering him straight into the main office, a Ban-Garda listened to him wearily at the hatch, ignored everything he said and told him to take a seat on the public bench.

Sergeant Corrigan eventually brought Coyne inside. They knew each other from a little spell they had spent together in Store Street Garda Station in the city centre. Corrigan was a tough policeman,

always whistling with menacing intent. His nickname was Whistler, given to him by an unknown criminal and adopted by the rest of the force. It was Corrigan's style to leave long silences while questioning a suspect. Made people really uneasy to see a big Garda walking up and down the cell, whistling *The Homes of Donegal* to himself.

It's not an accident, Pat.

What?

Your son may have something to do with Tommy Nolan... the Sergeant stopped and rephrased what he wanted to say. He may be in a position to help us in our enquiries.

You must be joking, Coyne said. Let me talk to him. Corrigan explained that there was a serious matter of some damage to property. Sabotage was the word he used at first before he changed it to vandalism. Malicious damage.

There was no mention of a stolen van. It did not even enter into the Garda log, because it was never reported missing. Some tiny nugget of wisdom shone through Jimmy's madness at the right moment, and he had parked the van on the seafront, where all the stolen cars usually ended up, sometimes burned out, sometimes crashed and looted, sometimes perfectly intact. Skipper Martin Davis did not have to go far to find it. The van was undamaged. But the holdall bag with the money was missing.

Jimmy Coyne never had to look for trouble. It came to him. He had been expelled from two good schools and barely scraped through his leaving cert exams. Now he was almost a year out of school with nothing to do but get drunk and wreck people's property. He was basically a good lad, Coyne always felt, just given to a temporary spell of self-destruction. Just like his father. But where Coyne had always been dedicated to sorting out the world, his son had a vocation for pure mayhem. The black hole of youth.

Hogan's yacht was the main focus of attention, for the moment. Councillor Hogan was suing for the damage and Jimmy Coyne was the obvious culprit. He had left his jacket in the cabin. A video store membership card inside belonging to Coyne.

I'd like to know where Hogan got the money for that yacht, Coyne muttered. As far as he was concerned, Councillor Hogan was a big fraud. He was the town killer, involved in every planning scandal going.

But this was the wrong thing to say. If anything, it made Coyne look like he had sent his son on a mission of destruction. Whistler stood like he was in a wax museum, warbling silently. Patience running out fast and his mouth shaped into a little O, ready for the last verse of *Avondale*, but the notes refusing to chime.

Jimmy sat in the cell with his head in his hands, more from a hangover than from remorse. Hardly even looked up when Coyne entered. So they sat in silence. There had never been very much communication between them.

Coyne had no words. He looked around the cell and saw for the first time what the world looked like from the reverse side. Even started reading some of the graffiti. Fuck the Law – Macker! Dope the Pope! Coyne and his son stared everywhere around that small cell but at each other. Until eventually Jimmy met his father's eyes by accident, in a brief glance. As though they had both been hiding behind bushes and suddenly had to give themselves up.

Coyne felt all the instincts of a father. Stupidity. Jealousy. Anger. Concern. His first thought was to ask his son about drugs.

Did you get yourself connected? he asked.

Jimmy was stunned by this new DJ vernacular. As though they could talk together openly in rhyming rap lyrics from now on. He thought he was elected.

Did you get yourself injected, is what I'm asking?

No! Jimmy responded.

Coyne maintained a stern face. What would Carmel say to all of this? What's more: what would her mother, Mrs Gogarty say? His reputation was on the line here.

You think you're cool, Coyne said.

Jimmy looked up. He saw that his father was a decent man. There was remorse and embarrassment in his eyes now.

I'm sorry, Dad!

So you should be, Coyne said. You know you've just fucked up any chance of me and your mother getting back together again.

Coyne was too soft-hearted. He could not be harsh with his son. He could not even bring himself to ask the big question. Did you have anything to do with Tommy Nolan's death?

Coyne sat listening to the familiar sounds of Garda activity outside – radio voices, computer terminals humming, people closing doors.

He was close to tears, with his chin quivering. Not just because of this situation but the entire shock of what being in a police station meant to him now: a mixture of nostalgia and contempt for the profession which had taken up so much of his life. It made him more compassionate than ever before for his own son. He was desperately searching for more words to soften the impact of his anger towards him. Something more trivial. Warm. Something in rap language that would allow him to look into his son's eyes again and tell him that everything would be fine in the end. Something that rhymed with cool. It was the only way that Coyne had of keeping faith with his son in this difficult time.

You think you're cool, but you're only in the vestibule, Coyne said at last.

It was exactly the right thing to say – cross but hip. Jimmy sat up. It allowed them to look each other in the eye. Coyne got up and went across to his son. Put his arm around him.

You're only in the vestibule, son.

It was Carmel who ultimately got Jimmy out of trouble. She went straight down to the Chamber of Commerce and asked to speak to Councillor Hogan. Left her red Toyota parked outside the Town Hall. It was embarrassing having to go in to sit in front of him in his office. Hogan was looking at her legs.

She offered to pay for all the damage to the yacht, but he would not talk about money. He was more interested in her.

I hear you're into some kind of healing, he said, smiling.

Yes, Carmel said, totally surprised that her reputation had reached so far around the borough already.

I've got a very bad back, you know, Hogan appealed. Can't do anything with it at all.

How long have you had this?

Years! I've been all over the world. I even led a fact-finding delegation to Europe to study back pain. Nobody can do anything for me. It's an atrocity. There's no other word for it. An atrocity.

So they ended up talking about lower back pain and osteoporosis. It was Carmel who ended up offering sympathy and solace to Councillor Hogan. She was off, asking intimate questions about his diet, exercise, medical history. She soon had him bending over and

arching back for her. All kinds of people turned instantly humble in front of a healer.

What kind of healing do you do? he asked.

Stones, she said. I do things with stones.

There was no need to mention the grubby business of the yacht any more. Carmel said she would insist on paying for the damage, but Councillor Hogan waved his hand. The charges were dropped, without question. All it took was a phone call. It was sub-verbal.

The next thing on Carmel's mind was to straighten Jimmy out. There was little she could do for her estranged husband, but she could set her own son on the right road at least. So when Jimmy was released she brought him directly down to the Haven nursing home and got him a job. Told him to stay at home for a while so she could keep an eye on him. She was not going to spend the whole summer looking after a delinquent son. One delinquent ex-husband was enough for the time being. There was no need to get angry or triumphant about any of this. She was being practical, that's all.

On top of everything else, Coyne was a bit of an insomniac. Middle of the night, he sat bolt upright in the bed, talking to himself like a deranged man. He was in no mood to make any more terrorist phone calls and shuffled around the flat instead, muttering and staring out the window at the ivy-covered garden walls at the back of the houses.

He was wide awake, confronted by a particular image of the famine which he had heard of in school and which still haunted him – how a dead couple were found inside a cottage with the woman's head cradled in the man's lap for the last bit of warmth. The final act of unselfish loyalty against such a cruel fate. Coyne could not get past that point in history.

He searched the whole kitchen but found nothing. Not even a cracker. What kind of housekeeping was this when he woke up at night like a famished man?

He rang Carmel, got her up out of bed and started babbling to her over the phone. 3:33 – the time of revelation.

For Godsake, Pat! This is crazy.

I'm starving, he said.

Jesus, Pat. Are you still in therapy?

Carmel was rubbing her eyes, speaking in a woolly voice on the

other end of the line, trying to sound more angry than she really was. This was a serious invasion of privacy.

Pat, what are you trying to say? What are you calling me for like a baby in the middle of the night?

I need you, Carmel. I can't live without you.

Go back to sleep, Pat. Jesus! Is that psychologist any use?

Carmel tried to calm him down. Was this another annual suicide alert, she wondered. She talked to him for a while until he began to sound normal again. Brought him back down to earth.

I forgot to do the shopping, he said.

I don't believe it, Pat, she laughed. You mean to tell me you phoned me up looking for food.

Please Carmel. I haven't eaten anything all day.

What do you expect? Meals on wheels?

It's an emergency, Carmel. There's nothing.

Is this some trick, Pat? If you're just trying to get me over to your flat, you can forget it. Because that would be really vile, and I'd never forgive you.

I swear, Carmel.

Going into Coyne's flat would have been a step beyond. Forbidden grounds. Mrs Gogarty, who was working against Coyne like a renegade in his own former home, kept telling Carmel it would be a big mistake ever to enter Coyne's lair. Put your foot inside that door and you'll never come out again.

Carmel was still half asleep as she drove the car.

Coyne stood at the door and looked at his ex-wife with a kind of haunted expression in his eyes. Her hair was in a mess. The dressing gown showed under the green coat, and she wore shoes with no socks. She was annoyed that he had forced her to get out and walk up the steps, having to ring the bell and hand over the sandwich at the door instead of him coming out to the car.

You can give me back the lunchbox when you're finished, she said.

She took the opportunity in return to examine her ex-husband, fully dressed, but looking a little harassed and thin. He was obviously not eating properly. Going into decline since the separation. She was hoping he would go for acupuncture, get himself sorted out and stop being a burden on her conscience.

Coyne asked her if she wanted to come inside.

She asked about his health. A neutral enquiry.

I'm not sick, he exclaimed suspiciously.

What are you off work for, Pat? For Godsake, just listen to your chest.

Coyne smiled. He held up the sandwich box and winked at her. Thanks!

You don't take care of yourself, she said. I'm not going to allow you to take that attitude towards your health. Your energy has become trapped.

Ah now, Carmel. Take it easy.

Coyne didn't like the sound of this consultation on the doorstep. He knew where it was leading to. How *are* you? How do you *feel*? Soon she would start going on about psycho-neuro-immunology again – all the stuff about prolonged stress in the aftermath of trauma. She seemed to be overheating a little these days, using strange new words that whooped like a car alarm around Coyne's head. Words like energy flow and centreing. She said Coyne would have to embark on a journey within, whatever the hell that meant. He had lost the map.

You know me, Carmel. Anything that can't be cured by a pint is not worth curing.

That's where you're wrong, Pat. You've got to cross the threshold.

What threshold?

Coyne deeply mistrusted this new faith-healing vernacular. These were the words of betrayal. Besides, there was too much healing going on in this town. People being healed who had nothing wrong with them in the first place, except that they might have required a good kick in the arse. Too many strange and unnatural practices going on. One thing was certain: Coyne was going on no journey within; or without, for that matter. And he was not going across any shaggin' threshold either.

We're messing, he said, looking into her eyes.

Carmel backed away from this sudden rush of intimacy. Protecting herself at all costs, she turned and walked back towards the car.

Carmel, it's you and me, he said with great feeling, following her out through the gate.

Is this what you got me up in the middle of the night for? She

turned back and faced him on the pavement. You're not hungry at all. You just tricked me into coming over.

She was determined not to slide back into this marriage. Losing all her independence. Having to live with Coyne's madness again. Listening to him shouting at the radio every day. Indulging his theories, nursing his phobias, and watching him cast his overwhelming spell of paranoia and doom all over the house. She had to keep things on a practical level.

Coyne stood on the pavement with the lunchbox in his hand, bending down to try and talk to her through the window. But Carmel started the car and drove off. He wanted to tell her that her dressing gown was hanging out through the door of the car. Flapping as she went around the corner out of sight.

Carmel's mother felt Coyne was simply beyond help. She prayed for him. He was beyond redemption. She behaved as though her son-in-law was dead already.

Each night as she knelt down alone at her bed and began the prayers for the deceased, like a rap hit litany of departed souls. Coyne the living dead man, walking around like one of the lost souls in purgatory.

Dear Lord have mercy on the souls of my dear Paddy, Nance, Eva, Mammy, Daddy, Granny, Auntie Mary, Auntie Essie, Eamon, Ned, Uncle Charlie, Uncle Paddy, Auntie Olive, Uncle Dan, Uncle Tom, Uncle Denis, Uncle Mick, Auntie Girlie, Auntie Olive, Father Moynihan, Frank Donnelly, Kathleen Boyce, Lilly Whitelaw, Jenny Pollock... for Aidan Martin, Father Joyce, Father Brady, Father Collins, Bobby Hayes, Mary Fuller, Michael Collins, Sean South, for poor Kevin Barry and for Pat Coyne and all the souls in purgatory especially Lord for those who have no one to pray for them in the hour of their death. Amen.

Coyne's therapist, Ms Clare Dunford, had her own professional anxieties about his frame of mind. She had never met so much resistance before in her entire career and had to devote a lot of attention to his case; putting on the rubber gloves, in other words. She wore glasses on a chain and looked over the rims at Coyne as if to say – listen here, my friend. I've dealt with all kinds of maniacs

in here, alcoholics, wife-beaters, rapists, murderers, you name it. I'm not going to be put off that easily by you, Mr Coyne. I'll sort you out if it kills me.

She was not convinced that the trauma of the fire alone, or even the break-up with Carmel, could have caused so much damage in itself. There had to be some other problem underneath that would stop Coyne from going back to work and behaving like a normal individual. Something substantial that went back to Coyne's childhood, perhaps. The fire was merely a trigger.

She tried to explain to Coyne that he had most probably become separated from himself. Her idea was that after the fire and the failure associated with this event, Coyne had walked out on himself and slammed the door. His inner self was really angry and vowed never to go back again. Basically, there were two Coynes now: the flesh and blood Coyne who went for a pint and lived in the real world and occasionally thought about committing suicide; and the other Coyne who had started messing about and being terribly difficult and looking down with great condescension on the real Coyne. They were like feuding brothers with separate entrances to the same house: the outside Coyne refusing to speak to the poor flesh and blood Coyne, because he had let him down on the day of the fire, through no fault of his own.

Coyne was an awkward subject. He was against all this psychoanalysis and feared categories. Next thing they'd be saying he was still in love with his mother, or that he was schizophrenic, or autistic or something. He hated the notion that there might be a recognisable syndrome or description for his state of mind. The only reason he was attending these sessions was to make himself eligible for compensation. Coyne's solicitor had advised him just to go along with the treatment, even if it was doing him no good. The state was going to pay out some serious money in aggravated damages.

Ms Dunford was in her late forties with a round, ill-defined shape. She usually wore a loose, silk blouse and blue-grey tweed skirt. Her bottom row of teeth jutted out a little further than the top row, and Coyne couldn't get over the idea that her face was upside down. Every now and again he wanted to bend over and see if she looked any better from underneath. As well as that, she wore massive shoes, and Coyne imagined large, webbed feet inside them, like a giant duck.

You're not fooling me, Ms Duckfoot.

He wasn't taken in by her motherly approach either. Coyne was thinking compensation as he answered all her routine questions with the maximum degree of neurosis, presenting an alarming impression of total human wreck. Depression. Irrational fears. Memory loss. Lack of concentration. Post-traumatic stress disorder! By Jesus, Coyne had them all.

Tell me about the fire, she said.

I'm trying to forget about it, he said.

You were on duty, weren't you? You attempted a rescue.

If you don't mind, Coyne said. I don't want to re-enact the whole thing again.

You've got to let go, she said. You're driving with the handbrake on, Pat.

Coyne looked up at her with a stunned expression on his face. Where did she learn all this cartoon psychology, he wanted to know. All these pert little phrases. All this shaggin' common sense. There was nothing worse than amateurs spouting superstition, pretending it was science. She tried to placate him by putting the proceedings on first name terms. He could call her Clare from now on. She sat up on her desk. Perched on the ledge with giant feet dangling.

You know, there's an old Chinese saying that you can't see your own chin, she said.

Here we go again!

Coyne was astonished by this latest remark. What in the name of Jesus was she getting at? What had Coyne's chin got to do with anything. All I can see is your chin, Ms Duckfoot, and it looks like a giant strawberry.

You can never grasp everything, she explained. It's a mistake to try and examine your own soul too carefully.

Listen here, you Jungian monster. I don't want to be normal. I don't want to be cured. I don't want to go back to work. All I want is the compensation. And so what if I can't see my own chin. I can't see my own arse either, but that doesn't stop me from grasping it, now does it?

Tommy Nolan's funeral was a quiet event. Coyne and a number of people loitering around the crematorium to hear the priest say a few charismatic words about the soul of Tommy Nolan. A great character

who would be limping no more in heaven. A man who would be missed by the whole community. Some people in attendance who hardly even said hello to Tommy while he was alive. McCurtain from the Port and Docks board was there, pretending he had been a lifelong friend.

And more surprising again was the fact that the burial at sea had been organised by trawlerman Martin Davis.

On a windy, early summer afternoon, around a dozen people stood on the deck of the *Lolita*. The priest remarked that it was strictly against the law to cast the ashes out like this. But he was defying it for Tommy's sake. The breakdown between church and state.

So that's how the ashes were disbursed in Dublin Bay. With the Superferry passing by a few hundred yards away, and the Dublin mountains in the distance behind the city. A decade of the rosary carrying out across the water. Another homily about the tragic nature of his untimely death and Tommy's sister casting the white dust and shards of bleached bone out from the stern of the boat with tears in her eyes. Seagulls coming to investigate. Hovering over a choppy grave.

The real farewell for Tommy Nolan took place later on that night at the Anchor Bar. Pints all round for the lads. The place had never been so jammed before, because people were of the firm belief that the only real way to honour the passing of Tommy was to get legless and locked out of their skulls. Mouldy in memory of the dead. That's what Tommy would have done himself.

Coyne was mute as a stone and full of resentment. He knew that Tommy's death was no accident, and anyone who took part in this event was under suspicion. There was something strange about the fact that the skipper of the *Lolita* was buying pints for everyone. Magnanimous Martin Davis was hiding something, standing centre stage at the Anchor Bar with his arm around Marlene Nolan.

This thing wasn't over and finished yet, as far as Coyne was concerned.

The rumour went around that Tommy had come across some foreign youths at the harbour. A conspiracy theory began to develop that he had been dumped in the harbour by a stag party on the return to the Superferry. A random attack on a poor defenceless man, killed

for no reason. Tommy Nolan knew the harbour too well to have fallen in of his own accord. People liked a conspiracy theory.

Everybody was langered. Sooner or later, McCurtain made his way over to Coyne and started talking indiscriminately into his ear, expanding on his own past glories. There was one of them in every bar, and Kelly's Anchor Bar was no exception. Given half a chance, McCurtain soon got down to boasting about his life as a playboy. Telling Coyne how the women of the borough used to go mad for him. Making himself out to be some kind of legendary Irish Don Juan.

There were more husbands after me than Indians were after General Custer, he announced, with a smell of diesel on his breath.

Sure, Coyne muttered.

Why this sudden rush of nationwide honesty, he thought. I mean, why couldn't people keep things to themselves any more? On the radio; on TV: everybody exposing themselves and trying to come to terms with their own psychological junk. Go and expose yourself to the Blessed Sacrament. Why don't you?

The women used to place bets on me, you know, McCurtain bragged.

Do me a favour, Coyne said, because he'd heard all these fantasies before, many times. Go home and decompose. Go on, back to your crypt, McCurtain.

But the thick-skinned Irish Casanova would not go away and Coyne was drawn into the unavoidable confrontation. One of those drunken funeral debates that took place at the bar with everyone listening in. Some vital point that had to be hammered out, as though Coyne had a civic duty to challenge McCurtain with the facts. Let him know that Coyne stood on the side of aggrieved husbands.

You're like the Irish Elk, Coyne said.

What are you on about now? McCurtain said, half walking away.

You're going into extinction, Coyne explained by way of a parable. Will I tell you what happened to the Irish Elk?

McCurtain pricked up his ears. He was ready for this kind of schoolboy abuse.

Go on, hit me!

You want to know why he became extinct? Coyne went on. Sex, that's why. Too much sex on his mind.

The barman was listening in, smiling to himself. This was a good

one. He even alerted the staff from the lounge next door to come in and catch this. Coyne talking extinction. Calling McCurtain an Irish Elk. Coyne was dead serious. Never before had the subject of sex been so openly debated in the Irish pub. Coyne delivering a vital message to General fucking Custer with masterful brevity and eloquence. Famous last words, spoken on the night of the funeral, in the shadow of mortality.

The Irish Elk never stopped thinking about sex, Coyne announced. He was obsessed with nothing else. That's what killed him.

Would you listen to him, McCurtain smirked.

The barman stood holding up a glass in his hand. Stalled with incomprehension.

I'm not joking you, Coyne said, raising his voice. It was one big snuff movie for the Irish Elk. Because he was so interested in attracting the female and fighting off other males that his antlers kept getting bigger. That was his downfall. Couldn't run around any more. Every time he bent down to drink water, he couldn't get his head up again. I'm telling you, they found a whole load of ancient elk horns by a lake up there in Wicklow.

Stick to bottled water, the barman said at last.

Would you fuck off, McCurtain bawled. Coyne, you're like an anthropologist. What's wrong with you?

You're in a cul-de-sac, Coyne said.

McCurtain winked at the barman. Exchanged a grin of consensus. Then McCurtain started laughing his head off, cackling like he needed to have his head examined.

Coyne had delivered his message with crisp profundity. That would give the bastard something to think about, he said to himself. The barman too. Each man before the jury of his own sex life. Every one of them reflecting on the decline of the Irish Elk at the height of his powers. Living on an island, with hardly any predators. His own worst enemy. Running like the prince of the species across bogs and mountains. Barking through the darkness of the oak forest. Standing with his heavy antlers up and his sad eyes staring out through the silent intimacy of dawn.

Somebody had brought a guitar. There was no band playing next door that night, so it was decided to do Tommy Nolan the honour of

a few songs. They sang *Galveston*, because Tommy had always been a bit of a cowboy at heart, a freak character from some memorable Western, a humble man, making a living in the shadow of the great legends – the local sheriffs, baddies, barmen, molls and dollar men. Perhaps he had been abducted by the Indians as a child and left to stalk the borough like an enigmatic figure with a strange past that nobody wanted to know. Until he was dead, at least. For a moment the Anchor Bar became a saloon as they sang Tommy's favourite number. *Three wheels on my wagon – and I'm still rolling along…*

Later it was *So Long, Marianne*, which they sang like some fiery republican ballad. And *Massachusetts*. In deep male voices. Belting it out with such masculine pride and testosterone dignity that you'd think it had to do with some ambush in the war of independence, a shoot-out with the Black and Tans.

I'm going back to Maaah-ssechusetts…

In the name of Jaysus, Coyne thought. You can't do that with a hippie song. It's meant to be all about peace and love and banality, with eunuch harmonies. You can't start that macho growl at somebody's funeral either. Strumming the guitar like an anti-aircraft gun. Pack of granite gobshites, turning a flower power hit into a Provo marching song.

And then it was McCurtain's turn to sing. The great Irish Casanova with the rebel heart who never discharged a shot in his life. The overspecialised Irish Elk, facing extinction and singing *The Fields of Athenry* with huge passion and fervour. McCurtain and his pals were in an evolutionary cul-de-sac, crooning the anthem of republican, auto-erotic perfection. A mythological country between the sheets. The great, all-time fantasy ride.

High-low, the fields of Athenry… they clapped and cheered in frenzied admiration as McCurtain raised his arms in the air, the bastard. Out of breath with post-coital exertion.

But then, at last, came something European. A Russian fisherman offered to do a solo number. There was a visiting trawler in the bay that night, a big factory ship which had brought Russians all over the town, reciprocating with more free pints. Must have thought there was a funeral in Ireland every night. Just like at home.

Hang on, lads! Pushkin here wants to take the floor.

A man with dark brown rims around his eyes and hollow

cheekbones started singing *Danny Boy*. Chest inflating. Letting out a gale of breath like it was going to bring ye back all the way to his own home town of Noril'sk.

Oh, Dannyol Boy... From glyen to glyen...

The crowd in the Anchor Bar was stunned. McCurtain said it was a travesty.

Bleedin' mockery, he growled. The Russian couldn't sing and shouldn't be let. If they hadn't put up all the free pints, they'd be turfed out of the pub. Back to the factory ship with a filleting knife in the back.

Fair play to you, Coyne encouraged the singer. Anything to defy the bellowing elk.

McCurtain muttered on about the Russians as new invaders, fishing every benthic inch and fathom around Erin's green shores, cleaning out the entire fish stocks. They had some audacity to come into the Anchor Bar and crucify *Danny Boy* like it was a karaoke night.

But everybody else loved this new rendition. It was the greatest version of *Danny Boy* they had ever heard. An old song of emigration, rescued from the graveyard of trite emotion and brought back to life with the fresh lungs of Russian loneliness. Great big Russian vowels hanging in the smoky blue air and the whole pub bulging with the sound of this man's epic voice. Veins standing out on his Caucasian forehead. And people joining in, even from the lounge next door. *Danny Boy* – from Donegal to the Urals.

Come forward! I want to come forward.

A number of witnesses had 'come forward' to say they had seen something going on the night Tommy Nolan was killed. A woman from one of the new apartment blocks overlooking the harbour said she had witnessed a struggle on the quay. From her bedroom window, no less than eight hundred yards away, she had seen two people either fighting or embracing. Later she saw people running. This was corroborated by a motorist who reported seeing car headlights on the pier and some youths fighting. Both gave a similar time frame – around 2:30 a.m.

Sergeant Corrigan was in his element, like the whistling gypsy rover, doing house to house enquiries all around the flash apartments.

He was chatting up the harbour police, nightwatchmen, caretakers, cooks; anyone remotely involved in harbour activity. Men in yellow coats. Torch carriers. Reflective sash and luminous donkey jacket wearers. He was seen drifting around the boat yards and yacht clubs, making a nuisance of himself all day. Then back to the woman in the apartment, just to confirm whether she had said 'struggle' or 'scuffle' in her statement. His handwriting was as bad as his whistling.

Tommy Nolan's postmortem had revealed very little. Officially, it was not quite a murder enquiry yet, but Corrigan was uneasy about the whole thing. The picture was not plumb, let's say. The funeral and a rousing farewell at the Anchor Bar were not sufficient to put Tommy Nolan's soul to rest, because society demanded some narrative conclusion. The full stop. Tommy Nolan had left behind a bit of a semi-colon, and Sergeant Corrigan was out there trying to finish the sentence with the right punctuation. He was besieged by the flat syntax of cop buzzwords and phrases, such as trying to close the book. Piece of the jigsaw missing. At the end of the day. In the heel of the hunt. He was always using words like complexion – oh that puts a different complexion on the matter. He was living in the world of the school textbook where Sean and Nora were always playing with the ball, Mammy was smiling in the kitchen making sandwiches while Daddy was outside mowing the lawn, and Rolo, the dog, was yelping at a cat in the tree. Something was not right in the early reader.

The problem was that all of this was pointing straight at Jimmy Coyne. According to Corrigan's linear logic, he was up to his neck in it. Corrigan was up at Coyne's flat on Cross-eyed Park, whistling silently in the living room. Prompting. Trying to make Coyne talk about his son. Double-checking statements and generally wasting everybody's time. You think we have nothing better to do than listen to you whistling some really thick, country-evangelical tune like *What if God was one of us?*

What has God got to do with us, you gobshite? That was Coyne's chorus. If God was one of us, he'd be a thick Garda sergeant, no question of it. A red-faced know-all, whistling through a bullet hole in his face.

I'm just trying to clarify a few matters, Corrigan explained.

Then he began to work up a line-of-enquiry. Just to demonstrate his capacity for lateral thinking, he looked around the front room

for clues, took in the picture of Coyne in uniform on the mantelpiece and behaved as though he was still treating Coyne like he was one of the lads, only to turn on him with a tricky little question. Like a left hook. Real Garda tripwire tactics. Straight out of the manual.

I believe you went to school with him? Corrigan asked.

Yeah, Coyne answered. So?

Coyne had nothing to hide, but he was far too bellicose. Definitely uncool. He should have waited a moment and then given a more composed reply. He just didn't want to fit in with the logic of daily Irish grammar any more. Those formative links that went all the way back to school. He didn't subscribe to neat Garda solutions. Motivation. Causality.

Sergeant Corrigan turned his back and looked out the window. In the hope that Coyne could not see what he was doing, he started picking his nose. Coyne couldn't believe it. This was not some discreet little knuckle wipe or nosewing scratch. This was explicit soil excavation. Hardcore. Over eighteens. Corrigan's index finger penetrating diligently and his head tilted conveniently to the left in order to dislodge big stalactites on to the floor.

Should have seen the look on Coyne's face. You'd think he'd just been handed the joke shop lighter, with the electric current running halfway up his arm. Pulled his fist back suddenly as though he was going to box the sergeant in the back of the head. Give it up! Stop that unnatural practice in my home. Go and carry out your dig in somebody else's place, you disgusting bastard.

Corrigan turned and looked Coyne in the eye. Held up the foraging finger and pointed towards the door. Coyne was more interested in the finger than anything else. Followed it wherever Corrigan pointed.

I think your son is involved in this, Pat. There may be a connection.

Forget it, Coyne exploded.

Calm down. I'm only telling you what I think.

Corrigan got ready to leave. He put his hand on the doorknob.

I'm only trying to warn you, he said. As a member of the force and all that. You should have a word with him. He knows something, Corrigan said.

Jimmy Coyne settled down very quickly at the Haven. He was transformed. He was suddenly making money and found the two

things that gave meaning to his life – love and morphine.

From the first day, he took to gerontology with great dedication. The exclusivity of being the sole youth among old people gave him a sense of immortality. They were on the way out – he was on the way up. He appreciated the feeling of indestructible health bestowed on him by the aged. Even the simple pleasure of passing by an old man on the lino corridor made Jimmy feel like he was travelling at ninety miles an hour, accelerating into the future.

His duties consisted mostly of helping sisters and nurses to lift the infirm in and out of beds and baths. Driving wheelchairs around. Bringing patients to Mass and back, up and down in the lift.

Jimmy enjoyed a sense of vigour and power, not just of his sudden athleticism, but also of moral superiority. At the Haven nursing home, he quickly assumed the role of God. Around these old people, he became the Lord of the Haven – a figure of immortality, bursting with the insurrection of youth. He was in a position to grant favours and to punish. If he felt that one of the old people was becoming too demanding, he would send them back to the end of the queue. As he passed by the rooms in his white coat and heard the helpless calls from inside, begging him to pick up a book or a ball of wool, he exercised divine power to leave them in their misery, or to reach into their fusty, apple-smelling rooms and help.

It was like final judgement day, with Jimmy Coyne as the Almighty. At times he was extremely kind and warm-hearted. But these old people occasionally incurred his wrath, and he would be forced to exact revenge. He punished old Dr Spain for being so cruel to his bedridden wife who was unable to defend herself. He left him turned the wrong way round in the church, with the brakes on his wheelchair, leaving him looking away from the altar with a smouldering pipe in his jacket pocket.

Little incidents like that made Jimmy's life worthwhile.

There was also access to pharmaceuticals. And Nurse Boland. She was a lot older than he was, a refugee from a marriage in Cork who had settled in Dublin. He spent every day of the week changing bed sheets with her. He liked her accent. He discovered that he liked to be on the left-hand side, because there was a small gap in her buttoned-up uniform that allowed him to see inside. You couldn't keep Jimmy out of the Haven nursing home.

In due course, Jimmy paid his debt to society. With his first wage packet he was determined to pay off the damage to Councillor Hogan's yacht, more for his mother's sake than his own. The job at the nursing home seemed to have changed his outlook on life and he became generous and thoughtful. His first wage packet knew no bounds and he bought gifts all round, for his mother and his grandmother. A new kettle for the flat.

Even then, there was still enough money left for Jimmy to buy new clothes for himself. His spell of nihilism was replaced by a spell of opulence. A golden age of affluence. He had become cool at last, buying the right clothes, drinking the right drinks.

It was really all about being cool, Coyne thought. Cool probably meant the same as being 'holy' used to mean. Being right and sacred and with God and all that stuff. Nowadays it was all to do with listening to the right music and being with the right women. 'Cool' was the new word for 'holy'. And Jimmy looked like he had just come out of confession, with a halo over his head. Or some kind of exclamation mark emanating from his scalp. In a state of grace! Walking with a new swagger of divine self-confidence, 'I've got the power' emblazoned on his face.

Jimmy was so full of generosity and good will that he became a bit of a philanthropist and extended his largesse to the marginalised sections of the community too. He stopped outside the shopping centre and gave the poet with the four dogs and the dreadlocks some money. People in the borough usually had more sympathy for the poet's dogs. But Jimmy gave him a bunch of dollars.

In God we trust, the poet said in amazement.

Don't mention it, Jimmy said.

The poet jumped up and started reciting bits of Yeats, bits of Heaney, and bits of his own garbled up work with renewed self-esteem and enthusiasm through his stained teeth. A listener with money. This was too good to be true. The cognoscenti had discovered him at last and he recited his work in a low monotone voice, almost inaudible at times with the weight of passion and pathos until he was whispering into Jimmy Coyne's ear. He tried to force his portfolio of scribbled gems on him, but Jimmy wanted nothing in return for his feckless donation. He smiled and walked off again, on his way back

towards the Haven nursing home, looking over his shoulder as he went.

The banks were shut and the poet with four docile dogs and dreadlocks had difficulty in finding a shop to accept the dollars. They all thought it was fake money. Even the man in the local off-licence was reluctant. Held the notes up in the air with no idea what the exchange rate was. McDonald's politely told the poet to fuck off. They didn't want him feeding Big Macs to his dogs outside the door either, because the customers might start thinking about what they were eating.

So that's how the dreadlock poet ended up in the Anchor Bar, late the same evening, desperately trying to persuade the barman to look up the paper and strike a rate.

We're not a bank, the barman was saying.

Did you rob a tourist? one of the men asked. But the docile poet was in no humour for jokes and the Anchor Bar finally obliged him with a pint. Plain ham sandwiches for the dogs tied up to the drainpipe in the laneway alongside the pub.

The news travelled fast. Somebody at the Anchor Bar was aware of the significance of dollars entering the local economy. Word got around to skipper Martin Davis and he came up to have a look for himself. Ordered a pint and casually asked the barman if he could have a look at the money.

Bud in a fuckin' sheasamh, he said to himself. It was genuine American money all right. And the docile poet was sitting in the snug, babbling to himself again with a pint and a short in front of him.

Mongi O Doherty made it out from the city to the Anchor Bar before closing time.

Hold him there, he said on his mobile in an upbeat tone. He had a feeling it wouldn't be too long before the money forced its way back into circulation. Money had gravitational pull. Money had homing instincts.

I want to hear some of that poetry, he said. Nobel stuff. With lots of Greek gods and Greek mythology. All that shite about Persephone and Philoctetes.

Mongi didn't actually make an appearance at the Anchor Bar himself. He waited outside patiently until the poet came out in his

own good time. You couldn't rush these artists. Skipper Martin Davis stayed well out of sight; he was a local man with a familiar face.

When the poet stumbled out at last, he was gently led down the lane in an exalted state of perception. He had hit a phase of great clarity and prolific creativity. He waved to the four docile muses tied to the drainpipe and was already climbing into an empty skip before he knew what was happening. For a moment, he thought he was stepping into a Greek ship. There was nothing inside except for a few bits of broken wood and cast-iron guttering. It was very private, and perfect for a spontaneous poetry reading. Mongi climbed in with him to be his audience. His hollow laugh echoing around the galleon as he walked up and down, while the poet sat on the floor of the skip, leaning back in fear and handing over a fistful of dollars from his pocket. The dogs were whimpering in the background.

I thought you guys were supposed to live in penury, Mongi bawled as he searched through the grubby portfolio. Where did you get this money?

There was a sudden loss of imagination. The poet could not think of an answer. Said he thought it was a tourist who gave it to him. A fan maybe?

How could you have a fan?

Take the money, the poet blubbered. It interferes with my art anyway. Keep the portfolio too. Some powerful stuff in there. Really good ones that would scald your hand while you were reading them.

Never get a proper bleedin' answer, Mongi muttered.

He was losing his cool. He was an entrepreneur, with no time for all this subtlety and reflection. He counted the money and put it in his pocket. Where was the rest of it? he wanted to know. Found a piece of wood with a bent six-inch nail sticking out of it. Dropped it in favour of a piece of cast-iron guttering which looked more inspirational. He knocked the poet over and put his pump-up runner across his face. Started belting scrap metal into his shins and kneecaps until the lyrics came spouting out through his trousers in blood red ink. We're supporting enough of you bastards. You do nothing for this country. You're in every pub, dead or alive, staring at people while they drink their pints. You're all a waste of food and drink, he shouted, while the docile poet was howling haikus. Stream of unconscious.

Coyne felt guilty about his son. Since Jimmy had been involved with the law, he thought of all the things he should have done with him while he was still a boy. All the fishing trips they never went on. All the football matches that other dads had brought their sons to but Coyne had no time for. He thought of all the casual conversations he should have had with Jimmy. All the moments when they might have laughed together.

It was too late now.

Or perhaps not. Perhaps Coyne could make another last-minute effort to bond with his son by taking him up to the Dublin mountains. One Saturday morning, he got him up at the crack of dawn to make egg sandwiches. Dozens of them. Enough for a whole Scout camp. They got to the outskirts of the city by bus and started walking along forest paths, not saying much. Just acknowledging each other's presence. With the wind whistling in their ears.

Maybe it was really a way of getting back in touch with Carmel. All day he walked with his son in silence. They were completely lost up there in the mountains, in awe of the emptiness. All that rocky and barren space with muted colours. The most deserted landscape on earth. Not far enough away from the suburbs to be exotic and not close enough to feel like home. It was nowhere. A bleak, disused back garden on the edge of the city.

Coyne was desperately trying to be close to his son but missing it by a mile.

Look at the stones and the rocks, he said, pointing to a moss-covered boulder with age spots of lichen marks, like an old man's face. The landscape was full of rocks. There was nothing to appreciate, only rocks and stones, and Coyne spoke about them with great passion, as though he had never seen them before.

All these years in the Gardai, Coyne said, putting his hand on Jimmy's shoulder, I've been blind. I never understood the significance of ordinary things like rocks.

The breeze across the open spaces was relentless as they sat down to eat the egg sandwiches. It hummed as Coyne unwrapped tinfoil packages and blew a hollow note from the rim of Jimmy's Coke bottle as he placed it on the ground between his feet. They smiled at each other briefly, and then looked away again, out over the purple distance of the bald mountains. In that moment they were closer than

they had ever been before, united by the ritual of food.

Except that Coyne could not go for too long without having to talk. He feared the silence. Felt the need to make some kind of speech about the petrified beauty of the place. These rocks were timeless. Rocks were all that mattered. Rocks were kings. They outclassed all the false building materials of the city, and Coyne talked about the purity of rocks with such emotional ballast that it made Jimmy cringe and long to be back in the Haven nursing home. Jimmy was begging the aliens to land right there in that desolate spot and take him away, rescue him from his father's sobbing intimacy.

Think of the infinity contained in those rocks, Coyne said with caramel sentimentality. The history they've witnessed. The link with the past.

Jimmy started wrapping up the left-over sandwiches. Anything to release him from this choking passion.

I know, I talk too much, Coyne said.

And then, at the last minute, he suddenly remembered his fatherly duty. Carmel had urged him to have a man-to-man talk with Jimmy. On top of all he had said about rocks, he tried to introduce Jimmy to the facts of life. At the worst possible moment, in a casual, laddish way, Coyne started asking him what a condom was. Then started talking about real love with tears in his eyes.

It's a hoor to be in love, he said.

I wouldn't know, Jimmy answered.

You'll find out one of these days, son. It's a hoor to be in love.

As they descended from the barren heights into the more populated foothills, the forest sanctity of their walk began to disappear. Something about the sight of civilisation put an end to the special status they had achieved on their journey together. The escape was foiled. Jimmy saw that his father hated going back home. Expected him to go straight into a monologue about low-density, car-dependent housing schemes that had ruined the outskirts of the city. But instead, they had something else to think about.

Who should they run into but Sergeant Corrigan? On his day off. After trekking all over the mountain range, they came back down to greener spring meadows where people stepped out of their cars for a breath of fresh air.

They felt entitled to a kind of sad elitism as they re-entered society. They had endured the intimacy of rock and bogland. They had endured each other. They had survived silence and discovered a deep spiritual link with the emptiness and the wind and the sun sloping across open spaces. A brown landscape disappearing into the postcard distance over ridges. And beyond, banks of clouds that looked like even taller mountains rising up into the sky. All that melancholy attachment was carried back into the city by Coyne like a flame of resentment. What they had to contend with now was not anonymity and loneliness, but recognition. They were welcomed back into the arms of banality by Brendan Corrigan and his family.

Corrigan out there playing the father with his own two sons, aged around eleven and twelve. He was virtually sending a message to Coyne, saying – look, I'm a father too. And I've got every right to walk around here as well, you know. You're not the only one.

It destroyed the experience of being alone in the mountains. The bastard had conspired to be there when Coyne came back. Just when Coyne had created a fragile bond with his son, they were dragged brutally back into the crass reality of everyday existence.

Coyne – the man without subtext.

And what was that in Sergeant Corrigan's hand? A hurling stick. Coyne could not believe his eyes as he watched Corrigan walking up the grassy slope, taking out his *sliotar*, giving it an almighty whack and sending the ball up into the meadow for the boys to chase after. Two strong young sons, running as fast as they could to get there first. Searching around eagerly in the grass until one of them found it and they came running back again. Off-duty Sergeant Corrigan with a fierce red face on him as he repeated the whole thing all over again. Whack. Sending the ball in a beautiful arc all the way up along the slope again with the boys chasing and yelping.

I mean, what the fuck was this in aid of? Coyne thought. The man didn't even see the symbolism of what he was doing. Training the sons of Ireland to fetch, like dogs. Like greyhounds.

From his hospital bed, the docile poet renounced all forms of personal wealth. He made a vow of poverty. Never again would he allow money, and especially foreign money, to corrupt his creative soul. From now on, he told the nurses trying to wash his dreadlocks, he would rely

only on the hospitality of the people. He would return to the ancient bardic order of praising those who lavished courtesy on him and heaping derision on those who abused him. He was writing sonnets to the nurses, even if they wouldn't let him smoke. And God help the man who worked him over in the skip, because the poet was far from docile with words and was already working on a red hot, scrotum-burning, invective epic against Mongi O Doherty. Though he didn't know the name of his tormentor, the poet wished him the most eloquent forms of ill health and everlasting death throes – may you live for ever on a life-support machine, may you watch yourself dying in the mirror.

The poet was reluctant to show the curse-poem to anyone before it was finished. Detectives were mystified because he gave no explanation apart from the fact that there seemed to be a bad omen around American currency. In God we trust, at our own peril. In God we trust to snatch the money right out of our hands again. In God we trust, the tight-fisted bastard!

I cursed all foreign money... the poet began to sing, and Sergeant Corrigan finally made a vague connection with the exchange of dollars at the Anchor Bar, but there the trail foundered in a fog of superstition and lyrical obfuscation.

I can't ascertain a thing from that poet, Corrigan said.

Coyne went to visit Tommy Nolan's sister Marlene, a small nervous woman with a ponytail and freckles all over her face. She wore a shiny tracksuit with FORCE written across the front. Spoke with a smoked-out voice and lit up various cigarettes that she never finished as she brought Coyne inside and talked to him about Tommy.

There was a huge TV in the living room.

He loved watching snooker, Marlene explained.

There were pictures on the mantelpiece of Marlene and Tommy as children. Happy times by the harbour with their father. Another one with all their cousins outside, on the street. Now she was the sister of a murdered man.

The Gardai had already gone through everything in Tommy's room. Coyne was proud of him for keeping his place so tidy. He admired Tommy's sense of order. His snooker cue standing in the corner. A shelf with Western videos. And one of the neatest toolboxes ever. A masterpiece of originality and adaptation: a six-pack wine

carton with a handle that had been remodelled as a toolbox containing a hammer, screwdrivers, chisels and tape measure all in their own little compartments where the Australian wine bottles used to be.

Marlene had tears in her eyes thinking of it.

Coyne made an effort to console her, but said only stupid things. Rushed into great superlatives of praise and condolence. Tommy will be remembered, Coyne said with great feeling.

Marlene looked surprised. It sounded almost like a threat to her privacy. People like the Nolans didn't want to be remembered. They were afraid of public acknowledgement.

There should be a monument, Coyne said.

What monument? She didn't like the sound of this at all.

He was better than all the rest of them put together, Coyne blubbered. He was suddenly overcome with a great limestone lump in his throat and his lip quivered. Here he was, trying to console Tommy's sister and he ended up crying himself. It was pathetic. Maybe it was all this counselling that had begun to open the floodgates.

Do you want any of his things? she offered. She didn't know what to do with them.

Coyne looked around the room. He was thinking Tommy thoughts. Trying to imagine Tommy's day. As though they were going to be best friends from now on. In retrospect. The great posthumous friendship between the living and the dead. He went home with red rims around his eyes, carrying the wine-carton toolbox.

Coyne was entertaining his emotions. He was getting personally worked up. Involving himself in every local tragedy. Allowing every piece of collective blame to impact straight on his psyche. He was prey to every small downturn in the weather – every little sign of ecological doom. He shouted at the radio, railing against corruption as if it affected him personally. Every change in his country, every sign of progress was an assault on his persona. As though he had become the custodian of purity.

Ms Dunford felt he was overburdened by worldly matters. She continued to try and unlock his mind to find out what made him so vulnerable.

You can't take on the whole world, Pat, she said. You can't solve everything.

She mentioned the possibility of joining group therapy. Perhaps it would be good for him to do something like psycho-drama. Come to terms with his past by re-enacting the traumatic events in front of other people. There was a lot to be said for group sessions.

The first duty is to yourself, Pat. You must enjoy life. That's what we're here for – to have fun.

Coyne was appalled by such a selfish construction of life. That's exactly what the problem was. There was too much fun. People with no other aim in life but gratification. Stuffing themselves.

We're not here to enjoy ourselves, Coyne said.

He would not submit to the tyranny of fun because he was devoted to sorting out the world. His heart went out to all kinds of people he never met. A lot of things had to be put right first before he could start enjoying himself. He was thinking global stuff here as much as local. And what about people in history. How could you forget what happened? How could you turn your back on all that and start tucking in?

Coyne's friend and mentor Fred Metcalf felt it was something more congenital. Coyne had inherited a lament in his head. It was the lonely echo of the Irish language across the Connemara shoreline. He could only think of what was gone, keeping faith with what had disappeared.

Our likes will never be seen again.

It's the sad gene, Fred said. We all have it.

In the blood?

Yes, in the blood. And also not in the blood.

What do you mean?

Whenever they say that people have something in the blood, they're usually talking about exactly the kind of thing that's not in the blood. A nation of people can carry things in various ways, Fred explained. You know the way animals carry their genes from one generation to the next, along biological lines. Well, human evolution is different. We carry genes outside our bodies, through songs and stories. Race memory.

Fred was right. If you thought of Joe Heaney or Caruso – the greatest singers of all time – their genes travelled the world through crackled recordings. Sex was very limited. Samuel Beckett's genes were

always more likely to be carried forth into everybody's consciousness through his work than through procreation. These people sent their spiralling messages out like floating dandelion seeds, like parachuting regiments of words drifting across the fields.

Coyne was facing extinction. He remembered being in Connemara as a child. He remembered the sad coastline of Béal an Daingin where he learned Irish. He carried with him a kind of elated loneliness, a great melancholia that sprang from people and the surrounding peninsulas and inlets where he lived.

The all-or-nothing impact of the sea on the shoreline formed his imagination. Every day the landscape changed beyond all recognition when the water receded and left the shore behind. In the morning, the tide could fill the land with great blue and white hope. By afternoon, it migrated almost a mile out from the coast road and the houses, leaving nothing but a vast disillusioned coast where he played alone among the rocks, watching the crabs running sideways at his feet in surprise. Breathing heavily with asthma, with the constant cry of snared prey in his lungs. The high latrine tang of the seaweed in his nostrils, and the thirty-five different Irish names for seaweed in his ears.

The ebb and flow of Coyne's psyche. Standing on the deserted tideline as a boy. A lifeless landscape from which the sea had been drained away and the entire foreshore had been left uncovered, like a great weakness. Limp manes of black seaweed draped across abandoned rocks as though the coast had been struck by a fatal disease. Nothing but the swirling shrieks of curlews and gannets and dogs barking in the distance with deceptive echoes. Everybody had gone off to America and left him behind.

Coyne made another call to Killmurphy, this time from a coin box. Just to keep the pressure on. Early one evening, just when the household was sure to be entering a nice relaxed atmosphere and Killmurphy was probably having his first gin and tonic.

You shouldn't have done it, Killjoy. You and your wife. Nora, isn't it? Living up there in your nice house.

Coyne recalled all the reasons why he was angry at Killjoy. The writ coming in the door. Carmel in tears every day for weeks, thinking

it was the end, with disgrace descending all around them. Until her mother finally came to the rescue and put a financial package into place that made Coyne fully subservient and beholden. A failed breadwinner.

Killjoy, you bastard. You'll pay for it. I'll be keeping in touch with you.

The moment had come for Coyne to try and get back with Carmel. It was her birthday. A perfect day for reconciliation. For the past few weeks Coyne had woken up every night talking to her. Dreaming about her rubbing lotion on his back. Dreaming about her eyes. And her laughter.

How had things got this bad?

We belong to each other, Coyne kept saying, like the words of a cheap pop song. He was trapped in the eternal Euro hit of sentimental longing, trying to find some more original way of saying the same thing.

Baby, this is serious! Stop fucking around with my heart, 'cause it's tearing me apart. And don't close the door, because I can't take it any more. You know, love can be so cruel, it will turn me into a mule. Coyne had the fire inside, that cannot be denied.

He hung around the cosmetics department of Brown Thomas trying to choose a gift for her. Something generous but not feckless. Nothing worse than giving her an over-signified birthday present that would be misinterpreted, ultimately, as an audacious advance. He needed something romantic and perfume was by far the most conventional method of approach. To hell with it, Coyne thought, why not buy something expensive?

Trying to make up his mind, he sniffed enough bottles to wipe out an entire colony of laboratory rats. He was suffocating. Any minute, he would be forced to get his inhaler out. Collapse on the floor, gasping, with a little crowd of people standing over him saying: oh my God. Who was he?

What evolutionary platform had the Irish arrived at now, Coyne thought. Their identity was what they purchased. All around him tills were ringing, credit cards sliding, people making choices with great conviction, while Coyne was stuck at the same counter in a state of perplexed consumer panic. Incapable of making an expedient decision.

The assistant with the orange face mask was doing her best in the circumstances, spraying jets of expensive effluent on her bare arm in polite desperation. The Irishman was becoming very fussy altogether. Used to be a time when they would sneak in with a newspaper, point to the nearest bottle and say: wrap it up, love. But Coyne was the new breed of Irishman, choosing conscientiously, by way of elimination. After all, it was no longer that straightforward. The tricky territory of postmodern separation, of ex-husband and wife relationships, required some thought. Maybe even an environmental impact study. You couldn't buy any old slurry stink like Eternity that her mother had probably given her already. Was there nothing called Obnoxious?

Coyne, the great prevaricator. The multi-optional man, terrorised by choice. Give me the reek of rotting seaweed. Give me haystacks and horse shite. Dunghills and decomposing leaves. The department store stocked every malodorous whiff in history except the one he wanted – the scent Carmel wore when he first met her. He could still remember it clearly. Like fuchsia hedges, laced with cut grass and a subtle background hint of diesel exhaust fumes on a late summer afternoon. Some cheap and ordinary perfume that had long disappeared off the shelves along with his innocence. That was it, the simple romance of the ordinary was no longer available.

Coyne became distracted by a young woman carrying a shoulder bag. He watched as she discreetly sprayed a quick blast of perfume on her wrist, then dropped the bottle into the bag. It was that easy. Only took a second.

Coyne was fascinated. For a man who had spent so much of his life upholding the law, the subversive elegance of this crime suddenly seemed attractive. An act of civil disobedience that confronted his entire devotion to order. Self-service socialism. Coyne had observed her before in the handbag department where he had already spent hours loitering around, sniffing leather, feeling the texture of imitation snakeskin, going through the whole existential breakdown over handbags and finally coming to the decision that it would be an insult to give Carmel a gift like that. I mean, what kind of total gobshite would buy his ex-wife a handbag?

Here! I hope you get mugged, is what it was saying.

Coyne was amazed, as much by his own tolerance as by the sheer

audacity of the shoplifter. It seemed easier to steal than to buy. He noticed that she was wearing high-heeled shoes. Strange, he thought, because Coyne's advice to Carmel was always to think of escape. Never make a purchase without assessing the flight implications. Always wear shoes that you can run for your life in.

But it was already too late. The young woman was surrounded by security guards. An older woman in plain clothes approached her, and there was a minor struggle when two security guards took the shoplifter by the arms. One of them speaking into a walkie-talkie.

Coyne told himself not to get involved. You don't need any more complications. Don't jeopardise the compensation claim, like a good man. But he had seen too many of these arrests in the past in the course of his work. Some of them genuine thieves. Some of them just doing it for fun. Others that would break his heart. For the first time, he allowed himself to sympathise with a criminal.

Excuse me, he intervened, before they had a chance to lead her away.

The security personnel looked troubled. He drew the store detective aside and explained that the young woman was not right in the head. Mentally challenged, he said. A ward of court, just out for the day. He apologised for letting her out of his sight. Said he would pay for the goods in question and tried to take the young woman by the arm.

Coyne was proud of himself, thinking all this up on the spot.

The shoplifter assumed a sad, orphaned appearance.

Hold on a minute, one of the security men said. His chest was bursting through his uniform from over-exercise. He had short brown hair, cut neatly into the shape of a square at the back of the neck. A real neck box. In addition to which he possessed a really dangerous set of canine teeth. Coyne returned to the fundamental implications of Darwinism in contemporary Ireland: whether you still needed all that primitive weaponry to bite into a Whopper. He watched the teeth with the fascination of a natural scientist as the security man spoke in his talking clock voice.

I am not at liberty to discuss with you the particulars of this case.

I'll pay, Coyne said, holding out his money.

It is the policy of this store to prosecute offenders, the security man persisted.

Somebody switch off this shaggin' neck box, please.

Coyne had always seen security staff as his allies around the city. His friend, Fred Metcalf, was a security guard. They were on the same side of the crime war. But something was happening to Coyne. He suddenly felt like destroying the shop and sending this red-haired primate with the hyena teeth crashing into a rack of Calvin Klein sunglasses. Coyne the great liberator. Of course, he was out of his mind getting into this. He could be charged as an accessory. And what if he made a run for it? They would come after him with video evidence. Coyne would appear on *Crimeline*, like a national celebrity. Have you seen this man? And sure as hell, Carmel's mother would spot it. That's him, she would hiss with glee in her armchair. Delighted to turn him in. Coyne, like an eejit on TV, running towards the exit with a young woman in high heels. That would be the end of Coyne and Carmel.

You're in this together, the sabretoothed security man said.

Coyne became a great persuader. He was on higher ground. Told them he was an off-duty Garda. Paid for the handbag and a bottle of Eternity, as well as some luminous green underwear. Coyne was a little embarrassed by these items being paraded so openly for all to see. The cashier demonstrably folded them at shoulder height. Republican underwear. The wearing of the green!

Her name was Corina. She was Romanian. She offered to buy him a cup of coffee, which, she felt, was the least she could do after him mounting such a daring rescue. Coyne gratefully accepted his reward and they stood in the street for an awkward moment before they walked away in the direction of an Italian café.

The city was changing. There was a greater selection of cafés in the capital now, and people were beginning to enjoy the notion of diversity as they sat over narcotic cups of coffee, with shopping bags at their feet. They had moved away from the mono-culture of tea and gaudy pink cakes, of rock buns and cream doughnuts with the worm of bright red jam. There was a time when Irish life was concealed with enormous skill behind cups of tea. When the paraphernalia of kettles and teapots provided the stage props of the nation's drama and gave people things to do with their hands while the subtext of ordinary life remained hidden behind the clatter of delph and stirring

spoons. Now, things were beginning to look more European. More cappuccino.

Are all Romanians such bad shoplifters? Coyne wanted to know as they sat down.

I never did it before, she said.

Fair enough, it was a promising début, he had to admit. But he wanted to know why she needed to put herself at such risk in the first place. Was shoplifting an act of revolution? His experience told him that there was something else behind this. There was always a cause. A Garda narrative.

I have to make money fast, she said in a burst of anger. Clearly, she objected to this interrogation. Coyne saw defiance in her brown eyes.

Stands to reason, Coyne said. He was also trying to make money fast, through compensation. Who wasn't?

I owe a lot of money, she said. I can't pay it.

She was already working as hard as she could in a fast food restaurant nearby but there was no way that she could meet her debts. She had expected affluence. Streets paved with gold.

Coyne would have suggested some insurance scam. It would make more sense, financially. She would be dealing in larger amounts, with less risk. Maybe a whiplash claim. People were getting rich on car crashes.

Corina began to apologise for her crime. She wasn't really cut out for it, she hinted. As though Coyne was the host and she was the visitor who had been caught pilfering the silver cutlery. Her momentary remorse allowed Coyne to ask more questions, and slowly she revealed how she had come to Ireland. He got the information in small increments – the journey by sea, the long hours locked inside a cabin.

Christ, he thought. These were the Blasket Islanders coming back. The tide of emigration was turning. Here they were, the first of them – thousands who had fled poverty and were now returning at last.

You're coming back, he said.

She didn't understand this enigmatic shift of gear in Coyne's attitude. He was speaking with great feeling now. Looking at her through watery eyes.

The islanders, he said.

Corina shook her head and smiled at this complete misunderstanding. It had nothing to do with any language barrier either, because the Romanians were the best linguists in the world, and she had already picked up a number of key Dublin colloquial phrases, such as I'm broke. I'm skinned. Altogether!

She had difficulty understanding what Coyne was saying now. He was entertaining his emotions again. He wanted to help her, give her money. Then he decided to write down his phone number for her. But she looked at him accusingly. Pushed the piece of paper away.

What do you want?

If you're in trouble, he offered.

I'm going to split, she said. This had obviously gone too far. She got up from her seat. I have to meet somebody, she said. She pushed the handbag and its contents into Coyne's lap. Thanked him and walked away from the table, leaving Coyne behind, looking up with a helpless expression of rejected kindness.

Wait, he said. I'm serious. If you're stuck?

He went running after her through the café. Knocking his own chair over with a great clack of undignified urgency as he chased her with the shopping bag in his hand.

The Anchor Bar, he said.

But it sounded sad, like he was looking for a favour from her in return for the rescue. She turned around and squared up to him. Looked as though she was going to punch him. She didn't trust Coyne's hospitality any more. Didn't need his help. Like she was saying: I can look after myself, you know. I don't need a man to sort things out for me. Then she was gone. And Coyne went back to his seat and sat down.

Mongi O Doherty was such a dedicated capitalist that he perceived cash as an awkward medium, an obstacle to the flow of capital. The physical collection of money was a nuisance which slowed down the whole process of amassing wealth. The trend was towards the virtual transactions of credit cards, to ease the resistance and make the concept of money more spiritual. Payments should be like prayers. Decades of the rosary. Novenas. In God we trust! Cash was a grubby, secular substance which he didn't like to handle personally.

Corina first had to pay her money over to a third party in a city

pub. It was a lodgement, so to speak. After which a phone call was made on a mobile phone, and she was then instructed to go to another specified pub to meet Mongi O Doherty himself. An audience with the money Buddha.

The instalment was disappointing, is what he was there to tell her. He appreciated the sight of hard currency coming into his possession, but the amount was too small, that's all.

I mean, how do you expect any of your ex-Soviet countries ever to integrate fully into Europe if you can't speed up the rate of repayments?

We're doing our best, Corina said.

Mongi forced himself to be pleasant and courteous. He had an idea that might help her. A kind of Marshall Plan, if you like, that would enable her to make better use of her natural resources and generate income more rapidly. He bought her a drink, which she tried to decline, looking at the daiquiri with the cherry and the plastic sabre with some amusement. If only this could be converted back into money to pay off more of her debt.

Initially Mongi was offended by her lack of gratitude. He explained that sometimes it was good to look like you had money. Money had a sacred element that gave off an aura. It made people 'holy', or cool. As a former moneylender, he was in a position to tell her that the appearance of wealth was often enough to achieve paradise.

Corina looked at Mongi's dress code to see if it matched the philosophy. He wore shiny blue tracksuit bottoms with white stripes down the side of the leg, and a T-shirt with sleek greyhounds running at great speed across his chest. He wore white socks and black slip-on shoes.

I have some contacts who could point you in the right direction, he said. You could buy some plenary indulgences, if you get my drift.

Indulgences? Corina was listening. Sipping poison.

It doesn't need to be that difficult, Mongi said, looking her up and down. If you put on a bit of make-up. Rob some decent clothes. I know people in that line of business who could see you right.

What are you talking about?

You have a great body, he said at last. You know what I'm saying. You could use it.

Dracu, she said, getting up to leave.

Mongi put a firm hand on her arm. There were debts to be paid, he insisted. A boat trip on a luxury trawler, with cabin accommodation. He needed a quick repayment schedule. His patience was running out.

I'm not doing purgatory for you, he said.

It was like the old days. Carmel's birthday and everybody sitting around the table in the happy Irish home. Coyne and Jimmy back in the bosom of the family and Carmel's mother bringing out the cake that looked like a UFO with a forest of lit candles on top. It was Carmel's idea to bring everyone together for occasions like this. Even if they were separated, there were some essential family rituals that need not be lost.

Mrs Gogarty was sceptical. Coyne noticed that she had started using the word 'actually' all the time. It was a theatrical distancing technique, and Coyne wanted to call her Mrs Actually, only that he was on his best behaviour and didn't want to squander the privilege of being allowed to attend the party. Coyne had a few drinks before he arrived. Heavy smell of alcohol all over the birthday cake.

Jennifer and Nuala were the only ones who were misbehaving. Fighting among themselves, calling each other bitch and cow over some clothes they had borrowed and not given back, until Mrs Gogarty said she'd had enough. This was Carmel's birthday. They should all respect that.

Carmel was stupefied by Coyne's gift. A real leather shoulder bag and a bottle of Eternity inside. How did you know, Pat? she exclaimed. She had nearly run out of perfume. And it was her favourite too.

Jennifer and Nuala took it off her and sprayed themselves immediately. The air was thick already.

While they were occupied with the scent, Carmel put her hand into the bag and took out the green underwear. Looked at it for a moment in disbelief, then pushed it back quickly, out of sight. Mrs Actually missed nothing. She had seen the outrageous, ex-husband sexual proposal that was contained in this gift. Generosity is a form of conquest, she always maintained.

You shouldn't have, Carmel said, holding up the bag and feeling the leather. It's too generous, Pat.

I'll be getting compensation, Coyne blubbered.

She kissed him dutifully. A courtesy kiss. Cheek to cheek, with a large slice of air in between, and Mrs Actually monitoring the whole thing at close range like a referee in a boxing ring. Ready to shout 'break' and separate the contestants.

Coyne was chuffed with himself. So much so that he started cracking jokes with Jennifer and Nuala. Taking the sweeping brush and pretending to sweep the kitchen floor. Then helping to carry cups and dishes out to the kitchen until Mrs Actually blocked his way, taking things out of his hands.

Mrs Gogarty, they should name a drink after you, he said. She gave him a fierce look and spun around on her hind legs.

This is the way things should be again, Coyne thought. Of course it was all his fault in the first place. He was the first to admit it. His drinking. His fooling around. His moods. But he was ready to go straight over that waterfall of domestic bliss as he watched Carmel laughing as she used to in the old days. He could not see why they had ever separated.

It's insane, Carmel, he wanted to shout.

Despite all the good will, Coyne could not persuade Carmel to go to the pub with him. Take one step inside a public bar with that man, and you'll never come out, Mrs Gogarty warned. Actually, taking one step in any direction with that man is a fatal mistake.

Carmel didn't know how she could allow herself to go out with her ex-husband on her birthday. It would mean that she had nobody else in her life and was still depending on Coyne for emotional partnership. It was for the sake of the children, she told herself. And in some respects she took pity on Coyne since the fire. Was it possible that his victim-hero status was slowly winning her over? She considered the expensive gifts he had bought for her. The least she could do was go for a walk with him. But she was not ready to give up her independence to be seen in some squalid pub.

Instead she suggested Irish dancing. I need a partner, she said.

Coyne didn't catch the irony.

You've had bad experiences with Irish dancing, Carmel.

She was willing to put it all behind her. Everybody is into it now, she said. There was a set-dancing revival club in every suburb, she added with great enthusiasm.

Riverfluke, in other words, Coyne muttered. People hopping around to *The Stacks of Barley.*

Carmel was keen to relive her childhood. She had won a lot of medals doing Tara Brooch dancing as a little girl. A cross between show jumping and the goosestep.

The country is changing, she said. People are proud of their heritage. It will be good for your chest as well.

Irish dancing was no way to repair your lungs, or your marriage, Coyne thought. But what could he do? He agreed to join her, even just to carry out a discreet little quality control check on this latest revival. He was the custodian of heritage. Coyne had learned a few steps himself when he was a young lad. Of course, he could have done with another drink beforehand, just to work up the courage. With enough drink he might even have felt he was rejoining society. Getting into the new Ireland.

But it was too much to expect. Coyne was off on his own ideological counter-attack.

For fucksake, he muttered when he saw the incompetence of the dancers. What a graceless pack of heifers.

Pat, come on. Just get into it, she said. You'll love it.

Coyne waited on the sidelines. What was going on here? These people didn't know the difference between Irish dancing and a haka. A woman wobbled past him with a low-cut dress, breasts churning around like she was making butter. Tina Turner gyrating on the Cliffs of Moher. A man stomping around with her like a cowboy, kicking dust and waltzing on bandy legs, like he'd been sitting on a horse all day. Coyne wanted to go up to him and give him a clout on the back of the head. Give that up. Dance properly. Stop moving your neck, you blackguard. And stop that pelvic thrusting, all of you. That's got nothing to do with Irish dancing.

Don't be such a purist, Carmel said. It's all evolving.

Look at them wiggling, Coyne said in despair, pointing directly at the woman shaking her fuselage. He watched the new hip movements with great alarm. Where was the subtle introspection of Irish culture? The secrecy? The provocative understatement?

You're stuck in the past, Carmel said.

This is all wrong, Coyne raged.

As far as he was concerned, it had everything to do with the

past. Irish dancing had its own unique swing. It was a triumph of control, with none of this cheap Riverfluke grandeur. How could you hope to merge humility with tacky exhibitionism? It was a cultural contradiction in terms, like a convertible Ferrari with a thatched roof. Where was the grace that made old women in Connemara look like young girls with their lightfooted dignity?

Coyne had lost it. The one chance he had of getting back with Carmel was about to be aimlessly thrown away on this primitive argument. He was determined to show these people what Irish dancing was about. An exhibition they would not forget. He took a puff on his inhaler and leapt out like an okapi. Like he had fallen out of the sky. With stunning poise. His shoulders twitching in time to the music, a look of abject dementia in his open eyes, and his self-raising hair standing up on his head with great vigour. He moved as steadily as a ship. Only the heel every now and again slamming down on the wooden floor, punctuating the beat with an emphatic bang as he swung Carmel around the dance floor. He was back in the Aran Islands, dancing in the Kilronan Hall, with the generator purring outside.

But as usual, Coyne went too far. People looked up in shock. Suburban novices, frightened by the sheer authenticity of his movements. They left a big gap of respect around him. Coyne the mountainy man, as cold and passionate as the dawn, yahooing and leaving casualties all around him. Swinging the wiggle out of Tina Turner and sending her practically into orbit. Until she was so seasick that she had to sit down with her head between her legs. White in the face. And her husband holding out a glass of water towards her.

Carmel was furious as she dragged Coyne outside. He was a bogman. Dancing was all about courtesy. Not some contest of strength.

Go back to aerobics, he shouted over his shoulder. You pack of flatfooted gobshites.

And then outside the hall, Coyne started coughing like he was going to die before he could justify his crusading intervention. Stood there with his hand against the wall for a clear ten minutes, rasping and dragging up a string of emerald green rosary beads which he spat on the ground outside like a warning to all dancers.

Take the wiggle out of Irish dancing!

Carmel drove home in silence. Couldn't wait to get rid of him. Coyne had definitely blown it this time. It was the end all right. Though when she pulled up outside his flat, he tried to cling on to some hope of a reunion. Refused to get out of the car and asked her straight out if she wanted to come inside for a cup of coffee. He still had a lot to say about Irish culture.

The idea of it. She looked astonished. *And I'd like to know where – you got the notion*, is what she was saying with her eyes. Trying to make a pass at your ex-wife, for Godsake.

I've got to go, she said.

It's you and me, Carmel, he said with another gust of passion, as if he'd met her for a tryst. We're inextricably linked.

She pushed him out of the car. Alarmed. Drove away and left him standing.

We're inextricably linked, he repeated to the empty street.

Coyne's attitude to women needed urgent exploration. Ms Dunford thought he was not only psychotic but dangerously unbalanced. He was in love with Carmel but he couldn't take his mind off women in general for more than a minute at a time. He admitted to having an uncontrollable fetish about tartan skirts, bra straps and knicker lines.

His relationship with women was more like a contest. Some big gender warfare, brought on perhaps by the way he was educated in single-sex schools, and the way the men and women gathered on opposite sides of the dancehalls in Béal an Daingin and in the Aran Islands. Or the men gathered in groups together outside Mass. And men together in the pub. It simplified everything into a clearly defined go-get-them role, but also left him without a vocabulary to deal with women, except as a lover. Love was easy. Talking was hard.

Why did you leave your wife?

I don't really know, he said.

Was it freedom? Some need to liberate yourself?

Coyne resented the question. This was like a mental grope. Scraping at his innermost secrets. He protected himself, speaking in riddles. She had identified the problem, something awry in the nature of men; some deep, ongoing crisis that they carried around with them all the time, even when they looked happy and amused and well adjusted. Coyne was restless. He could not trust himself.

I'm not in control, he said. I never was.

You need control?

I just never know where I stand, that's all.

While Coyne was living with Carmel, he wanted to get away. Now he couldn't wait to get back with her. Maybe there was some profound contradiction in the male psyche that could never be reconciled, except through the active pursuit of desires – women, goals, music, football. Men like Coyne were never stationary. They were like mackerel, without the air-bag necessary to maintain a steady place in the water. They were forced to keep moving all the time, chasing around the pelagic depths of the ocean at forty kilometres an hour, all day and all night, unable to stay still for any length of time. Coyne the restless mackerel, like a channel surfer's nightmare: obsessed with what he was missing.

You should join one of those men's groups, Ms Dunford advised.

What?

A lot of men are starting to meet and discuss their problems these days.

What the hell was she on about? No way was he going to join up with some bunch of wackos in short trousers talking about their feelings and getting in touch with their instincts. Out there in some forest with bow and arrows, dancing around the campfire, chanting and bawling like lost elks. Primordial men, getting it all off their chests.

In any case, what Coyne wanted could never really be discussed out in the open without destroying it. There would always be something dark and unspeakable about his desires, some innate contradiction. Coyne was a walking paradox.

Sergeant Corrigan was trying to expand his investigation. He was casting a wider net, so to speak, and the biblical metaphor was appropriate since he had begun to investigate the entire fishing community. He went through every trawler. Spoke to skippers and sailors, some of whom had been asleep below deck when Tommy Nolan met his death. They must have heard something.

He encountered a conspiracy of ignorance. Empty nets. Fish-head silence.

Normally Sergeant Corrigan was more inclined to employ DIY

metaphors. He was one of those who never stopped improving things. A true handyman. Every available minute off duty was spent sawing and drilling. At the weekend, he wandered around his home, measuring everything in sight.

He had come down one morning early to do a few measurements at the harbour. As far as most of the fishing people were concerned, Corrigan should stay at home and measure his own mickey. They were seriously pissed off with this DIY stuff. Watched with contempt as Corrigan climbed down the side of trawlers, measuring the gap between boats and the quay. The angle of fall. The slack of mooring ropes.

Sergeant Corrigan seemed to concentrate on skipper Martin Davis.

Is the tide coming in or going out? he asked.

Martin Davis was a busy man, and if the sergeant had nothing more serious in mind, he would like to get on with his work. Corrigan got a bit testy. He didn't like to be rushed on his DIY jobs. He was the type of man who asked questions a second time if he didn't get an answer. He belonged to the measure-twice-cut-once persuasion.

You facilitated Tommy's funeral, he said accusingly. You helped dispose of the ashes.

Tommy did a few jobs for me, Davis answered with a hint of genuine respect for the dead. I was indebted to him. He was a great guy.

But Corrigan was never going to be happy with the answer. He was there to measure things again and again. Maybe everything was not quite fish fingers at the harbour, he thought.

The skipper squinted against the sun. The glare reflecting across the surface of the harbour was suddenly too much for him. Besides, Martin Davis was getting very irritated at being mistaken for a plank of timber. Sergeant Corrigan had a pencil behind his ear and looked at Martin Davis as though he could build shelves on his face.

From there, Sergeant Corrigan went straight on to the Haven nursing home where he interviewed Jimmy Coyne again. Another vital piece of information had emerged – a discrepancy, if you like, between Jimmy's version of events and his friend Gussy's. Of course, it had to be taken into consideration that they were both drunk and stoned on

the night in question. Neither of them was reliable. The Sergeant was trying to work out why Jimmy had stayed at the harbour after Gussy went home.

I don't know, Jimmy said. I fell asleep.

A real schoolboy answer, Corrigan thought. This time he found Jimmy's behaviour strange. A little distant. Not quite in touch with reality. He formed the opinion that Jimmy was either very guilty, or else he had taken some kind of narcotic substance that prevented him from thinking clearly and giving rational answers. It was like talking to somebody with senile dementia.

Did you encounter Tommy Nolan?

You're in the vestibule, Jimmy said.

What's that supposed to mean?

Jimmy shrugged as though he didn't know what he meant himself.

Look, I can take you into the station if you like, Corrigan threatened.

They quickly reached a kind of stalemate in the reception room of the Haven. It was clear that Corrigan had nothing more than suspicion on his side. Just a gut feeling. Hunch science. They sat looking at the calendar depicting a smiling over-seventies couple jogging through a forest and a schnauzer running beside them, trying hard to keep up. Lactulose! Like clockwork! Corrigan's mouth had gone into the silent whistle formation. Like he could have done with a spoonful of lactulose himself.

Jimmy Coyne was in love. At the old people's home, surrounded by all that morbidity and decline, he discovered a great longing for life. He followed Nurse Boland around wherever he could. He brushed against her accidentally and she punched him back, accidentally. They slagged each other all the time and brightened up the mausoleum wards, as she called them. The age difference was meaningless and Jimmy told the old people he loved her. For the inhabitants of the home it was like a live soap opera unfolding in front of their eyes.

The nuns who administered the nursing home felt that Jimmy was a deeply caring person. He understood the needs of these people, the casualties of time clinging on to life day by day. Sad old people and happy old people, holding on to their memories, encouraged by visits from their relatives. He understood the frustration of age and observed

how Mrs Broadbent would grope for an hour or more, trying to find a mini-torch that she kept under her pillow. Others were fumbling around with their memories. Asking what time it was. Whether they'd had their breakfast yet when it was already time to go to bed.

One of the patients, Mr Grogan, always had trouble putting his trousers on. A former high-ranking member of the Civil Service, he was still determined to fend for himself but came down to Mass every second day with some garment inside out. Once Jimmy found him in his room, late in the evening, with one foot in his jacket sleeve.

But this was nothing when compared to the bodily failures which characterised this home. The entire place was held together by ointments and eye drops, baby oil and disinfectant. Not to mention slow-releasing morphine. Key words that had entered into Jimmy's vocabulary. The old people were infants at the latter end of the arc, losing words. Saying Ma Ma and Da Da for the last time, their skills reducing by the day. Jimmy soon got to know their smells: fish, sardines, leather and banana. He knew the pungent stench of their incontinence sheets, the blend of perished rubber and urine. But he also knew the softness of old people. The frailty of their bones. The beauty in their wrinkled folds of flesh. He helped them to the bathroom. He helped Nurse Irene to wash them. Lifted them in and out of the bath.

Jimmy loved the squeaking sound when Nurse Boland put on the rubber gloves. Every day he helped her with fresh sheets and pillowcases. Most of the time, he hindered her. Playing games and trying to annoy her; throwing water at her until she picked up a stick belonging to one of the old people and started chasing after him, through the rooms, across the beds and along the corridor. Nurse Boland at last managing to whack Jimmy on the backside and extracting a yelp of pain and helpless laughter out of him.

The shocking speed of their games made the old people dizzy. They could see what was coming, as though this romance was being played out for them vicariously. And one day, like a leap of evolution, the exhibition took a new twist. While Nurse Boland stood there with her rubber gloves in the air and her back to a row of nodding patients in their wheelchairs, Jimmy lifted her uniform and showed all the old men and women Nurse Boland's underwear. Just a quick semi-consensual glimpse which sent them all nodding into infinity.

Nurse Boland's white lace underwear for all to see. She turned around but Jimmy was already on the run, driving a wheelchair at high speed down the corridor. Looking back at the last minute to see Nurse Boland with her rubber gloves in the air, looking like a nuclear physicist with a burning smile on her face. I'll get you!

Coyne was fighting with everyone these days. His father had come from Cork, the rebel county, the part of Ireland perhaps best known for its noble tradition of insurgency. Michael Collins country. But what use was all that rebel greatness now? What could you do in times of advanced peace and prosperity with the faculties of rebellion, nurtured over centuries? It was like an overactive immune response that was long obsolete.

He had a brief altercation with Martin Davis outside the Anchor Bar one night. As the skipper came out and he was going in, he allowed his suspicions to reach the surface.

You're not doing much fishing these days, Captain.

Bud focain asail, Martin Davis responded, walking away.

So the skipper was a garlic speaker, Coyne thought. Delighted with the chance to show off his links with the past, Coyne took up the challenge. Struck back with his own range of expletives, shouting down the street after him, like he was performing in some outdoor pageant. *Poll séidigh!*

Diúg mo bhud, a mhac!, the skipper said over his shoulder.

A hot battle of insults as they vilified each other outside the Anchor Bar in the mother tongue. It drew respect and admiration, as though they belonged to an elite little club of Irish speakers who would greet each other in the pub every night from now on with this barbaric invective.

Coyne was besieged by the past. All the ghosts were coming back to stalk him. One day he ran almost straight into Mr Killmurphy.

Maybe the phone calls were working, because Killmurphy seemed to give Coyne a very serious and inquisitive look when they saw each other on the seafront. Coyne was walking towards the gentlemen's bathing spot. Forty foot gentlemen only. Not for a swim or anything healthy like that. Just to have a look. And who does he see only Killjoy?

He hadn't laid eyes on him for years. Assumed he must have moved to a different branch, because Coyne was dealing with a younger manager now. But the sight of Killjoy brought out all the old animosity. The basilisk-eyed bank manager. Staring at him. For a moment, it even looked like Killjoy was going to come over to Coyne and talk to him; perhaps start accusing him of sabotaging his garden.

The past was full of atrocities.

Coyne threw him a look of triumph. It was a moment of moral superiority when Coyne remembered exactly why he had gone to such extremes. The siege mentality.

Yes, Killjoy, you're absolutely right. It's me. Coyne the patio terrorist.

Coyne still had friends in the force. He was trying to find some way of getting his hands on Tommy Nolan's postmortem report. People owed him favours all over the place, but there was nobody around who would risk their neck on that one, let alone know how to go about getting it in the first place. Leaking out a pathology report was a tricky one, so Coyne had to ask Fred Metcalf. He was the only contact who could deliver when it came down to the wire. Even though Fred was retired now and living alone, he still had important connections in the detective branch.

It was a matter of life and death, Coyne explained. He wouldn't be asking, if it wasn't. And Coyne swore that he would never ask another favour as long as he lived.

I'll have to twist a few arms on that one, Fred said. It wasn't that he didn't trust Coyne. It was just a bit of trouble getting possession of documents like that. He was really looking for a good reason, that's all.

Coyne had brought him a box of Kentucky Fried Chicken. His favourite.

Tommy Nolan was a friend, Coyne said.

Coyne gave no further explanation. He sat down and drank tea. Watched Fred put the chicken meal away for later and eat a half-dozen pink Mikado biscuits instead.

Fred was an old man now. He was slow, and struggled with the simplest of tasks. He had a scratching disease that drove him insane at times, sitting in his armchair all day trying to keep calm. If he was a dog, Fred explained once to Coyne, he'd have a lampshade

around his neck to stop him scratching. Coyne took pity on him and occasionally thought he would end up like Fred himself, sitting in front of the TV all day, eating biscuits and scratching.

Coyne had promised to bring his two daughters out. Took them into town one afternoon because they wanted to get their bellybuttons pierced. How could he argue with them. He just had to make sure it was all cleared with Carmel and Mrs Gogarty first.

The girls had reached an accommodation over who was going to do what piercing. They agreed that Jennifer was going to get her bellybutton done, and Nuala was going to get her nose pierced. Coyne was utterly malleable. In situations like this, they could walk over him. He went along with personal freedom of choice. If his daughter wanted to put in an extra nostril in her nose, then he couldn't stop her. Even agreed to pay for it.

But things were different when they got into the Body Culture store: a dark little studio with pictures of mutilated victims all over the walls.

The owner came out from behind a curtain, stooped with the ton of steel hanging off his face. There was a hole in his earlobe the size of a large coin. His arms were covered in tattoos, blurred snakes and daggers which had stretched with age and elongated flabbiness. The girls began to get a little nervous and self-conscious.

Coyne told the man he wanted a nose and a bellybutton job. Pointed at his daughters.

The piercer produced a disclaimer agreement and explained that the piercing wounds might take months to heal. And if anything went wrong, if there were any medical complications later on, he could take no responsibility. It looked as though Mr Body Culture himself was beginning to regret each one of his own mutilations.

Coyne insisted. On behalf of Nuala and Jennifer, he was ready to sign the form. Until one of them began to get worried.

I don't want to, Nuala said, and the whole thing began to go into reverse. The great confidence which they had worked on for weeks slipped away. It was the picture of pierced nipples on the wall that got them. They left the dark little torture studio in a hurry.

Jennifer and Nuala were silent, walking with their dad through the warm sunlit Dublin streets. Off along Grafton Street, not

knowing what to say any more because their great mission was abandoned. Coyne could see they were disappointed. They were still only children. Though they were too old to be told stories, he was still able to spin a kind of fantasy for them. He bought them clothes. Bracelets and eye make-up. Helped them feel better. Took them in for cakes and cappuccino.

He got the bus back and walked with them as far as the gate of his old home. Nuala asked him to come inside. He was reluctant at first, but how could he refuse? His youngest daughter's mind had not yet understood the partition in her parents' life and still saw them as one entity. Still saw her father as the man who had sat at the end of the bed telling stories.

Carmel was out at the time, so Coyne decided to go inside briefly. What harm was it to behave like a real father. To go and examine Nuala's school project on the Dalai Lama. Coyne felt a strange sensation of regained memory as he climbed the stairs, as though he had dropped back in time. He was bewildered by his old home. Sat for a while admiring Nuala's work, asking questions, adding things that he knew about the subject.

What's that for? Coyne asked suddenly, when he noticed a white line drawn with chalk on the carpet.

The peace line, Nuala said.

The girls looked at each other and began to explain how they had drawn a demarcation line in the middle of the room, dividing it into halves, one for Nuala, the other for Jennifer. A virtually invisible boundary across which they were not allowed to step. While Coyne was in the room on his rare visit, they suddenly struck an unspoken truce which allowed them to ignore the normal rules of engagement. Coyne the great peace envoy.

When they had shown their father everything, and it was time for Coyne to leave again, they suddenly became very hospitable. Urging him to stay for a while longer, they offered him tea and went downstairs to put the kettle on. Get the biscuits out.

Coyne was on his way down after them when he caught a glimpse of his own former bedroom. He stood on the landing for a moment, tempted to take a look inside.

Why not?

While the girls were busy downstairs, he stood in Carmel's bedroom, towering over the bed he had slept in. He looked at the curtains and the window where he had so often stood at night looking out at the nocturnal golfer next door. Everything was so seductively familiar that it began to wash over him until he felt that nothing had changed, a ghost-like figure in his own life.

Carmel's paintings were on the walls. Along the vanity desk, her painted stones which reminded him of one of the last arguments they had. It drove Coyne mad that she had begun to make use of stones from the shore. How could you possibly hope to improve them? They had an authentic seashore look; an integrity that had taken millions of years of erosion to achieve until she started mutilating them with silly little dots and faces. Tarting them up with zigzag colours. Systematically eliminating the last unspoiled link to prehistoric purity.

On the bed there was a big white teddy bear that Carmel had won in a raffle at one of the local shops on Valentine's Day. On the duvet were more stones. Not painted stones this time, but stones in their original beauty which Carmel had collected for their healing qualities. I want to touch people, she had once said. My talent is in giving. She had selected these stones for their shapes and their beneficial potential. They contained infinity, polished and smoothed by time. Lying on the side of the bed, where he had once slept, he now saw a variety of stones and pebbles, some grey with white markings, some white, one with what looked like a planetary ring. Another stone that she had picked up from the tunnelling workers – a white granite ball like an ostrich egg, excavated from the big new sewerage tunnel, deep under Dublin Bay.

Coyne sat at the edge of the bed. The stones rolled together with the click of pool balls. He was looking at the sun-heated shoreline on the bed, transfixed as if sitting on a remote strand, with the red sunset of a bedside lamp going down on the horizon. Carmel like a topless sunbather, sitting at the edge of the water, smiling. Sheets and duvet lapping around her knees. A handprint on the sand where she was propped on one long sloping arm, with a dimple above her elbow, the other hand toying with the stones. Shifting them around self-consciously with her fingers. He imagined her taking one of the smallest polished pebbles, red in the glow of the sun, and placing it against one of her breasts.

Coyne reached out and picked up a stone – cool at first, then warm in his hand. It was the one with the white Saturn ring. It fitted perfectly into his cupped palm, like a sculpted breast. He felt the weight of it, threw it in the air a little and caught it again with a satisfying smack. He liked this stone and wanted to keep it. To steal it from her and hide it in his own flat, like a secret possession, a memory, a physical souvenir of Carmel. He put it in his pocket and went back downstairs, triumph and guilt on equal rank as he felt the stone against his leg.

The following day, Coyne collected the postmortem report on Tommy Nolan: the last details on a posthumous friend. At a glance, he could see references pertaining to a head injury. Pages and pages, all about the one injury alone. But he closed the document again because it would be wrong to read it on the bus, like a copy of the *Star* newspaper. Reading about Tommy's death as if it was a soccer report.

He waited till he got back to the flat. Decided to have lunch first, though he was not really hungry. Food was more like a rite of passage that marked the separation of one part of the day from another. He put the report on the kitchen table, hung his jacket around the shoulders of a chair and began to prepare some eggs.

Coyne was inefficient in the kitchen. He switched the cooker on too soon and allowed the blue flame to hiss away urgently while he fumbled around in the fridge getting out the eggs. He found a bowl and cracked one of the eggs against the rim, not vigorously enough, so that the egg still held together and Coyne had to force it open, getting egg all over his thumb in the process.

Normally, Carmel would have taken over at this point. Come here, give it to me – I can't bear to watch this! Either that or her mother Mrs Actually would have become involved and Coyne would have found himself barred from the kitchen. But he was taking control of his own food now. The second egg cracked with far too much force and Coyne spent more time picking out bits of shell. Then he whisked the egg and started enjoying the rhythm.

The timing was wrong. He went back to the fridge more than three times. First for butter, then for milk, then for a scallion. The toast was done long before the scrambled egg was started. He cut the toast into triangles, just as Carmel would have done, but then forgot

to make the tea. And when he finally sat down to eat his lunch, he had lost his appetite. Somehow, it was the achievement of producing the meal that mattered more than any physical need. He ate the first few forkfuls voraciously, like a starving man, chewing on the crisp bread and the soft, salty egg. Sipping the tea. Looking at the brown envelope containing the postmortem report.

Coyne had become a furtive eater. He looked around as he ate. He crossed his legs and began to swing his foot in and out. He was uncomfortable with himself. Instead of feeling gratification and calmness, his mind frequently made the lateral jump to something distasteful, as though disgust had become the most prominent, overstated instinct of self-preservation. At moments when he sat down to eat his meal, he would suddenly think of the worst possible image. Faeces. Violence. Blood. Pictures of psoriasis. Worms emerging from a wound. A drowned dog he had seen floating just beneath the surface of the water in the harbour, with an orange rope around its neck, eyes gone white. A chain reaction of ugliness asserted itself in his mind every time he sat down to his food. His stomach churned in revolt, and he was already pushing the plate away.

Coyne had begun to develop a serious eating disorder, according to his psychologist. Perhaps he was experiencing some belated race memory. She didn't want to overemphasise it for fear of fuelling the problem. Coyne was now losing his appetite during the day, and then waking up in the middle of the night with a raging hunger. Ms Dunford tried to minimise it by blaming the years of shift work and bad dietary habits in the Gardai.

A feeling of guilt made it impossible for him to celebrate food in the normal way. There was no word for *bon appetit* in Irish. There was no way of rejoicing in bounty. No formal language, no vocabulary with which to encourage people to eat, except perhaps for some of the more crass expressions that had emerged more recently, like dig in! Eating remained a clandestine thing, and the only traditional phrase Coyne could remember in connection with food was a vicious, begrudging one to do with choking. All manner of things, even entirely unrelated to food, were brought under that vicious curse.

Go dtachtfaidh sé thú! May it choke you!

Besides, Irish cuisine had a long way to go. They had started experimenting with things like black pudding, but the Irish would

basically eat anything as long as it was dead and came with french fries. They were either starving or stuffed. And they would never go so far as to prefer food to singing. If it came down to the straight Pepsi challenge between *moules marinière* and *The Town That I Loved So Well* – no contest.

Sergeant Corrigan had his lunch at the Marine Hotel. It was the main meal of the day for him. Carvery lunch in the lounge. Chefs in white hats and red faces behind a self-service counter. Corrigan was not interested in the smoked cod pie or the *boeuf bourguignon*, so he opted for the bacon and cabbage with potatoes in their jackets. Just what he loved.

Corrigan was accompanied by a younger colleague who chose the *bourguignon*. The chef wiped his hands on a blue and white checquered apron before handling the food. Sharpened a short carving knife with a musical interlude before cutting fresh slices of bacon. Smiled and gave the sergeant extra, knowing that he was in the force. Corrigan rubbed his hands in anticipation.

The Marine carvery had the atmosphere of a sanctuary. Plate sounds and cutlery clash. The low hum of monotone voices: a rising babble of sufficiency. Corrigan and his colleague sat at a round table in silence. For them, food was still of such primary importance that a curfew prevailed. Until they crossed the hunger threshold they could not really afford to get into any serious conversation.

How are the wardrobes coming on? his colleague attempted.

Fine, Corrigan said, and normally he would have been only too delighted to start talking about the cult of home improvement. Every screw, every measurement, every tricky corner. His new black ash veneer built-in wardrobes with tinted mirrors were a matter of great pride. But this was not the time for it.

Corrigan opened the buttons on his jacket and sat leaning forward, knees apart on either side of the round table. One of his feet curled round the leg of his chair for support. Red napkin on his right thigh like a piper's patch as he peeled one of the potatoes. The noble spud. Big as a lumper. He picked it up in his hand and stripped away the freckled skin with meticulous care, catching it between thumb and knife and exposing the bright and steaming pulp underneath. There was a slight frown on his forehead and a barely concealed smile on

his face as he concentrated on this intimate task. He respected the potato and seemed to be talking to it all along. Come on, take your jacket off now, like a good lad. You're far too hot. He undressed it quickly, juggling the hot core around on a tripod of his fingers until he had finished and dropped it gently on to the plate, right beside the cabbage. Jacket folded away neatly on a side plate. Then he plunged the knife into the centre and the yellow-white, powdery landfalls of flesh fell apart. Steam bursting up from the scalding interior. Butter melting into a golden pool.

He ate with gusto and possessed excellent food management skills. He cut a triangle of pink bacon, anointed it with a touch of mustard and moved his torso forward so that his head came to meet the fork. Again and again, this repeated welcoming motion. Bowing to the bacon. Following it up with a forkful of cabbage and potato. He held the knife like a fountain pen, deftly levering a bale of cabbage on to the fork and bonding it temporarily with the adhesive potato mash, before moving his body forward again to meet the oncoming food.

The potato was still too hot, so he whistled a bit to cool it down. Then he remembered to drink his cordial, before starting the same routine again. His eating was carried out in a series of well organised clearing operations. Demolition and disposal. Keeping an eye on the custard trifle to follow.

His eyes were in fact semi-glazed. He looked out the window towards the seafront but failed to see the band of blue water. He half noticed people coming and going. But his eyes stopped seeking information. His vision was impaired. Women and men could have danced naked on the other side of the room. He was virtually blind to anything further away than two feet around him. A kind of voluntary blindness. As if there was an area cordoned off with crime scene tape, beyond which everything was a watery blur.

John McCurtain had lunch at the Anchor Bar. It was as convenient as anywhere else. He intended to make a right pig of himself. He was starving and Kelly's did a great sandwich.

Port and Docks! That's what McCurtain worked at. Nobody ever knew what exactly that meant, or what kind of duties he performed. It could have been anything from sweeping the offices to designing lighthouses. It didn't seem to matter much. The Port and Docks

board was a kind of vocation that embraced a great number of men and women under a cloak of respectability.

McCurtain walked into the Anchor and slapped the *Star* newspaper on the counter. Sat up on the stool and started reading the front page. Ordered a ham and cheese toasted sandwich with relish. An American touch. He also asked for onion rings. The truth lay in between the slices of a sandwich at the Anchor Bar.

It was more like a meal, both in price and handling. Not the kind of sandwich you could hold in one hand while you had a pint in the other. It was a knife and fork situation, with thick, generous rivers of relish running like lava out from between the slices. McCurtain lashed into it. Cut smartly with a downward motion of his elbow, and a look of disdain on his face which seemed to imply that he actually reviled what he was about to eat and enjoy. His nose was curled up. Mouth shaped into a grin. And his eyes leering at the food like a voyeur.

He sat up straight, inhaling deeply as he chewed and stared at the topless woman in the newspaper on the bar counter beside him. He gazed at her arm cradling her massive breasts. Jesus, she had to hold those things up, they were so big. Almost like an arse. His fork was like a crane hire service, delivering chunks of ham and cheese sandwich. He started humming with pleasure. No particular song; something more like a speeded-up version of classical Western film music like *Big Country* or *A Few Dollars More*. He took a great draught of creamy black milk. He hummed and swallowed and chewed and looked sideways at the woman, as if he had something against her.

It was feeding time at the Haven. Jimmy pushed the trolley carrying trays along the corridor, the smell of tomato soup drifting before him. The nursing staff helped to distribute the trays to the various rooms: Mrs Broadbent, Mrs Bunyan, Dermot Banim, Bernard Berry, etc. Some of them were still able to handle their own lunch, more or less, though they sometimes dropped their spoons and had to call for help. Some made a big mess of themselves. Jam and butter all over their faces. Bernard Berry instantly slobbered soup all over his trousers.

Each tray had a bowl of soup, a knife, fork and spoon, a side

plate with two slices of white bread cut diagonally across with a pat of butter. After he had delivered the trays, Sister Agnes asked him to take care of Mrs Broadbent who had already spent twenty minutes trying to open the butter. At this rate it would take her five days to finish the soup. Jimmy slipped the tip of the knife into the pat of butter, unfolded the edges and spread the soft yellow butter across the white triangles. Then he stuck the spoon into Mrs Broadbent's hand, a slice of bread in the other and stood back.

Off you go, Mrs Broadbent. I'm timing you.

Some of them wanted to go to the loo as soon as they saw the food. Others had to be spoon-fed. Nurse Boland normally spent a half an hour over soup with Mr O Reilly-Highland, pinning his head back against the armchair to stop him nodding. Even the triangular slice of white bread was a problem for some of them, because the tip flopped down and took them forever to aim at their mouths. Bernard Berry was trying to stick the bread in his ear.

Finally, when this daily drama was over and the Duphalac had been administered, Jimmy sat down in a wheelchair, looking out the window over the harbour, to eat a bowl of soup himself. He was hungry enough to be able to censor the grotesqueries of the old people's home out of his mind for the time being. Tried to convince himself he was not eating flaky skin and bedsores. Incontinence sheets. Mrs Spain's shrunken breasts. Polyps. Corns. Lesions and festering melanomas. Jimmy was beginning to feel jealous of the old people. And when Nurse Boland came into the sitting room, he started rattling his spoon against the side of the stainless steel bowl. Pretending to spill it all over the floor. Threatening to slobber and pee all over himself. Throwing slices of white bread around like paper aeroplanes until Nurse Boland smiled and knelt down in front of him to feed him with a mock frown.

Skipper Martin Davis had lunch on the move. He parked the red van on the pier and stepped out, took the wrapper off a tuna sandwich and opened a can of Sprite. The seagulls perched nearby and watched each movement of the food towards his mouth. He left the door of the van open so that the music on the stereo played to the open air.

It was a rushed meal, because Mongi had asked him to deliver a box of fresh fish.

Martin Davis threw the crust out on to the oily water where the gulls shrieked and fought for it. Then he walked over to the ice-box where the women sold a variety of fish. Two men from a Japanese restaurant nearby were picking and choosing. The skipper bought a full box of mackerel and the women were surprised that a fisherman would be buying fish. But Martin Davis side-stepped the enquiries by saying it was a special delivery to a catering firm.

Mongi O Doherty was a great man for the kiddie food. Beans, chips and sausages. He had not progressed to an adult diet yet, and his mother was cooking up some prime pork sausages for his lunch. She had crossed the city on a bus to get his favourite Hick sausages and now stood in the kitchen, staring out the window as she listened to the radio, all about a young boy who had been inducted into a religious sect and brainwashed. It would never have happened to her son, Richard.

Mongi was in the living room watching Sky news. Every now and again they would break in with the latest stock market reports and share index, which irritated him no end.

Does my head in, he said to himself.

For practical reasons, much of his money was tied up in property. He had recently bought the house and put it in his mother's name, though it was understood, of course, that an unwritten contract between mother and son was more binding than any legal document. His present address was at a city centre luxury flat where he spent most of his time with his present girlfriend, Sharon. Cooking was not one of her strong points, however, and Mongi usually ate at home with his mother.

Mind, the plate is hot, she warned, placing the meal of ebony sausages in front of her son. A life in waitressing had taught her how to distract from the food at a crucial moment.

What's this? Mongi demanded, looking at the disaster on the plate.

I was listening to this programme, she said. I got kind of carried away, son.

Don't call me son, Ma.

There was no excuse for incinerating a man's food. Unforgivable. It was worse than any double dealing. Worse than snitching.

Worse than being fucked over by the law. His own natural mother, destroying the best of Dublin sausages as though she cooked them with a blowtorch.

They're black!

I'm sorry, Richard.

And look, Ma! Did I ask for parsley?

No, she said. I just thought it would look good.

What use was a touch of garnish when the rest was totally inedible?

It's pretentious, he said, picking up the lettuce and dangling it in the air. Especially when you go and burn the shaggin' sausages.

I'm doing my best, son.

You know what lettuce and tomatoes says to me. It's a set-up. A stake-out. It's just the kind of thing the cops would hide behind. I can see them hiding under that lettuce in plain clothes. Lettuce and tomato is a dirty Garda operation.

He picked up the knife and pointed it at his mother. Even if it was only a butter knife, it was enough to terrify her. Nobody had more power to scare a mother than her own son.

You're trying to shop me, Ma.

No, son. I'd never do that. I swear. My own flesh and blood.

Mongi ruthlessly pushed the greenery off the plate. His mother went back out to the kitchen and sulked, while he sat in the living room, trying to make the best of his meal alone. He took one of the ebony sausages and placed it on a slice of pre-buttered bread, drew a red line of ketchup along the top and rolled it up like a sleeping bag. He saw food basically as a victim. He bit the poor little sleeping sausage with a ferocious bite of his yellow smile, expecting it to scream in pain.

Mongi had subliminal thoughts about eating raw food. He looked at the Sky newscaster and imagined taking a big bite out of her arm. He wanted to return to the wholesale savagery of eating in the jungle, as though food didn't taste right unless he killed it himself. Perhaps he should have been a butcher.

He pushed the sausages away and turned to a bar of Toblerone. Something about the pyramid shape made it more of a challenge. He bit off a slice of the mountain, leaving the satisfaction of his teeth markings behind. Chewed and took a good sip of Southern Comfort. Churned the mixture around in his mouth, inhaled through the grid of his brown teeth and swallowed.

There was a knock on the door. It was the skipper, Martin Davis waiting outside with his box of mackerel.

Marlene Nolan opened a tub of Hot Cup, poured in the boiling water and watched the metamorphosis taking place in front of her eyes. It was a miracle each time, like the resurrection of Christ. The room lit up as the golden light radiated from the Hot Cup. The smell that permeated the flat was something close to a block-layer's armpit. She had got used to that reek and even began to crave it. Missed it when it was gone. It was like the bad smell they put into natural gas so that it could be detected by the human nostril, a scent that was designed to be thoroughly offensive but that you could get attached to, in a peculiar way. Maybe it reminded her of her father – his big overpowering, testosterone presence in a small two-roomed council house. Smiling with his white shirt rolled up at the sleeves, and the smell of stale smoke in his clothes mixed with his all-embracing Parmesan scent. A hundred thousand paternal armpits processed into one concentrated cup and brought alive with boiling water. She sat down and switched on the TV. A programme about dogs and dog owners. Taking care of your pet. How to vet the kennels.

Councillor Sylvester Hogan took a light lunch at the yacht club. He hadn't eaten there in a long time and was told the food had greatly improved. It had always been more of a drinking haunt, for meeting up with people from the Chamber of Commerce. They had changed some of the kitchen staff and had since received a Sense of Excellence award, as if excellence was some kind of absolute in itself. Excellent what?

Who knows. Perhaps the dining room was worth another go, Hogan thought.

The waiter greeted him with huge enthusiasm and behaved like a method actor as he ushered Hogan to a table, bowing and practically genuflecting; speaking in a broken French accent. But Hogan knew he came from Sallynoggin, just up the road, and had picked up the strange hybrid dialect as a commis chef in Paris.

Hogan could have told him that Irish people didn't like all this attention to be drawn to themselves when they were entering a restaurant. Eating out was still a stealthy engagement. And they

didn't want it broadcast around the world on Euro News every time they had a snack in public.

The waiter stuck a menu into Hogan's face and stood back with gleaming pride.

Hogan went for the Seafood Symphony and bore an expression of supreme satisfaction when it arrived on the table. It was a dish in the great Irish tradition of pink prawn cocktails with orange mayonnaise sauce on a bed of lettuce and soft cherry tomatoes. A prizewinning College of Catering creation that came with slices of home-made brown sodabread which began to crumble in his hands as soon as he touched it.

Magnificent, he muttered, as he opened the four provinces of the butter pat and tried to bind the breadcrumbs together.

Some day Hogan would start a gourmet charter for his country. Show people what a real gastronomic sense of excellence meant. He could talk. Some of the meals he had eaten on his fact-finding missions to Europe were absolutely stunning. Such class. Such aesthetic masterpieces. The German *Schweine-haxe* ranked among his favourites.

Hogan skipped the main course and moved straight on to the pudding. The new chef had concentrated on minimalism. A tiny piece of apple pie sat at the centre of a massive dinner plate. A piece of confection which came with a knife and fork and looked like a secluded thatched cottage on a deserted plain, with icing sugar and frosted snow covering the frozen landscape. Rural desertification, with boreens of chocolate designs all over the empty plate to signify a trend away from the land. A humble apple pie in a Southfork setting, with a dollop of cream like a marquis tent on the ranch.

Any other day, Hogan would have been a little disappointed with the portion. But that afternoon, he had set up an appointment with a healer. Carmel Coyne was going to meet him at his home to cure his back. He was smiling to himself as he demolished the apple cottage.

Corina Stanescu ate a plain hamburger and french fries. Initially, when she started working at a diner-style, take-away restaurant, she was excited about this kind of food, with its new world taste of prosperity. But she had by now watched at least a million customers devouring the same meal. It seemed to her that it was fantasy food;

customers who came there were just mentally hungry and ate an imaginary meal. She had seen people impatiently cramming french fries into their mouths as if they could never get enough. There was something insubstantial about them, as though each person knew they were being cheated.

She remembered how in Bucharest people had taken the McDonald's trays home with them at first, thinking that everything was free, or else thinking that they deserved a little more. People had flocked with great excitement to the new fast food restaurants, as if they represented a new freedom. Her attitude had changed since she'd started working there herself. All she could think of now was the temperature of the deep frier, and the length of time it took to cook a hamburger, and the correct procedure with the garnish. At first, she hadn't noticed the distracted looks on customers' faces. Or the people who sat alone, not eating anything, just staring into the street outside and the passing traffic. Women with buggies. Men holding on to styrofoam cups.

The manager said Corina was very good at her job. He had told her that he was going to promote her permanently to the till. No more mopping up and collecting trays. No more frying burgers and preparing french fries. She was on the counter from now on, he said, with a great big smile that must have meant something. He fancied her, that was for sure. He said she was very intelligent and that she had the ability to become a manager herself. But this only worried her even more.

As she finished her hasty meal, she understood at last what the hamburger and french fries were supposed to do. They triggered off subliminal memories of other food. Meals back home in Romania, like *sarmale*, and *mititei*. And *papanasi*.

Mr Killjoy was having his lunch at one of those wholefood restaurants, run by a co-op of local women. Chicken in white wine sauce, with rice and pineapple. Every dish on the menu at the Whole Earth restaurant was his favourite. Especially the desserts.

He took out the *Irish Times* and set it beside him on the table. It was not a newspaper as such, but a device for distracting attention from food. A utensil, needed for eating your lunch; some kind of mental fork or psychological shoehorn, on a par with any other

cutlery. Killjoy needed a decoy to make onlookers think that he was more interested in the news than he was in food.

The presence of the newspaper allowed him to enjoy his lunch without thinking that he was being watched. He could eat heartily, uninhibited by the casual gaze of other people. He could remain inside the closed circuit of his own world, forking the chicken dish with one hand, pinning down the paper with the other.

It was a platform of deceit. A form of food denial. As usual in Ireland, everything operated on the reverse. If you said one thing, then you meant something else altogether – usually the opposite. Words and gestures were a bluster, meant to convey what people wanted to hear.

It was only when Killjoy had finished his banoffee that he could raise his head again and look around. Then he was suddenly curious about what other people were eating, looking at the mound of food the man next to him had on his plate. And finally, when Killjoy sat back over his coffee, he began to take on more global interests. He actually started reading the paper.

Mongi was running his own catering operation, feeding fish to the visitors out in Clondalkin. It was basically a piece of monetary realism that helped to speed up what he called the wet-back repayments. Because he had failed to persuade Corina to enter into a more lucrative line of work, he would have to convince her in some other way. By leaning on her relatives.

Some of the Romanians were living in the low-density, car-dependent suburbs of Dublin, while Corina and a few other women lived in a flat in town. Her brother and cousin lived together in Clondalkin. Apart from some occasional shifts on building sites, they had found no permanent employment yet.

Mongi forced his way into a semi-detached house and found them sitting in the living room watching TV. Martin Davis put a box of mackerel down on the purple carpet. Looked around at the pattern of damp black stipple coming through the floral wallpaper in the corner. At first, it looked like he had brought them a gift. Some freshly caught fish. And though this turned out to be true, it was not quite what the Romanians had in mind.

Mongi was getting really pissed off, the skipper began to explain.

He was there to give them a new deadline. He couldn't care less where they got the money. They could steal it if they liked. He wanted to be repaid in full by the following Friday.

Right, you fucking wet-backs, Mongi took over himself, making a call on his mobile. The amusements. It's time for some A-M-U-SAMENTS, he said, pronouncing the words as though they understood no English.

Caius and Tudor looked at each other.

Amusements, Mongi repeated. Amusamenteees. Amusementescu or whatever the fuck you call it over there.

What are you doing? Martin Davis asked. He was beginning to feel nervous about this.

Mongi asked to speak to Corina Stanescu on the phone. There followed an altercation, along the lines that Corina was busy in the restaurant. So Mongi stressed the urgency of the situation. Said he was a surgeon at St Vincent's hospital. Talked about having to notify the next of kin, so the manager of the restaurant eventually capitulated and allowed her to come to the phone.

Corina Stanescu, Mongi said.

Yes, she said.

Mongi handed the phone to Caius. Then he took out one of the fresh mackerel – first of the season – and began to hold it up towards the young Tudor, brother of Corina. Caius talked quickly in Romanian, as if he was reporting on the scene.

Fresh fish, Mongi said. How do I know? Because it's stiff.

Rigor mortis, the skipper added, but he was not happy about the idea of fish being used as a threat. Fish were sacred.

Erect, Mongi pointed out, holding the freshly caught fish with its blue, green and black tiger stripes up to Tudor's face. Later on it will go limp again. That's how you can determine the time of death.

It was like a party line. Mongi indirectly communicating with Corina in the restaurant, through Caius and a thousand years of the Romanian language over the mobile phone. In turn, she was trying to deal with the restaurant manager who was getting angry behind her at the time she was spending on the phone. And he in turn was trying to deal with starving customers.

Mongi said no more. Just held Tudor's head back against the wall with one hand and pushed the fresh mackerel into his mouth, head

first. Tudor struggled, but Mongi was in a dominant position for this force-feeding programme. Soon there was little more than the tail end sticking out. Like an unexploded torpedo.

This was all in the nature of a parable. Mongi was not seriously trying to feed fish to foreigners. It was merely a gesture, a liturgical offering which was relayed to Corina as an indication of what might happen if she didn't clear the debt by the given date. For the moment, Mongi was at pains to point out, this was strictly a symbolic feeding. The next time it would be real. And maybe not oral either. Then he took back the phone and spoke directly to Corina.

I'm giving you a week, Mongi said. Then they left.

Fred Metcalf was too old to eat lunch any more. He opened the box of Kentucky chicken and fed it to a range of cats which instantly arrived as though they could read his mind. He stood on the doorstep of his flat and threw them the chicken legs that Coyne had brought. In the background, the TV was on all the time, with the sound turned down. Silent figures of a daytime soap opera.

Fred's stomach had come to a standstill. All he ever ate these days was biscuits and tea. Mikado, custard creams, chocolate Kimberly. Anything that people brought to him at his small flat. But especially pink biscuits. Flamingo pink sponge. By now there was a large concrete block of pink, reinforced cement lodged in his abdomen. Surgeons said there was no point in operating. He was too far gone.

When the cats had been fed, he went back inside and sat down with a cup of tea. But even then he had no appetite. Instead he was transfixed by a commercial on TV. The agility of young people dancing and skating around in front of him was stunning. Here was the landscape of the future, full of young people leaping around and eating Pringles. Music punctuated by the amplified crunch of their mouths around the wafer-thin food. That's what youth was – hunger and energy and fun. Crunch! Crunch! Fred watched this high-speed meal with great awe. Once you start you can't stop. These people were eating themselves sick.

The take-away restaurant suddenly became packed with schoolboys in their crested college blazers. The windows were steamed up. You couldn't get in the door. They were all there for their usual burgers

and hot dogs and french fries. But they were also there to look at the new woman behind the counter in her blue gingham overalls. Something about the way Corina looked each one of them in the eye as she served them. Something also about her foreign, East European accent drew these boys down from the nearby college every day. Some of them asked her irrelevant questions, trying to get her to smile. They laughed about hot dogs. Muttered in baritone voices as they ate. Threw straws of french fries at each other. Called each other wankers and gave each other wedgies, especially those preoccupied with the Romanian woman behind the counter with the smile and the shadows round her eyes.

The girls from Loreto Abbey were hanging around outside a local newsagents' shop. Mr Kirwin did a little pizza business every lunchtime and Jennifer and Nuala bought a slice each. Most of the older girls were having cigarettes: more tar, less calories. The convent girls were using as much bad language as possible, making up for lost time, when girls were sweet and full of Catholic ethos. Mr Kirwin seemed to put up with it most of the time. Will you fucking give us a fucking light you fucking bitch! Which was as sweet and polite as they were ever going to be to each other. I'll give you a kick in the clit, you cow! While Jennifer and Nuala ate their pizza, they watched as two older girls threw down their bags and challenged each other to a fight. There were no rules among girls any more. Biting, scratching and kicking were all legal. Knickers in the air to passing motorists. Skin and hair flying until Mr Kirwin, the United Nations shopkeeper, had to come out and separate them, saying Girls, Girls, Please! and offering Kleenex to the one with the bloody nose.

Mrs Gogarty had invited Carmel around for lunch to meet some of her friends. Nothing was spared in terms of effort and style. It was lunch in a formal sense. The full orchestra. The best delph. Silver cutlery, silver napkin rings and silver knife and fork rests so as not to stain the white tablecloth.

The main course was fresh grilled salmon steak with hollandaise sauce. New potatoes and fresh garden peas. All organically grown, as Mrs Gogarty was only too pleased to point out.

Carmel gave her some help in the kitchen, but everything had

already been prepared. All Mrs Gogarty had to do was cut the fresh brown bread, and Carmel noticed how her mother leaned forward in a special bread-cutting posture, with the knife in one hand and the bread in the other. Everybody was equal in front of bread.

The women in Mrs Gogarty's circle had elevated the business of lunch to a showcase. It had less to do with food or the gratification of appetite than with the whole pageantry around the meal. For them it was more like a ritual. A stage drama which they revived and re-enacted every now and again to elevate food and remove it from the vulgarity of need.

Conversation ran along the lines of a daytime talk programme. Should drivers be allowed to use mobile phones while driving? By gum, one of the women said, they should not. Mind you, in defence of the mobile phone, another one of the guests said, it was great security to have one in the car. Finally, they moved on to horrific accidents. The fact that there was no crash barrier along the central reservation on the new motorway. The idea of a car coming across that central reservation straight into the oncoming traffic.

The idea behind this great lunch was to defy the existence of hunger and appetite. They had a way of eating salmon and hollandaise sauce without damaging their lipstick or leaving lip marks on wine glasses. It was more like a hunger test, to establish who could best conceal their appetite. Mrs Gogarty had learned all of this at boarding school down the country. Ladies ate bread before they went to a meal so they didn't end up behaving like a starving peasant. Never go to dinner hungry, Scarlett O'Hara's mother used to say. Because Irish people, no matter where they ended up, were taught to present a noble abstinence. It was food warfare. Mrs Gogarty ended the meal with a flourish, placing a basket of exotic fruit on the table with lychees and kiwis. The guests surrendered.

The poet with the four docile dogs was great on food phrases. He possessed a number of key lines in praise of food. Even though it was hospital food and he wanted to dig in as soon as the nurses brought the tray, he didn't feel right eating in public – in the public ward – without ritualising the meal with a few of his phrases. Letting the other silent patients know how hungry he was. Fucking starving! The Irish had refined many lyrical disclaimers to allow the naked savage

in his wine-coloured, leaf motif pyjamas to attack his food with as much right as anyone else and not feel guilty about it. I could eat a farmer's britches through a hedge. I could eat a camel's balls through the eye of a needle. I could eat a pregnant nun's arse through a chair.

Ms Clare Dunford was trying to keep her weight down. It would be a lifelong struggle. In the same way that people once struggled to keep fed, she now had to fight a daily battle to keep from being overfed. Life will always revolve around food and money, she thought. Whether you have it or not. That day she skipped breakfast, or more correctly, postponed it until lunchtime.

She decided to take in a sandwich at the hairdressers'. There was not enough time for the hair appointment, and lunch afterwards, before she rushed back to her patients. She opted to combine the two, and had already taken a bite out of a cumbersome chicken and salad submarine when she was asked to lean back to have her hair shampooed. There was a momentary loss of reality as the hairdresser rubbed vigorously, almost forgetting that Ms Dunford was human. Just another disembodied head for shampooing, like pots were for scrubbing. Ms Dunford chewed and examined the ceiling. Cool rim of the basin on her neck, hot water on her scalp. She savoured the combined taste in her mouth, even as she obediently leaned forward again with a red towel over her head. Eventually, she got back to the sandwich and coffee while the hairdresser started clipping and talking.

It was a new experience, Ms Dunford thought. A little disconcerting too, to watch her reflection struggling with the submarine. She observed a menacing grimace on her face as she bit into the roll and the contents of chicken bits and tomato squirmed awkwardly out through the sides. Hand like a safety net underneath. Lower set of teeth coming forward, round cheeks rotating, a little frown on her forehead and her marsupial nose curling up as she sipped from the styrofoam coffee cup. She was appalled at the vision of her own animal desires.

By now, everything was covered with a layer of clipped hair. Under the gusting blow-drier, she thought about the concept of food. It was cerebral as much as physical. Phantasmal, even. Perhaps it would become a revolutionary new dieting technique, to look at yourself eating and to see at first hand the singleminded greed in your own

eyes. Ms Dunford was so astonished by her eating habits that she pushed the submarine away. Only then did she notice that, with a touch of mousse, her head had begun to resemble a Donegal ram which had stopped grazing for a moment to look at a passing car: two great hanks of hair curling dangerously forward on either side of her face, and her lower jaw still swinging relentlessly.

Coyne took his time reading through the postmortem report. There was nothing in it that pointed the finger at any murderer. Nothing that indicated foul play as such. Only the cause of death by drowning. The rope burn marks and an injury to the head which was assumed to have been caused by Tommy's head striking against the side of a boat during his fall. The report mentioned injuries consistent with motion.

Coyne was struck mostly by the details on Tommy Nolan's intestines. The pathologist had found considerable amounts of alcohol in his body. There was also evidence of chips, partially digested. Tommy must have gone up to the chipper before he went down to the harbour. That's why Coyne could not find him on the night in question. Because Tommy was standing in the Ritz waiting for a bag of chips. Probably looking at himself reflected in the convex stainless steel front-piece of the chipper. His face clownishly elongated as he waited.

Salt and vinegar?

On his way to the psychologist that afternoon, Coyne could not help thinking about Tommy's stomach. He imagined what everyone else had in their stomachs that afternoon. Like some laser vision, he could see into stomachs all over Ireland: a cross-section of the food that was consumed at lunch on a single day. Mikado biscuits. Sausages. Tomato soup. Chips. Fresh salmon. Chicken in white wine sauce. Chicken submarine. As though Coyne had carried out a national autopsy on the potato republic. Fresh garden peas. Beans. A slice of toast here and there. Biscuits with cheese. Cabbage and boiled potato. Hot dogs, doughnuts, sausages, Pringles and lychees.

Ms Dunford asked Coyne to sit in the usual chair while she started strolling up and down her office. She looked out through the window with her back to him.

Coyne appeared to have something to say that afternoon. He was unusually eager to talk, and lifted the embargo on his schooldays. Without realising it, he was giving Ms Dunford what she was looking for.

I'll tell you about the bread and seagulls, he said.

It was in the school-yard. There were two gangs, with two dens. It was always like that, gangs running through the yard, clashing somewhere in the middle and retreating. The physical force tradition of the Irish school-yard. Coyne always kept his back to the wall and watched as they came. And then one day, in the middle of the yard, he saw one of them punch one of the younger boys full in the stomach. An innocent bystander.

He just doubled over, Coyne said. I turned around and saw him there with his mouth open, leaning forward. Holding his stomach with one hand. His sandwiches in the other. His mouth was wide open. But there was no noise. It was like a silent scream.

Coyne remembered a piece of masticated bread slipping from the boy's mouth. It hung on to his lip for a moment and then fell to the ground. And then all the other sandwiches wrapped in tinfoil also fell on the tarred surface of the yard while around them the warring continued. Boys with sticks and cardboard shields, shouting and flailing at each other in combat. The boy who was hit in the stomach, right in the middle of the war. Speechless. Screaming silently.

It was Tommy Nolan. Everybody was patting him on the back and asking was he OK. Are you all right? When the gangs retreated to their fortresses, Coyne picked up the sandwiches and put them back in the tinfoil wrapper. But Tommy's hands were limp and he dropped the sandwiches on the tarmac again.

He was winded, I suppose, Coyne said. That's why he couldn't make any noise. They called for his sister Marlene and she looked after him from there on.

The worst thing was afterwards, thinking about it. Coyne sitting in class looking out at the yard, all empty, with the echoes of the shouts still left behind. And the seagulls coming down to pick up whatever sandwiches were left lying around. They got Tommy Nolan's. They got every bit of crust and jam-tinted bread. They even got the half-masticated bit of dough that Tommy had in his mouth and let fall down with a dribble as he began to cry. Coyne was locked

into these helpless endings. Condemned to repeat them in his head, unable to move on.

It was extraordinary, the amount of intimate details people were willing to give a healer. Because Carmel had the ability to take pain away, she was often entrusted with all kinds of personal matters. She commanded complete trust. Pain normally brought people to their knees. In the belief that she could take it away, they told her everything.

Carmel was, in the first instance, a good listener.

Because all else had failed, Councillor Sylvester Hogan was now relying on her to sort out the alarming state of his lower back. In his position on the borough council, he had been on junkets and visited healers all over Europe. No cure available.

Carmel sat in the living room of his house, with the bay window looking out at the stone lions on the gates and the harbour beyond. Hogan's wife Norma had gone for extensive beauty treatment. Leg wax, bikini line: she would be wrapped up like a mummy for the next four hours. A charity dinner engagement after that. Hogan asked Carmel to look on this session as open-ended.

I've tried everything, he said in despair. What I'm telling you now is monumental, he seemed to be indicating with his eyes flashing. Nothing was quite as destructive as back pain. He was close to tears.

It must be hard on you, Carmel encouraged.

It's hard on my wife too, he explained, on an updraught of emotion. Heels sinking into the carpet of humility.

Carmel was swallowing hard. She was moved by his honesty. In the silence, she heard a very audible stomach gurgle which could not be clearly attributed to either of them. They gave each other a look of denial. Hogan with libidinous recognition in his eyes.

Carmel told him to lie on his stomach, on the carpet of his own front room. In his Salvador Dali, melting-clock boxer shorts and with a pair of white porcelain greyhounds standing guard on each side of the fireplace, she began to examine his vertebrae, feeling each disk and then moving on, while Hogan pinpointed the pain.

Yeah, just there, he said. That's exactly the place. It's an atrocity.

She placed the big granite egg straight down on the base of his spine. Hogan was in ecstasy. Groaning into the carpet with relief. Submitting fully to the sorcery of stones. His energy flow was coming

back slowly as Carmel counterbalanced the granite with other small basalt and limestone rocks and stones, until Hogan was covered in a pattern. Stoned to death in his own home. Call it accidental if you like, but Sylvie Hogan allowed his hand to make contact with her knee and take in the smooth sensation, like a soft, round, washed stone.

Late afternoon, Corina managed to appeal for compassionate leave. She went to the Anchor Bar to try and contact Pat Coyne.

I want to talk to Pat, she said.

Lot of people come in here by that name, the barman said. Besides, there was a matter of discretion here. A barman had to stick to the non-disclosure ethic of the confessional.

There was nobody else in the pub at the time except the poet, sitting in the snug with his crutches. He looked up at her and saw a vision of great beauty.

Raven black hair, he said. Sign of true Celtic blood.

Corina wrote out the name and number of a city restaurant on a beermat and handed it to the barman.

Who would he give this document to? The barman shrugged. She had to give him a bit of a description at least.

A goodlooking man, she said. With hair standing up on his head.

Lot of goodlooking fellas in here, the barman said.

Many a man in the Anchor Bar who'd do anything to receive a message from a woman like her, is what he wanted to say. She remembered that Coyne had told her something about being in a fire. So that narrowed down the handsome men of the Anchor Bar to a short list of one. The barman nodded and placed the beermat between two antique stout bottles behind the bar. Corina left.

The fact that she had mentioned a goodlooking man caused great derision around the bar. Throughout the afternoon and early evening, every crock of a man in a donkey jacket was sized up for the message like some male Cinderella. The whole pub was talking about Coyne's mystery woman.

Should have seen her, the barman kept saying. Fucking gorgeous, I swear.

What was her name? McCurtain wanted to know.

Corina, the barman answered.

The poet said she had to be a supermodel. Surrounded by all the men in the bar, he leaned on his crutches and drew an exquisite word-painting. A lyrical Identikit photofit picture of the young woman. And because McCurtain was such a good customer, the barman showed him the beermat.

It was a miracle. Sylvester Hogan got up from the stone therapy and walked. He was suddenly free from all pain. Carmel had liberated him from the greatest curse on earth and he wanted to jump around like a goat. Spring in the air and dance. He was a new man and put his arms around her with an exuberant embrace.

He was a man of property, he reminded her. But what use was all of this new wealth to him if he was a cripple who could hardly walk? At that moment in time, he was building a complex of fifteen Irish cottages on Achill Island. With the tax arrangements in place, they would effectively pay for themselves within five years. You couldn't help making money in this country: if you had any kind of intellect at all, the money was throwing itself at you.

Carmel sat on the sofa with Hogan. She had lifted the curse and saw the adoration in her patient's eyes. He wanted to repay her. Some reward fitting for this great miracle.

If you were interested in one of those holiday cottages, he said, I could see you right.

Ah now, Mr Hogan!

Sylvie, please.

Wait until you're absolutely sure the pain has disappeared, she said.

With a bit more regular treatment he would soon be in a position to go horse riding again. Golf at least. But you were never sure. Sometimes people went into remission. You didn't want to be making any rash promises and giving away Irish cottages. Carmel looked out at the lions on the gates. She wanted no reward, is what she was trying to explain. Her satisfaction came from the knowledge that she had done some good. She had brought the gift of health.

Thank the stones, she said.

You're a genius, he insisted. He was euphoric. Kissed her full on the mouth.

Jesus, Carmel! How could you have anything to do with a fraud merchant like Hogan? I mean, backache is the least of the things he should have. Somebody should go and break his back for him. Fold his vertebrae in two like a deckchair. Snap! He deserves all the suffering he can get. He's a moral cripple with a derelict imagination. Did she not know that bastards like Hogan were responsible for all those trendy little Toblerone cottages, with high-pitched roofs and big PVC windows?

Those weekend love-shacks have nothing to do with Irish heritage. They're so fake, they wouldn't even put them on a John Hinde postcard. And that fucker never even goes to Achill on his holidays. So he doesn't care.

Have nothing to do with Hogan, Carmel. He's the town killer. He's the landscape killer. Give him back his low back pain. Make him suffer. Ram the stones up his arse. Snap his lollipop spine. Put him in a wheelchair and send him up to the Haven nursing home.

Again and again over the last year since they separated, Coyne had continued to act as Carmel's conscience. He tried to warn her and protect her from marauders and con men. But she was no longer listening. She had left behind the stone wall solidity of her relationship with Coyne. It was goodbye to poverty and peril. Goodbye to indigenous humility. Instead, she was entering into the spirit of new building materials. The security of arched doorways and Doric pillars. Fake stone façades and garden furniture. White balustrades and stone lions.

Carmel allowed Councillor Hogan to open some buttons on her dress. A summer outfit she had bought the previous day. She was at the forefront of a new healing age. Of PVC windows and draught-free doors. Of double garages and outdoor lighting. Underneath, she wore the new luminous green bra and knickers that Coyne had bought her. Eternity behind the knees and between her breasts. She was turning her back on the old Ireland. A consummate betrayal of the past. She was leaning against the wall in Hogan's living room, allowing him to lift her dress and remove her rebel green underwear.

Mind your back, she said, her breasts already spilling out of her dress.

Break his back, Carmel. For Godsake, cripple the bastard.

But Hogan couldn't care less about his back. Pain had a short

memory and he was already laughing at it. Laughing at Ireland. Dancing on the graves of generations. Fecklessly snapping his spine in and out, like a great athlete. Man and superman! With his melted boxer shorts around his ankles and his buttocks flexing like the rump of a great stone goat god of mythology. One hand was propped against the wall for support. In the other, he held the luminous green knickers up to his nose and inhaled deeply.

Jimmy Coyne was out there spending money like a profligate son. He was with God and with Money. Every second day he was down at the foreign exchange desks in the various banks, looking up the rate of the American dollar. It was time he moved on to a new set of banks. These tellers were getting nosy. Soon they would be asking questions.

He was lavishing attention on Nurse Boland, taking her out to dinner in hideaway restaurants, buying her gifts – chocolates, drink, drugs, jewellery. Even got to the stage where Nurse Boland was beginning to ask where the money was coming from. The wages at the Haven were known to be the meanest in Dublin. The nuns had even deducted money for Jimmy's white overalls.

Most of Jimmy's expenses went not so much on material gifts as spiritual improvements. Occasionally, he was able to buy drugs from his friend Gussy. And Gussy accepted foreign currency, though he normally levied a stiff exchange fee. He also asked questions about where it came from and was promptly told to mind his own fucking business.

Jimmy declared himself to be independently wealthy.

He was only working to see Nurse Boland. In the boiler room at the Haven he had hidden the holdall bag containing an endless flow of dollars. Happy ever after amounts of money.

Mongi O Doherty made a fortuitous breakthrough late in one afternoon. One of his dealer friends quite casually mentioned dollars. From time to time, Mongi used a bit of high-quality dandruff, but the coke circle was quite small. Initially he thought it was some kind of bad joke when the dealer asked him if he wanted to pay in dollars.

Are you fucking ragging me? Mongi said.

Jesus, no! I'm only saying, like, everybody else is paying in foreign money these days.

So there was a little spontaneous enquiry. And the trail very quickly

led to the young Gus Mangan, a part-time dealer in coke, who was Jimmy Coyne's best friend. Mongi went around to visit Gussy, put a lighted cigarette up to his eye and asked him if he wanted to see the sun. Caught up with him in his granny's living room and showed him what the inferno looked like up close. Eventually came out with the name of Jimmy Coyne.

Jimmy was incredibly unlucky: the day he moved from virtual love into active love was the day that he got sacked from the old people's home. Most of the afternoon had been spent putting people in wheelchairs and bringing them outside where they sat overlooking the harbour with parasols overhead. Jimmy had done it all efficiently. It was not a problem with his work that finally caused his dismissal, but his desire for Nurse Boland.

He was caught in the act. The nuns were all outside with the old people. Only two or three of the residents had been left upstairs. Mr O Reilly-Highland, Mr Berry and a Mrs Cordawl who was so infirm she could not be brought down any more. Youth was a faraway country of the past.

In front of this audience of three distinguished guests, Jimmy finally managed to win Nurse Boland over. He opened her uniform. She was a willing accomplice and assisted by removing her underwear. With the wheelchair audience gazing with open mouths at the sheer agility of their movements, Jimmy made love to Irene Boland for the first time. On a hot early summer afternoon.

Until big Sister Agnes dropped in.

Jimmy could not understand why Nurse Boland pulled away so suddenly. Was it some contraceptive instinct that made her jump and hide in the wardrobe? Leaving Jimmy with his trousers down, looking out over the harbour in a multi-dimensional dream.

What is going on? Sister Agnes shouted, as if there was an element of doubt. As if she was deceived by her own eyes.

Look, Sister Agnes, this is not what you think it is.

But the expression on Sister Agnes's face confirmed that she was not as stupid as she looked. She came from a farming background and knew very well what male buttocks were meant to look like.

I've seen all kinds of animals trying this kind of thing, she said, blessing herself.

She was built like a bodyguard. Should have been working as a bouncer in one of the nightclubs, the way she came over and lifted Jimmy up with one hand and dragged him half naked all the way along the corridor towards the sluice room. When Jimmy tried to resist, she threw a killer punch which almost knocked him out. As soon as he got dressed, he was dragged ignominiously out of the Haven on to the street. Lucky not to be taken away by the Gardai.

You beast! she shouted after him. Don't ever come near this place again. Ever!

Mongi O Doherty had a knack for being in the right place at the right time. He had been driven up and down through the coastal suburb all afternoon by an associate. He had passed by the Haven nursing home on a number of occasions, but eventually caught up with Jimmy Coyne later on as he walked past Fitzgeralds' timber yard.

Jimmy had compensated for his bad luck by taking some afternoon narcotics. He was artificially elated as he wandered back home in the direction of the flat. Hardly noticed anything until it was too late. He was preoccupied with the fact that he had finally made it with Nurse Boland. He was in a dream. A big grin on his face, despite the almighty punch from God administered by Sister Agnes's fist, which was still throbbing in his jaw. Maybe his jaw was even fractured by the blow. It was a hoor to be in love, no doubt about it. But that was nothing in comparison to what was waiting for him.

Come 'ere, you fucking dirtbird bastard.

Mongi got out of his car and crossed Jimmy's path, carrying a wheelbrace. His assistant came around the other side of the car to make sure Jimmy had no escape. Gus Mangan, Jimmy's best friend, stayed in the back of Mongi's car, with his head down.

Jimmy was at the height of his powers of alacrity and cunning, however. The drugs and sex should have induced a benign acceptance of the world, but they also elevated his self-preservation instinct. He realised that his genes faced rapid extinction. Something about the look on Mongi's face told him that he was facing a straight Darwinian contest for survival. It was like any ordinary Sunday afternoon wildlife programme, with Jimmy as the zebra cutlets, Mongi as the greater shovel-nosed debt collector. Capitalism equalled chaos, was the basic message to be extracted here. It was

the natural order of things, and Jimmy owed this man money, simple as that.

It is behoving on you to give yourself up, Mongi demanded. Surrender, you little fucker.

Instead, Jimmy made an instinctive detour. His legs were programmed to make a run for it, rather than attempting any kind of serious dialogue. This was not the time for conflict resolution. He ran towards the timber-yard gates, which were closed. Managed to get a foothold on a low wall and heave himself up. Mongi and his mate were close behind. As Jimmy tried to get across the gate, puncturing his hand and thigh on the barbed wire along the top, Mongi took the wheel brace and repeatedly jumped up, trying to hit Jimmy's head.

Always go for the head, Mongi explained, as though he was reading an extract from a Marxist manual. Everything feeds the capita. Always take the principal sum.

But instead of hitting Jimmy's head and eliminating any chance of escape, Mongi only managed to hit his arm and his elbow. Just as his prey was beginning to get away across the gate to safety, Mongi hit Jimmy another prizewinning blow on the ankle. The wheel brace sought out that perfectly rounded, cupboard knob of the ankle bone with such a clean strike that it made a note, like the sound of a tuning fork, resonating with pain as Jimmy fell down on the far side. He couldn't walk. He was hopping around on one foot, trying to contain the screaming musicality of this long note in his ankle. Humming and holding a high C across the whole city like a howling lament.

Mongi and his partner climbed up on to the wall. They both wore tracksuits which made them look very athletic.

Jimmy's problems were only beginning. He tried to limp away from the pain towards a stack of timber. Smelt the wood and creosote all around him. Noticed the gleaming blade of the power saw reflected by the yellow light from the street. Imagined the pain of his ankle being sheared away like a piece of turned mahogany and his foot dropping down on to the pile of sawdust like a cheap offcut. The sawdust going pink with blood. The psychedelia of fear.

At that moment he understood the full implications of survival. Why tabloid newspapers were always raising public consciousness of pain and pleasure, increasing the threshold of feeling. Why everybody had become so obsessed with violence and gratification. He longed

to be back in the arms of Nurse Boland. Felt the warmth of her body luring him into submission.

In his intoxicated state Jimmy saw the rotary blade of a power saw running towards him out of the semi-darkness. He knew it was a common Alsatian guard dog, but he perceived it as an electric saw, spinning and whining as it came bounding through the timber aisles on four legs. Tungsten-tipped teeth and a long, purple-pink tongue dangling. Jimmy took another final leap of gene loyalty on to a stack of cut-price batons. The law of the jungle. Where an enemy can suddenly become a protector. When the sum of what you owe to one predator is equal to what that predator owes another.

You're dead, Mongi shouted, as he threw the wheel brace at him. But it missed the target this time and clattered ineffectually along a shelf of planks. Jimmy was safe for the moment, protected by the dog barking continuously like a vicious peacekeeper. There was nothing they could do but watch Jimmy making his way to the other side of the timber yard, climbing from one island of wood to the next until he escaped across the far wall and limped off down a laneway.

Coyne responded quickly to the distress call from Corina. It was exactly what his life needed: a rescue operation, a humanitarian mission. He went to the take-away restaurant and found her wearing a paper hat and a uniform. Held up the queue of hungry customers, told them to have a bit of patience while he asked her some questions. She was reticent and embarrassed: kept looking around at the manager, who was staring at her with a smile that was like a slug curling up in salt. Corina kept telling Coyne to order something. This was no place to start explaining what had happened.

Is there some problem here? the manager eventually asked, and Coyne ordered a strawberry-flavoured milk-shake.

He said he would wait till she finished work, and sat there like one of the lonely men staring into the distance all evening as if struck by some evangelical vision. In the old days they would have hung around in churches. Coyne watched the customers coming and going. The same routine repeated into infinity over a thousand times. People entering with expressions of hope and joy, staring in awe at the board where the menu was written up, then sitting down in the

purple chairs, urgently hand-feeding themselves and leaving again in a bewildered state of grace.

Every now and again a young man came around with a brush or a mop to clean the floor or to clear away the trays. Outside the light was fading and giving way to night, while inside the restaurant was bleached in a bright fluorescent wash that showed up every blob and blemish.

They attacked my brother, she said, when Coyne finally escorted her away from the place. She outlined her predicament. The threats made against her if she didn't pay up.

She and twenty-four other people had paid their passage by boat, and now had to pay a second time because the money had been stolen. She had been forced to collect a levy from each of them and pay over the ransom in weekly instalments. Now the men were demanding the whole lot, within a week.

Don't let them give you a hard time, Coyne insisted. I'll deal with them. I'll sort out those bastards.

She smiled. It was a brave thing to say; gallantry from another epoch. He was ready to lay down his life for her and take on the agents of exploitation. He did not tell her that he was an ex-Garda, because he didn't see himself as a Garda any longer. And the Gardai were the last people to deal with this. As always, he had a plan.

You've got to get out of that place, Coyne said. You can do better than that.

It's a start, she said.

Your luck is going to change, he promised.

I don't know, she said.

She invited him inside her flat. He didn't want to intrude, or appear as though he was looking for a reward, but she begged him not to refuse her hospitality. Insisted on offering him a drink in the kitchen. Corina's brother and cousin were there. They repeated the story of their assault, detail by detail, and Coyne listened to every word with great anger. Vowed to kill the men who had carried out this attack.

Wait till they deal with me, Coyne said with an earnest expression, hair standing up on his head as if to prove he meant business. They made a big miscalculation, the bastards. Don't worry about it. It's all sorted out.

The women in the flat came and shook hands with Coyne. He had difficulty pronouncing their names, but he gave it a try. Smiling at them all.

It was like the old days in Ireland, when a visitor changed everything. The visitor brought the excuse to abandon life and step into a temporary fantasy. It was like walking into a house in Beal an Daingin when Coyne was a boy. Everything stopped. These people knew what the real welcome meant. They understood the feckless impulse of hospitality that was needed to make this the last great occasion on earth. They knew how to stop time; how to create a life-affirming moment of immortality. To laugh in the face of tragedy.

Coyne might well have stepped into their homes in Romania. They ushered him to a small table and made him sit down. Cleared the cups and food away and placed an unmarked Napoleon bottle of home-distilled plum brandy down. Filled tumbler glasses to the brim and stood back, talking all the time and watching him with pride.

Tuica, Corina said. Go on, drink up.

Coyne sipped the firewater. It was like *poitín*. Rocket fuel that went straight to his head. Jesus, they should mark that bottle with a skull and crossbones, he thought. He would be drunk for a week on this. Then start seeing white flashes. But he was ready to give everything to this spontaneous celebration. Nothing but complete abandon.

They offered him cigarettes even though he didn't smoke. Opened a new packet in front of him. Big white Smirnov ashtray. Romania was the last great refuge of smokers, they said.

Corina took on the role of interpreter. She described the journey to Ireland by trawler. Stuck in the cabins all the time, with no light and the smell of fish and diesel fumes in the air. Some of them vomiting because they had never been at sea before, not even on the Black Sea. Tudor recalled the fish diet he had been given. They were almost apologetic about it and kept saying how friendly the Irish were in general. OK, people kept mentioning Dracula, but that was easy to handle. It was the Irish who had invented Dracula in the first place.

Coyne raised his glass to them all. He was already spinning with passion. Toxic with emotion and charting the great undiscovered link between Ireland and Romania.

Of course, he thought, it was the sad gene. Here they were at last, the emigrants returning to Ireland. The Blasket Islanders. The

famine people coming back in their coffin ships. *A stór mo chroí, when you're far away from the land you will soon be leaving.*

It was true, you could never escape history. For Coyne, however, the past was far more real, far more genuine than the present; his imagination far more vivid than reality. He could only see those parts of Ireland that had already disappeared. The great paradox of emergence and loss. He should have taken more notice before it was gone, during the glorious pre-television peak of Irish civilisation. The past was like a lost lover. He should have known that this was the end of Ireland. Now it had leaped ahead into a new age of golf courses and windsurfing. Golf was the heart of Irish culture – that's what they were saying in the ads.

Coyne was trying to reverse time. Desperately clutching on to history in the same way that he was clutching at the lapels of Carmel – begging her to go back to the old days when love was simple. But she was having none of it. Coyne doggedly held on with that undignified and cloying embrace that eventually drives loved ones further away.

He was requesting the impossible. Trying to preserve everything like a museum. Begging the people of Ireland to wear the old clothes. The red dress and the lace-up boots. The Galway shawl. Pampootees! He was pleading with them to go back to currachs and Connemara hookers. Turf smoke and damp cottages. Put the rags up against the back door to keep the rain out. Hang the spiral fly trap from the light in the middle of the room. Carmel had become inaccessible. A figure of nostalgia, drifting away out of reach into the history books. Into black and white, Father Browne type photographic collections. Soon he would no longer recognise her, just as he could no longer recognise the Irish landscape.

Coyne was whirling with the effects of plum brandy. And still the Romanians were filling up his glass and pressing cigarettes on him which he couldn't smoke. He stood up with his glass to make a statement.

Welcome to Ireland, he said.

They stood up with him, and held their glasses up. To Ireland, they said.

It's not much of a country, but you're welcome as the flowers in

May to any part of it. As long as you don't start playing golf. That's the only thing I'd like you to do for me. Don't take up golf, for Jaysus sake. This country is blighted by golf courses already.

They thanked him, then swiftly moved into the dancing phase before Coyne got a chance to start talking again. It was only nine o'clock in the evening and Corina was urging Coyne away from the table into the middle of the kitchen.

You ain't nothing but a hound dog...

Corina led the way. In her loose, flowery red dress, she was showing Coyne how to relax and step outside himself. My God, these Romanians had something to show the Irish. They understood dancing the way it was meant to be. No more of the pseudo-Irish dancing with the wiggle of the hip. This was rock 'n' roll with gypsy blood. All they had to do was raise their arms, click their fingers, clap their hands and the whole room was dancing. One shoulder held provocatively forward and a look of powerful defiance in their eyes. There was no stopping them. Corina and Coyne jiving around at high speed with Caius and Tudor and some of the other women dancing in the background until the floor of the little kitchen was throbbing like a trampoline. The window shook in time to the music. As though rock 'n' roll had just been invented.

Coyne danced like a madman. A truly international epileptic explosion of boogie, shuffling, jiving and set dancing. Even if his head was incapable of commanding his limbs and the control of his legs was lost in a juddering mêlée, it was clear that he was having fun. He was enjoying this night in spite of himself. Having a ball for once without a single Irish person in sight. Perhaps his audience had finally disappeared. That night, Coyne appeared to lose all the inhibitions laid on his shoulders. He was abroad. Away from Ireland in a strange land of dancing and swirling plum brandy.

Later, when they were exhausted, he sat down with Corina alone. They talked for a while about Bucharest. About going for walks in the park every Sunday with her parents. There would be peony roses out now. She was homesick at times. And Coyne once again found himself in a fatherly role, as though he had adopted her as a daughter.

The familiar streets of the borough were like an anticlimax. He was back in Ireland, walking home along the usual route with the

sound of his own footsteps. Gateway after gateway, he passed by the gardens with their ornamental stones. All over the place, people were bringing more and more stones up from the shore. Every night Coyne noticed the latest additions. New oval-shaped boulders outside hall doors. Silly little lawn borders. Stone circles around rose beds. It was a great abuse of the natural world, forcing these rocks into suburban slavery. Coyne was ready to pick up one of their designer rocks and throw it through a front window. One night he would come down with a wheelbarrow and collect all of these stones and bring them back to the sea.

It seemed that the brief euphoria of dancing with the Romanians would inevitably be followed by some trauma. Even before he turned the corner into Cross-eyed Park and in through the garden gate to his own flat, there was a premonition of disorder. His flat had been ransacked. As he climbed the stairs, he saw the door ajar and the bootprint close to the lock.

Fuck, he uttered. His flat looked like a handbag turned inside out. Clothes everywhere. Documents scattered. Cupboards emptied out.

Coyne felt the calmness evaporate. He was suddenly exposed again, not only to the audience in his head, but to his enemies. The place no longer belonged to him. It was draughty and public, as though the doors could never be shut again and the intruders had taken away all sense of privacy. His flat was basically open to the street now. What worried him more was that nothing was taken. Just stuff thrown around the place as if they'd been looking for something specific. It was almost like a police search.

A box of photographs lay scattered across the bedroom floor. This is what he had taken away with him from the marriage: a tin biscuit box full of images. Not once since he had moved out had he opened that box, because he saw it as a last resort. Photographs of the children when they were small. Of Carmel and Coyne together laughing. Of Nuala and Jennifer on the swing. And lots of photographs of Carmel and the children from behind, looking out over the sea – the ones that Carmel always put away because she said they were depressing. Now they all lay on the floor. He knelt down and began to pick them up, looking at each one of them carefully before putting it back in the box.

It was the symbolic force of the intrusion that burdened him. The

thieves had stolen something intangible. Something that could not even be identified in words.

Coyne attempted to put a few things back in place. Lifted a chair, closed a cupboard door. He thought of reporting it to the Gardai and knew he should leave everything the way it was. He wandered around looking at the mess of his own home. Going from one room to the other saying fuck! Tried to convince himself that it was a normal break-in. He had dealt with a lot of this, as a Garda. But he was increasingly aware of the fact that this was a search, not a robbery. He went through a subconscious inventory of belongings. Maybe that invisible item would be found missing months later. All items of commercial value were untouched. TV. Video. Ghettoblaster. What else was there to break into Coyne's flat for. The toaster? Bath towels that Carmel had given him last Christmas?

Where was Jimmy? Coyne phoned home and talked to Nuala. Carmel was out and Jimmy was taking a bath. Coyne knew that his son had something to do with it. What kind of stuff had he got himself involved in? He suspected drugs. He had seen the result of these hasty searches, normally accompanied with a dead body. He was unable to close the door of the flat because the wood around the lock was split.

He walked briskly to his former home. It wasn't far away, but the landscape began to unnerve him. When he turned the corner into the familiar street, he was assailed by the memory of his old life. The fact that he had left home had less to do with Carmel than with the oppression of this neighbourhood. It's these bastards he was getting away from, with all their own suburban ideologies. Mr Gillespie, the nocturnal golfer next door. And Mrs Brindsley across the road, with her B&B and dog minding service. At night, the tourists checked in and in the morning packs of dogs emerged with grotesque regularity. Dogs barking at the gates of hell every time you passed by the garden. Mrs Brindsley with her authentic seashore pebble driveway and her DIY identity.

There was a car parked outside his home. A Mercedes.

He stood back. Took cover behind a hedge that hung over the garden wall on to the pavement. He could see Hogan and Carmel in the car together. Leaning towards each other. Talking and kissing.

Coyne reached a depth of depression. There was nothing he could do, in spite of the fact that his methodology had always

been characterised by instant action. Insurrection! A call to arms! Everything in Coyne's life had to be solved by generous deeds, often involving great personal sacrifice. He wanted to go and rescue Carmel from this bastard. He was ready to make his move, ready to drag Hogan out and impale him on the Mercedes emblem of the bonnet. He'd break his fucking back for him. Jesus, Hogan would be in a wheelchair, pissing himself.

The problem was that Carmel did not want to be rescued any more. She had been seduced by the new Ireland. And if Coyne resorted to force, he would end up driving her into Hogan's arms. Coyne was helpless, hiding on his own street. Standing in semi-darkness behind a hedge with a shadow turning his face half black half white, and with strands of spider silk drifting across his head around his ears and neck. He looked like he was waving at Mrs Brindsley's bedroom window for a moment. A frantic signalling in the dark, struggling with a web, thrashing his arms around to free himself from these fine strings.

He saw Carmel stepping out of the car with a bag of stones in her hand. She leaned back in for a moment before stepping away and laughing across her shoulder. Waving goodbye without looking back at the Mercedes as it pulled away.

Jimmy had been immersing his ankle in hot water, but it was not doing him much good. He was still limping when he emerged from the bathroom an hour later. His ankle had turned dark purple. He got some of his clothes together. He would go on the run. The flat in Cross-eyed Park was no longer safe. Nurse Boland was the only person who could provide a safe house away from the attentions of Mongi O Doherty. Away from the attention of his own father.

He had left it too late.

Coyne was at the door already, ringing the familiar bell. Nothing had changed here except that Coyne was now an outsider. A stranger.

Is Jimmy there? he asked when Carmel opened the door. He was so disturbed that he could not bring himself to be civilised and say hello.

Carmel laughed. She was nervous. Had Coyne been following her? She had just had time to take off her coat when Coyne had pounced on the doorbell.

Pat! Look, it's past midnight.

Coyne looked desperate, standing on the doorstep with the porchlight casting a melancholy shadow around his eyes. A hurt man. He had forgotten to shave and looked stubbly. Out of touch with civilisation. Like he needed somebody to bring him back to earth and tell him when to change his shirt and brush his teeth. Carmel's heart went out to him. That orphaned boy-at-the-window look. But she could not invite him in. Not now. He would make her feel guilty. Kill all her privacy.

Come back in the morning, Pat. Let's talk tomorrow.

Coyne snapped out of his trance when he saw the bag of stones at the foot of the stairs behind her. Can I borrow your keys? he asked.

In the moral confusion, Carmel didn't know what to say. It was a spontaneous payment. She was buying silence. The fact that she put up no argument, and didn't even ask why he needed the car, said it all. An admission of guilt.

I need it in the morning, she said, dropping the keys into his hand. Not allowing his hand to touch hers. Not allowing his eyes to look into hers.

Jimmy came down the stairs and Coyne told him to get into the car.

Where are you going? she asked at last, but there was no explanation.

We're going to sort this out, he said.

He drove away as though they were never coming back. With an alarming yelp of tyres, he turned out into the street. Jimmy was afraid, not knowing what his father had in mind. He was almost craving the quantifiable threat of Mongi O Doherty. At least that was simply a matter of money, whereas Coyne remained utterly silent, locked into a kind of ideological riddle with no answer.

Coyne drove like a maniac. There was no other way to drive the small red car that Mrs Gogarty had bought Carmel. Past the Garda station. Screeching around the corner on to the main street. Feckless and furious. Turning towards the harbour and down to the very spot where Tommy Nolan had met his death.

Not here, Jimmy pleaded, looking around and expecting to see Mongi lurching towards him with the musical wheel brace.

Why not? Coyne said suspiciously. Was the truth coming out at last?

He stopped the car and left the engine running. The moment of reckoning.

They were parked near the edge of the quay. Nothing between them and the harbour now, not even a rope or a bollard. Just a step away from the surface of the black water. In the distance, some moored yachts swinging from side to side. Trawlers elbowing each other as they rose and fell on the tide. Nobody around: not a soul to witness this impromptu courtroom in a car. Just the cheap whine of the engine and the utter silence between them.

Did you do it? Coyne asked with great solemnity.

What, Dad?

Coyne revved up the car. The engine hummed.

Tommy Nolan? I want the truth. Why have they ransacked the flat?

I don't know, Dad. I didn't go near Tommy.

The truth, Jimmy, that's all.

Coyne let the handbrake down. Edged the car forward as if he had already made up his mind. Collective suicide. The most honourable way for them both to go. The truth involved sacrifice and he was ready to go with his son.

Jimmy began to cry. He was still only a boy, for Godsake.

What could he say? He was dealing with Coyne's justice. A kind of double-bind test. The self-implicating verity fork. Because no answer could reach the absolute standard of truth set by his father. If he denied the murder of Tommy Nolan once more they would both be in the harbour, struggling with the fuel-laden gunge coming into the car.

The headlights of another car flashed over the water in front of them. It was like a door opening, letting in a shaft of light across the boats. Perhaps it was Mongi O Doherty coming to rescue Jimmy from his own father, inching slowly past the shipyards, down to the quays. Casting huge moving shadows, a candle coming down the stairs. Past the barracks. Right down to the foot of the pier where it stopped and the headlights went out, as if the door had closed again.

Coyne looked straight ahead. His breath was noisy, making a big sawing noise, keeping time with the crisis.

Jimmy looked around at the yellow half-darkness where the other car was now parked. Yellow eyes watching. Jesus, if it was Mongi,

then he might as well die, here and now, with his father.

Go ahead, Jimmy said at last. Go ahead and drive.

Coyne turned to his son. He was clearly surprised and elated by this response and looked right into Jimmy's eyes as though he had witnessed a great redemption. He pulled the handbrake up and switched off the engine. Tears in his eyes. Tears in Jimmy's eyes too, knowing that he had given the correct answer by sheer accident. Jimmy had shown himself to be made of the same noble stock as his father. He was ready to die to uphold the truth.

By Jesus, Jimmy!

Coyne got out of the car, went round to Jimmy's side and opened the door. Nodded to his son to step out, then embraced him with a vice-grip hug. Jimmy's ribs were nearly crushed right into his spine. His shaggin' vertebrae were coming out through his mouth and his lungs punctured with the weight of paternal affection. Coyne kissed his son vigorously on the cheek to complete this extraordinary ritual. The trial on the pier.

I knew you didn't do it, Coyne said in triumph. I knew all along.

Then he let go of his son and they both stood for a while looking into the solemn black water below. They had just dumped some great secret into the harbour and were watching it long after it disappeared. They understood each other fully – they had entered into a great lie together.

You're my son, Coyne said with great feeling. I'll protect you.

Thanks, Dad!

Jimmy wiped his eyes with the back of his hand, trying to look like a man, and nervously glancing up the quay.

In perpetuity, son. I'll protect you in perpetuity.

Coyne slapped him on the back, a reward for his bravery. Of course, there were other questions that needed to be asked, but the communion of minds put matters of a practical nature on hold. It was a genuine father and son, funicular type relationship – pulling each other, but in opposite directions. An equal and opposite interdependence. Coyne didn't want to know anything else, because that bright blue kernel of understanding had been located. They didn't need to say a word more. They had postponed the truth. A dizzy reprieve, with the smell of fishboxes and engine oil all around them.

There was somebody whistling. It echoed across the water towards them and Coyne turned to see a figure approaching with a torch, beaming along the quay. Jimmy thought of making a run for it, but Coyne pushed him back into the car and got ready to drive away again.

It was Sergeant Corrigan. Whistler of all people had to come down and catch father and son staring into the harbour. This didn't look good at all, Coyne realised. Whistler, the plain-clothed Holy Ghost standing on the pier with his torch shining from below, making a mental note of the circumstances.

Coyne rolled down the window and smiled at the sergeant, as much as to say: what the fuck do *you* want?

Are you looking for Jesus or something? Coyne said as he drove away.

Sergeant Corrigan staggered backwards, a strange epiphany glowing across his face. A grin of sanctity. An apostle in plain clothes, standing on the pier with the beam of his torch entering his open mouth and lighting him up like a luminous souvenir.

Were you really going to go in? Jimmy asked on the way home again.

No way, Coyne said.

You were only bluffing?

Christ, Jimmy. Do you think I was going to kill us both?

It was a strange denial which increased the terror in retrospect. In the awkward silence that followed, Jimmy began to experience the full aftermath of fear, when the moment of crisis had passed and the clarity of this bizarre Russian roulette sank in.

They had started building a wall on the street where Coyne lived. As he came out of the flat the next morning, he saw that a truck full of granite rocks had been delivered and men were out there already with their cement, laying the foundations. A piece of twine had been spanned from a gatepost to the far end of the front garden and one of the men was placing the first of the granite rocks into an open trench.

Coyne watched them for a moment with fascination. The same way that he had watched men building dry stone walls in the west as a boy. Here at last was a job Coyne would like to have done himself. He could ditch his career and become a wall builder like these men.

He admired the simplicity of the job, the plain sense of achievement.

One of the men wore a woollen hat on the side of his head like Toulouse-Lautrec. Coyne watched him slap cement on to the surface, then cautiously select a granite rock and place it on the cement. He tapped it into place with the handle of the trowel before stepping back to examine the progress from a distance.

This was a real job, Coyne thought.

Coyne went to visit Fred Metcalf, bringing another box of chicken nuggets with him, and some Kimberley biscuits. There was a time when he used to tell Fred everything that went on in his life. But now he had become a little more guarded and they talked merely in an agreed tone of melancholia.

Fred was going through a bad time. He was on multiple medication and had finally received a hopeless prognosis from his doctor. The obstacle lodged in his intestines was immovable. Fred Metcalf, the security guard, was going to die like Elvis, with a cement block in his stomach.

Coyne put on the kettle and they sat for a while and talked, because that was all that was left to do. Fred didn't even eat biscuits any more. Packets of them were piling up on the kitchen cupboard. He was wasting away.

They're not being honest with you, Coyne said. Doctors are liars.

Nothing they can do now, Fred whispered.

I'd put them under pressure. Demand the best consultants. I'm sure there's something they're not telling you.

But that was far too much hope for one afternoon. There is nothing more irritating to a terminal patient than the sound of blind optimism. Fred had no time for hospital waiting rooms. He was basically like Coyne. He didn't want to be cured. What was the point?

Diabolical, was how Fred put it. He was not just talking about his own health but the health of the nation.

It's not fair, Coyne said.

Look at them all dancing around, eating Pringles, Fred said. Everyone smiling at each other all the time. You'd think they had some disease or other that was making them soft in the head. Happy as pigs in shite all of them.

I know what you're saying, Coyne agreed.

Everything is great, Fred said. Everything is cool and wonderful. Everything is a masterpiece. A *tour de force*. A triumph. The whole country is praising itself out of existence. All these empty superlatives. One of these days they're going to run out of superlatives, Pat.

Absolutely, Coyne colluded. There's nothing ordinary.

Fred and Coyne had long been of one mind about the decline of civilisation. They were staring up the same areshole of gloom, so to speak. Two men with grave expressions on their faces, belonging to the elite club of global paranoia, with only a minimum of sunlight entering the room through the small window, and the certainty of Fred's slow but imminent death underpinning the decline. Both of them brought up on tragedy, war and doom expectancy which they were forced to remain loyal to. An ancestral readiness for disaster. As if they were waiting for the return of the bad days and deeply mistrusted the new optimism and fun: the forces of darkness and remembrance fighting a constant battle with the forces of brightness and forgetting. One of these days that optimism would fall flat on its face. Then Coyne and Fred would have the last laugh.

Yeah, but are they happy? Fred asked triumphantly.

Good question.

You can see right through all this aerosol happiness. It's fake.

They're only putting it on, Coyne said. Maybe Fred was right. Maybe the Irish were basically a sad people who pretended they were happy, just waiting for the next calamity. Going to all kinds of clownish extremes to deny their melancholia.

It's the dogs of illusion, Fred concluded, shaking his head.

In the afternoon Coyne almost ran into his bank manager again. This time he was standing outside the book shop in the shopping centre. The town-killing Dun Laoghaire shopping centre. The ubiquitous Killjoy was now beginning to follow Coyne around, it seemed. Coming to haunt him after all the telephone calls. Maybe the Bank of Ireland had a long memory and had started cloning dozens of Killjoys, distributing them throughout the borough to stalk Coyne.

Mr Killmurphy was staring straight at him. Giving him the evil eye. Ready for confrontation.

It reminded Coyne to make more phone calls and to be more consistent in his campaign. Killjoy looked a little too happy. In fact,

it appeared that Killjoy was saying something to Coyne across the distance. Killjoy looked like he was going to come over to talk to him.

In the background, George Michael was screaming *Freedom!*

Coyne had to make a swift detour to try and avoid Mr Killmurphy who was now coming towards him with a big grin on his face. Even had his hand up to indicate that he wanted to engage Coyne in conversation. To accuse him. Or maybe to ask for a truce.

Fuck off, Killjoy. You can't talk to me.

As Coyne made his escape along the rail, sprinting almost, with a shopping bag dangling beside him, he could see in the corner of his eye that Killjoy was diligently giving chase. It was like one of those Olympic walking races, where the contestants are not allowed to run. Killjoy galloping along with lots of torso movements and elbow power.

Coyne managed to get to the elevators, but then discovered that both were going up. It was typical of the town-killing shopping centre management to trap people on the upper floor to prevent egress. The twin elevators of no return. The inward and upward valve of shopping mall psychology.

Coyne, almost caught, got away just in time. He had to act fast, and eventually escaped by running down the hallway towards the next exit. Killjoy calling after him: Hello! Excuse me!

By late afternoon, the wall outside Coyne's flat was almost finished. He stopped to admire the work. The men had gone home and a temporary barrier had been erected around the site. Coyne stood for a while examining the pointing and the skill with which the builder had selected his rocks. The cement was still drying, but the wall was already indestructible.

It was a masterpiece, of course, but he didn't want to start breaking into superlatives, going over the top and saying it was a brilliant wall. Or that no wall had ever been built like it. It was such an original wall. A new wall. A *tour de force* wall.

For Christsake, no. A wall was a wall.

He admired it quietly for a moment and went inside. The different shades of granite merging into a pattern. It was a fine wall.

At the harbour bar, McCurtain was drunk and acting up. He was annoying two local lads who had come back home on a visit with

their German wives. They had just returned from Munich for the first time, visiting relatives, spending money and buying pints for all their local friends and neighbours. But McCurtain was full of drink already and took exception to them. He felt that these two feral homing pigeons didn't look quite right. They were too tanned and well dressed, taking their affluence to extremes, laughing and joking with the locals in a thick Dublin accent laced with a Bavarian swagger. The language of lederhosen made McCurtain bitter. It was sheer jealousy. One of the women was wearing glossy lipstick, and the pink print of her lips was embossed on the rim of a pint glass.

Where are you from? McCurtain asked.

Munich, one of the women answered.

Munickers!

It was a dodgy moment and the men exchanged acid looks. There would have been a row straight away only that one of the women smiled and acknowledged McCurtain's shabby joke with an equally shabby response. Pouting her glossy lips, she shifted around on the barstool and said they weren't half as tight as Dublin knickers.

McCurtain was taken aback, and after a moment's silence, everyone laughed it off. But he kept up his resentment. Wouldn't believe that the men were local.

You're not fuckin' Irish, he bawled. No way.

Bloody sure we are. York Road, born and bred.

Would you shag off! McCurtain waved his hand.

I swear to Jaysus. My passport has a fuckin' harp on it, you know.

But it was a big mistake to defend your origins in the Anchor Bar. McCurtain refused to accept their credentials. Challenged them to prove they were Irish by singing a song in the Irish language. And while McCurtain was looking the German women up and down with lascivious interest, the men sang *Cill Chais*. They got most of the words right and were clearly delighted at their excellent powers of retention. Working in a Bavarian printing firm with the noise of big machines around them every day, drinking abundant litres of German beer every night and still able to remember a sad old classroom lament to the ancient Irish oak forests. *Tá deire na gcoilte ar lár...* but even then, they didn't look Irish enough for McCurtain. I mean, how Irish do you have to be?

Krauts! You can't sing either.

Fuck off, one of them retorted. I'm as Irish as a Hiace van.

Ah! McCurtain exclaimed. Now why didn't you say that in the first place? At last he began to believe them. The Hiace van. A true icon of Irish life.

They shook hands and embraced each other like brothers. In turn, they called McCurtain a Hyundai hatchback, and everyone became instant friends. Hyundai and Hiace suddenly became more indigenous than the Irish themselves. More pints were called for, and there was laughter all around until one of the women suddenly slapped her hand on the bar counter and said she could not let it go. There was a point to be made here about the whole issue of ethnicity. Furious at the slur against her husband, the woman with the glossy lipstick laid the matter to rest once and for all with a short eloquent burst.

You fucking *Arschloch*, she said, pointing at McCurtain. What is this problem with you Irish? I don't care who is what here. And even if you are some kind of Celtic prince, you are still nothing but a big *Arschloch*.

Ah, take it easy, McCurtain said, holding his hands out in supplication.

The Anchor Bar was silent. The barman stopped serving just to watch McCurtain being put in his place with a Bavarian *oomph*. She gunned him down with a big tirade while McCurtain looked at his shoes and leered. The twisted grin of shame.

Big Celtic *Arschloch!*

Coyne sat on his own with his pint, trowelling away the excess foam from his mouth with the back of his hand. The Anchor Bar was gaining momentum. Heading towards closing time fast. One of the visiting emigrants on the far side of the partition was still trying to put his origins beyond doubt with a new song. *You may travel far far, from your own native home*, he kept thrashing out again and again with fiery pride, but he couldn't really get going at all. The lyrics stopped there every time. Like a drunk trying to get up on a bike, cycling along with one foot but unable to swing his leg over the saddle and take off properly.

McCurtain wasn't going to listen to this philistine any longer. He spotted Coyne and went over to him. Bought him a double whiskey without even asking. Coyne was stunned at this generosity. What was

happening? Had he won some money or something?

I hear you're dancing with strangers, McCurtain said.

Who?

Stranger came in here looking for you recently. Young Romanian supermodel.

How do you know?

Word of advice, Pat. Lay off the wet-backs, unless you want a visit.

Coyne laughed. The whiskey was placed on the counter beside his pint. A double Jameson. Ten years old and beaming through the glass with a reddish, gold glint. McCurtain threw out a fifty-pound note.

A visit from who? The Pope? Michael Jackson? Dana?

Look, I'm only the messenger, Pat. As a friend. Stay away from the strangers.

Shag off, Coyne said.

He turned on McCurtain. He was ready to put the Irish Casanova on his back. Nobody was going to tell Coyne who he could consort with. But there was something else behind this threat. Coyne looked at the whiskey on the counter, a strange contradiction of generosity and domination. What was this about a visit? Coyne knew what it meant. He was getting the hint, from a sacred organisation. Coyne tried to counter the threat with cynicism. Imagined McCurtain going up to the Provo army council and saying: lads, did you pay a visit yet?

What have you got to do with the Romanians?

Don't push your luck, Pat. I'm talking balaclavas here.

Coyne was vulnerable. He could fight McCurtain, but not the entire Provo hinterland. Maybe McCurtain had something to do with the poet getting beaten up outside the pub. Maybe McCurtain had something to do with Tommy Nolan. Everything was suitably enigmatic, and McCurtain's uncharacteristic generosity made Coyne think it was the end of freedom. What did it mean if Coyne accepted this drink?

Sláinte mhaith! McCurtain toasted.

Jesus, Coyne thought. Another closet Irish-speaker.

Coyne placed his hand around the poisoned chalice, rage and fear simultaneously taking hold of his motor neurons, while McCurtain smiled and nodded beside him. Coyne told himself not to be stupid. But he could not go along with the pretence. Instead of raising the

glass up and tasting the precious drink of quiescence, Coyne turned it upside down on the counter. The alarming clack of glass on wood reached other customers. The barman looked up in horror, instinctively aware of that strained silence that presided over pre-violent moments of intense anger. People in the bar listened to all kinds of irrelevant, faraway sounds, like a car reversing at the back. The cooler shuddering. A shuffle of feet.

Smoke stood still. The Anchor Bar was a big lung holding its breath, ready to cough. Free molecules of single malt Jameson lifted into the air as Coyne stared straight ahead of him. His outstretched hand was still holding the glass, like a high-voltage fence, defying anyone to come and touch him as the whiskey slowly ran across the shiny surface of the counter, finding its own meandering course towards the ledge and dripping down at McCurtain's feet. Soaking into the dark, seasoned wood of the floorboards.

Coyne was back with the psychologist. This time Ms Dunford was determined to make some real progress and wanted more facts, stories. Anything that led the way back to Coyne's childhood where the underlying trauma lurked.

What has my childhood got to do with it? Coyne asked.

The fire has probably triggered off something in your memory.

No way! Coyne insisted. There's no bad memory. I'm clean.

She kept trying. There had to be some dirty childhood scandal somewhere. Nobody could even begin to sort themselves out until they went through all the historical stuff. OK. You didn't want to throw Coyne's identity out with the bad memories. But he would stumble through the rest of his life like a wounded animal if he didn't try to reconcile himself with it.

I can't remember a thing, he said. He gave the impression of a man who was firmly rooted in reality. His life was based on avoidance.

Ms Dunford was like a dog with a rubber femur. Snarling with Bonio excitement at the thought of discovery. She took a different angle.

Pat, you have a truth fixation.

Sure. I want the truth.

Yes, but you can't live with truth. We all live with symbols. We need dreams. Fiction.

She was pushing Coyne into a box. Next thing she would be asking him if he belonged to those who were afraid they were being watched during sex, or those who wanted to be watched during sex. Next thing she would be encouraging him to go back to work, like a child being forced back into a buggy and screaming in the street with stiff-backed resistance.

It's all about fantasy, she said. Lives are stories.

So?

The brain is basically a storyteller, she said. And maybe she was right, Coyne thought. Maybe the function of intelligence was to tell lies and detect lies. The Irish were such good liars. All that beautiful dishonesty. Force of history had made us into 'a craftie people'. Great storytellers with no resources but their imagination.

I'm not going to start spouting superlatives, Coyne declared.

Coyne's truth fixation centred on Carmel. He could see nothing but Carmel, corrupted by Hogan. He was blinded by her infidelity. He could see her leaning against the wall in Hogan's house. He could hear her little voice, the tiny gasp of pleasure that still resounded like a fading echo in Coyne's head. He was obsessed with that.

He thought of other stories in his life. He shuffled through the big data bank of dodgy memories. The bees killing his father. The language war. The hedgehog in the car. His own attempted suicide. The abandoned shoreline of Connemara. He searched through his childhood looking for big-time recovered memory.

I was put in the girls' class, he said finally. In primary school.

You remember being put in the girls' class, she echoed. As punishment.

Three times, Coyne said. Maybe more.

Ms Dunford took it seriously, though he expected her to show more astonishment. Maybe it wasn't the great character-breaking incident he'd always thought it was. Maybe all kids experienced some gender angst. At least Ms Dunford wasn't laughing at him. At least she didn't just dismiss it and say: we all went through that sort of thing. Toughened us up, emotionally.

What were you being punished for?

Coyne could not remember the crime involved. All he could remember was the punishment. They said he was a bold boy: *buachaill*

dána. Then they dressed him up in ribbons and led him across the playground into the girls' school.

Yes, she encouraged. Go on.

Well, you know, he stammered. They brought me into the girls' class and put me sitting down. At the back of the class. Fourth class senior infants! *Rang a ceathar, cailíní.* The girls all kept looking around at me and laughing.

Ms Dunford tried not to smile. You poor thing, she wanted to say, put in there with all those girls. Humiliating. And terrifying too, I bet. Finally she was getting down to the real trauma. The Irish classroom. The austere rooms of childhood captivity, with high ceilings and cornice plasterwork. The grandeur of aristocratic homes, remodelled as Catholic schools in the new republic. All that bleak Georgian architecture of Dublin, casting a spell over innocent minds.

Do you equate women with punishment? she asked. Did this make you afraid of women?

No, not at all, Coyne said. I just wish they'd put me in a room with all of those *cailíní* now, wherever they are.

But that was sheer bravado. That was the small-boy macho line of defence he had always resorted to among his peers. The hero status he awarded himself when he was back with the boys again. Jesus, you don't know what you're missing, lads. You better do something really bad and get yourselves in there to *rang a ceathar, cailíní*. Underneath, Coyne was still trapped in the girl gulag, unable to get out. Unable to talk to women as equals. Still seeing everything in absolutes. Male and female. Black and white. Good and evil.

He recalled the fire. There was no fire brigade. Only neighbours running with buckets and basins. And children crowding on the pavement with bikes and rollerblades, stating the obvious in their own childish words. Look at the flames. Look at the mother screaming. There's a child left inside.

Coyne understood what was needed. The seconds were critical. He wrapped a wet coat around his arm and burst through the front door. His final act in uniform. He ran into a wall of smoke and toxic fumes behind which he saw the stripes of yellow flame and heard the growl of crackling wood.

I remember shouting, Coyne said. As though he could frighten the inferno off with his rage. Pushing through the smoke and punching at the flames. Choking and coughing until his lungs seemed to burst. His arms and knees felt the sharp stab of heat, as the anger of the fire turned on him. Coyne on his own. Just blind heroism.

He reached the return, halfway up the stairs. People were shouting at him not to go any further. The stairs were about to collapse. He stood on a mass of gleaming red cinders, as though the floor beneath him had been eaten away by red and black ants. Thousands of them with their red-hot pincers. In his urgency, Coyne had put his foot right down and felt the wood shifting underfoot, biting through his shoe. Hundreds of them gnawing through the leather at once.

His eyes were flooding with tears and smoke. He could not see a thing. Blindly lashing about him and shouting. Making one more effort to disperse the smoke and see up towards the landing. Because he heard a voice. And then momentarily saw the child at the top of the stairs crying, before his feet gave way. The cinder ants had eaten through the supports. The entire staircase collapsed underneath him. It was too late. He fell back down and his colleague dragged him out again on to the lawn.

That's what Coyne remembered. The endless loop of heroic failure. The sadness of defeat. The sound of voices all around him. And the rage of the fire taking over, given new life with a draught of wind gusting through the house, from the front door to the back window. Glass panes bursting in the heat.

Ms Dunford suggested psycho-drama again, getting together with a group of other wackoes so that Coyne could re-enact his traumatic moments. She was getting excited about the idea. Jumped up from her swivel chair and started plodding around the room in her big webbed feet again. Put her hands on Coyne's shoulders and gently pushed him back in his seat when he attempted to get up and escape.

Relax, she said. I'm not going to do anything to you.

Then she waddled around the room again.

I have an idea, she began. *Vergangenheitsbewältigung!*

What? Coyne moved back in his seat when her face came close to his. He was afraid of this new fiction. Give me back my truth fixation.

Why don't we bring you back to that school. Why don't we turn you into a little boy again. Just for one day.

Are you serious?

Why don't we put you in short trousers and bring you back?

You mean physically go back?

Yes! Why not?

Jesus Christ! Coyne should never have opened his mouth. Now look what he was getting himself into. An encounter with the past. Back to the classrooms of fear. Sitting in with the *cailíní*, just to see what effect it had on his psyche. You must be joking, Dunford.

The Anchor Bar was closed for renovations. Coyne was hoping to do a little group therapy with McCurtain and went around some of the other bars looking for him. McCurtain had some questions to answer.

In the meantime, Coyne started re-enacting all his own gear-grinding memories. Raking over his childhood with an increasingly reductive menace which was either going to destroy him or funnel him out through a gateway of pastoral calmness perhaps. For the moment, it was doing nothing but damage. The fire had taken hold of his intellect, standing out as the leading symbol of all his losses. Cuckold. Failure. Burglary victim. A cumulative powerlessness driving him on a self-destructive mission.

Somebody had to pay for this. It had worked before. Direct action!

Coyne phoned Killjoy once more, this time just bawling a string of abuse down the line, all about Killjoy's wife Nora. It was the only way to make Killjoy wake up and take notice.

It was time to put a few things right in this town: not just Killmurphy, but Hogan as well. The man who wrecked his dreams and blasphemed against his erotic mythology.

As he walked up towards Hogan's house, Coyne swept through the full traumatic economy of his existence. All the landmarks of hurt and defeat. Starting with the beige door of his school, going through all the wars and arguments in his life, all the way up to the fire that had put him out of work. The crackling fury of the red cinders under his feet. The victorious laughter of the fire and the hollow apology of his own static inadequacy. He could visualise Carmel's transgression with Hogan. Her breasts offered up to Hogan's eyes like an exotic

confection, the forward thrust design of the green bra exaggerating the gift-wrapped effect. A coy gaze downwards to undo the bow at the back and allow the harness to float away freely. And Hogan's boyish hands testing the spontaneous white Plasticine bounce of her emancipated breasts. The blind curiosity of his thumbs slipping across her illuminated nipples.

After all, Coyne knew her body so well: a territorial knowledge that was all the more vivid for the intrusive gaze. Hogan was looking in, disturbing the phantasmal secrecy of his love for Carmel. Bastard voyeur! Peeping into Coyne's dreams. Shattering the frail intensity of his sexual illusion.

He found himself marching towards Hogan's mansion – a land agitator finally driven by the limits of endurance to confront his landlord. Some kind of attack on his person or property is what Coyne intended. He didn't care what appalling ramifications would ensue. It was an act of passion. Of moral justice.

Along the way, Coyne passed by a building site and saw an earthmover parked quietly in a little compound. A corporation JCB which belonged to the new South Dublin sewerage scheme. They had spent months drilling through the granite crust of the earth under Dublin Bay, laying concrete pipes in order to carry Hogan's precious little nuggets of personal waste out to sea. It was time to move the earth under Hogan's feet. Just watch Coyne arriving on the doorstep with this JCB. There would be no time to cut the ribbon on the big sewerage scheme. No time to get to the bathroom even. Hogan would experience an embarrassing little solid accident in his trousers.

There were no witnesses. Coyne got into the cab of the JCB, hot-wired the starting motor with a bent nail and drove out straight across a plywood hoarding with shocking force. No need to open the gate. Such liberation! Such triumphant empowerment of the underclasses! It had the democratic mandate of a rebel song. The man who drove this egalitarian vehicle had the ability to change not only the face of the earth, but the course of history too. No earthly obstacles could impede the onrush of inevitability. Coyne, the revolutionary, driving steadily around the corner until he could see the stone lions coming into view. This was a poetic strike. The JCB chugged along the coast road like a dinosaur. A giant T-Rex making its way towards the home of Councillor Sylvester Hogan with primordial vengeance.

Coyne saw the pebbled driveway and the cluster of three birch trees on the lawn. For Christsake, he thought. That's a real give-away, Hogan. That's nearly as bad as the three ducks on the wall, you fecking *leibide*.

Coyne had now mastered the lifting gear. The T-Rex was opening his mouth and growling with voracious intent as he headed for the stone guardians. One lurching mechanical movement forward was all it took to lift each of them into the air. The lion on the left had an indifferent plastercast expression on his face as though he was about to ignore this great prehistoric predator and continue peacefully licking his own balls. The dinosaur moved through the gateway and towards the house, crashing right through the big bay window with the ruched curtains and spitting the animal out in disgust on the living-room carpet with a huge crescendo of breaking glass. When the JCB reversed, there seemed to be even more noise as it pulled the buckled PVC window frames out with it, lurching back and forth a little to maximise the destruction. Coyne then drove back for the other lion, which yawned imperviously as Coyne delivered him on to the doorstep of Hogan's home.

Coyne parked the T-Rex in the porch, taking one of the Ionic pillars down with him and breaking through the front door into the hallway before jumping down from the JCB and walking away. A primitive parable. He was sorry he couldn't stay and look at the disaster in more detail. But he carried with him the image of the lion on his back in the living room, surrounded by glass, the heavy velvet curtains moving in the breeze and the tangled PVC bay window frames lying in the rose bed. The JCB with its nose embedded in the front door.

Good lad, he said to himself. Give that man a doughnut.

As he walked away along the seafront, he seemed to be followed by a big cheer of appreciation, the roar of a football stadium. Coyne the suburban terrorist.

The lights came on in Hogan's house. Hogan and his wife came out and stood at the front door in slippers surveying the damage, appalled and horrified. Beyond belief. The moral outrage meter returning all Hogan's troubles at once. He was suffering from an acute form of back pain. A painful tingling around the back of his thigh, as though he and his long-suffering wife, St Norma of the

waxed bikini line, were doing some kind of sciatica waltz on the doorstep.

Mongi O Doherty was in a particularly asexual mood that evening. Having gone back to visit Sharon, the woman in his life most likely to represent carnal solace and least likely to fulfil a role in domestic economy, he was now curiously uninterested in sex. What he really needed was a mother who could cook, play the sex kitten, offer Oedipal comfort and also give breathtaking advice on business matters. As well as shut up and stay out of sight from time to time.

Sharon was a lousy cook; but she was all over Mongi with affection and sweetness, full of Rose of Tralee kindness. Her palliative, chimebox voice got a bit stifling at times, because all Mongi wanted to do that evening was to lie around bollock naked and watch football. Above him, the festooned canopy of the bed with its peach lace drapes hanging down like two half-moons. It was one of the last games on the soccer calendar. A testimonial, he called it. And what could be more unerotic than end of season, drag on, scoreless draw football. The referee hadn't even produced a yellow card yet.

Sharon was doing her best to liven up the situation, instantly assuming that there was something wrong with her if her partner preferred soccer. She was practically maiming herself. Trying to wrap her legs around one of the mahogany poles at the foot of the bed, vaulting across the massive TV in a red, cheese-cutter thong and recklessly reversing her centre-spread backside into his face, without even as much as a blink from Mongi.

I can't fuckin' see! You're blocking my view, he said. Sharon sulked.

Sport was the end of imagination. It was a refuge from sexuality and engagement. A mushroom cloud of sterility. She could tell by the heartburn look of bitterness on his face that he was not even satisfied by the game. He was gnawing like a badger at his already depleted fingernails, and it looked like the only thing he wanted to do with Sharon was to start biting her false purple-black talons. He was self-absorbed. He had failed to get his hands on Jimmy Coyne. In addition to that, he had been questioned by the cops in relation to the murder of Tommy Nolan. Sergeant Corrigan had put a number of awkward scenarios to him earlier on at his mother's house while his hamburger was going cold.

Sergeant Corrigan was now presenting Mongi with all the evidence he had collected. Amazing the amount of witnesses he had found. Mongi was a cornered rat, ran the theme of his message. And the Gardai were thematic, schematic bastards. There was only one thing Mongi hated more than all this unwanted attention, and that was being called by his real name, Richard. Pronounced by Sergeant Corrigan as Rigid! Spoiled his appetite and fucked up all his *jouissance*.

To make matters worse, Sharon started talking to Mongi's mickey. Mongi thought he was hearing things. Addressing his pecker, she was, in dulcet, nursery tones. She knelt down and had a private conversation with it as if Mongi didn't exist and this floppy little instrument of power and pleasure was the only friend she had in the world. As though Mongi's half-stiff ego was located right there in his ragdoll member. Careful not to get in the way of the lacklustre images of soccer, she chatted away.

Come here, my little pet! What's the matter with you tonight, you poor little peckerhead?

At first, Mongi ignored the use of these diminutive adjectives. All lovable items were little to the women he knew. A nurturing instinct to reduce everything to manageable infant dependency. A Sindy doll universe. Venerating his fragile id, kissing it and shaking it playfully from side to side, trying to spark a debate against the background noise of indifferent football cheers. Until she used one Lilliput superlative too many.

My sweet little sprat, she said, nudging it with her nose and whimpering.

Mongi looked down and discovered that his mickey had indeed taken on the blue-green stripes of a lower infant class mackerel. Flapping about and hyperventilating like it was out of water in an over-oxygenated environment.

What did you call it?

Darling little sprat, she repeated, looking up at Mongi with great concern. It was the wrong word. She tried to swallow and withdraw her face.

Too late! Mongi lifted her with a punch in the mouth that sent her across the room. There was a neat, audible click of her lips as the fist made contact. A wasted string of libidinal saliva was left hanging in

the air and Mongi wiped his knuckles on the bedspread in distaste. Then he jumped up and grabbed a lamp in the shape of a black nude bearing a yellow globe on her shoulder. Held it like a joystick, took Sharon by the hair and threatened to electrocute her womb if she ever used that term again.

You're saying it smells like a fish! he shouted.

No! Jesus, Mongi. I didn't say that.

You insinuated that I'm a fishmonger.

Mongi, no! Please. I swear!

Sharon was shaking. Her lipstick had turned to blood. She was astonished by the level of aggression involved in the preamble to sex these days. Thug foreplay. A bit of rough. A multi-pack of bruised breast fantasies delivered in one terrifying domestic assault. Gratified only by the stuttering sound of her Rose of Tralee voice begging for mercy, he switched off the TV, ready to punish this grievous misappellation.

Never say sprat again.

I promise, Mongi, she whispered, white in face. Counting her teeth with a scarlet tongue. Please don't mark me.

He kissed her mouth and sucked her swollen lip. Mongi the vampire, swallowing the taste of terror. But in that moment, the cellular phone rang. After him getting all worked up for it, then came the crass intrusion of the mobile phone. Another setback. An urgent business development that put an instant dampener on Mongi's dark desire. It was Jack McCurtain. A serious problem had arisen in the wet-back situation.

Of course. Why hadn't Coyne thought of this earlier? If McCurtain had been chosen to deliver a paramilitary message to Coyne, then he had to be in a position to lead the way. They expected Coyne to be afraid, they expected him to shrivel. Like all those people who had their windows painted black in final warning. They thought he would be cowering in his flat at the mention of balaclavas. Coyne felt vulnerable at first. Any man with a family would. But he had nothing to lose any more. He would not fret for the rest of his life like a frightened rabbit. Not Coyne.

He found McCurtain's house, rang the bell and waited. The door opened and emitted a waft of curry. McCurtain saw Coyne and

instantly tried to slam the door. Like they used to slam the door shut on all the Mormons and Latter-day Saints and Poppy Day sellers. Feck off back to England. Anyone who didn't conform with Catholic republican ideals. Coyne's own father was the same, slamming the door so the whole street would shake.

McCurtain didn't care for any creed at his door after midnight. He whacked the door like a tennis racket, creating a hostile gust in the hallway. The rebuff on the Irish doorstep. Except that Coyne was too fast an opponent. Stuck his itinerant boot in the door, close to the hinge at the angle of least resistance. Caused the door to bounce back ineffectually.

Sorry to disturb your dinner, Coyne said.

I'm busy.

You shouldn't be eating that kind of stuff so late at night. Give you nightmares.

What do you want?

I'm looking for your friend, the man with the mackerel.

Listen, it's got nothing to do with me. I don't take moral responsibility for anything else. I'm only the messenger, Coyne.

The dove from above, is that it?

Coyne pushed his way into the house and closed the door behind him. The smell of bindi bhaji was overpowering. He pushed McCurtain along the hallway towards the kitchen where he had been eating his take-away and watching hardcore porn. Tarka dhal and simultaneous ejaculations. For Christsake! Coyne was not easily disgusted by other people's proclivities, unless they included golf. But the thought of McCurtain horsing into his erotic Indian dinner was a sight too far. Indian food was the pornography of world cuisine.

Where is he? Coyne shouted.

Who?

The bastard with the message.

McCurtain claimed he had no way of contacting him. It was all operating on a strict cell system now.

Coyne had had enough of this evasion. Grabbed him by the neck and pushed him back into a chair, so that McCurtain suddenly found himself reclining gracefully with his legs sticking out straight for balance. Arms flailing around trying to grab hold of his take-away and sending basmati all over the kitchen floor.

For one minute, McCurtain thought he could get out of this by force. He got his hands on a fork and started stabbing the back of Coyne's neck, like some Jurassic bird pecking, until Coyne threw him down and cracked his head on the terracotta tiled floor.

Coyne felt his neck. Like a zip had been opened, letting in the air. His hand was red. The television was making appropriate gasping sounds of agony.

McCurtain, you Casanova bastard. You shouldn't have done that.

McCurtain huddled in the corner with his fork. Tried to gouge Coyne's eye out this time, until he was dispossessed of his weapon. There followed a straight, *Ryan's Daughter* style punch-up in the kitchen. McCurtain at times gaining the upper hand, throwing tarka dhal straight into Coyne's eyes. But at last Coyne won the battle and pinned McCurtain to the floor with the chair.

You're forcing me to do this, Coyne said.

He took a bottle of Tabasco sauce and stuck it up McCurtain's nose. A jet of the fiery liquid made its way down the nostril, burning through McCurtain's sinuses, making him sneeze half a dozen times in quick succession. This was chemical warfare. Red-hot lava trickling around the nasal cavity more powerful than any caustic toilet cleaner.

I swear, I don't know!

Another squirt of Tabasco in McCurtain's eye caused him to weep convulsively. Red-eye McCurtain, crying for Ireland. His eyeball bathing in a socket of acid. It was the only way of dealing with the situation, the physical force tradition. Fighting fire with fire. The inherent paradox of all warfare. Violence to end all violence.

Wait! McCurtain shouted at last. Can I make a phone call?

Mongi was furious. Right in the middle of a delicate moment in the build-up to love he had to negotiate with McCurtain. Jesus, the pong of garlic coming down the phone line was enough to put him off sex, if not football as well, for a year.

McCurtain was trying to speak in code. Explained his predicament in the most eloquent Irish. *Tá mé i sáin*, he said, using a common chess analogy. By the grimace on his face, it looked like McCurtain had surrendered.

Have you ever wondered what happens after checkmate? Coyne asked. The game doesn't end there. Tell that to your friend. The next

move is even more interesting. The defeated king gets roasted alive in a cauldron of Tabasco sauce.

Mongi put the statuesque bedside lamp of the black nude on the floor as he listened to this arcane gibberish coming at him across the phone in the middle of the night.

Gabh' agus fuckáil thú féin, he said.

Mongi didn't care about McCurtain. Why should he care if this ex-cop gave McCurtain a hiding. Let him give McCurtain the vindaloo treatment. They would get Coyne back in good time.

Meigeal an Mhaighdean Mhuire, McCurtain was screaming. He'll kill me.

Coyne started laughing to himself. What was all this garlic lark. Didn't they know that Coyne was a fluent Irish speaker? Coyne the true native. Not like these half arsed Irish speakers who spread a patina of the language all over the country like low-cholesterol margarine. Abusing the mother-tongue, turning it into an incendiary device. Gaelic as a weapon of war.

Coyne grabbed the phone from McCurtain and spoke directly to the leader.

Listen here, *a mhac*, Coyne shouted. Those new visitors from Romania. They're my friends. If you ever lay a finger on them again I'll incinerate your pal here. Every grain of that basmati rice is going into his urethra. Then I'll come over to your place and do the same to you, mate.

Mongi was calm. His fury had not had enough time to percolate into his nerve endings, still tingling with sexual promise. In the background, Sharon was tousling her hair. Exaggerating a rip in her belly-top and lying back as though she'd just been knocked off a horse or a tractor. Simulating a farming accident: absentmindedly taking blood from her mouth and smearing it on her cheeks. On her left ear.

Stop that, Mongi barked at her.

Coyne burst into another poetic string of golden Irish treasures. Cursing at Mongi with real *blas*. Mongi could not help being impressed. *Beidh tú sínnte, a mhac, le bud asail I do bheal agus méar an deabhail I do thóin*. Coyne was advising Mongi to put his mackerel in his mouth and smoke it.

Diúg do roinneach.

Mongi responded with a few lacklustre expletives and threw the

phone across the room. What was the point in talking to this crazed native speaker?

Mongi sat back on the bed. He had no real interest in the language, except for its fetish value And there was no way that he could resume the intensity of his love for Sharon, after all that garlic. Not with the same sadistic brio. He looked down and saw that his mickey had been reduced to a minnow. Paucity pecker! It was money he was thinking of. Because there was nothing as erotic as money. He was thinking hard.

Coyne found himself on shaky emotional ground after the encounter, as though there was some benign hand laid on his shoulder by the Irish language that made him tolerant again. Those few words made him realise what he had been missing. That sense of lost friendship. The consensus in adversity. Now at last he knew what was wrong with his country. They had lost that close-knit sense of support and good will towards each other when things were poor and everyone spoke Irish.

McCurtain was snivelling and nursing his eye while Coyne was struck by a huge wave of remorse. It was an unforgivable thing to do, to interfere with a man's meal.

It was just like the bread and seagulls incident where Tommy Nolan dropped his sandwiches in the school-yard and let out a silent shout of pain.

I'm sorry about that, Coyne said. It's not right.

What? McCurtain said, looking up with fear, still coughing and spitting.

I want to apologise for doing this to your food. I didn't mean to. It was wrong.

McCurtain was amazed by the sudden kindness and didn't trust such a dramatic personality change. He wished Coyne would stop talking about the food. Leave it alone. The damage was done now.

Can I get you some more rice? Coyne asked. Look, I'll go down and get anything you want. I feel terrible about this.

But it was too late. The Indian take-away was already shut. McCurtain gazed in astonishment at this bizarre reversal as Coyne picked up the grains of rice one by one. Coyne straightened up the chair. Swore he would make up for it as he lifted McCurtain up and

ushered him towards the table, begging him to resume his meal. Hoping to Christ he still had his appetite.

Here, have some more of this bindi bhaji. I didn't touch it.

There was remorse in the air. Skipper Martin Davis was also feeling a deep new unspeakable guilt on account of the death of Tommy Nolan. Even though he had no part in his death, he still felt he had contributed with his presence, with his words and with his tacit support. The force-feeding incident with the mackerel had changed his mind and he was now hoping to erect some kind of memorial to Tommy Nolan. He began to make a collection. Or effectively a bogus collection, because very few people could spare more than a few pence for a memorial and it was Martin Davis himself who put up the money. Then he consulted McCurtain, the guru of all commemoration, to see how best it could be set up. Perhaps some kind of plaque outside Tommy's council flat, or somewhere at the harbour, near to where he died. But that was a little too close for comfort, perhaps. They discussed the idea of a brass plate at the Anchor Bar, to show public appreciation for what Tommy had meant in their society.

Sergeant Corrigan was up early, standing on an outcrop of rock, looking out to sea through a pair of Garda binoculars. The lenses were a bit blurred, but he could see the *Lolita* just out beyond the bay, returning with a catch of fish and the trailing seagulls. What mystified him was that skipper Martin Davis had so suddenly decided to return to fishing. With the blue sky of an early summer's day, he was out there in the Irish Box hauling in the first mackerel shoal of the season, listening to them slapping about in the hold.

If the binoculars had been any stronger, Corrigan would have detected a smile of plain pleasure on Martin Davis's face as he sang to himself through his beard. Belly to the breeze. With the seagull chant in the background, the drone of the engine underneath him and the swell of the sea lifting the boat like the chorus of a song, he was reverting to a simple lifestyle. An ancient devotion to the sea. There was nothing to beat the frenzied sight of fish throwing themselves helplessly on deck in their thousands. Multitudes of green-blue mackerel. Better than the sight of money.

Coyne was on his own in the flat. He hadn't seen Jimmy in days. Since the big incident on the pier, his son had disappeared.

Coyne was decapitating a late morning boiled egg. Many people would have expected him to regret what he had done. To feel fear. To acknowledge some sense of impending reckoning for taking on the might of Mongi O Doherty. There was a lot of unfinished business out there.

Instead, Coyne was in a fighting mood. Shouting at the radio again.

Good, he roared, when the news broke that an oil company drilling off the west coast had failed to discover any commercial yields. After initially positive indications from geologists, shareholders had their hopes dashed. Disaster! A spokesman for the company said they would be exploring further sites, but that the field closest to the Aran Islands had sadly proved uncommercial.

Well, I'm glad, Coyne shouted back at the radio.

Jaysus, the country was in a state of bereavement. Flags should be flying at half mast and Coyne was laughing. Great news. One last reprieve! Leave that fucking oil where it is, you bastards.

There was a knock on the door. He was in the middle of his tirade, pointing a lump of egg yolk at the radio. Squinting with hot idealism at the invisible oil spokesman as though he was going to kill him with a spoon. He stood up and went to the door.

Carmel.

Somebody had let her in at the hall door. Maybe Coyne hadn't heard the bell with all the shouting.

Great, Coyne thought at first. Finally, she had decided to visit him. He asked her to come inside and sit down. She had ignored her mother's warnings. Into the den of thieves. But there was something solemn about the way Carmel stood in the middle of the room and looked down in disgust at the frugal egg on the table. Smell of toast in the air. One of his familiar T-shirts on the radiator. And a colourful kiddies plaster stuck on the back of his neck.

I'll never forgive you, she said, tears in her eyes.

What? Coyne with his schoolboy innocence.

What you did to that man's lions.

What lions?

You know very well what I'm talking about, Pat. It's disgraceful. Destroying his home like that. And for what?

Coyne reached over to the top of the fridge and grabbed a feckless amount of tissues out of the box. Handed them to Carmel. Jesus, she was starting to cry and Coyne would not know what to do then.

Don't expect me to get you out of this, she said. You can go to jail for this one, I don't care. I never want to speak to you again. So you needn't come up to the house. You can talk to Mr Fennelly.

Carmel had threatened the solicitor before, but this seemed more serious. She moved towards the door and opened it so that all his neighbours could hear his most intimate affairs. She wanted the public on her side.

You've nothing to say for yourself, have you?

Carmel, please. Sit down.

Piss off, she said. Doing a thing like that. And you've no explanation, have you. Because you're full of spite and jealousy. You're full of hate.

Carmel, look!

You're nothing but a vandal. A civic disaster. It's an abomination.

This was a smear campaign. She had no evidence that Coyne drove the T-Rex into Hogan's house. She was just making a wild assumption. Totally unfair.

Don't smear me, he appealed.

Besides, any fucking eejit with lions on his gatepost deserved to be dismembered and devoured in a Colosseum of plastercast artefacts. An audience of garden gnomes grinning at him and an eternity in the kitsch kingdom of hell at the end of it. With Christy Hennessey singing in his ear twenty-four hours a day. What about all those Toblerone cottages in Achill Island. What about that for a civic disaster?

You've nothing to say for yourself, Carmel said bitterly. Do you realise that poor man has a very bad back. He was just starting to respond to therapy. Showing great signs of improvement. And now look what you've done. He's virtually an invalid with all the pain.

Brilliant, Coyne wanted to say.

You've ruined his life.

It's you and me, Coyne said at last. But it was the wrong moment entirely. The timing was atrocious. Instead of showing some modicum of contrition, he was now going in the wrong direction altogether. He was in another world and could not connect with her anger. He was more inclined to start singing a cheap new love song to her. Let's get

it on, baby. It's you and me, maybe. Lovers keep on loving – darling keep on pushing – 'cause I'm gonna keep on gushing!

She looked at Coyne as though he was completely heartless. Have you no feeling?

At that moment she saw the rock on the mantelpiece: the rock with the white Saturn ring which had mysteriously gone missing from her room one day. There it was now in Coyne's flat, like a piece of her life that he had misappropriated and kept hidden. She looked at the stone, then back at Coyne. Fury and sadness in her eyes at the same time, knowing that she would always be stuck with him in some way or another.

She threw the tissues in his direction and turned to leave. They floated towards him and down to the floor, descending gradually like individual feathers. His reaction was to try at all costs to prevent any of them from reaching the floor. Grabbing and clutching at them while she ran out the door and down the stairs.

We're inextricably linked! he shouted after her. Neighbours downstairs looking up in disbelief and nervous curiosity.

Sergeant Corrigan was taking an even more grim view, standing at Coyne's door later the same day with a sombre look on his face. As a colleague and a local Garda ambassador, as an impartial agent of justice and a father of two boys himself, it was his painful duty to take Jimmy in for questioning once again.

This might come as a bit of a shock to you, Corrigan said. But we have reason to believe that your son has taken some kind of revenge act on Mr Hogan. With a bulldozer.

Coyne chuckled at the glittering irony of this accusation. Once again they had levelled at the child the crimes of his forefathers. Blame and moral responsibility passed on like a genetic inheritance. An heirloom of guilt and knock-on atonement.

He's not here, Coyne answered. And I don't believe he would have done a thing like that. Jimmy's changed.

I'm afraid he'll have to answer a few questions, Corrigan insisted.

I don't even know where he is. Haven't seen him for days. Weeks. You'll only make matters worse.

Sergeant Corrigan sympathised with the fact that Coyne would want to back up his son. But it was better not to push a man with

Whistler's reputation to the limit. This was a criminal investigation. He would be back.

Coyne suddenly changed the subject altogether. It was the only thing to do. Just as Corrigan was about to leave in frustration, he dropped a crucial cultural test.

Do you mind if I ask you a personal question, Coyne said.

Go ahead.

Did you watch *Forrest Gump* last night?

Yeah! Great movie, Corrigan said without reservation. Marvellous!

Thousands of people had watched the film on TV and the country was already divided into polarised camps – those who thought it was great and those who thought it was complete and utter rubbish. The same old breakdown of affinities. Except that from now on everything boiled down to what side of the Gump divide you were on.

I thought it was crap, Coyne eventually said with a grin.

Corrigan was shocked. He took it personally. Lashed back from his mono-cultural barricade and told Coyne he was going to be in trouble.

One of these fine days I'll sort you out, he warned.

But Coyne was smiling with elitist superiority. Corrigan raised his eyebrows. As far as he was concerned, Coyne was the odd man out. The loser. The uncool heretic who didn't get the message.

Jimmy was hiding out with Nurse Boland in her small, top of the house flat overlooking the seafront. His life had been syncopated into a timeless fantasy; the spatio-temporal vacuum of a high Georgian love nest with tall ceilings and large sash windows going from knee height right up to the ceiling. Every day, when Irene went out to work, he looked out over the blue sea and watched the ferry appearing on the horizon, enjoying the langourous repetition of people parking their cars and getting out to walk along the promenade towards the pier. Summer clothes were coming back at last. Buckets and spades. Children going swimming and playing ball along the waterfront. Dogs running in circles and figures of eight.

Jimmy Coyne and Irene Boland had struck a rich vein of bliss. He would never have to leave that apartment again. Every night she nursed his fractured ankle. Bathing it, drying it carefully, rubbing ointment into the swollen, purple stain around his foot and mummifying it in

a new binding. After which they made love and danced and loved and drank and took their drugs.

He missed the Haven nursing home. He missed shaving old men and speeding down the long lino corridor with the wheelchairs. Acting the fool with residents. Cracking jokes and doing interpretations of Coolio or James Brown in front of them. Instead, he undertook the housekeeping at the flat, hoovering and dusting and cleaning the big windows; even tackling the sticky, salt-encrusted stains of spring storms on the outside, so that when Irene came home she thought there was no glass at all, they were so clear. He discovered a natural talent for cooking; started producing some magnificent Italian masterpieces. Goat's cheese lasagne! Mushroom and Stilton risotto. Homemade spinach ravioli. As they sat over dinner in the evening, looking out at the solitary cargo ships moored in the black bay, he talked about getting married and going to live in Italy with her.

I have money, he said. Loads of money.

I'm nearly twice your age, she argued.

So? Why should that matter?

He stood naked at the window in the dark, with his skinny white body and his bony backside, making up stories while she sat in the armchair behind him, all bulbous and plump. They were a perfect couple as long as they remained in hiding and eluded their pursuers. Like Diarmuid and Gráinne.

They're after me, Jimmy said. We have to go away. They're going to kill me.

She laughed at the way he announced this threat with such gravity, as though she had anticipated this sex-induced paranoia. He had begun to invent a kind of fugitive mythology; a beleaguered mindset that became an essential part of their relationship. Love was not possible without these vital ingredients of fear and forced exile.

They're going to kill me, he said at least once every day, like a mantra.

It provided a context of ending. Of exclusion. A terminal narrative in which every moment was stolen. They were living with a fatwa.

Coyne took on the role of tour guide one afternoon. He had promised to show Corina and some of her Romanian friends around Trinity College and other landmarks of the city. He talked to them about the

famous writers. About historical facts. Here and there he stopped and told them about a bank raid, giving them the exact details, with dates of arrests and convictions. In some instances he was able to tell them the calibre of weapons used and the number of shots fired. He gave them a legal tour of the city – fraud cases, murders, abductions. It was all told with great enthusiasm, as if Dublin was famous for its crime. As he brought them up towards Stephen's Green he had something to say about every shop and every building. He stopped and gave them a brief history of the State. It was not unlike the Soviet Union.

Worse, Coyne said. At one time, every Irish child had an invisible listening device planted in its head.

Corina laughed.

Marlene Nolan was contacted by a number of people from the Anchor Bar in connection with a memorial plaque which they wanted to erect. It was explained to her that some of the fishermen including Martin Davis had made a collection to honour Tommy Nolan at the newly refurbished, soon to be reopened, Anchor Bar. McCurtain had been appointed treasurer and spokesman, so he called on Marlene to hammer out the wording at her small corporation flat. The place was blue with smoke. TV on at ten in the morning: another documentary on the death of Diana.

I don't know what to put on it, she appealed.

She was not used to this kind of decision. The power of words had always been the domain of the Catholic Church, poets and politicians.

What do you think Tommy would like? McCurtain asked.

But it was not what Tommy might have wanted, so much as what the community wanted. Some phrase or sentiment had to be found that would expiate their guilt. Like a candle in the wind. A local deification process by which the victim was becoming a contemporary saint and martyr, raised to the status of suburban hero. Not because of anything he did in his awkward, uneventful life, but because of the way in which his life ended. The people of this coastal Dublin borough needed to raise his memory out of the dirty harbour water in which he had drowned. Tommy Nolan, up there along with Princess Diana and Bobby Sands.

Here sat Tommy. Here sat Tommy and drank his pint. In memory of Tommy Nolan who was a regular here.

McCurtain was looking for something more legendary and dignified. Marlene smoked a dozen cigarettes trying to think, but her words seemed too crass: May the man who sits on this seat never be short of the price of a pint. May God bless Tommy Nolan. Even the old religious invocations sounded trite and misplaced in a pub.

McCurtain suggested a line from a song. *Four Green Fields*, he thought, would have had a good, resonant line in it, so he quickly went through the lyrics to see if anything stood out, half singing or speed reciting his way through it. In the end, she picked something from Tommy's favourite number. *Three wheels on my wagon, and I'm still rolling along. The Cherokees are after me....*

Perfect! At last, with tears in her eyes, Marlene made up her mind. It was the ideal way to describe Tommy with his limp, as though he'd always been missing a wheel or two but still managed to keep going. The symbolism was right. *I'm still rolling along!*

Clare Dunford was of the opinion that Coyne would profit from a session under hypnosis. Perhaps something would emerge that Coyne had suppressed all his life.

You can try all you like, he said. I can't be hypnotised. I'm not the type to yield under pressure.

If you'll allow me, she said, smiling. We can take it from there.

You're wasting your time, he argued. My personality isn't taken in by a dangling watch. Besides, I'm too much on edge. I'd never be relaxed enough.

Just let me try, she said.

Go ahead, he said. Be my guest, but it's not going to work.

Ms Dunford pushed him gently back in his seat, trying to disarm him. But the softness of her approach made him even more tense and hostile, determined not to slip into her power. He had become an expert at resistance. Insurrection. Repulsion.

She suddenly changed her style and began to turn Coyne's inner defiance into an advantage.

You're trying to resist me, she said, looking right into his eyes. You're really concentrating hard on staying awake, aren't you? You're using all your energy to counteract mine.

And finally he succumbed to her commanding tone, or perhaps it was more to her teeth, which forced him to imagine that he was floating upside down in the room. He was soon spilling out all kinds of debris from his cluttered mind, like an attic of stored memorabilia, a Gothic novel of psycho-babble.

The dogs of illusion, he repeated over and over. First he went into confessional mode, revealing a range of misdeeds that took Dunford by surprise. Then he began to rail against his enemies. He was cursing and swearing in the most vicious language known to man. *Téigh g'an deabhaill!*

By suggestion, Ms Dunford lightly steered him away and began to probe a little deeper to see if there was a more passive Coyne underneath. What she found was a benevolent maniac, because Coyne instantly snapped over into a phase of generosity in which everyone became his best friend. He was spouting superlatives.

Marvellous. I think you're all bloody fantastic, he said. Magnificent.

Dunford was alarmed at this sudden transformation. He was lashing out hysterical blandishments and hugging the world with new optimism. He was positively sentimental, full of cheap good will and gleaming TV commercial virtues.

It was a worrying development. She had unlocked Coyne's head and watched him descend into a spate of uncontained adulation, sitting in the chair and waving his hand about like a pontiff, giving his blessing to all. His fighting exterior had concealed a vulnerable intellect, given to bouts of indiscriminate praise. Beneath all the aggression and dereliction she found a vulnerable boy. He was a walking paradox, a victim-oppressor, an exhibitionist and a shy recluse, a mess of contradictions ready to switch over at any moment to benign pathos.

We are all bloody great, he announced. We are the best in the world. Nobody can match us. The rest of the bastards are only trotting after us.

Dunford could not bear it any longer and clicked her fingers. Coyne snapped out of his trance looking unusually relaxed.

Bet you I didn't say anything, he said cheerfully.

Ms Dunford would not respond at first, as though she was afraid to reveal the truth.

I knew it, he laughed triumphantly. I wouldn't break under torture either.

I'm afraid you did, Pat.

What? Coyne sat up. Eyes open. What did I say?

You started praising everything in sight, she told him. You said everything was good.

No way, Coyne barked. You're making this up.

He sat back again, obviously distressed. Betrayed by the Coyne within. There was nothing he could do about it.

I think it would be a good idea to go back to the school, she suggested.

It won't do any good, he said.

She came over and put her hand on his shoulder.

Coyne went to visit the grave of his mother that same afternoon. No matter what crisis might arise, he could not miss going to the cemetery on her anniversary.

It was his mother he thought of first. He could hardly remember his father's death, it was so long back. As he walked up to the grave, he thought the headstone should have something more written on it, not just the names and dates. There should be a descriptive sentence. Sean Coyne, murdered by his own bees. Jennifer Coyne, who died after a break-in at her home.

It was another mild day, unlike the day she was buried three years previously. Coyne remembered the rain. The relatives. The priest speaking a few words.

Busy place, a cemetery. Even in the short time it took Coyne to seek out the grave of his own parents and stand there to reflect a few minutes, at least five other funerals had taken place. People in Dublin were dying all the time. Every day. At all hours. Coyne heard the familiar sound of prayers coming across the gravestones but couldn't see the mourners until he moved a little and saw them huddled together, heads down, mostly in black.

Our Father who art in heaven... somehow, the sound of another funeral was so much more vivid. The gash of an open grave, the raw look of wreaths and the fearful smell of flowers.

As Coyne started making his way back along the path, he almost ran straight into the man he had been trying to avoid for weeks.

Mr Killmurphy. Killjoy, for Christsake, the man for all seasons now appeared to be hanging around the graveyard waiting for him. He was standing with his hands folded in prayer, pretending to be grieving. Coyne walked past him with his head down, but Mr Killmurphy turned around and spoke up in a calm voice.

Pat, he said. Pat Coyne.

Coyne's first reaction was to walk on. Ignore the bastard at all costs. But Coyne softened almost instantly when he saw the name of Nora Killmurphy on a gravestone. She had been dead all the time while Coyne was making his abusive phone calls. Jesus, Coyne should have known this. She never answered the phone.

Coyne stopped. The sound of a decade of the rosary on the breeze behind him.

Mr Killmurphy, he said.

I saw you in the shopping centre a few times, Pat. How are you these days?

Killjoy stepped forward and shook hands. Coyne found himself talking to his enemy: the man who had made his life hell and the man he had victimised for years in return; the man he would never forgive. Coyne looked at the grave-stone and felt instantly sorry for him. He was overwhelmed with remorse and saw everything from Killjoy's perspective for the first time.

She died of cancer four years ago, Killjoy said, with his head down.

I'm sorry to hear that, Coyne said.

They exchanged some words of encouragement and Coyne ended up reciprocating with his own grief.

My mother, he said. Three years ago.

Killjoy said something stoical about life having to go on. He was always one for the daft and ceremonious, looking for some kind of financial parable to spout at you across his desk. And he was still wearing those pink shirts. But you couldn't be hard on a man in his grief, and Coyne's heart went out to him. Jesus, he was close to bursting into tears. Any minute he would be begging Killjoy for forgiveness. Please forgive me for damaging your property. Forgive me for the patio stuff, and all the phone calls.

I retired early to look after her, Killjoy said.

Coyne felt helpless. Tried to remember some of the anger that

had sent him up to sabotage Killjoy's house that time. Killjoy had it coming! But it was all so far in the past now and he was unable to stop himself becoming Killjoy's friend. Here in the graveyard. United in mourning.

Coyne slowly opened up, baring his soul to Killjoy as though the cemetery had brought out some deep conciliatory unction. He explained how he'd been injured in a fire. How he was out of the Gardai now. And separated.

You always seemed like a perfect couple to me, Killmurphy said. I never would have thought... I'm sorry, you know, about all that trouble in the bank. I wish I could have been more generous.

Ah, no, Coyne said. You did your duty, Mr Killmurphy.

No, Pat. It's not good enough. I should have given you a break. It was wrong to call in the debt on a young couple like yourselves. I should have rescheduled. I should have written it off, in fact.

The conversion in the graveyard.

To hell with the bank, Killjoy kept saying. To hell with all their money. I should have been more generous.

No, Coyne insisted. It's me who should be apologising. I'm sorry about all the trouble I caused. You know, all that damage, like.

Will you go away out of that, Killjoy said. You were a customer. You should have been treated better.

There was no need for the damage, Coyne said. And the phone calls. That was wrong.

What damage? Killjoy smiled. What are you talking about? Then he came around and slapped Coyne on the back. Told him not to mention it. His behaviour had been exemplary in the circumstances.

The truth lay hidden. It was clear that Killjoy had not made the connection. Coyne had come right out and admitted everything and Killjoy still didn't get it. He had no idea that Coyne was a terrorist. Perhaps some time in his sleep the whole thing would click and Killjoy's suburban arithmetic would finally reveal the formula. Coyne didn't have the heart to drag it all up again. I mean, that would have been worse than the original crime. Jesus that would kill him, to tell him now, at this late stage.

They walked away towards the gates together.

It was nice to meet you again, Killjoy said. Always like to keep in touch with my old customers. He even told Coyne to look him up in

the telephone directory: perhaps they could go for coffee some day, now that they both had so much time on their hands.

Mongi O Doherty was not idly standing by. He was not the type to sit on his arse, *pro bono publico*, waiting for Sergeant Corrigan to come and point the finger at him. He was on the move, pursuing his own ambitions, looking at ways of recouping his losses, still hoping to extract the capital repayment from Jimmy Coyne. A pound of flesh if he couldn't actually get it in liquid currency.

The problem was that Jimmy Coyne had disappeared off the face of the earth, leaving no trace, not even with his family or friends.

Early afternoon, Mongi decided to call on Carmel Coyne to see if she could help. Stood on the threshold of the family home with his hoof in the door.

I'm looking for Jimmy, he said brusquely. He was getting desperate now, and there was no point in trying to pretend he was a friend or a Garda. No foil better than the blunt truth. Stare the mother in the eye and tell her you want to whack her son. Nothing more profoundly disturbing than that.

I don't know where he is, Carmel said, fiddling with the lock. Honestly.

The line was hard to sustain. It wasn't even worth saying, even if it was true. A mother who didn't know where her son was? And there was something even more dishonest about the way she tried to bang the door shut on Mongi O Doherty's footwear. As if she didn't notice the big pump-up runner stuck in her hallway.

Do you expect me to believe that, Carmel?

She was shocked to hear her own name. Then he stepped inside the house and produced a knife. Stood in the hallway and closed the door quietly, silent, solicitous, like a priest with bad news, looking her up and down and choosing his words carefully while his assistant went around the house searching the place for the money. Carmel could smell his smoky breath. The electrical hum of his nerves. He told her he was devoted to the physical force tradition – guns and blades, concrete blocks and glass shards, metal objects and syringes. He liked the sound of accidents and natural causes. He was particularly good on car crashes and was also the type to do most of his own creative dirty work. Held the knife up to her neck as though he was proffering

it to her. Here, I'd like you to feel the edge on that. Sheffield steel – diamond sharpened.

You have no right to come in here! she shouted, all righteous and proprietorial. As if the whole thing was a matter of assertiveness. But the conviction had already left: she detected a kind of misfired irony in her own voice.

My husband is a Garda, she announced. He's due back any minute.

Oh, I see, Mongi said. He's not living in that flat any more?

Carmel had never felt so exposed. It was such a comprehensive defeat. Victim embarrassment. It was the lie, more than the attempted defence.

Leave us alone, she cried. Once again the plural, inclusive concept of the traditional family.

Look, don't start bawling like a fucking baby, Mongi shouted. He slapped her across the face and Carmel was suddenly left holding her burning cheek, blinking through tears, unable to cry. Didn't notice the trickle of blood flowing down her chin. She tried to swallow, but couldn't do that either.

The search of the house yielded nothing.

I'm going to clean this thing on your tits if you don't tell me where he is.

I swear, I don't know, Carmel whispered and then sank down. Collapsing in slow motion, trying to close over her light blue summer blouse.

He fucking owes me money! Mongi shouted.

He opened his mouth wide to pronounce the words. I'll be back, he said. Like news for the deaf. Then he prepared to make his point with a graphic illustration. Took Carmel's hand as though he was going to dance with her. Come dance with me, in Ireland!

Maybe it was some kind of parting handshake. Or more like a quick manicure. He pointed her index finger out and tucked the tip of the blade under the painted nail. Just one sharp little stab of dilated pain to drive his message home. Up through her arm and straight into the smarting tear ducts. By which time he had already stepped back and opened the door, pausing for a moment to look out before he disappeared. But as with all intruders, part of his persona still remained. Under the fingernails. As though he had only stepped out

temporarily and would be back again any minute to continue. As though he was moving in. A new resident. Like a husband.

Coyne came across the poet with the four docile dogs outside the shopping centre. His face was very familiar from the Anchor Bar, but Coyne had never really had much to say to him. This time, in the street at the entrance to the town-killing shopping mall, there was something that attracted his attention. The poet had pinned a rough charcoal drawing of a man with a shaven head up on the wall behind him. Underneath was written the word 'Foe', in bold black letters. By induction, through the medium of verse, the poet was teaching his docile dogs to bite. Trying to turn these timid animals into selective killers. If they ever encountered this shaven-headed monster, alive or dead, they were instructed to turn instantly vicious.

Would you like a poem, sir?

But Coyne didn't see the point. I mean, everybody was spouting the stuff these days and nobody was listening. Poets vastly outnumbered readers. Coyne's advice was to change his career immediately. Offer himself as a listener. He'd make a fortune.

Coyne was more interested in the Identikit drawing. It was pinned up almost like a religious picture. Something to be venerated.

Who's that?

My enemy, the poet responded. Then he hunted through his portfolio for his best invective poems. Greatest hits of hate! Here, he said, and began reading out cantos of abuse and denigration, so that the dogs started growling at the drawing again. May you choke on a chicken bone. May you be thrown out in the rain. May you contract distemper and ringworm and the mange. Forsaken even by your own fleas. All the empirical suffering that dogs understood so well.

Coyne knelt down and examined the drawing. Finally interrupted the epic poem in order to extract some explanation for all this hatred. There was a time when every poet had a muse: some figure of great beauty that inspired him to place the chaos of the world behind him and seek perfection in words. Now they only had figures of great contempt. A poet could not work without a formidable enemy: some malicious bastard who had offended his honour and humiliated him. It made better source material. The poet as victim.

Coyne examined the drawing and became attracted to the notion

of an anonymous, clearly defined but nameless adversary.

Can I buy it?

It'll cost you a fair whack, the poet said. Besides, what would I do? I'd be lost. I'd have to go back to writing love poems.

I'm offering you money for it, Coyne insisted.

Thou shalt not covet another man's enemy, the poet warned. You'd be taking your life in your hands. I'd feel responsible.

He was underestimating Coyne. There was no situation he was unable to handle. No enemy that he hadn't unceremoniously dispatched to the dustbin of history.

Except for himself. As enemies went, Coyne would never find anyone more formidable than himself. The battle with himself is the only one he would never win. The Identikit face seemed like a walkover. A skirmish. He haggled until the poet took the drawing down and handed it over, along with the strict advice that this man was armed and dangerous. Do not approach! The dogs snapped at the paper in Coyne's hand.

Slowly, Jimmy Coyne started changing his mind. The totality of his love affair with Irene Boland was under threat. He wanted to re-enter society and abandon the refuge of love in which he had become imprisoned like a captive.

I don't care if they kill me, he was now saying.

Don't go out there, Irene warned, trying to preserve the sanctuary of their relationship at all costs. Once Jimmy set foot outside, he would be murdered. It was like the archaic legend in which Jimmy would fall off his white horse and grow instantly old.

I'm going to renounce my wealth, he said.

In the long hours that he sat in the flat looking out to sea, he realised that he had been trapped into happiness. This was Jimmy's big re-think. What he now wanted was to be able to see both sides of the coin at once. Love and freedom at the same time. The great opposites.

He asked Irene to get the money. In the boiler room, he told her. Just reach into the back of the boiler and you'll find a bag. It's full of money, Irene, so be careful. I'd get it myself only I can't go in there any more.

What money is this? she asked.

Don't let anybody see you with it, Jimmy said, ignoring her enquiry.

Coyne was in the supermarket at the town-killing shopping centre when he was approached from behind by Irene Boland. He was standing close to the cornflakes. Jumped back in shock and smiled awkwardly.

It's about your son Jimmy, she said.

Where is he?

He remained non-judgmental. This woman standing in front of him like a store detective was almost Carmel's age. Jesus, she could be Jimmy's mother for Christsake. But Coyne could also see the attraction. The warmth in her eyes. The husky voice.

You've got to protect him, she said.

Why? What's wrong?

They're after him. They're going to kill him.

Coyne pulled out the Identikit picture, right there in the supermarket with the sound of Frank Sinatra going his own way in the background and the voice of a woman breaking in telling them the price of chicken legs.

Is that him? Coyne asked.

I don't know, Irene said. I never saw any of them.

There were two women talking in one of the aisles not far away. One of them had a baby on her arm. She was listening to the other woman and rocking the supermarket trolley with her free hand. Back and forth, back and forth, making the groceries go to sleep. The hand that rocks the supermarket trolley.

I had to give him shelter, Irene Boland said. They attacked him and broke his ankle.

They'll hear from me, Coyne vowed. They better not lay a finger on him again or I'll kill them. He picked up a packet of Bran Flakes, realised he didn't normally buy that kind of thing and put it back.

They're after the money, Irene said.

What money?

Irene handed Coyne a bag full of dollars. Coyne opened it briefly and saw bundled notes inside.

They're the same people who killed the man at the harbour. Jimmy said that to me. He saw them.

Coyne looked all around him. At the meat counter there were some men in white coats and white hats that you could see the shape of their heads through. And matching red faces. On the wall was a gathering of these men smiling and standing around a table full of raw meat. Smiling at this slaughtered animal with their red spotty faces and white hats and canine eye teeth. Beside them another poster of a bull like a map dissected into territories. Cantons of rib roast and rump steak.

Where is Jimmy now? Coyne demanded. I need to speak to him.

No, she said.

There was something troubled about her: a kind of shakiness in the eyes. Then she turned and Coyne watched her walking away. She was small and plump and wore an ankle bracelet. He stood there with the bag of money, looking at the ankle bracelet under the tights. The red-faced butchers with their meat cleavers suspended in mid-air were joking and laughing among themselves.

Coyne went looking for Jimmy. Found out from the Haven nursing home where Irene Boland lived and stood ringing the bell early that evening. Irene was not there at the time but Jimmy was looking out at his father below on the steps. He moved back from the window, but then sneaked forward again to watch Coyne ringing on bells next door and speaking to an old man for a moment. Once again he came back and rang on the right doorbell but got no answer.

Jimmy, frozen, held on to his fugitive status and allowed his father to knock and ring until he gave up and walked away, a vulnerable figure pacing away along the seafront in the closed cyberspace of his own thoughts.

That's my dad, he said to himself, and saw his own father for the first time with the brutal clarity of a curt description on a shampoo bottle – dry, damaged. A man with a limited vision. An absolutist. A sad bastard, carving a polite but determined path through a crowd of pedestrians who had come out for the evening with their children and their dogs and their buggies. His father was at odds with the languid mood of the evening, walking among the ordinary people of the city, locked in mortal combat with his phantasmal adversaries.

Jimmy felt sorry for him. It was unforgivable to ignore his own father like this. He changed his mind and decided to run after him.

Wanted to re-enter his force-field of trust, perhaps walk out to the lighthouse together and talk about things the way they used to when Jimmy was still a child, convinced his father knew everything. Maybe hear some of the stories that were going on in Coyne's head and pretend that everything was all right again in the little republic of Coynes.

Mongi O Doherty had been awaiting this opportunity. It was inevitable that luck would fall his way at last, after so much scratching. It was like three identical numbers on a lottery card. He was there to intercept this emotional reunion between father and son. He and his assistant caught Jimmy crossing through the boat yard this time, asked him to sit in the back of the car and drove the short distance to the *Lolita* with a tape over his mouth to keep him quiet. Took him on board for a conference-style meeting, once the sun had gone down and the light was beginning to fade.

Jimmy was brought down below into the main cabin. There was an altercation with the skipper, Martin Davis, who refused to allow his boat to be used as an interrogation centre. This is not Castlereagh. I can't have any inhuman and degrading treatment on my boat. He said he was finished with all of this stuff. He was going back to fishing.

I'm going clean, he said, but Mongi laughed out loud with his protruding teeth. What was clean about fishing? Besides, Martin Davis was in this business up to his neck. It was too late to get out now. So he agreed to take the *Lolita* for a spin around the bay. Started the engines and set off into the evening with the smell of diesel fumes all around.

They sat Jimmy down and pulled the tape off his mouth. Mongi sat down beside him and began to talk to him in a very polite tone.

Put yourself in my shoes, Mongi said. Don't you think I've been very patient?

Jimmy gave no response. Mongi's helper also remained quiet and the skipper was up on deck in the wheelhouse.

You're not listening, Mongi said, disappointed. I'm trying to enter into meaningful dialogue with you, for fucksake.

Hum! Jimmy looked up at Mongi. His ankle was beginning to swell up with referred pain. As though he was already suffering future injuries.

OK, let me give you an example, Mongi said. We've got plenty of time. I'll make it easy for you. What would you do if somebody robbed your dinner off you?

Jimmy looked helpless.

Just say you're in McDonald's, Mongi continued, and somebody comes up and swipes your Big Mac right off you. And it's your last money and you could be facing starvation. Snatches it out of your hand when you're just about to bite into it. How would you feel?

I don't know, Jimmy said. I hate McDonald's.

Abrakebabra then, or whatever?

That's worse.

OK. Bad example. What kind of grub do you like?

Italian.

Gimme a dish! Mongi clicked his fingers. Spaghetti or what?

Risotto.

Right, Mongi started once more, sitting back, not looking at Jimmy at all. You've got a bowl of risotto in front of you, and you stick your fork in. Then some fucking dickhead comes up and takes the fork off you, and the dish, and starts eating it up himself. And it's the last can of risotto left. What would you say?

I don't know, Jimmy said.

The boat was moving up and down on the swell. The engine was rumbling and sending deep vibrations through the boat: everything that wasn't fixed down was jumping with epileptic madness. Mongi's shoelace was swinging rhythmically, doing a lasso imitation on its own. A key hanging on a hook along the wall was dancing around in a frenzy and a newspaper opened on the sports pages was shivering.

Mongi sighed. I'm asking you a simple question, Jimmy. I want you to dignify me with an answer. I bet you'd be a little bit upset, wouldn't you?

I suppose.

I'm trying to do a quid pro quo with you, like. You're not helping me.

I suppose I'd be upset all right.

Bloody right you would. You'd be fucking going apeshit, man. Throwing a tantrum like a bawling baby. Mongi felt he had been very understanding. He had acted like a gentleman. That's what this

is all about, Mongi said philosophically. It's about taking food out of somebody else's mouth.

Mongi decided to proceed to the amusements, as he called them. We can do this the easy way or the hard way, he said. If Jimmy told him where the money was, right now, then they would go back in to the harbour and everything would be cool. Mongi would be very lenient and let him off with a battering. But if Jimmy did not make a full disclosure straight away, Mongi would be forced to go the extra mile. Jimmy thought of giving the money back, but it was too late for that now. His father had it.

Amusements! Mongi shouted.

Coyne decided to walk along the pier. The anglers were out, standing at the edge with their fishing rods, cigarettes and sandwiches. At their feet, some stained newspapers with live lugworm; one or two plaice already caught. From a small radio a crackled and distant news-on-the-hour dispersed in the open air.

The pier was thronged with people. Some sat in the seats by the wall – brown rust marks of bolts and metal supports bleeding across the flaky blue wood like a crucifixion. The stigmata of seaside benches where people paused for a momentary review of life. Greatest moments. Worst disasters. End of century millennial self-analysis with the sunset over Dublin city leaving behind a sky of candy-floss streaks. Atomic dust particles turning the night over Dublin into a curtain of darkening pink and orange. The red glow on the granite rocks slowly faded and a white moon was already out on the far side of the wall, along with one or two bright stars. The wind gauge was not spinning like a propeller, for a change. Everything was calm. The Superferry slipped out with a moan of its siren echoing through the suburbs. And the lighthouse started casting an elliptical ring around the bay, whipping a long red finger across the black water, while the banjo player was playing the sad theme from *Doctor Zhivago*, warping the notes with added pathos.

Coyne saw the trawler making its way out through the harbour mouth but by the time he got to the top of the pier it was too far away to make out the name. The banjo player had moved on to other tunes – mazurkas, a waltz, ballads and polkas – all of which he covered in a blanket of trills and grace notes. Maybe it was all grace notes, in fact.

Coyne stood below the lighthouse and leaned against the wall facing out to sea. He was taking his time now. Things had become less rushed. Perhaps he should start letting things go a little more, become a tolerant man. A man without subtext. Perhaps he should do something useless. What a brilliant notion, he thought. It could be the great new catchphrase of our time: do something useless. There was far too much purpose in the world. It was all too productive and good and esteemed and valued. Why not something less viable.

Do something useless, he repeated out loud. He liked the sound of it.

He stared out to sea and listened to the music coming and going on the breeze. It was not quite summer yet and people were treating the good weather with great suspicion as usual. There was warmth left in the air, and a kind of afterglow in the rocks. As he leaned against the wall he felt it in his stomach, the latent heat of the sun stored in the granite. He was surprised by this sensation and it struck him almost like human warmth, pressing against his body. He had experienced nothing like it in such a long time. *Bolg le bolg!* Belly to belly! As though he was holding Carmel. Slow dancing with her to the music on the pier. The human warmth of the rocks.

Everybody was packed into the Anchor Bar that night when it opened its doors to the public again. Free pints for the first hour. All the familiar faces were there. Red-eye McCurtain was in early. And the poet. Free drink was all that mattered now.

The whole pub had been changed beyond recognition. There was no need for a snug any more. The curtains on the windows were also gone, allowing people to look right inside. It was an open society now. Nobody was hiding anything any more and the basic need for anonymity had gone. People wanted to be seen drinking. Young people sat in the window seats with bottles of foreign beer saying: look at us, drinking and having fun. We are well-adjusted people, able to speak up for ourselves.

They had changed the name from the Anchor Bar to the Anchor Café. Gone too were the little partitions and the nautical artefacts. The interior architects had gone for transparency. Accountability! Generous open space and judiciously placed art objects. The Irish bar had evolved as a communal living room, allowing people to meet

on neutral ground – a place of anonymity and fantasy. Now the Irish drinker was coming out at last. Spending more and drinking less.

Some of the local people were a bit put out by the price of the pint. Some complained about the music, said they couldn't hear themselves think. The poet was already lamenting the snug of Europe and said he was boycotting the pub, once the free beer ran out. The management was confident that the whole café idea would take off. There was an atmosphere of celebration and anyway they didn't give a shite whether they had a poet in the bar or not. Everybody was a poet as long as they had money.

The plaque to Tommy Nolan was unveiled quietly by Marlene Nolan. *I'm still rolling along...*

It was a Celtic disco pub. But already the little contradictions had crept back into the Anchor Café. Like the weekly golf tournament. And the weekly pub lottery. And the cliques and local gossip columnists. McCurtain had donated his *Playboy* calendar, which the barman quickly pinned up on the side of the fridge door. Otherwise, it was a controlled environment, with a CD blasting out over the new sound system.

Martin Davis reluctantly steered the *Lolita* out into the Irish Sea. There was another altercation on board when the skipper told Mongi that he was meant to be in the Anchor Bar. He was meant to unveil a plaque.

Time for the amusements, Mongi said. Spectaculars!

Leave him alone, the skipper said from the wheelhouse. It's not worth it.

You do as you're told, Davis. Shut your jaw or I'll give you the mackerel.

Poll circe, the skipper muttered through his beard. If I woulda-hada-known there was this much violence involved, I woulda-never-hada-got into this.

Mongi had tied Jimmy to the railings on deck and had put him on a diet of stale fish. Just as he had done with the immigrants, he was shouting: Fresh fish! Despite the fact that Jimmy now had limp mackerel stuck in his oesophagus, coughing and gagging, with his eyes bulging out through his purple face, the force-feeding programme was not working any more.

It was counterproductive, Mongi decided. He took the mackerel out of Jimmy's mouth, like a stopper, and threw it to the seagulls. Then he lashed a long rope over the bow of the boat, working quietly in darkness with only the instrument panel lighting up the skipper's face in the wheelhouse and everybody's lips trembling with the shudder of the engine.

Did you ever see *Mutiny on the Bounty*? Mongi asked.

Martin Davis looked up. No, you can't do that, Mongi, he said.

Just a little dip. A little trip round the underworld.

Jesus, you'll kill him.

We'll be there on the other side when you come up, Mongi said to Jimmy. We'll be there to hear your confession.

But even as Mongi and his friend tied Jimmy's feet and hands and began to lower him down the side of the boat, with the utter darkness of the sea beneath him, Jimmy held fast to his ideals. Because that's all he had. He was blindly holding on to his faith. He could have given the money back. It would have been simple. But he went down into the inky black sea vowing to fight to the death. No Surrender.

Carmel had tried Coyne's flat once before that afternoon without success. Now she stood at the door again ringing the bell, with the engine of the car left running.

A man from the ground-floor flat came out and spoke to her. Coyne had not been in all day, as far as this man knew. So she decided to leave a note.

We need to talk, she wrote. Perhaps Coyne would read some subtext into this. So she wrote out a fresh note: Please contact me immediately regarding Jimmy. Then she posted the note through a crack under Coyne's door. Pushed it as far as she could with the pen, and left.

The darkness beneath the trawler made it seem like the underworld to Jimmy. There was darkness in his lungs too and he was coughing up an awful lot of water when he was pulled back up on deck again, retching grey spurts of brine and producing all kinds of sea debris. There was a cut over his eye. They sat him on a winch and gave him a minute to recover.

OK, Mongi said, slapping him on the back to help him breathe.

Let me ask you one last time. If somebody took food away from you, what would you say?

Jimmy could not face the black water again and spoke up. Looked Mongi in the eye with great sincerity.

We're all in the vestibule, he said at last.

What's that?

You're in the vestibule, me and you.

Mongi turned his back on Jimmy in anger. His fists were balled as he looked towards the land and the string of lights along the coast. The sky above the city was reddish and inflamed.

You're making me do this, he said, turning back to face his victim.

They lifted him and brought him back to the side of the boat, Jimmy violently coughing up more in protest and the skipper standing by, pleading with Mongi to stop. For Jesus sake, Mongi. He's not going to last.

He has a choice! Mongi shouted. It's not as though we didn't give him a chance.

Carmel walked straight into the Anchor Café amid all the celebration and commemoration. Just when Coyne was lifting up his pint and examining it at eye level in a moment of eucharistic admiration, she suddenly appeared, standing right behind him and calling out his name over the music. There was a worried look on her face, though she tried to smile back politely at all the local people who greeted her.

Great, Coyne thought. Jesus, things were looking up. If this is what the café idea was intended to achieve, then he was all for it. More openness! More reconciliation! The only thing he regretted was that he didn't have a gin and tonic ready and waiting for her. The one day she decided to walk into the Anchor Café, he was not prepared.

I'm not staying, she said.

Ah, Carmel. Just have one, while you're here.

No way. She shook her head. And even when Coyne ordered a gin and tonic, she refused to touch it. We need to talk, she said.

Of course Coyne got it all wrong, thinking that she was trying to get back together with him at last. He was all flushed and emotional. He ran around looking for a barstool she could sit on.

Jesus, Carmel. I've been waiting for this moment.

What moment?

You know! Us, Coyne said. Us getting back together.

Jesus, Pat, she sighed. You've got this all wrong as usual. She quickly explained why she had come to the pub – the attack, the threat, the bandaged index finger. She hadn't come all the way down to the Anchor Café for her health.

Coyne was taken aback, not only by the blunt way in which she expressed her mind, but at the thought of her vulnerability. There was a little frown on her forehead that he had rarely seen before. He had always thought of her as being rock solid and could not imagine her unable to cope. Now he realised that she had come for help. She had not entered the Anchor Café of her own free will. She was calling on him as a protector of the home.

I should have gone straight to the police, she said.

I'll look after you, he said, still trying to salvage his pride.

It's Jimmy, she said. He's involved in something. This man says Jimmy owes him money. Big money.

I'm not a cop any more, Carmel, Coyne said at last, hurt.

You're his father.

She said none of the things he would have expected to hear. And he could say nothing to reassure her. It was the wrong place for intimacy and Coyne was suddenly raging at the music. Called one of the barmen over and told him to switch it down. How could anyone talk while REM were howling and wailing their self-important, self-obsessed dirges all night? *Shiny, happy people holding hands!* For Jaysus sake!

Coyne and Carmel looked at each other, like they both agreed silently that this was a big disaster. There were things to be said but they were entirely out of context in this meeting. She was standing with her arms folded, a fortress of resentment and anger.

You're his father and you don't even know where he is, Carmel said, and then she started crying. With McCurtain looking on. And the poet. And the barman. It was a true sign of transparency when customers in the new café began to show their feelings in public. Crying openly without shame.

Carmel turned and left. Coyne ran out after her and caught up with her just as she reached the car. He took the keys from her hand,

opened the passenger door and ushered her inside. Got in and drove her home. Stopped short of the house and took out the Identikit drawing from his pocket.

Is this him? he asked.

Yes! How come? she said, looking up at Coyne as he stared out through the windscreen.

I'm going to look after this, he said, putting the drawing away again. Leave it to me.

Then he got out and brought her into the house. She was overwhelmed by the sudden conviction with which he assumed he could open the hall door, as in the old days, and lead her inside.

Everything will be OK, he said. I might need to use your car for a day or two.

He was a father again. He was the man of the house. Pat and Carmel Coyne on the doorstep looking at each other for a moment through a blaze of confused emotion. He did something instinctive, something audacious that he would not have done if had thought about it. He threw his arms around her and gave her a hug: an awkward embrace that surprised him as much as it surprised her. It lasted only ten seconds and was over before they knew it. Before either of them could respond in words or work out what it was meant to signify. A gesture that was deep and lighthearted at the same time. It was over within seconds, but it lasted long enough for Coyne to feel the warmth of her body against his stomach, the latent heat of the sun, the slow dance with granite. The sensation that he had experienced on the pier earlier that evening. Human warmth.

Coyne drove back to his flat for the money. He left the engine running and ran inside to pick up the bag. On his way out he saw Carmel's stone on the mantelpiece and put it in his pocket. Then he bounded down the stairs and out to the car, only to find Sergeant Corrigan waiting for him.

Corrigan was always going to be one step behind, like a transmuting virus piggy-backing on small details of information. At times he tried to get one step ahead of the action, but he found himself shifting back as though he was dealing with a relativity principle in which he was constantly catching up with crime, his time-travelling twin brother. One day he would arrive before something happened.

Sergeant Corrigan stepped forward out of the shadows, whistling, just as Coyne was getting into the car. Where is he? Corrigan demanded.

Coyne looked around and saw two other officers sitting in an unmarked Garda car. They were so obvious. For Christsake. You give yourselves away. It's like you have a big sign on the roof of the car saying: we are watching you! What kind of surveillance is this, he thought, when you can spot them a mile off. Corrigan should have brought his hurling stick so he could whack the ball and his two greyhound colleagues could go and run after it.

Do you know the one about Achilles and the tortoise? Coyne asked.

What are you getting at?

You know, Achilles, the guy with the wings on his hat. The fastest man on two feet. Well he has this race with a tortoise and gives him a bit of a head start, on account of him being so slow, you follow me.

I'm warning you, Coyne. I've had about enough of this shite.

Hang on a second, Coyne said. You see this fella, Achilles, no matter how fast he is or what medals he's got for running, is never going to catch up. Because every time he catches up, the tortoise has moved on a fraction. And so on into infinity.

So! What's your point, Coyne?

Well, that's the way it is with the law. That's why I got out of the Gardai. No matter what you do, no matter how fast you can get your greyhound detectives there to run, you never catch up with crime, 'cause it's already moved on a little bit.

Look, Coyne. Would you mind stepping out of the car. I think we'll have to sort this out at the station.

Wait, Coyne said.

He took out the Identikit picture of Mongi O Doherty, gave it to Sergeant Corrigan and asked him to take a good look at the face.

That's the man you want, Coyne said.

Who's this? Corrigan demanded.

Mr X. He's the man you're after.

Then Coyne drove off, leaving Corrigan on the street staring at the drawing. Coyne turned the corner with a little too much fervour, giving another characteristic yelp of the tyres to wake up the neighbours. A statement of great hope, echoing around the canyons

of suburbia while Sergeant Corrigan looked up and beamed out at his colleagues with epiphenomenal satisfaction. He seemed to have made the big breakthrough at last. A confluence of evidence. As he folded up the tattered drawing of Mongi O Doherty, he felt everything was finally beginning to sit perfectly. As though the map of Ireland had been folded up incorrectly for years into an awkward bulging mess, cartography forced together in a strained and hasty arrangement. Now at last it was beginning to fit more snugly, collapsing effortlessly into the intended folds.

Coyne drove at great speed towards the harbour, full of renewed determination. He knew what had to be done. The war to end all wars. The final showdown.

Along the way, however, Coyne put his foot on the brake and brought the car to a halt with a howl that cut through the quiet streets, piercing through dreams and half-sleep. Rubber burning and a blue cloud rising from the tyres. It looked like he had suddenly remembered something and could go no further. The car was stopped dead in the middle of a side street. He opened the door, got out and stood for a moment, looking around and listening, struck by a vision. The street was empty. Most of the lights in the bedroom windows were out. The city was asleep.

Yes! He would start here. At Clarinda Park. This is where he would begin his modest enterprise. He had Carmel in mind now. Inspired by the granite warmth of her stomach. No question about it. He would start here.

Coyne opened the hatchback door, laid out a rug along the boot and went off searching in the gardens. It wasn't long before he came across the first rocks. Grey boulders like dinosaur eggs lined up along the path. He lifted the first of them and brought it over to the car, placed it in the boot and looked at it with satisfaction before going back for the next one. With the engine running all the time, crooning the neighbourhood back to sleep, he worked away quietly, lifting the rocks one by one and putting them in the boot of the car. Each time he stopped for a brief moment to stand back and look at the progress of his work. When the boot was full, he put some more on the back seat. Already, there was a sense of industry about all of this. Coyne was becoming efficient. And when the car could take no more,

he drove away, listing to one side as he dragged along the road up the hill. He could hear the moan of the suspension as it laboured in second gear all the way.

He had chosen a place already, long ago on one of his walks. Like any visionary, he had seen the end result in front of his eyes many times. All that remained now was the execution – the physical birth of the idea.

He was doing something useless at last. Something less viable. Something gloriously unproductive and unacclaimed.

He parked the car as close as he could and began to carry the rocks up to the nearest seaward point of the hill, a promontory high up overlooking Dublin Bay. It was deserted there at night, and he found he could easily work by the light of the moon. There was a metallic sheen across the bay too and the night was now almost as bright as day. One by one, he carried these boulders quietly, heaving them out of the car and lumbering all the way up the hill, then stopping briefly to look at the bay surrounded by its necklace of yellow lights out to Howth. He was sweating now and breathing heavily. It seemed to him that his rasping breath could be heard all over the city as he worked. Now and again he took out his inhaler and had a quick blast before going back to work. He never looked at his watch once.

When this consignment of rocks had all been delivered to the site, he drove back down into the suburbs looking for more. Got a large bottle of water at one of the chippers and stood there drinking it while other people walked away with chips. He went back to work immediately, tiptoeing through people's front gardens and taking their precious rocks from under their eyes without as much as the sound of a footfall or a cough. It was a stunning crime, one that nobody would be able to explain the following morning. A local mystery. Why would anybody steal rocks that were free in the first place? It was an incomprehensible assault on the idea of suburbia.

Coyne dragged the next load up through the back streets towards his site. Worked again like a labourer with unlimited endurance until the stones were delivered to this strange construction site. This would be a decent monument, he thought to himself, as he sat back and drank more water. This is one that will mystify them all, an overnight monument erected by the spirits. Underneath would be a bag full of dollars that nobody in the world knew about except Coyne.

As he worked, all kinds of random images floated into his consciousness. Pleasant thoughts of when his children were small and he used to let them jump off tables and cupboards into his arms. He remembered some of the stories he used to tell them. In particular the one about the woman with the silver voice. He stopped to think of that one. The woman had such an exceptional voice, such a beautiful and powerful voice, that she placed the whole country under a spell. Everybody was compelled to listen to it. People in cars stopped at the side of the road. People on the streets of Dublin stopped to catch her voice emerging from a radio through open windows of upper rooms. Even robbers trying to break into a house would have to drop everything. A curfew reigned over the whole country while she sang, so that even if there was a war on, they would have to stop. Years later, the children still half believed it. He half believed it himself as he went back to work and started building his foundations.

Out on the bay, Mongi was preparing to send Jimmy down to the black waters for the last time. He gave his victim one last chance, but Jimmy had no way of saving himself now. In the end it was the skipper, Martin Davis, who came to his rescue. This was going too far. He was already crippled with remorse over the death of Tommy Nolan and was not willing to face another one. He stepped into the wheelhouse and got the flare gun. Shot the bright red star into the sky, turning their faces pink and turning the water all around them into a wine-coloured bath as it dropped down over the sea.

Mongi looked up. He shouted at the skipper and ran to the bridge, trying to restrain him from firing another shot. There was a fierce scuffle but it was of no consequence. The lifeboat was already on its way out of the harbour towards them.

Coyne saw the activity in the bay. He looked up and saw the flare shooting into the sky, arching down over the sea like a red comet. He noticed the lifeboat heading out towards the furthest point, close to the horizon. It was such a clear night that he could see the white parting of foam on the side of the boat as it rode the swell. Down in the town there was more activity. Blue lights of Garda cars and ambulances at the harbour, sirens whooping through the main street.

Coyne was locked into his work. He grafted right through the

night, not feeling the slightest fatigue. At one point he placed the stone with the Saturn ring down into a neat gap in the foundations. Back in the town collecting more rocks, he saw a figure coming towards him along the street with a dog. He thought he was caught now surely: one of the neighbours coming to investigate. Soon they would call the Guards. But then he saw that the person was accompanied at a distance by various dogs. Four dogs, he counted. Just as Coyne was having trouble with an extra-large boulder, the dreadlock poet came on the scene and started asking what he was up to.

It's a folly, Coyne explained.

The poet watched Coyne struggling with the rock and saw the great determination in his face. A folly, he said. You mean, like in the famine times.

Yes, Coyne said.

The poet gasped with admiration. He wanted to belong to this. He liked it. The great unacclaimed, non-functional, existential beauty of it. His entire body of work had been marked by obscurity. He was emotionally and artistically close to all things unremarkable and unnoticed.

He offered to help and Coyne agreed to bring him along up the hill after first swearing him to secrecy. It was important that nobody ever found out who constructed this folly. They talked about dry stone walls for a while and the poet was good at selecting the right kind of stones. Along the way, they came across a mound of granite rocks which would do perfectly for the outer shell. Nor was the poet averse to physical endeavour.

The work was beginning to accelerate. All through the night this pair of labourers worked diligently, with very little talk between them, except for a moment here and there when the poet thought of something and said it out loud to commit it to memory. The dogs sat close by, one of them looking out to sea and the others curled up asleep, or just keeping an eye on the work. At one point, the poet stopped to ask Coyne a question.

What did you do with the enemy?

I gave him away, Coyne said.

Pity, the poet said. You don't often come across enemies as good as that.

Maybe he never existed at all, Coyne said.

Maybe Ireland never existed, the poet laughed.

Perhaps he was right, Coyne thought. Maybe Ireland was not a real place at all but a country that existed only in the imagination. In the songs of emigrants. In the way people looked back from faraway places like Boston and Springfield, Massachusetts. Maybe it was just an aspiration. A place where stones and rocks had names and stories. Maybe this was the glorious end. The end of Ireland.

By the time they finished building the cairn, the light was coming up over the horizon, seeping along the coast from Wexford. A nascent brightness edging the sky closer and closer to blue. From where they stood beside the overnight monument they could see the shape of the world and the texture of the water: choppy, like elephant hide at that distance. Slowly the colours were emerging. Around them, the grass turned green and the hedges took on a dark blue. And the shapes of the rocks became clear, so that Coyne could now see the individual shade of each rock they had used. Now he could appreciate the full effect of his achievement.

Up above them the seagulls were on the move, flying from right to left as they did every morning at that time. Flying silently with the same determination with which he and the poet had worked all night on his construction. The birds seemed to have somewhere specific in mind as they flew across the bay from Wicklow or Arklow up to Dublin and on past Howth and Lambay Island. Silently. Many of them in small V-shaped formations with leaders and followers; others just going it alone. The great exodus of dawn. Not stopping for anything. Not remotely interested in food or in anything on the surface of the sea. They were crossing the bay at a great altitude, like vectors all going in the same direction across a screen. Hundreds of them emerging with the light in the south and flying with great self-knowledge towards the north.

Coyne went to the hospital the following morning to see Jimmy: sitting up in bed with a blue tube across his nostrils, he looked pale and serene. Beside him the usual bottle of Lucozade and some grapes that Irene Boland had brought in before she went to work. Coyne was completely overwhelmed by events and only slowly began to emerge from his obsession with the cairn when he met Sergeant Corrigan in the corridor.

He's co-operating, Corrigan smiled. A vital witness for the state.

Jimmy had become an overnight hero. Martin Davis was there too, anxiously hoping to hear how the young lad was doing. And Sergeant Corrigan was clapping Coyne on the back, thanking him for the Identikit picture.

I know what you're going to say, Jimmy whispered as Coyne entered the room and stood beside the bed looking at him.

No, Coyne said. As a matter of fact, I wasn't going to say anything. The vestibule!

Coyne put his hand on Jimmy's shoulder. Things had shot ahead beyond his control. It seemed he had only briefly controlled anything in his life once or twice when the children were very small. He listened quietly now as Jimmy talked.

When Carmel came into the room some time later there was more silence. It looked like the big reunion in many ways – Coyne and Carmel back together again in the hospital, sitting on either side of Jimmy's bed. Carmel holding Jimmy's hand. Coyne unshaven and exhausted, waiting for her to say something, to make a move, perhaps to hold his hand as well as Jimmy's. He thought of showing her what he had built. But the cairn remained undiscovered. He kept it to himself.

Coyne picked up one of the grapes in the basket and put it in his mouth. Carmel looked at him as he crunched on the seeds.

Have you had breakfast yet, he asked her.

No, she said.

Do you fancy a rasher?

Ms Dunford had arranged everything. She had contacted the school and set up the whole thing with the principal. Psycho-drama. Ms Dunford would write books on the subject one day. Coyne's uncharted emotions, like discovering America.

Some weeks later she collected him at his flat, smiling at him with her bottom row of teeth as he came out the front door. She was dressed up for the occasion. Perhaps a little too much make-up for Coyne's liking; it looked like her face was already beginning to crack into little lines at the side of her eyes. But she was very happy. And quietly excited by the fact that Coyne had finally agreed to this visit.

They drove towards the city on a warm morning in mid-June.

The school was still open and there were a few days left before the summer holidays. There was no pressure on Coyne to do this, she explained once more in the car. He was doing nothing against his will. And he understood that he could pull out of this at any moment if it made him uneasy. Ms Dunford kept talking all the time while Coyne remained silent. Anxious.

The familiarity of the school surprised him; nothing had changed since he was a boy. The ancient stuffed bird display in the glass case outside the principal's office. The shiny banisters. Echoes of children floating through the stairwell and the smell of chalk and dusters as Coyne was ushered into the classroom like a school inspector from the Department of Education. *Rang a Ceathar – Cailíní!* The girls turned and looked at him with awe and curiosity, perhaps also with some amusement as he smiled awkwardly and tried to fit into one of the benches at the back of the class with his big clumsy knees. He compromised by sitting sideways in the end. He listened to the teacher resume her geography class, all about the Nile. Now and again, one or two of the girls still looked around at him furtively. But he was lost in a slide of sense memory, sifting through a gallery of mental possessions. He could remember his mother wearing a summer hat and a blue polkadot dress as she collected him from school. He remembered a plastic water-squirting camera on his first Holy Communion. And there was a familiar sensation at the back of his throat, like the sweet and slightly nauseating taste of custard.

It was lunchtime when he got around to the boys' section. A hastily built blockwork extension, never plastered. He remembered the familiar grey, tin wastepaper bins. And there was nothing quite like the silence left behind in an empty classroom, with the collective voices of boys and girls coming in from the yard outside. It induced a kind of dreamy surrender as he wandered around the abandoned desks. He read a sentence in the Irish language on the blackboard. Found his own former desk and examined a copybook lying open on it. Remembered the opening lines of a poem he once learned off by heart about a hanging in Ballinrobe.

Out in the yard, as he walked into the full volume of children's voices, he thought of the sandwiches falling out of Tommy Nolan's hand. He stood at the spot where it happened, but was distracted by the sight of two small girls talking to each other and eating their

lunch. No more than five years old, they were oblivious to the noise and action around them. One of them was trying to pull the hair away from her eyes, and her mouth. She held her white bread sandwich up in her hand and Coyne could see the shape her bite had left behind. Like a little ticket-machine bite. A small, neat semicircle. A perfect crescent.